NORTHTOWN ECLIPSE

This edition first published 2018 by Fahrenheit Thirteen, an imprint of Fahrenheit Press.

ISBN: 978-1-912526-28-4

10 9 8 7 6 5 4 3 2 1

www.Fahrenheit-Press.com

F 4 E

Northtown Eclipse

By

Robert White

Volume 1: Raimo Jarvi Investigates

Fahrenheit Thirteen

An Imprint of Fahrenheit Press

For Chris Black, writer, editor, and mate

Chapter 1 - August 1

Visitors to Raimo Jarvi's office on Bridge Street that morning, had there been any, would have found the temperature uncomfortable. If yesterday was an indicator, daytime heat would proceed from pre-dawn warm through stifling to downright oppressive by noon. Heat like this was unusual for Northern Ohio after mid-July. That typical turn in the morning air as day broke could be felt in the blood and was expected by early August. Everyone knew summer was ending, and fall was on the way. Not this year; just an oppressive, blanketing heat for the past two weeks.

When he bought the two-story building, Raimo renovated the upstairs into living space for himself and sealed off the area behind the downstairs office with a partition. He was a one-man outfit and didn't require more room. Behind the desk, a door with the transom window—strictly architectural fou fou circa 1909—led to nothing. A single row of fluorescent lighting down the center worked, but the long, narrow room held no furniture except for a lovely cherry table desecrated with nicks where old George O'Mullan used to wrap up his customers' shoes like a butcher in thick brown paper and tie it off with string unspooled from a cast iron dispenser.

Raimo had one vague memory of the old salesman from a visit with his mother before she turned recluse. She brought him to O'Mullan's store for a new pair of dress shoes for his fourth-grade Confirmation. O'Mullan's bald pate shone from the same overhead lighting, his navy-blue suit and bone-white shirt were crisply pressed. His voice had an actor's timbre, not unpleasant but something odd lurked in the earnest expression, something his mother had picked up. While George talked to himself searching among the racks of shoes honeycombed along the wall, she snatched Raimo's hand, jerking him from the seat, and hauled him out of there. She never spoke about it later.

Raimo wasn't superstitious and didn't consider it ominous he had acquired the building occupied for decades by the mad shoe salesman.

The boxy air conditioner that he inherited with the building sat directly above his office door facing Bridge Street and hissed like a basket of snakes. It spat fat drops of water onto the sidewalk below where Raimo watched it evaporate in seconds.

People walking too close by his window couldn't see in through the glare, but he could see them in every detail. Some were as familiar as species of water birds—tourists traveling by car wore brighter clothing than locals and shopkeepers, other tourists arriving by port from pleasure craft all over the Great Lakes possessed the shabbily genteel look of people with money, locals visiting the shops, bars, and diners of Bridge Street wore a smug ordinariness like a badge of contentment. The occasional drunk wandered past, a fact of being sandwiched between a pair of the busier taverns, one catering to twenty-somethings, the other rabidly country-western.

Couples chattered past and would sometimes try to peer inside. Raimo sat rock-still as if he could be seen. His straining a/c unit, however, drowned out any words. The out-of-towners were more alert and took a wider detour to avoid being hit by the spray. The evening drunks were reckless, some acting as if they'd been doused from a bucket instead of sprinkled. The heaviest drinkers plowed past oblivious of any dotting of hair or clothing.

Raimo thought of it as street theater: humanity's parade. He even looked forward to the goat skip of some passersby as the drops flew and landed. Several stared balefully upward at the unit before moving on. Occasionally, an abrupt curse followed a hostile look through the glass. The higher the temperature outside, the more droplets ejected from his rattletrap machine.

One familiar drunk, a grizzled Bridge Street veteran with a graying ponytail, put himself on display in a mime show for Raimo's benefit. He opened his mouth, tongue protruding like a wide-mouth bass snapping at bugs on the water's surface or he impersonated a man showering, his black-and-gold tee speckled from the falling water; he rubbed his armpits energetically with invisible soap while bellowing something that sounded like Waylon Jennings or Willie Nelson. That morning Raimo caught a good look at the man because—drunker than usual and earlier than usual—he'd pressed his face against the plate glass, his hands forming a bridge over his brow to penetrate the glare. Raimo beheld the aging peeping tom with a crosshatched Appalachian face, narrow as a fox's, eyes red-rimmed from drink.

"There but for the grace of God," Raimo muttered, quoting his mother, and felt himself blushing. It had taken him years to overcome his ingrained discomfort of being stared at by strangers.

Raimo had never exchanged a word with the man in the three years since he'd become a private investigator with a license and an office to go with it. The light's angle of refraction guaranteed his security behind the glass until mid-afternoon. Then he'd be obliged to wave back at the few boulevardiers who acknowledged him as a visible, if not a busy, man inside.

He leaned back in his executive office chair, an impulse buy from Office Max, and realized that if he didn't start drumming up more and better clients he was going out of business. As if to affirm that resolution, the air conditioner released a final gurgle, a death rattle, and ceased.

While he stared at the water pooling on the sidewalk the

office phone trilled.

Raimo heard the familiar opening: *Mister Jarvi, I am Leotis Pennimann here.*

Leotis began every phone conversation this way and thereafter followed the *in medias res* logic of the epic, backing up and filling in. But it was always the same epic, his personal tragic one, that Raimo knew he was about to hear yet another rendition of.

It baffled him so completely the first time Leotis called that he begged him to come into his office "to explain his situation." Now, he was used to him, and could piece together enough of the scrambled narrative that never varied: *Tanisha was cheating on him again, follow her, get proof.* Leotis Pennimann was the opposite of drumming up new business.

The sixty-six-year-old, retired track laborer for Norfolk & Southern Pacific was his first and oldest client. Leotis had raised five children, all of whom at one time were threaded into conversations centering around Tanisha's infidelities. Rhonda was a heroin-addicted prostitute living in the projects in Cleveland with arrests for drugs and solicitation. Darnell, Deshon, and Demetrius were either serving time or were back under the patriarchal roof for the shortwhile their freedom lasted. Anthony, the youngest, was also the most dangerous of his sons. He'd eluded a homicide charge by the narrowest margin and was usually mentioned in the police-beat section of the *North Coast Tribune* as "a person of interest" if the crime was unsolved or suspect if it wasn't. Raimo had met Anthony when he'd been forced to squire his injured father around after an accident on a ladder left Leotis in a leg cast. He was polite, like his father, but remained silent once his father unleashed his impassioned rhetoric about Anthony's mother's latest infidelity. Raimo noticed a twinge of Anthony's hands in his lap as his father concluded the visit with a denouement Raimo had heard before: "She a bitch, Mister Jarvi."

"She been seeing this dude every Thursday," Pennimann said for the fourth time.

Raimo cut through Leotis' mournful diatribe and told him

to drop by the office at two o'clock. He was tempted to ask Leotis to put his wife on the phone. Tanisha was probably the easiest spouse in the state to follow, and it would save everyone a bundle of time and Leotis' fee if she would simply give her husband the details that Raimo was going to have to spend two days gathering for yet another report. Raimo kept his fee down as much as possible, but nothing could persuade Leotis to divorce Tanisha. His love for his cheating wife was bullet-proof, beyond comprehension, and as immortal as any lyric poet had ever lamented in sonnet or ode.

Cutting Leotis' woeful pining about his marriage short only brought Raimo face to face with his own nearly monastic love life. His parents were married forty-one years. Comparing them to Leotis and Tanisha, he thought his parents not that much superior—his father cowed his entire life by a stronger, more intellectually agile mate. Raimo's mother, a staunch and fierce Catholic who never darkened the church's threshold once she retreated inward, died as she lived—raving at the world, bitter, convinced she'd been short-changed in everything with Raimo's older brother the sole exception. Riekoriki, formally, but "Rikki" inside the family and "Rick" to outsiders, was the exceptional son and family darling: handsome, athletic, and admired.

Under the battering of name-mockery by classmates during his first recess at school, Raimo came home and demanded to be called "Ray" from then on. Rikki, however, had the swagger and toughness to hold on to his Finnish heritage if he chose, but let the assimilation happen naturally with friends, family, and teachers abetting the swindle.

The copperplate gothic lettering of Raimo's name and profession — RAY JARVI, PRIVATE INVESTIGATIONS — rebuked him with the knowledge he'd lost one of the earliest battles of life by letting others take away his birth name.

As he did unconsciously every time that thought occurred, he brought up his hand to touch his face. Raimo had known a greater loss at a young age: "Freak!" chanted by a wolfpack of classmates surrounding him in a tight ring and shoving him with thumps on his back reminded him of his difference from them forever; the scars in his psyche oozed open daily with some reminder that, since the age of ten, he did not look like other people.

Raimo decided that sitting at a desk with an empty in tray made little sense on a day without air conditioning. He checked out some portable air conditioners online, clicked on one with an elephant-trunk extension and checked to see if the town's trio of hardware stores had it for purchase. It was something to do.

He set the desk phone on record and stepped into muggy heat laced with its familiar river smells of diesel fuel and rotting fish. Raimo had made a decision one day in the pre-op room before another skin graft surgery. He had listened to his parents talk about the weather on the drive over. They missed what he thought was a gorgeous display of cloud cover over the lake—huge, boiling clouds with battleship-gray cores running through tree-rings of pewter to finish in silver-brite fringes at their edges, all that tumult backlit by a fuzzy white disc of sun, and everything below dappled with shades of gray. All they could see was the misery of snow, ice, and dark skies. Even Rikki, along for the ride, complained that the mud-spattered snowbanks looked like "diarrhea." Hearing two doctors in the outer room complain, he decided to add days to his life by never talking about weather again.

Raimo usually parked above his office around the corner on Hulbert Avenue but decided to meet Bart Massey by walking to the diner. He knew each establishment on the street from childhood. None seemed on the verge of going out of business except his. The man who had first encouraged him to hang the PI shingle was always upbeat about his prospects. *Dastardly crime,* Bart Massey, deputy sheriff, liked to exclaim—especially after a couple rounds of lubrication at one of Bridge Street's drinking establishments—*is on the rise in Northtown. . .*

Most of the noontime crowd in the Poseidon diner were

just settling into their menus when he entered the foyer of what had once been a chandler's shop. The upstairs led to the dining area. Heads swiveled toward him as if on cue and abruptly swiveled away as he paused, scanning for Bart. Today, he occupied a booth near the window facing the river traffic. Raimo sat opposite his boyhood friend and noticed the show: the *Arthur M. Anderson* was unloading stone just across the river not fifty yards distant.

Raimo hoped it wasn't going to lead to stories of Bart's sailing days out of high school. Not because he'd heard them all by now, but because he envied him. Every Finnish kid who grew up in the Harbor wanted to go sailing on the big lake freighters instead of getting stuck in factories and stores like their fathers. That included two boys from Raimo's class who went down with the *Fitz*.

"Bart."

"Ray, what up." Mumbled without Bart looking at him, mesmerized by the ore boat's activities.

"I could be an assassin, a serial killer," Raimo said. He sat and picked up a menu.

"My keen ears recognized your footsteps," Bart said. "That's why you need me as a partner."

Bart had hinted more than once that, if he ever left the Sheriff's, he'd like to come in on Raimo's "gig" as the town's sole shamus. Raimo had known Bart for twenty-five years but wondered if he, too, needed a moment to adjust like the other diners. Always one or two nearby would steal a second or even a third glance. Raimo wasted years breaking the habit of touching his face whenever that happened.

"Fighting crime this morning or are you coming off shift?"

Bart yawned. "Coming off. I switched with Barrick. His wife's in labor again."

Bart was nicknamed "Black Bart" for his heavy stubble, which seemed to start just below his eyes. His five o'clock shadow was darker than most men's beards. Part-Sicilian, "part-Heinz Fifty-Seven," he liked to say, for the many genetic contributors to his personal genome. His clan had as many blondes as black-haired, dark-complected in his family.

"I should have guessed," Raimo said.

Deputies had to be close-shaved and Bart would sometimes have a piece of bloody tissue sticking to his face or neck. Raimo, on the other hand, could go days without shaving before he felt stubble. Rikki could sport a noble Viking's red-gold beard in a few weeks. Bart was un-nicked today.

"I envy you, Ray," he said. "You never have to get in a fight with your razor."

"They sell styptic pencils in every drug store nowadays, Bart."

"You won't believe how many uniform shirts I've ruined," he lamented.

"Sartre said a man should never let hairs invade his face."

"Who?"

"Forget it. How's crime in the backroads?"

"It's up, way up. You know about the body dump off Cato-Springs, right?"

"Three women."

"Four," Bart corrected.

He told Raimo about another decomposed body found within a thousand yards of victim number three off Cato-Springs Road in the southern end of Northtown County.

"We think there's more," Bart said.

"We?"

"Sheriff's, FBI, Northtown PD, Highway Patrol. It's called a multiagency task force, my boy, and I'm angling for a slot."

"Good luck," Raimo said.

"Luck, shit," Bart said loud enough to draw stares. "It's politics. Who gets plum assignments and who gets the broomstick up the wazoo." Bart meant third-shift rotation "to the ass end of the county among Amish barns where there's nothing but a barbed-wire fence and a lobo wolf."

Bart's complaint, by now a song with a refrain and interchangeable lyrics, was warranted by the politics of cronyism and aggravated by the fact he and the Sheriff butted heads in the past. Complaining loud and long in the bars on

Bridge Street did little to endear him to his boss.

A blonde waiter, wearing the unisex black slacks and white shirt to match the all black-and-white décor of the walls, floor tiles, and Ansel Adams prints on the walls brought them coffee. Bart was a ferocious eater and gave all his concentration to the meal. Raimo silently thanked her for not overreacting when she handed him the bill. He had other kinds of scar tissue to thank for that.

"You eat like a rabbit, Ray."

"I like salads."

"You must."

The diner specialized in hamburgers half the size of a dinner plate and sides that were a meal in their own right. Bart's appetite was as robust in a heat wave as a blizzard.

"I heard your bro's coming back this way for his reunion."

It was a subtle admonishment. Rikki had never come home for either of his parents' funerals.

"He told me he was wrapping up some business commitments," Ray said, hearing how hollow that sounded.

"Why cover for him?"

The waitress returned while Raimo considered a response to that. Apologizing for Rikki was new to him. It had been the other way around for most of his life.

Bart was in touch with the town's gossip. He'd attended the same schools, been married in the same church Ray's family worshiped in. He remembered when Rikki was a football god in the halls of Sts. Stephen and Basil. Bart had ignored Ray then, ran with his own jock crowd, which was no more than Rikki had done.

"He wants to see you," Bart said.

He, Kris' husband, not Rick—her husband. Her killer.

"How can you ask me that?"

"Don't shoot the messenger, man," Bart said. "I'm just saying. He's being transferred to the holding center for assignment."

"Good. The Youngstown State Pen, right? Maximum security. I hear it's crawling with Aryan Brotherhood."

"Don't get your hopes up. He goes to a holding pen. They'll assess him there and then assign him somewhere."

"Lucasville, I hope," Raimo said.

Bart snorted. "Fat chance of that, man. Only the baddest of bad boys go down the river."

"He murdered his wife."

"So? That's like littering nowadays. The guy's filthy rich and connected to half the state legislators. He has college background, country club, *yadda-yadda*, he'll probably get minimum security or a work camp."

"There'll be wire fences around it. That's the main thing," Raimo replied.

"If I had to bet," Bart said. "I'd guess Chillicothe, medium-security. He'll be out in ten, maybe sooner. What do you expect, Ray? He isn't the reincarnation of Charley Manson."

"She didn't deserve it," Raimo said. They both knew his anger was pleading his own guilt.

"Jury didn't think so after they heard all the juicy stuff about her."

The juicy stuff. Meaning: all those men she had cheated with. Him included.

"I'll give him your best," Bart said.

"Tell him to hang on to the soap," Raimo said.

Raimo had attended Kristine's husband's arraignment in Jefferson; he felt eyes boring through him from all over the court house during the brief proceedings. His name never came up in the investigation, he was left off the witness list by the defense, but he was known as one of Kristine Radebaugh's lovers.

Raimo had a view of people coming from the marina. They looked happy, tanned, laughing in their groups despite the sweltering heat. It would be cooler on the lake where they'd been sailing in their yachts, shiny with brightwork visible from the breakwall where he'd fished as a boy. The bridge siren screamed through his thoughts.

Bart tore the last of his fries in half and stabbed it into a pool of viscous ketchup on his plate. He checked his watch and declared he had to run.

"Crime doesn't wait," Bart said.

"You're sticking me with the check."

"You invited me, remember? Besides, you've tapped my crime-fighting brain for insider info as usual, so it's a fair swap."

"Go easy on those Amish buggies," Raimo said.

"Not me. I'm incorruptible. All are equal before the eyes of the law."

"That tells me the Sheriff's got you filling quotas again."

Bart grimaced, said nothing, and headed for the door. Gun on hip, athletic swagger coupled with bulked shoulders from bench-pressing, he made an impression on females in public. Bart savored the glances when he exited or entered a place. Raimo once called him a reverse Marilyn Monroe.

"What do you mean?" Bart asked him. "You saying I have an ass like a woman?"

"I'm saying," Raimo replied, "you like to make a big splash when you exit."

"What can I say? The camera loves me."

Raimo had time to kill and a dessert would have made him logy for his two o'clock appointment with Pennimann. He left a tip to cover both dinners and headed out into the blast-furnace heat. Opposite the marina past the lift bridge, the city had landscaped a small plot with geraniums and impatiens and placed park benches. Recreational fishermen tossed their catch back into the river. They'd all been warned about carcinogenic PCBs dredged from the bottom in a recent Superfund cleanup.

Raimo sat on the far bench closest to the coal docks to avoid being spoken to by passersby.

As a child, Ray accompanied his father to this very spot when the tug shanty leaned out over the river. Fridays were payday for the tugmen and Raimo looked forward to a stop at the Wyandotte following his father's picking up his check. He was bought a bottle of orange soda and given some quarters for a few games of Skeeball while his father talked to men from the docks and lakeboats. In those days, the Wyandotte was a private club.

The shanty was long gone, and the tugs were tied up opposite the coal docks for the little towing business left. The coal storage docks would be emptied soon because Canada, the major purchaser, had opted to go nuclear and would have no more use for the hundreds of thousands of tons of coal shipped up from the mines of Kentucky and West Virginia. He watched the *Anderson*'s conveyor crew moving about on deck below the self-unloading boom as the thunder of falling gravel from the moving belt disgorging stone from the hull created rising pyramids of stone ashore. Deckhands stood face-to-face and shouted to be heard; others moved amidships toward the stern closing the open hatches with giant steel square covers set into place by an iron deckhand. The conveyor belt crew had the filthiest job aboard any lakeboat; whether coal, taconite, or stone cargo, the men were blackened with dust by the time their vessel was ready to leave port. A casually dressed, stubby man in a hard hat held a walkie-talkie and peered around the stern tiller. Raimo watched the dock supervisor check the Plimsoll numbers and relay them to the captain in the pilot house.

Just beyond the *Anderson* was a span bridge connecting the dock to the railyard where the gondolas packed with "on the road" loads with bituminous coal were overturned in the hopper shed and dumped. The coal was fed onto a boom that led to a conveyor belt. Gulls shrieked and broke ranks to dive for fish, pleasure boats came and went, halting at the bridge waiting for the siren to go off. All of it a scene imprinted into Raimo's neocortex. He could tell the time from his office by listening for the half-hour tandem of siren and clanging of the warning gates at both ends of the bridge.

One thing never changed: the smell of the river. Putrid with dead shad from the recent die-off where thousands of the tiny silver fish came ashore to perish, iridescent with a rainbow slick of fuel coiling around the dock pilings, it reached down into Raimo in a way he couldn't describe. With a dash of diesel, it smelled like home.

Warmth saturated his pores, and he forced himself to get up and head back to his dismal office. At this time of afternoon, light sheared off anything shiny and bounced back from windows, putting him on display for the restaurant diners and the bar patrons. Sweat poured down his back and stuck his shirt to his belt. He put on sunglasses just as he noticed a grinning Leotis Pennimann staring at him from his office doorway.

"Mister Pennimann, you're early. I hope you haven't been waiting long."

"Naw, man, five minutes. Mister Jarvi, you know, there's this solar eclipse comin' soon."

"Yes, I heard. Please come in."

"A total solar eclipse, man. Going to block out the sun! Darkness at high noon," Pennimann said and looked for the seat he always took. He liked the phrase and repeated it: "Darkness at noon. Be like the, you know, *caveman* days."

Raimo thought there wasn't far to go for that.

"I'll be sure not to miss it then," Raimo said.

Leotis thought that was worth a bark of laughter.

Pleasantries over, Leotis sat in the chair and placed his hands on his knees and rocked. His brown face was open, expressive despite the hard look in his eyes. He was shades darker than all his children. Tanisha was biracial. Anthony could pass for white.

He looked at Raimo with a crooked smile on his face, stared straight at him but didn't speak. Raimo knew the sign: *he's gathering his thoughts, part of the ritual.* The emotional onslaught of Tanisha's latest infidelity took some time to corral and organize.

Pennimann cleared his throat, a drumroll.

"Nisha be cheatin' on me again," he finally said.

"Mister Pennimann," Raimo began, "do you know the expression 'glutton for punishment'?"

"'Course I do, Mister Jarvi. I know she ain't gonna change. I know that. But I have to know."

Leotis dropped his big fists. Rubbing them on his knees was a solace for pain. Raimo thought the man needed an Aladdin's lamp, not a private investigator, something to release a genie to make things right.

Raimo took notes, recording the sordid details of Tanisha's latest betrayal with pedestrian, if not pornographic, fidelity. As he spoke, Leotis' vocabulary became less profane, as if he were setting the scene of his betrayal in his mind and it had to be just so.

Raimo had learned fast how much of his job required some element of the confessional; after all, people didn't come to him because things were going smoothly in their lives. His last few cases, spread out over the prior year, had boiled down to a pair of opposing tasks: his clients either wanted him to get something from someone or else they wanted him to keep someone from taking something from them.

But I can't absolve you, Raimo thought, continuing to note the final details of Tanisha's rendezvous with her man. Raimo made the usual conciliatory comments out of habit and saw him to the door.

Leotis shook hands. His tightening grip could crack open a walnut. It reminded Raimo of his last client, a concert pianist from Cleveland who had sought an out-of-town investigator to avoid bringing down scandal on Severance Hall where he performed. That man's fingers were steel bands that could prolong a lovely Chopin etude to an exquisite final *appoggiatura*, a grace note climbing to the rafters. Those same strong fingers had fashioned the elaborate hangman's knot by which he ended his life in his basement a few weeks later—after Raimo delivered the report on his runaway daughter's death. Redacting the harsh details from the police report describing her death in a squalid motel in Melbourne, Florida had not diminished the pain.

Raimo promised Leotis a report in a few days. In fact, he had no ongoing case to occupy him. If the father of another runaway he had tracked to an Insane Clown Posse "gathering" in San Diego didn't pay up soon, he'd have to file a suit in small-claims court to get paid. The fact that the man's child was a math prodigy who had sabotaged her Harvard interview and bolted for California to huff paint with a pack of wild street kids seemed less important to him than quibbling over Raimo's line items. His voicemail the day before claimed Raimo was "treating himself to luxury five-star hotels" instead of the freeway motels he'd itemized on the bill. That was Raimo's break-even case for the fiscal year. He could always draw from the remainder of his trust fund, but siphoning off a little at a time made no sense and masqueraded his so-called career into being just an expensive hobby.

Raimo adjusted his computer screen to obscure him from the view of passersby as the blinding waves of daylight lengthened into longer wavelengths of late afternoon. He opened a drawer and took out his wireless earphones. Satie's *Gymnopedie* No. 3 wouldn't unstick his shirt from his back or beltline, but it would slow that nervous tick of desperation ratcheting up in his mind. He spent long minutes listening to the silver notes and staring into a screensaver of the Horsehead Nebula on his monitor. The fraud hiding behind the look of the busy professional with his Bluetooth and computer screen.

The door opened and a man in sunglasses stared back at him. Not a tourist. There was something familiar about the chiseled jawline, the predatory smile.

"Hello, Handsome," the man said.

Only one person used that insult, always out of Rikki's hearing. Brian Kevin Tuomey, Rikki's former classmate, fellow jock, and drinking buddy was the only person in Northtown who might have a reputation bigger than his brother's. Not a better one, just wider and more complex, depending on whom you asked.

Rikki's football prowess was legendary, only diminished by time as other athletes overshadowed his accomplishments. But B. K. Tuomey covered a wider swath that went beyond athletics as the quarterback of Sts. Stephen and Basil High's only State Division 2 championship team. Prom King of his graduating class — followed by whispers of date rape. Most Likely to Succeed — dogged by rumors of drinking and drugs. Pranks that went beyond schoolboy revenge and crossed the border into criminal mischief. Episodes of rage against adversaries from other schools that led to hospitalization of Tuomey's enemies but never criminal charges. His family was entrenched in social and political circles from the time the Irish had come to Northtown from the famine ships and had taken over the docks from the Swedes.

Some in his circle of peers knew him as "Beak." There was an intuitive aptness beyond the semantics of his initials for the image of a hawk among sparrows.

Rikki once told him Brian's father had grounded him after another accusation of date rape, barely resolved with a check to the girl's family, which was followed by an assault against a boy from another high school that resulted in a broken jaw. Rikki refused to believe half the stories about his friend. Not Raimo, although he knew that being the great Rick Jarvi's little brother was a talisman even Brian Tuomey wouldn't lightly dare to violate. When he heard that Tuomey had left town, he breathed easier.

"I thought you were—somewhere else," Raimo said.

"Rick's little bro. Look at you now. All grown up—and a tough guy, no less." He motioned to the lettering on the glass.

"Rick's in California," Raimo said.

"My, you've come up in the world."

"Did you hear me—"

"Still riding your famous brother's coattails, Handsome?"

Contempt lay beneath the words like a snake coiled under a rock. Tuomey was as good-looking in his thirties as he'd been when he quarterbacked the football team Rikki starred on. His attire would have been excessive on anyone else in this heat but not on Tuomey. He didn't look away from Raimo and he didn't flinch.

Raimo didn't get up to shake hands. Tuomey ignored that as if the idea had never crossed his mind. His face wasn't greasy with sweat like everybody else's on the street; the three-day beard belied the care that created the effect. His masculine face was still handsome but not in the current Neanderthal Hollywood style—more the chiseled good looks from a bygone era when Clark Gable set the standard. He hadn't put on much weight since Raimo had last seen him, a time Raimo recollected when he and his brother had come home in the wee hours from one of their boys-will-be-boys' escapades, Rikki vomiting in the yard and Tuomey wickedly laughing, clutching the post on the porch.

How would he have fared today? Raimo wondered. Few parents or teachers were as willing as then to turn a blind eye to vicious bullying and roughhouse sexual aggression.

Compared to Tuomey's casual dress, Raimo's rumpled, powder-blue suitcoat draped over the back of his chair looked like something off the racks at Goodwill's; certainly, the scuffed shoes beneath his desk were sorry-looking compared to whatever foreign brand Tuomey wore. *More than my whole outfit cost,* Raimo guessed. They probably had some name that spoke of continental bravura or discernment. Even Tuomey's tousled hair had the professional look of an expensive stylist.

Take away the fine cracks at the corners and the eyes that looked out from that handsome face were the same. Still beholding an adoring world every bit as much as they had when he was a teenager.

"Before you ask me, I haven't heard from Rikki in weeks," Raimo said.

"That puts me one up on you, private eye. Your big brother flew in from LAX last night."

"How do you know that?"

"Because he's shitfaced on Moscow Mules across the street at the Wyandotte right now."

"Why didn't he come himself?"

"Maybe he had to down a few before he could stand that pretty mug of yours."

Raimo stood up as if his chair were electrified. He had been insane to take Tuomey on back then, but every last restraint of common past had been severed; besides, he was forty pounds heavier and four inches taller than the last time he'd taken a run at Tuomey.

Raimo wouldn't forget it because the arm bar Tuomey held across his windpipe while he pinned him into the dirt knocked him unconscious. The first thing he saw when he came to was Rikki yelling and pulling Tuomey off him. Tuomey frothed at the mouth like a mad dog. Had they been isolated somewhere, Tuomey would have killed him. Raimo compensated for his loneliness and absent social life by lifting weights and punching a speed bag.

"Sit down, shithead," Tuomey said, the smile never leaving his face. "You'll get your chance."

Before Raimo could cross the desk, the door opened and struck Tuomey in the back of the legs. He whipped around, but it was only a small child, barely past toddler stage, holding a dripping turquoise and cherry popsicle in her small fist. Her mother came rushing in behind her and stopped, looked at both men, first at Raimo, then Tuomey. When she realized her mistake, she tried to hustle her little girl out the door.

"Oh, I'm so sorry," she said. "We thought this was the Finnish bakery."

"Across the street, next to the law offices," Raimo said, his voice husky from the adrenalin surge.

The situation was turning ludicrous. Tuomey's tight smile relaxed a fraction.

"Come on, hon," the girl's mother said. "So sorry . . . I d-didn't realize. . ."

But the little girl stood rooted where she was, right beside Tuomey's pantleg, unmoving despite her mother's hand. The popsicle dripped over her tiny fist and spilled parti-colored drops to the floor.

She let out a high-pitched wail and pointed a tiny arm at Raimo. "Mommy, monthster, Look!"

The child's gaping stare took in the bumpy, livid purple scars crisscrossing down the left side of his face. He'd received a tempered version of that look thousands of times before from adults but children who had not cultivated the same filter gave him the brunt of their horrified reaction. Her mother's flushed face deepened a shade to crimson, and she gripped the little girl firmly, spun her, and half-carried her out of his office. They disappeared across the plate glass window in a blur of colors and sounds of protest from the squealing child.

"See, Ray?" Tuomey said, his smile curling up to his glittering eyes. "Out of the mouths of babes. I delivered my message. See you around, Handsome."

Chapter 2 - August 2

"Is Rikki here?" his mother had asked.

"No, Mom. Not yet," Raimo had told her for the seventh time in an hour. "He's on his way."

"You sure?"

"I'm sure," Raimo lied again.

She asked more often lately and with greater urgency as her condition deteriorated. The hospice nurse said it was a matter of days. It was a call-and-response by now, a sad chant between a younger son and a dying mother who yearned for her first born.

Raimo was never called "Ray" by his mother, but she'd acquiesced to her older son's Americanized name without demur. Raimo couldn't recall the day she started calling him Rikki, too, in the confusion that was like a blanket being pulled over her mind, but he could remember hearing her saying "Riekoriki" in his early youth long before puberty and athletic fame gave his older brother all the clout in the house. It was so vivid it became an auditory hallucination in his mother's dementia, that double-click of syllables betokening an occasional exasperation but more often pride and love.

Raimo was grateful for the hospice care nurse and the shots of morphine that reduced the number of times he had to endure the game of "Where's Rikki?" Raimo's bigger fear, however, was the sundown syndrome that caused her to hallucinate back to the past. She asked him once to tell the priest hiding under the dining room table to leave; another time to find the little girl who kept dashing from room to room, hiding in closets and making a mess in the kitchen. Raimo dutifully went on these mental snipe hunts for her ghosts, usually smoking a cigarette on the porch, stifling a sob, before returning to her downstairs bed. By then, she was often asleep or too dulled by morphine to remember.

Her funeral came a month and a day after Raimo's father passed away. He died hard compared to her. A bloody, rust-colored stain followed the carpeting down the stairs when the ambulance men had to carry him down while he leaked from a duodenal ulcer the surgeons at the Cleveland Clinic were unable to fix. He'd been home recovering from a prior surgery that gave Raimo hope until the day he called out from his bed. A big strong man, his voice was reduced to a whispery croak.

Raimo arranged both funerals and they lay side by side in St. Joseph's Cemetery. Raimo's Lutheran father never stood a chance against his wife's virulent Catholicism and both boys were educated through parochial schools right from kindergarten. If his mother had been a practicing Satanist, Raimo's father would have gone happily along with her decision. It was an early lesson in the irrationality of love as well as the mind's superiority over physical strength.

It wasn't that his mother stopped loving Raimo because of his disfigurement. She was the one who kept his appointments at the doctor's, gave him his medications—all the topical analgesics and opiates—applied the gel sheets and Mederma cream, all while soothing him with lies that the scars would disappear. Years later, as the surgeries to make the skin grafts allow for the growth of his bones began, the lies no longer accommodated the reality. He understood, deeply and profoundly, that his scars would never go away. "They're less noticeable, smoother," she'd croon, as if she were reciting a TV commercial for fabric softener.

Blunt-force trauma tended to wipe out victims' memories of the events, but not so with burn victims. Everything is there, every ghastly moment. Raimo recalled coming awake in his backyard tent where he and his brother were "camping."

Rikki had complained all day to his mom he was too old to be playing with his kid brother but agreed after Raimo begged him to help set up the tent. Raimo was ten, just beginning to understand the vastness of the night sky and the constellations, and he wanted to find as many as he could on that summer night in July. He remembered falling asleep with his flashlight and the big library book of stars across his chest and the stuttering *pop-pop-pop* of firecrackers going off late at night. Fourth of July celebrations were over but the neighborhood kids were still firing off their dwindling supplies of fireworks including the cherry bombs and silver salutes his mother didn't know Rikki kept stored under a sock drawer.

They said it was a bottle rocket that went astray. It dropped into the maple in the backyard where the tent was staked. It dropped to the tent, still sizzling, and ignited the plastic material. In seconds, the whole tent was ablaze. Raimo's eyes snapped open beneath an inferno. He remembered that helpless feeling over and over, how long seconds could be, spaghettified in the black hole of pain, and how mesmerized he was by the colors of the flames even as the heat scorched his face. The zipper of his sleeping bag was stuck and he couldn't wiggle free. He thrashed and looked beside him for Rikki's sleeping bag but he was all alone with swirls of black smoke filling his lungs every time he opened his mouth to scream for his brother to save him. When flaps of the burning tent fell on him, he remembered how it stung at first, like a hive of angry wasps let loose on his face and shoulders.

Then a white-hot *blitzkrieg* of pain, all-enshrouding, total, and beyond anything his young mind had the comprehension to absorb. It was everywhere and nowhere at once: his hair on fire burning his scalp, maddening ripples of pain sent straight to the top of his head that he didn't realize until later weren't blows from someone outside actually hitting him but his very animal being blasting one message into his neurons, informing him *he was going to burn to death. . .*

They told him later that Rikki saved his life by pulling him feet first out of the flames, the sleeping bag on fire. Rikki's hands remained pink for weeks afterward and he had to have a special salve applied several times a day.

He never saw his mother apply the ointment to his brother's hands yet in his mind he can see it. He was in the burn unit of the Cleveland Clinic and wouldn't come home for several weeks.

All of that was clear in every detail. Even the parts his family claimed he couldn't remember, such as the regressing that happened when he finally got his release: the loss of speech, days without talking, the bed-wetting, the refusal to leave his room, the nightmares.

Some memories leached downward to the paleocortex, all there, every second, and it took nothing more than pure chance—a smell on the street, a look from someone passing his office window, a pause between sips of coffee—for portions of it to come raging back. His imagination and his memory intertwined at some point and he elongated certain memories, others he collapsed in a rush of imagery and sound. As time went by, he became the director and scriptwriter of his own biopic, "The Burning Tent," he called it; INT. RAIMO'S BACKYARD. NIGHT. Establishing shot of neighborhood. ZOOM to tree where the bottlerocket lands. SMASH CUT to flames. ZOOM on RAIMO thrashing in sleeping bag, helpless, his face melting under the burning tarp. Enter RIKKI. He pulls RAIMO free. PULL FOCUS to fully engulfed tent, a huge ball of yellow-orange-red with a massive plume of black smoke like a rooster's comb in the backyard of an ordinary street . . ."

Dissolve, dissolve. No wrap, no credits. It replayed on a loop in his head. Over and over, just waiting for the next mental trigger to restart the film.

Raimo considered it his personal version of the lemniscate, infinity's symbol, the figure eight lying on its side, endless memories that follow the same grooves like a toy car in a child's racetrack.

Rikki home—but not more than a few words from his brother despite Raimo's urgent texts to come home before his mother drew her last breath. As the hospice nurse gave him the time left in increments of weeks, then days, and finally, mercifully, hours, his texts to Rikki *come home now she's dying* were answered with briefer replies until an hour after paramedics arrived on the day she died, a last lengthy appeal was answered in six words: *Complicated. Busy. You arrange funeral. Thanks.*

Raimo checked the clock. His reverie consumed just enough time to force a decision to close the office. The brutal heat had by now infiltrated every cubic meter inside so that sitting still was uncomfortable. He'd get that portable a/c unit first thing tomorrow. He made a few notes for "the Pennimann case point four" on his digital recorder, shoved it into a drawer, dimmed the light, set the phone to record on three rings and locked the office. He regretted not buying the HD security camera with its four-channel system—an indulgence he couldn't afford for his tiny operation—but it would have saved him a lot of time and energy from dashing out to see who was at his office when half the time it was salespeople or a lost tourist. He could have had all the images sent right to his upstairs computer instead.

The building had no access to the upstairs except through a door around back that required a short walk around the corner, up Hulbert Avenue about a hundred feet to the parking lot. A short footbridge connected the lot to his door. It bothered him at first to have a single entrance and exit. Since the fire, he never walked into a closed space without knowing how to get out. His brain automatically mapped exits every time he entered an unfamiliar building or residence.

If I do go bust, Raimo thought, *I won't have far to go.* In the three years since he bought the building from the former owners who had converted it into a restaurant many years after George O'Mullan was rescued from his senility by relatives, the upstairs was strictly used for storage. At first, taxes were minimal. But as the harbor district grew economically after the recession of '08, and stores expanded or new business came in, he saw his own business decline. All the empty lots and abandoned buildings sold at sheriff's auction had been gobbled up by developers and tourists were no longer a novelty but a staple of the Harbor. *All except me*, Raimo thought. He seemed to be the only "novelty store" left on a street that catered to antiques, folk art, beach glass, bars, and diners. Where outlaw bikers once parked their black-and-chrome steel horses outside the Windward Lounge, a cozy boutique offered "gavage-fed" *foi gras* and imported wines.

The kitchen was the first part of the rectangle, followed by a dining area, and a work station overlooking Bridge Street. A small U-Haul truck had carried everything he needed in a single run. Raimo fixed a Tom Collins from a sideboard near the fridge, sat in his father's old lounge chair with fabric nap rubbed to a shine where his arms rested. He watched CNN with the sound muted. Acting on a hunch, he got up, threw the dregs of his drink in the sink, and left after just a few minutes.

The family home was a five-minute drive up Third Street, which bisected Hulbert just above his building. A forest-green Victorian with little left to distinguish it from its construction by a lakeboat captain in the days of wooden ships; the extensive ginger-breading had fallen away, the front porch rotted and was demolished by Raimo's father, one colored-glass window remained, but the widow's walk in an old photo had never been replaced when a portion of the roof had burned up in a past fire. When he pulled into the sloping driveway, he found Rikki sitting on the porch steps smoking.

"You are a detective," Rikki said.

"The dog returneth to his vomit," Raimo said getting out of the car. "I guessed you'd be here."

"I was on my way to your office but I thought I'd swing by the homestead first."

"Take a good look because soon it'll be somebody else's" Raimo said.

"What are you talking about? Half this place belongs to me."

Rikki reached out to steady himself against a pillar as he

stood up. Thin gold bracelets dangled from one wrist. Raimo noted the bloodshot eyes and a three-day stubble that was the opposite of Tuomey's crafted look. Rikki sported gold chains and one necklace with a small cross depending from his neck half-visible in the unbuttoned blue silk shirt. Arabic mosaic pattern—or maybe an Aztec design, Raimo thought, but something you'd never wear in a working-class town.

Same old Rikki. No mincing words, no apologies for missing his father's long decline into senility or his mother's funeral. Just: *Where's my cut?*

He had changed since Raimo last saw him a few Christmases ago. He might even be leaner. He looked less like the running back who matched himself against the team's biggest lineman when it came time to go "Round-and-Round-the-Mulberry-Bush," his moron coach's post-practice game of sending two players in opposite direction at full tilt around a small tree at the far end of the practice field to butt helmets like mountain rams. Raimo wondered if that Neanderthal ever got the memo about CTE.

"What are you doing here, Rikki? I'm assuming you aren't here out of guilt to lay flowers on Mom and Dad's graves."

"That's it. B. K. said you looked 'spiffy.'"

"It must be something important for you two to hook up again,"

"Wrong, fucko. Just the twenty-year reunion. Brian talked me into it."

"You and Beak couldn't pass up an opportunity to bask in the adulation of your peers one more time," Raimo said.

"The last time you called him that I had to pull him off you," Rikki laughed. "Your face was bluer than that friggin' sky."

Rikki tottered a couple steps on the porch before recovering.

Raimo headed to the porch with the key and opened the door. Without a word, Rikki brushed past him and left a reek of alcohol in his wake.

"Nothing's been removed except Dad's La-Z-Boy," Raimo

said. "It's in my apartment above the office. I'll give you half the value."

"Keep it. I don't want the fucking chair."

Raimo saw how drunk he was. Intense heat and booze were a bad combination. Dark patches of sweat under his arms and back turned the blue shirt a patchwork of cobalt and lighter shades.

"You ever hear of air conditioning, hillbilly?"

"California living has spoiled you, Rick."

Rikki's transformation from small-town Midwesterner to West Coast sophisticate with his gold chains and thin gold watch and Oxford shoes with double buckles was all but complete—yet he looked wretched in his expensive, sweat-soaked shirt. His eyes carried a worried glint besides the drunkard's foul temper.

"Your room still has bedding," Raimo said. "You can sleep here tonight."

A triple blast of car horn from the driveway ended the conversation in mid-sentence.

"I'll swing by your office tomorrow," Rikki said. "We need to talk about this goddam house."

"The letter's in the drawer if you want to see it now," Raimo said.

Rikki ignored that. He had to concentrate all his effort into leaving the house in a steadier manner than he had entered it.

"Regards to Tuomey," Raimo said.

He parted the curtain over the window in time to see his brother settle into Tuomey's black Spyder convertible. He didn't react when Tuomey spotted him and threw up a middle finger.

Raimo left the papers from the insurance company in the kitchen utensil drawer; he didn't need to look at them. His mother had signed a reverse mortgage three years before she died, before her mind started to go. He tried to talk to her about it but she shut him off. It was useless to go to his father, whose health was beginning to fail, and who'd never stood up to his wife when he was in his prime. Raimo didn't want the house, but he didn't understand why his mother needed money when his father's pension was sufficient and the cash Raimo took from his trust fund bought a new furnace, shingled the roof, and paid for every car repair.

The only answer that made sense was that Rikki needed money out in California. His mother would have crawled on her knees through broken glass to get it for him. Her decision to sell the house for monthly sums of cash would have been a no-brainer: If Rikki needed money, Rikki would have money. He sometimes wondered if the milk from her teats was tinged with some astringent like Witch-hazel leached from her bloodstream when it came his turn to suckle.

Rikki's football career came to an end his sophomore year in college when his scholarship to Western Michigan in the MAC was revoked; he was caught with marijuana in the athletic dorm, not unheard of, but Rikki complained he was white and that made the difference. Raimo thought his brother never learned the hard lesson high school stars from backwater schools all learned eventually; few made it big when the competition became keener. Rikki's habit of abusing his status in high school was another thing that didn't transfer to college, and he quickly fell out with his coaches. Rikki complained they were "racists" and wouldn't put him because he was white and being a running back was strictly an African-American position the way quarterbacking used to be for whites. Raimo mentioned the string of black quarterbacks for Ohio State but that provoked him worse.

"You mean *The* Ohio State? Those nigger-loving cocksuckers wouldn't even scout me. That's how racist they are."

Arguing with his brother went so far before Rikki flipped the switch that narrowed his eyes and furrowed his brow. Rikki turned into a dirt-pawing bull with flared nostrils who did everything but snort before he charged.

It took three years after his burns subsided before Raimo could engage in the roughhousing all brothers took for granted. Some of his scars were as thin as a spider web strand;

others began under his left eye like an out-of-control birthmark rimmed with ridges of cadaver-pale skin coursing in zigzags down his face over his shoulder and back and ending below his elbow where most of the flaming tarp had fastened itself and melted. The red wavy lines that intersected with those gray bumps gave him the appearance of a walking topographical map and were the result of the many surgeries designed to replace the grafts. He was clotted with flesh's transformation by the element of fire.

Raimo lacked the inborn skills of a private eye and he knew he didn't have the physical courage to be a bounty hunter. He was mostly shy around people and had no idea how to make social contacts. He was as lousy at talking to people as he would have been at throwing a bad guy over the hood of a car, a feat his deputy friend had performed many times. It was one reason why the outgoing, muscular Bart would make a good partner if the business expanded. At the moment, it was barely surviving despite some success at finding runaways. Raimo made up for his lack of people skills with a dogged persistence that kept him going.

Rikki hadn't said much but what he said and how he said it, right down to the glassy stare, told Raimo there was more than booze at work and Tuomey's pressure to come home for a reunion didn't cut it. He decided to go back to the office and see what his brother might be hiding among his parents' papers in the strongbox his mother kept under her sick bed even as she lay dying. Alive, he'd promised to protect it "from the bad people" she saw lurking in the corners of the room; dead, her claim subsided into pathos. Still, he found himself touching the furrowed ridge of dead skin, pale as a toad's belly, all down his forearm to his wrist. It was a nervous habit, something he did only when he felt the ground loosen up beneath his feet.

His upstairs apartment was a sweat lodge; beads of perspiration burst on his forehead by simply breathing in the stuffy air. He used a tire iron he kept under his bed to free the boxy unit from the window. He set it on the floor, dismayed by the water leaking onto the tongue-and-groove floorboards he had spent long hours refinishing; he threw the window open to the late afternoon air but the curtains were as stiff as a sculptor's statue. The outside brick was still hot to the touch and the air pungent with odors baking from the street. Rising above the exhaust from the parade of mufflers going back and forth was the burnt sugary aroma of Nissua bread.

Raimo didn't like invading his brother's life, but the idea Rikki might be in trouble gave him the final nudge to do some work downstairs in the morning. Raimo knew his brother's shock at being told the house was lost was phony. The next step was Rikki hitting him up for cash; he considered Raimo a soft touch so he had to know what Rikki was up to before he allowed him to siphon off his cash reserves from his dwindling trust fund. Rikki could turn on the charm as well as threaten, and Raimo had a lifetime of hero worship to overcome.

He fixed a Tom Collins and stripped down to his underwear. First, some digging around in the strong box. He had a variety of master and skeleton keys and a set of burglar picks locked in his drawer downstairs, but finessing wasn't required for the job. He noted the Made in China label and set to work levering the bar's grooved end into one corner and began prying the lid up a few millimeters at a time until he had a small finger-sized opening. One good stomp of his foot on the side of the plastic-reinforced box increased the crack wide enough for his fingers to reach inside and begin withdrawing the contents.

A couple more Tom Collinses later, drenched in sweat, a pleasant buzz had settled over his eyebrows. Raimo worked through all the papers and memorabilia but found nothing significant: crayon drawings, homemade Valentine cards to his mother, scapulars from his and Rikki's Confirmations with dour saints' portraits on each, some utility bills dated twenty years ago, yellowed newspaper clippings from Rikki's many sports accomplishments. A third-place medal at the state tournament during his brother's senior year.

One legal letter from the trust fund lawyer dated eight years earlier. Apparently, his mother had written to see about having the settlement money released to her. The denial was crisp despite the legalese. Raimo learned for the first time that his father had set the terms of the award, not his mother, and the money would be released "solely to the injured party, namely Raimo T. Järvi, juvenile, pending his twenty-fifth birthday and pursuant to the Tax Benefit Rule as established to the extent includible under IRC § 111. . ." Leave it to lawyers to include the umlaut in his name, he thought, but he was grateful they did what his father asked.

At the bottom lay a long-bladed knife. A family heirloom he hadn't thought about in years. Raimo's great-grandfather was one of the original dockworkers from Finland who settled the Harbor with other Scandinavians before the Irish clans arrived. The Italians wouldn't arrive until mid-nineteenth century when they assumed the dirty work of excavating the city's sewerage system. The knife, Raimo's father told him, was found in the back of a dead man—"an Irishman"—floating in the harbor. How his great-grandfather acquired it remained a family mystery, but the story of the knife, the famed Finnish *pukka*, was brought up from time to time but never during Thanksgiving or Christmas dinner when Nora Jarvi's Irish clan descended on the house.

It must have galled his mother to be thwarted by her tame husband, especially when it concerned Rikki's welfare, feigned or real. Raimo had no doubt it aggravated the tensions of the house at that time and furthered the widening gap between his parents. Raimo paused, grateful to add a footnote to the memory of his spineless father and his courage—for once, and for his second-born son's sole benefit, the mouse had stood up to the tiger's wrath.

All he had to show his brother was the insurance company's registered letter informing him, as executor of the estate, that he had thirty days to vacate the premises. It would have to do. Of course, Rikki could deny receiving any money from his mother, but what had he done to ask for it in the first place? All his calls home testified to his success in one business venture after another. The last thing he mentioned to Raimo was a night club in West Hollywood he owned "a half-share in" and was then managing for a silent partner, a woman he said he met through Tuomey. Rikki was big on name-dropping and bragged about celebrities who showed up in "his place."

Rooting among the papers, the faded and forgotten memories gave him a stab of sorrow he didn't expect. There was nothing from him during that two-year period of convalescence as if he had stepped out of time before resuming his damaged childhood. Salt-sweat stung the corners of his eyes, and he had to wipe the sheen of perspiration from his forehead every few minutes. He made a mental fix-it note to get two of those portable units in the morning. Not having eaten since his salad at the diner with Bart, the liquor exerted a strong influence abetted by the sauna warmth; his reading and concentration steadily eroded, so he decided to quit before the booze fog descended. He'd call California in the morning allowing for the four-hour time lag.

Raimo fell across his bed and remembered he'd left the reading light on. It wasn't worth the effort to get up so he turned his head toward the wobbly rectangle of light from the window. The street's sodium arc lights cast an orange glow throughout his rooms he found soothing. His last conscious thought was that he should angle his head on the pillow more toward north. His mother, for some superstitious or private reason she never divulged, insisted the boys' beds face north.

"Why do we have to face that way?" Raimo asked his father one night. "What happens if I sleep at the other end?"

His father (he remembered with a sudden jolt) was in the doghouse for drinking with some tugmen at the Wyandotte Club: Piecho Saari, a bantam-sized, hell-raising captain, Ari Lehtinen, and Eino Karppinen, an oiler from the engine room who never spoke ten words when none would do. His father straightened up to his full height and pulled his pants higher on his belly.

"Sleep any goddamned end of the bed you want, son," he said.

Raimo gave up willing the fire to stay out of his dreams before sleep. A month out of the hospital, he awoke in the middle of night rubbing his hands together and slapping his legs to put out invisible flames. Rikki's threat to "put him out" until morning was enough to quiet him down but not still the hummingbird thumping of his heart. Rikki's relationship to him chilled from that day on, and Raimo thought it the result of the strong despising the weak or infirm, some throwback to our earliest origins as bipeds fresh out of the trees. After all, he learned in grade school Vikings used to hurl handicapped newborns off the fjord cliffs into the frigid sea.

Too much alcohol at night was a risk because any internal braking system was bypassed and the sensory details became even more vivid when he dropped off that cliff into the black void of sleep.

The induced coma the doctors put him in was the only blank in his memory. From one eye, he saw Rikki's face pulling him out of the inferno, the other saw nothing because of the burning tent fabric plastered to the side of his face. He wouldn't see out of either eye after the coma because of the grease slathered into his sockets and the puffed skin of his face. The surgeons worried he might lose his left arm from infection; trying to free himself from the sleeping bag had only cocooned him tighter in the folds. His legs received only second-degree burns because Rikki had cut him free and his pants, being corduroy, had not burned as easily as the cotton tee-shirt they pulled off in fiery ribbons.

He often wondered where he was in that dark period between the first waves of pain and the second, when the nerve endings came back and he felt doused in acid. It made him doubt everything the nuns taught him about religion. Where was his name saint? Where was the merciful God who let that bottlerocket tumble onto the tent? If Rikki hadn't been there, he'd have burned to death.

Raimo spent two hours in his office racking up a big phone bill with calls to California, including the manager of the condo where Rikki was staying on Santa Monica Boulevard. Raimo easily recognized a Midwesterner without that obnoxious California lilt.

"Alameda Arms, concierge speaking," chirped a pleasant voice that failed to indicate its gender.

"I'm calling about a rental," Raimo said. "My company is transferring me next month and I wondered if you could give me some basics."

"Certainly," the voice replied.

"First thing," Raimo said, "is the cost. Can you tell me—"

"Twenty-four, sixty-five per. Extra charges for certain amenities, of course. One month in advance, two months' security deposit."

"That's a bit steep for me," Raimo said.

"For *that* price, in *this* location," the reply came, "you must understand, sir, the amenities alone are among the best available in Hollywood." Less warmth now and a touch of exasperation for the density of anyone who didn't immediately recognize the obvious.

"No, no, that's fine," Raimo said, apologetic for being so thick: *Hollywood*, of course. "I'm sure my company can afford it," he added. "However, I was wondering—you see, my brother lives there—and he says your place has first-rate accommodations, is just outstanding." Rikki's word for everything Ohio was not.

"Ah, I see. Your brother is one of our guests. I'm glad to hear he gives us a good name."

The brightness came back in the voice but waited for him to volunteer the name of the particular "guest" able to pay almost three thousand for a single month's rent, which term suggested more of an oxymoron to Raimo.

"Rick Jarvi, perhaps you know him?"

"Yes, yes. I do," the concierge replied.

The delayed response dropped two octaves in pitch and several more degrees of temperature, but it said plenty about Rikki's personal relationship to this concierge. Loud parties? Unpaid rent?

"Can you tell me—"

"Sir, our website should have all the relevant information you need to make an informed decision. Thank you for calling Alameda Arms. You have a *won-der-ful* day."

The California lilt, at last, saddled to the chirpy brush-off.

Raimo looked up the Alameda on Google Earth and the closest precinct: West Hollywood Sheriff's Station. Bart would still be awake from his third-shift tour. Massey liked to brag about getting by on five hours' sleep, which didn't include the cooping he managed to sneak in whenever he patrolled those back-country roads south of Route 45.

"*Kemo sabe*, I need a favor," Raimo said when he heard Bart answer.

"I was just about to hit the sack, Ray. Can it wait until noon?"

"I'm buying lunch this month."

"I get to choose the place?"

"Within reason," Raimo said.

"Fair enough."

Raimo told him what he needed.

"Can't you make that call yourself? You're supposed to be the gumshoe."

"I want you to call early. Maybe the desk sergeant's bored and will talk to a brother officer."

That wasn't a stretch. Northtown cops gave him a cold shoulder or were grudging in their cooperation the few times he'd asked. The Sheriff's wouldn't return his calls and Bart would know that too well as he mentioned a rebuke from the Sheriff when it got out at headquarters he was a friend of Raimo Jarvi.

"Give me an hour," Bart said.

Raimo's ringtone jolted him from his thoughts.

"What have you got?"

"That place your brother said he had a fifty percent share in? It burned down three weeks ago. The state arson investigator still hasn't released his report."

"Arson?"

"They can't prove it. Something about 'saddle burns' but no evidence of an accelerant, which is rare. They're using some fancy 3-D software to study the burn pattern."

"What else?"

"They've interviewed your brother and the owner," Bart said. "She's from San Pedro. Owns a few rental properties in LA, including Sallie-O's, your brother's club, and a strip mall on South La Cienega. By the way, that place is—was—no dance club for the beautiful people. The desk cop told me it was a sleazy tit bar at the wrong end of Santa Monica responsible for a dozen call-outs a week. Not a high-class joint, he said."

"Text me the station number and the name of your contact, Bart. And that bar owner's name."

"Okeydoke."

"I owe you."

"And you shall pay."

So Rikki lied about his bar. It didn't mean or prove anything other than he didn't want to be considered a failure back home. Everything for an athlete who enjoyed success at seventeen was going to be anticlimactic if he couldn't follow it up with bigger triumphs. The arson was problematic, however. If Rikki did it, or paid to have it done, what could he gain that would justify the risk of going to prison for a serious crime? A share in a strip club wasn't enough to risk his future for—or was it? He and Rikki hadn't spent much time together in the last few years. They used to Skype when he left for California. Raimo was still living at home, champing at the bit, though he promised his mother he'd stay. She needed help with his father, whose health was caving in faster, no more inch at a time but every ailment produced a cascade of other symptoms and resulted in more trips to the pharmacy.

Mama's boy, Rikki chided. *When are you going to cut the apron strings?*

A good question. The past was like the scar tissue on his body: always close enough to remind him that chance could pulverize his dreams into dust.

It was time to go. Tanisha Pennimann had a rendezvous at a trysting motel on the outskirts of town. She made it easy for Raimo. Always the same two or three places, pastel-trimmed freeway motels, popular trysting places for cheating spouses, and often the same time of day—between 3:30 and 5:00 o'clock. The lovers themselves were the only thing that changed.

He thought about taking the directional mic he'd purchased online but decided it was overkill. The last time, he'd sat in the parking lot while she waited inside the room for her new lover, an owner of a used-car lot where Leotis bought his SUV. Raimo counted the empties already lined up on the sidewalk for the maid. He imagined the bedbugs and chiggers these randy couples had to be oblivious to for the sake of consummating lust. Her lover finally arrived, fashionably late, a lanky bald man in cargo pants and a LeBron James jersey. Before him, it was a gray-haired elder at People's Baptist church she and Leotis attended on West Avenue. He'd snapped Tanisha getting out of her car and going into the lobby before going to her room. He used his expensive Canon to snap the man in profile, mid-stride, then full-faced as he turned around at the door, which the guilty always did. Bart told him guilty suspects always slept in an interrogation room or put their heads down and tried to sleep. This was Raimo's axiom for the guilty, man or woman: they always turned around to see who might be looking. *Nothing more than your guilty conscience*, he would mutter to himself.

Unlike the shy elder, this man had a purposeful look on his face. Then several more snaps before Tanisha let him into the room. She was a large woman, not at all a beauty, and with a Dolly Parton-sized red wig and make-up applied with a trowel. She was a formidable thing to behold in a bright sari dazzling with tropical flowers and petals the size of bratwurst. Leotis always insisted on more than the arrivals and departures, so he knew he'd have to crawl up to the window with his Nikon pinhole camera for the money shots. It wasn't something he looked forward to and reminded him why private eyes were held in such contempt by real cops.

Twenty minutes later, he steeled himself for the ordeal ahead and walked across the lot with an eye toward where he might best position the camera, fastened to a sling and attached to his belt; a bottle of Jack Daniels, a prop, was cradled in his arm like a football—just another party-goer on his way to a room. The drapes of Tanisha's room were suddenly flung wide apart and there she stood at the window, big as life, her hands on her broad hips staring right at him. He made a casual adjustment in his step as if he forgot his room number. Head down, he burned with shame under her gaze but resisted looking and hoped his imitation of yet another cheating husband might pass muster under her gaze.

No such luck. Out of the corner of his eye, he caught the crimson-painted mouth moving in words he didn't need to hear to know what they said; he caught the unmistakable message of the middle finger jabbed in his direction. No doubt, Leotis had made him a household name by now, and that knowledge flustered him more. When he risked a look, the drapes were closed again.

So much for capturing the dalliance *in flagrante delicto*. Leotis would be upset, but he'd take the fee down. Meanwhile, recalling Tanisha's stamina at love-making, he returned to his Wrangler, drove to the back of the lot and settled in for a long wait.

Raimo pondered the nature of love, the whole monkey nature of it with its rambunctious couplings and smells and wondered who or what had put this idea into the minds of human beings. It wasn't supposed to work, and mostly it didn't, he knew, yet somehow, deep in his core, he hoped it did for the lucky few who possessed the grace to deserve it.

Chapter 3 - August 3

"Did I stutter? There's nothing, Rick. The money's been paid out," Raimo said. "You probably have a better idea than I do where it went."

"What's that supposed to mean?"

He and Rikki had the last two seats at the far end of the bar. The Wyandotte was almost full at this hour, which—considering it was only mid-afternoon—was a testament to the power of the ongoing heat wave. Watering holes and thirsty animals.

"You think she sent me the money?"

"Forget it," Raimo said.

"Fuck you, brother."

This hadn't gone well. Raimo was hoping to glean a few crumbs from their conversation about Rikki's doings in California, but his brother showed up a half-hour late, in slovenly attire, and looked badly hung over. Rikki kept his shades on like a movie star slumming among the little people. He only removed them long enough to glance at the order-to-vacate letter Raimo slid across the bar.

"Fucking insurance companies. They like to take but never give," Rikki said. He pushed the letter back to him. Raimo wondered if he were talking about his torched bar in Hollywood rather than the family homestead.

"Look at these people," Rikki said.

He ordered another bourbon and water by wagging his empty glass in the bartender's direction. The bartender was new, too young to remember Rikki's feats on the playing field and showed no real hurry to break off his conversation with an attractive young couple halfway down the bar.

"What people? I see tourists mostly," Raimo replied. "I don't see anything different."

"Town's full of blacks and Puerto Ricans. Everywhere you look. What happened here? I been gone—what?—three years, and Northtown looks like a Rainbow Coalition of freaks."

He was sweating off the previous day's booze from his hairline down to his shoulders bunched in another damp silk shirt. Raimo thought of a fish rotting from the head down. The air conditioning in the Wyandotte was set at morgue temperature. Raimo knew Rikki was a believer in the hair-of-the-dog remedy for a hangover.

"You're from California and you say that about this town?" Raimo responded.

"Everything's going to shit and you don't see it."

"So we're clear about the house?" Raimo asked him.

"I can't fucking believe she would do this to me," Rikki said.

Raimo couldn't tell if his brother's outrage was real or feigned. Rikki always seemed to have money but he went through it like water. The summer he graduated high school he landed a cushy job on the railroad, thanks to an alumnus and football fan who also happened to be a county commissioner who had pull with a Norfolk & Southern vice president. When Rikki's Chevy pickup was found stuck in a ditch near a train siding and it was discovered a couple dozen cases of beer had been removed from a car while the train idled at a siding, he was fired but not prosecuted. Rikki denied it but there was no doubt he and his pal Tuomey were the thieves.

"What the fuck, hey asshole, I been waiting on this drink for an hour," Rikki demanded of the bartender as soon as he brought him a fresh drink.

"Take it easy," Raimo said.

"You fucking take it easy!"

The bartender glowered at them both but walked slowly back to resume his conversation.

"This shithole town. Fucking lowlifes." He downed the bourbon in a gulp and chased it with water. "This bourbon tastes like cat piss."

"This town's been good to you, brother," Raimo said.

"Kiss my ass, bro," Rikki said. Raimo doubted Rikki ever used his real name in California. Too ethnic.

Whenever Raimo broached the subject of California, Rikki turned it around to something else. Worse, he'd picked up the scandal of Kristine Radebaugh's murder, probably from Tuomey, and was badgering him for details.

"I banged that bitch in high school," Rikki said. "Bet you didn't know that."

Raimo felt like a punch had just been delivered to his solar plexus. He covered it with a sip of beer.

"Yeah," Rikki went on, reminiscing. "Had a sweet little box with a twist of hair right under her belly button. She stepped out of her panties, I see this caramel thatch, and my cock grew another inch right there."

"You mind if we talk about something else besides your limited jock fascination with sex?" Raimo tried to make it light, but his stomach churned.

I never knew, he thought.

"What's going on out there?" Raimo asked again, a misfired attempt Rikki picked off like lint.

"Nothing's going on out there. Mind your own fucking business," Rikki said.

Raimo intended to do everything else but mind his own business. Rikki's brush-off was going to become his quest. Maybe because his reunion was scheduled for that night, Rikki peppered him with questions about people they knew from the past—the old Finn, Irish, and Italian families from the neighborhood. Rikki's sexual preferences were eclectic like most adolescent boys, but he favored the darker Italian girls because "they had the biggest tits."

"Ask Tuomey. He was your class president."

"Brian has a shittier memory for names than I do. Half those people will expect me to remember them tonight, but if they don't have those Hello-My-Name-Is tags, I won't."

"Tuomey should have scheduled it for the twenty-first."

"What's on the twenty-first?"

"A total eclipse of the sun," Raimo said.

"Who gives a fuck?" Rikki said. "I've got to run. Great to catch up on old times and all that shit, but I have things to do."

"Why not stay at the house? It's empty. I'd put you up at my place across the street but—"

"Brian's putting me up at his condo on Lake Road," Rikki said.

"Tuomey doesn't do favors for free."

"Tell me about it," Rikki said.

Raimo noticed the bartender leaned more intimately into the girl's space every time her boyfriend got up to go to the rest room.

"I haven't seen that guy in twenty years and I still can't stand him," Raimo said.

"Say what you mean. Stop fumble-fucking around like some drag-ass loser in this shithole."

"So says the Dale Carnegie of Hollywood. I'll bear that wisdom in mind," Raimo replied; "for what it's worth, I'll be at the reunion tonight."

"What the hell for? It isn't your class," Rikki said.

His scowl lasted from the time he slid off the stool to the time it took him to take a twenty out of his wallet, toss it on the bar, and tuck his shirt into his belt.

"*Fungoo*, I've got to lose weight," he said.

Raimo said, "I still think Mom sent you the money from the house."

He didn't look at his brother. He waited for the explosion. But it never came.

Rikki slammed the whiskey glass down on the bar hard enough to draw the bartender's gaze from the girl he was chatting up to gaze in his direction.

Raimo waited a few minutes after Rikki left, put a twenty of his own on the bar to cover the bill and a tip. He liked this bar and he liked the memories it evoked. The transition from a working-class tavern where big men with tattoos and huge beer bellies used to sit and enjoy a chinwag with one another in their rough, spare vocabulary had been converted over time to a place where twenty-somethings sipped their flavored vodka drinks with obscene or silly names and discussed which vols-au-vent pastries went with whichever amuse-bouche ice wine. The randy bartender a few feet distant from him was separated by lightyears when it came to things held in common. His me-first millennial status, indolent walk, the silver loop earring, his half-shaved head and blue glyph neck tattoo all said defiantly he had nothing to do with Raimo's in-built fastidiousness or small-town mindset: *You're more than a half-beat out of tempo from your own generation, brother.*

"A day late and a dime short." Which was yet another of his mother's sayings about his father.

Bart put Raimo in touch with a Columbus private investigator when he decided to take the big leap on his own. The money was spoiling him and he knew it. He'd become a familiar Harbor rat, a bar-fly, someone inclined to sleep until noon, shave on weekends, and fall asleep in front of his hi-def plasma TV every night.

At first, he balked. "Is there a training program for it?" Raimo asked him one night at the Wyandotte.

"Training? Are you serious, Jarvi? If you haven't been adjudicated insane by a judge or been convicted of a felony or arrested for anything that falls under a moral turpitude clause somewhere, you can be a licensed, practicing private investigator in this state in no time," Bart proclaimed.

"How fast?" Raimo asked.

"How fast can rats fuck?"

Bart was in a sour mood as a result of being dumped the previous night by his girlfriend at the time, a married woman.

The ex-FBI man Bart hooked him up with, however,

impressed him as someone who looked and acted like a true professional, not some inebriated sloven reeling in his boots like some TV cop show. He spoke knowledgeably and compassionately about the "good" a private eye can do because a private investigator wasn't tied to legal procedures like cops and detectives. "Much more than spying on cheating spouses, believe me," he said with a wink. He gave Raimo examples, such as finding missing children, bringing runaways home to their families, catching scam artists, locating deadbeat dads, protecting people, especially women, from stalkers and regaled him with cases where he had done these things. Raimo thought he detected a tear in the man's eyes as he reminisced his best cases.

When it came to databases Raimo might need, he gave him a list: Tracers, Skip Smasher, SkipMax, IRBsearch, and several others he mentioned that could be "a little pricey" but were worth it. One kind of cellular phone-tracking technology called Stingray sounded like something the NSA used for international terrorism.

A private investigator's license allowed him access to driver's licenses depending on the state. The exam was a joke. A $30 fee, a background check, proof of liability coverage, and 5 letters of recommendation as to his integrity from "reputable" citizens unrelated by blood gained him his Class A license. That latter proved the hardest to obtain because his social life in town, not counting bartenders and bar-hoppers, was nil. He had to grit his teeth to get three of those references from people who easily extolled Rikki to the skies but had only a vague recollection of his existence.

The day after he hired one of his drinking acquaintances to hand-letter the sign on his window, he received a letter dunning him for "a consultation fee" of three hundred dollars by that very same investigator.

Raimo dropped half the databases, one by one, as the renewals came due. He just didn't require them for the little work that drifted his way. For better or worse, Northtown's need for his private investigative services all too often came down to exactly what the Columbus eye said would not be the only reason for being one but was, in fact, precisely the reason Leotis Pennimann first showed up at his front window, rocking from one foot to the other, racked with indecision about opening the door. Raimo grew so anxious about seeing the man standing out there staring in at him with such obvious anguish for the third day in a row that he finally got up, went outside, introduced himself, and practically dragged Leotis Pennimann inside. Now he wished he'd left him out there to be torn asunder by the demons of his own obsessive masochism.

The ayenbite of inwit—a phrase he'd heard on *Jeopardy*, came to mind: "The prick of conscience," the show's host defined it. Some medieval confessional work.

How little we've changed, Raimo thought.

Bart's text came in; he noted the woman's name, Darlene Cook, and set to work tracking her down. He fed her name into public records databases and turned up several phone numbers and addresses. She skipped around Los Angeles County, always trading up. Three kids, a husband, and other information accessible with a private-eye license gave him a skeletal outline of the woman; she was very well off, upper-middle class, licenses for everything from massage parlors to apartment complexes but no advanced degrees, plenty of holdings and businesses incorporated into a holding company. The husband's name was nowhere to be found. She also had a full page of real-estate listings and multiple numbers in the LA area. He clicked on the house address and got a good view of an angular three-story monster house built in to a hillside on Long Beach. He checked Zillow for comparable houses; hers was worth a couple million.

The most telling information about the woman came from an online site where people with specific grudges over their real-estate dealings could unload. Darlene Cook had made a lot of people unhappy over the years, especially tenants of her properties. The gleanings from the past year alone were telling: "I hope you rot in the darkest corner of Hell you

Bitch!" might be typical of the negative responses. Accusations of neglect, theft, insect infestations ignored, cheating on contracts, short-changing contractors and a multitude of petty and serious offenses were all attributed to her.

He called the number but was told it was out of service. It took him time and a little artful subterfuge—namely, lying—but he managed to get her cell phone from a handyman at one of her apartment buildings.

"Ms. Cook, may I speak to you for a minute?"

"What about?"

A masculine voice to go with the photos of a big-boned, handsome woman in her 50's who smiled big every time, a stevedore's face beneath a mop of unruly blonde hair too disheveled not to be expensively coiffed. Most noticeable in the bulk of snaps was the deep cleavage on display.

"My brother works for you, Rick Jarvi."

"You tell that motherfucker Rickie I'm not covering for him anymore. The cops want to talk to him and he damned well better call—Who did you say this was?"

"My name is Ray Jarvi. I'm his brother in Ohio.

"Fuck you and your whoredog brother."

Click, dead air. Silence.

He didn't expect much but he didn't expect that.

"May I speak to Ginny?"

"Just a minute."

He could hear *Hey, babe, it's for you.*

"This is Ginny?"

"Ginny, you don't remember me. I'm Rick Jarvi's brother, three years younger. He mentioned you were a class officer, so I thought I'd call you."

"I didn't know Rick Jarvi had a brother. What is it you're calling about?"

Virginia Dyson was the only one of Rikki's class he trusted not to mention his call to their former president, Brian K. Tuomey; she was National Honor Society, MENSA IQ, Yale and MIT grad. Her IT work was so advanced she worked from home for a major international corporation when most people were still using computers as glorified typewriters.

Raimo said. "Rick mentioned you might want some catering help tonight so I thought I'd volunteer my services—gratis, of course."

Ginny told him what time to show up and thanked him.

He had a foreboding about anything that went smoothly and scratched the livid worm of scar on his forearm; he thought he might be making a mistake. *Not my circus, not my monkeys.* He didn't like to freewheel anything anymore than he ever walked into a room without boxing the corners, searching out the exits.

Raimo entered his old high school around five and felt no nostalgia for the place. He hated it, every year and every room in the building, and most of the teachers who were as gutless as the students who mocked him to his face or behind his back. He was grateful social media was still in its inception in those days or the humiliation would have been far worse.

He passed the same lockers he'd once used, noticed the idiotic, badly written banners extolling the same events, clubs, athletes and cliques. Different names, same hero worship, and similar frenetic need to be accepted.

He proceeded down the corridor to the cafeteria. The same hallway smells assaulted his nostrils, reminding and surprising him at once how deep his hatred of the place was.

He saw a dozen people in caterers' uniforms preparing hors d'oeuvres, trays of drink glasses, and setting out cases of beer and wine. Leave it to Tuomey to find a way around the prohibition of alcohol on school premises.

Raimo finagled a spot serving at the bar based on his long experience.

"Bartender?" the harried supervisor asked.

"Drinker."

The class officers showed up a half-hour later and he waved to Ginny, but she didn't acknowledge him. Raimo looked at them bustling about setting up the table at the entrance and giggling over old photos and yearbook portraits; he discerned the youth hiding beneath the perms, mascara, the crow's feet, tummies, and balding hair like a double exposure in old film stock.

One guest not invited had already made his presence felt—namely, the Grim Reaper. Raimo overhead a discussion about when to introduce a moment of silence for classmates who had succumbed to the ravages of disease, accident, or some type of malfeasance that had to be euphemized. He heard "pancreatic cancer," "car accident," "Iraq," overdose," and then there was Donnie Morning. He died spectacularly on Bridge Street one night after the bars closed. Raimo, abandoning booze for his new profession, paid for the transition to respectability with insomnia and IG tract problems. He was moving into his new digs in the upstairs on Bridge Street when he heard voices in the street. A crowd was gathering down by the river. Donnie had left his favorite tavern and climbed to the top of the bascule bridge—no easy feat—and when the police arrived to block off the street, he performed a high dive to the river below. The Coast Guard vessel fished him out with a broken neck. Donnie's two hundred pounds and gravity applied a lot of force and, according to Bart the next day over coffee, had lacerated every internal organ from liver to lungs. "Flipped his head completely around," Bart told him, gleaning the gossip crumbs from the scuttlebutt on the street. An impressive number of dead for one class.

Raimo nearly attended his own tenth class reunion, had gone as far as to dress up for it, but his sole intention was mayhem; he'd wrapped his hands in duct tape around a couple pieces of sawed-off rebar and planned to go after three of his worst bullies. Sense or cowardice, something had changed his mind at the last minute. He got drunk instead and resolved to put the past out of his mind. That was the moment Raimo felt he had finally grown up even if the world wanted to deny him the right to live in the world as a man, not a victim of a childhood accident.

People began to arrive, mostly as couples but a few arrived solo. The din inside grew in volume as more people arrived and exchanged hugs and kisses, cried tears at seeing what time had wrought. The rising decibel level kept proportion with the flow of alcohol and Raimo found himself unexpectedly busy.

He saw his brother arrive at seven. When Rikki spotted him at the bar, Raimo's brother fixed him with a long look and shook his head. Around eight-fifteen, the class president arrived amid fanfare and ballyhooing with his arms spread out to the crowd like a guru beholding his devotees. Cheers, good-natured jeers, and laughter welcomed him inside. Tuomey milked it like a politician for every ounce of admiration he could squeeze out.

Tuomey, like Rikki, could charm when he chose. Raimo read somewhere that one of every one hundred people you passed in the street was a psychopath; few wound up in prison, many were successful. High school were breeding grounds for mastering and disguising an inner viciousness.

Another hour passed and the crowd noise increased in volume. Some were very drunk, others just feeling the buzz. Tuomey and Rikki were reliving their glory days on the field with long passes of beer cans tossed the length of the cafeteria. Rikki let a couple Tuomey passes drop and explode on the floor. The people at nearby tables hooted approval at the antics of their two former stars.

Among the people he served, Raimo picked out a couple of drunks who had come solo and shared a table. They were largely ignored by the tables around them. One was obese, the other slovenly. They weren't jocks, geeks, brainiacs like Ginny, band types, or druggies. Just average loners, rejects from the cliques that teenagers formed instinctively. When the heavier one approached the bar for the third time in an hour, Raimo chose the moment.

"I see Brian is still Big Man on Campus," he said.

He had thin ginger hair and his hands were small and puffed like a baby's.

He grunted.

"I hear Brian's made a ton of money in some business venture," Raimo offered, tossing a little more chum in the water.

"Business?" One hand wrapped around the plastic glass. Raimo made sure he had a double shot. "He's just a—he's just a marketing executive. No big deal."

Raimo watched him walk back to his table. He moved carefully, protecting his drink against his stomach like Saint Tarcisius, boy martyr, with his Eucharist.

That was more than Rikki had offered, except that Rikki mentioned Brian's headquarters was in Columbus.

The next drunk Raimo selected for a gentle interrogation was uncooperative and stared at him.

"What do you care?"

"Just curious," Raimo said with a shrug. "How's that drink?"

Then, appearing very late among the crowd, was someone Raimo recognized: Dino Caddio. He was part of the Rikki-Tuomey clique, one of their circle, more like Brian's flunkey and whipping boy. Andino Caddio had aged badly. Raimo took in the stooped posture, rounded shoulders that resembled a dowager's hump, the combover that failed to cover the ebb of baldness. The slicked-back effect made him look like an otter just out of the water with spiky bristles popping up in every direction.

Dino was a small man, slender, and unassuming except in his clucking servitude to an alpha male or his bullying attitude to his inferiors. Once upon a time, he'd been a good-looking, black-haired teen who ran with Rikki's crowd. His easy-going personality, popularity, and expressive eyes gave him an abundance of "guinea charm," as Tuomey derisively described it. The few times Dino had come over to the house, he'd either ignore him, as if the kid brother were invisible, or give him the Italian salute: *va' fa' un culo.*

Around eleven, things began to wind down, the drunks got quieter and the air was stuffy with exhaled booze and nostalgia; the music swapped Guns-N'-Roses, Bon Jovi, and Def Leppard for Phil Collins, George Michael, and syrupy love ballads. Gloria Estefan seemed to do the trick as wives dragged husbands to the floor for a slow dance. Some couples remained at their tables littered with empties, party whistles, sopped crepe paper, and spilled drinks. Raimo kept his eye on Rikki and Tuomey, the confirmed bachelors in the room, who hadn't been seated at any table longer than fifteen minutes. On occasion, they'd meet at a table where the talk was boisterous. Rikki seemed subdued and willing to let Tuomey shine as unofficial master of ceremonies. Wherever Tuomey went, his faithful shadow Dino Caddio would appear nearby.

Raimo was about to slip away, call it a night now that the bar action had slowed to a trickle of serious drinkers. The fat man came back several times and it fell to Raimo to serve him. He'd gone through most of a bottle of Scotch on his own. This time, he asked for a water chaser.

Raimo set the drink in front of him. The man's face was shiny with sweat. His face was pink and round as a pie plate.

"I want to tell you—I want to tell you—something," the man said. He was bleary-eyed and unsteady.

"Yes?"

"Your brother, my fren' Rick, old Rick Jarvi, he was the greatest. . . greatest running back in the county. Shoulda played pro ball. Shame, shame."

With that final pronouncement, he planted his elbows on the table and tucked his head between them like a honey badger sniffing out larvae in a hollow tree. Raimo just caught him under the elbows before his legs gave in altogether. He couldn't dead lift him to his feet and he couldn't drag him so Raimo allowed the man to melt from his arms to the inviting floor. The supine man burped once and passed out.

Raimo looked around for help. A dozen heads swiveled his way but no one seemed inclined to get up or move. He signaled the biggest male with the catering service to give him a hand; together they managed to hoist him, one under each arm and half-drag him to his feet and then guide him out to the lobby.

Ginny Dyson came out with them. She used her cell to call for a taxi.

Raimo had seen plenty of drunks over the years, and being one of those drunks carried outside to recover, he knew the humiliation and the accompanying hangover. He felt uneasy about dumping him in a taxi. The man might not be a heavy drinker and alcohol poisoning could wreak havoc on someone as badly out of shape as he was.

The big caterer told Raimo he couldn't stay. He looked down at the unconscious man once more and said, "He must have a heart the size of a canned ham."

Ginny found a room key for one of the cheaper freeway motels in his pants pocket.

The taxi arrived in twenty minutes. By then, the man had come to and was sitting up. He recognized Ginny but had no idea who Raimo was. He was able to get in the taxi with Raimo's and the driver's assistance, Ginny held the cab door open and climbed in beside him. She gave Raimo a wave as the taxi took off.

When he resumed his place at the drinks table inside, he was ready to pack it in. He scanned the room once more: no Rikki, no Tuomey, ergo no Dino Caddio, but a pair of fire doors propped open at the far end.

The cavernous room in dim lighting didn't call attention to Raimo's disfigurement but up close was another thing, and as he moved down the path of tables, he felt his face flush with that old sick feeling. The face was so integral to a human being's essential self and acceptance by others that even boxers had to train themselves to be hit there. It wasn't *natural.*

Hello, Handsome. Monthster. Monster. . .

Finally, he made his way to the back and followed the wall despite the swiveled necks and more stares tracking him.

Exiting into the warm night air Raimo had to adjust to the dark. Voices to his left.

Rikki's voice—but the words were slurred together like a curse wrapped in a growl.

Rikki had Tuomey by the shirt front and hoisted into the brick wall. A goose-necked light hung from one corner of the building and cast the trio in a sepia tableau. Caddio stood behind Rikki pulling at his sleeve like a child. Tuomey's face was obscured but he recognized the expression on Rikki. This wasn't play.

Caddio spoke first. "Hey, Rick, it's your bro. Come on, man, let go!"

Rikki turned his head slowly to gaze at Raimo as if he'd never seen him before. Raimo couldn't see what effect he was having on whatever he had just interrupted. Tuomey hung in the air by his brother's fists and was pinned to the wall. He didn't move or fight back. He was the last to turn his head in Raimo's direction.

"Hey, Handsome, what's up?"

"Fuck you, Brian!" Rikki said. He let Tuomey drop until his feet touched the ground. Tuomey pushed Rikki's hands away and fixed himself, his shirt tail hanging out, and his collar ripped to expose a white tee and a gold medallion.

"See there, Rick. You've got little brother all upset. He came looking for you. Better go nursemaid the freak—"

Rikki pivoted in place, a ballet move, swung his fist in an upward arc that connected with Tuomey's chin—a solid uppercut that snapped Tuomey's head back. He slumped against the wall where in slow-motion time he sank down to the dirt with legs splayed.

Caddio waited for Rikki to move before he hunched down to assist Tuomey.

Rikki passed Raimo without looking at him. Raimo said to his back: "I've been waiting twenty years for you to do that."

"Give me a hand here, man," Caddio called.

"I'm not his bitch, Dino. You are," Raimo said and followed his brother back inside.

No sign of his brother. Nothing but the silhouettes of heads and bodies at the same tables as before. Some still, some moving. It looked surreal, more like an Indonesian shadow puppet play where the characters walked, nodded, danced, fought, and laughed.

It reminded Raimo he was a puppet, too. Someone else had the control rods.

The desk sergeant at West Hollywood Sheriff's wouldn't talk to Raimo, but he agreed to put him touch with the detective working the case.

Raimo identified himself as the brother of the manager; he hoped that would entice Det. Fanducci to talk. He told Raimo the fire started an hour after the last customer staggered out into the pre-dawn night. The girls who'd danced the final sets sometimes hung around with their boyfriends drinking but not that night.

"Has the cause been determined yet?"

"No, we're still investigating."

The building was one of the oldest brick structures in West Hollywood. It wouldn't have to be razed as the fire was caught early enough. Mostly smoke damage. Fanducci gave Raimo his cell number for his brother to call him and Raimo said he would pass on the word.

"Is he a suspect?"

"We just want to talk to him," Fanducci said.

Translation: Rick Jarvi was a person of interest.

He didn't think his brother could be stupid enough to start a fire and be the last known person on the premises. That was like being the last person seen with a murder victim.

He had his report for Leotis to finish and then lunch with Bart, who left a message informing him he intended to begin collecting on his free-lunch debt.

Writing as objectively as he could, he presented his findings and conclusions. He added a final recommendation with his fee stating his client in future would have to contract with another agency as he would not accept future assignments of "this confidential matter."

There, Raimo thought, *I'm through enabling you, Leotis.*

Bart was sitting at a table when he entered Makki's. It was the best fish restaurant in the city. If Bart ordered the red King crabs, he'd renegotiate the deal right there.

"I've ordered the perch for us both," Bart said. "Hope that's OK with you."

Lake Erie yellow perch in season ran about $15 a pound. It wasn't much of a compromise but he let it go.

"You hear about the plane crash?"

"What are you talking about?"

"Some guy's plane went into the drink last night from Burke-Lakefront," Bart said. "Went down a mile offshore. No Mayday, nothing." He used his flattened hand to imitate a plane going up and then going down.

"It was on all the Cleveland news channels. Whole family, a couple neighbors along for the ride. They came up for a Tribe doubleheader."

"Any survivors?" Raimo asked him.

"No. Not so far. The city can't fly choppers over the lake at night. Civil aviation rules. The Coast Guard's out there now with search helicopters and marine craft."

By the time Raimo got home from the reunion last night, it was well after one. After what he witnessed out back, he figured Rikki wasn't going back to Tuomey's condo. He drove from his building up Third Street to the house but there were no lights on. He went back home, fixed a Tom Collins and read an article, "Keep Your Celebrity Safe from That Deranged Stalker." It sounded like something transplanted from an old issue of *Soldier of Fortune* and had a lot of information about closed-circle fighting techniques.

"Damn, this fish is good."

"Tastes better when it's free," Raimo said.

Rikki hated fish, even fish sticks, but Raimo would eat anything from the sea. He loved to fish as a kid. He'd had two extraordinary events happen to him before he was fifteen, one being the fire; the other was a rogue wave that came out of nowhere and knocked him off his granite slab where he'd been fishing with his friend Tony Kantorak.

A seiche on Lake Erie was a rarity but the conditions were right that summer day. The water wasn't its usual muddy green but an ominous milky white. Gentle white caps were coming in row after row like battalions all morning long and pretty much negating fishing for perch. Raimo didn't care. He kept throwing his silver spoon out and hoped something big would go for it—a gold carp, maybe, or a fighting muskellunge. Tony was behind him clambering over the rocks when the wave reared up, just a bump on the horizon that moved silently and steadily toward them west-northwest in his direction. When it hit, it knocked him backwards into the stagnant pool behind the granite wall where cattails grew wild and some fisherman tossed their garbage fish.

Luckily, he missed the jagged edges of the huge granite slabs, each weighing several tons. Tony had missed the brunt of the exploding water and recovered faster; he hauled a soaked and coughing Raimo up from the pool. He got filthy water in his lungs and developed a bacterial infection that forced him to spend a week in bed recovering.

"What are you thinking about?"

"Nothing," Raimo replied. "Fishing from the breakwall."

"You don't see kids doing that today," Bart said. "It's all cell phones, selfies, violent video games, dick photos."

"Somehow, old friend, it's easy for me to picture you addicted to video games if they were around in our day," Raimo said. Rikki's superior eye-hand coordination beat Raimo at *Super Mario Bros.* despite the hundreds of hours Raimo had spent playing after treatments.

"I could get into sexting," Bart said.

"Never too late to start, they say," Raimo told him.

"Oh yeah?"

Bart wrote some letters on a napkin and shoved it across to Raimo. "What's that mean?"

"It's gibberish," Raimo said.

He called over their teenaged waiter and showed her the same block letters. "Hon, tell my ancient friend here what this means."

She studied it for a moment. "BTDTGTTSAWIO. Been There Done That Got the Tee-Shirt And Wore It Out," she recited.

She handed the napkin back to Bart. “Nobody uses that anymore.”

“See?” Bart said to him and showed his teeth. “You’re too old, Daddy-O.”

Chapter 4 – August 4

The crash made national news. The plane that went down under clear, starry skies with twenty-mile visibility was a single-engine Cessna 206. It killed the pilot, his wife, their two sons, a neighbor and his fourteen-year-old child. The plane went up, and after one minute's flight, it went down again, straight into Lake Erie off Cleveland's Burke-Lakefront Airport.

Part of the fuselage was detected under ninety feet of water by the Coast Guard's thermal camera. Human remains were detected but divers were dealing with one-foot visibility and extracting would take time. Meanwhile, a task force of law enforcement and civilian volunteers were walking the shoreline westward to Mentor. The physics that applied to bodies submerged in warm water meant searchers would probably have to wait until bacterial gases in the bodies and rising water temperatures brought them to the surface.

The Cleveland news stations covered it with the same information: the pilot and plane's owner was licensed, experienced, and was the CEO of a small pharmaceutical company with a distribution center in Cleveland and headquarters in Columbus. Neighbors and relatives of both families were interviewed and all said the victims were great people, from decent, loving families and how devastated they were.

Raimo felt uneasy. He left messages on Rikki's cell but hadn't heard back. Bart called him at one that afternoon to tell him he was dropping by his office before his shift. He had some news about Rikki.

Bart knocked. Raimo let him in.

"You closing early, Ray, or cracking a safe?"

"I never opened," Raimo said. "I've got to drill through brick for this flex hose. What did you want to see me about?"

Ray took off his protective glasses and set the drill on his desk. His face was grimed with sweat and his arms and neck were dotted in white powder from the blasted masonry.

"I take it you haven't heard," Bart said. He took off his sunglasses. "Jesus, I'm half-blind in here."

"Heard what?"

"It's about Rick. He's been in a car accident. They life-flighted him to Cleveland."

"When?"

"Last night," Bart said. "He crashed on Route Eighty-Four. Must have been going fast around a curve or something. He sheared off a fender. Buckled his rental like an accordion."

"How is he?"

"I called University Hospital. I knew you'd want an update. He's stable. Banged up bad. A smashed femur and arm fractures. He's concussed but awake, according to the surgeon."

"Was he alone?"

"That's the other good news," Bart said. "He didn't take anybody out and he didn't have any passengers."

"What's the bad?"

"He was shit-faced drunk. They found an empty vodka bottle under the seat."

"That doesn't mean—it could have been there," Raimo said.

"Ray, pull my other leg. It has the bells on it. They take blood first thing. You think it's going to come back clean?"

"What's the worst charge?"

"DUI, failure to control. All in all, I'd say he's damned lucky, your brother."

"Lucky," Raimo repeated.

"Look, I've got to clock in. I'll call you if I hear anything."

"Thanks for telling me."

Ray was about to lock up when he heard the desk phone.

"Jarvi? Ray Jarvi," the male voice said.

"I'm on my way out of the office right now for a family emergency. Leave a message on my machine. I'll get back to you."

"This is Radebaugh."

Her husband. Calling from jail, he realized.

"I want to see you, Jarvi."

"What about?"

"I'm being transferred in a couple days. It's my last chance. Visiting hours are two to four. If you're not a total chickenshit, I'll see you then."

Did a man who cuckolded another man have a moral obligation to see him, especially if that man murdered his wife? How many angels can dance on the head of a pin?

"Fuck it," Raimo said to his empty office. He had to see his brother first.

It was a wasted trip. The surgery that repaired his brother's arm and leg was lengthy, and Rikki was unconscious the entire time Raimo sat by the bedside in ICU recovery watching his brother breathe in and breathe out. The steady tick and whirr of the monitors overhead attached to his chest and fingertip were punctuated with an occasional snort from his brother. Ray looked up to see if the red and blue lines reacted. The surgeon said he wouldn't regain consciousness for several more hours and he'd be too groggy for conversation when he did. The doctor gave him a full report replete with the anatomical jargon and was surprised when Raimo understood it.

"I've spent a lot of time in hospitals," he told the doctor.

The drive back to Northtown helped Raimo clear his head. He'd driven with Rikki drunk and sober and his brother was never so intoxicated he could not control a car—unless he didn't want to. Rikki suicidal wasn't a thought he wanted in his head.

He pulled into the parking lot behind his building and saw a woman standing by the door. He didn't get a good look at first; she was a brunette, long chestnut hair, well-dressed, too much so for the heat where everybody wore the least amount of clothing they could get away with in public.

She turned to greet him when he reached the halfway point of the walkway. Dark glasses, a pretty face. A prospective client would have gone to the office on Bridge Street around the corner.

"Hello, Ray," she said.

Raimo knew her in that instant: Irene Donovan, a high-school classmate.

"Come inside," he said.

Irene's voice carried a telltale impediment from childhood when rubella made her partially deaf. Her speech carried that distinct *-ng* back formation of her words. Her sweet nature and her pretty face made the number of students who mocked her speech decline over the years until, by senior year, it would have gotten anyone loutish enough to try braced by a clique of her friends.

Irene had a special place in Raimo's memory. She came from a big Irish-Catholic family from Appalachia. Many West Virginians came north to work in the factories, docks, and railroads of Northtown in those days, especially when Amtrak was featherbedding and hiring high-school graduates for section-gang work at ridiculous wages. She was too smart for the dull business courses fobbed on the dimmer students as opposed to the pre-college academic curriculum. However, she and Raimo wound up in the same history class in freshman year, both seated opposite each other in the back. The parochial school required its coaches to double up so the history teacher also happened to be Rikki's coach. He was an indifferent teacher who turned the class into a study hall.

Raimo kept a novel for reading in there but one day was different because that morning he'd dropped one of Rikki's football trophies and the figure's stiff arm had snapped off at the elbow. Rikki had just come in, saw what happened, and covered the distance in a half-step. Before Raimo could apologize, Rikki walloped him on the side of his face knocking him sideways. The noise was so loud it brought their mother into the room. When she saw the damaged trophy in Rikki's hand, she took his side at once and screamed at Raimo for being "a clumsy, stupid ogre."

Clumsy, stupid—that was OK, Raimo thought. The "ogre" part scalded. "Ogre" meant ugly.

The twisted look on her face made Raimo realize how far down in his mother's affection he was. The force of the blow despite the open hand had caused his face to swell up and he couldn't see out of one eye as the morning passed. While Coach Bedaki sat busy drawing up football plays at his desk, Raimo was overcome by an adolescent tumult and tears began to flow—not just a few tears but a copious draining of both eye sockets; worse, his nasal cavity opened up and he was a broken pipe in mere seconds leaking fluid down his chin. Trying to wipe away snot and tears, his entire face was smeared. A snivel burst from his throat and classmates swiveled their heads to see what the disturbance was; he noted their smirks and grimaces of disgust and that accelerated his distress until even Bedaki, oblivious to anything not related to football, jerked his head up. Irene Donovan, without a word to him, left her desk and took his wet hand in hers and gently led him out of the door past the astonished faces of the class; she guided him to the boys' lavatory.

He never forgot his shame at the outburst, as if his classmates would ever let him, but it was Irene's courage that stayed with him as other memories of high school miseries faded over time.

She declined the offer of a drink. He was thinking she was here because she was a class officer senior year and his class had also planned a reunion for the end of the month. He'd thrown the invitation card in the garbage as soon as he saw what it was.

"I want you to . . . follow my husband. I think he's having

an affair," she said.

Dino Caddio. When Raimo heard she'd married someone he saw as beneath her, someone who lorded it up in the hallways of school and swanned about with Brian Tuomey's clique, he dismissed her from his mind. But there she sat in his apartment, hands demurely folded in her lap, wedding ring winking in the light from the window, and sounding like the girl he once knew.

"Do you want to tell me about it?" His stock line with Leotis and the parents who came to him to ask him to find their runaway teenagers.

Beauty and maturity melded in the face. There was a pronounced curve to her upper lip, an attractive feature when she smiled and showed perfect teeth. No, her flaw was her choice of husband. Andino Caddio had become a stoop-shouldered, prematurely aged man, but he was something of a catch back then and she, a mere frosh with no family connections or country-club contacts, found herself envied by the girls in her circle when she agreed to go steady with Dino.

Irene started talking about other things first, a commonplace for clients; they had to work up to it, whatever "it" was. She spoke of her daughter Cassie, a girl now eleven, enrolled in the special-needs program at a public school because of her autism.

"Dino was crazy about the baby when she came," Irene said. "He adored Cassandra. He was afraid to hold her in the hospital because he thought he might break her." The marriage soured when Cassie was diagnosed autistic.

Raimo kept his apartment dark at night with a couple pole lamps at opposite ends; it wasn't for mood lighting but to keep his face in shadow. Daytime sunlight made that impossible. Irene, however, never betrayed those telltale signs of repulsion from so many people who first saw his face and the purple burn scars. Of course, she knew him from those days but still, to use Tuomey's words, he had the only face in town that could stop a clock.

"Tell me why Dino started to change, Irene," Raimo told

her. "Take your time."

Raimo took notes while she talked. His memory was excellent but it allowed him to avoid looking at clients as they spoke.

"Dino was so proud and everything was going so well. He went to school, got certificates. He was making good money at Cleveland-Hopkins. He was making more money than he ever could working the factories here like his dad and brother."

It reached that point where the turn was coming. He'd learned to expect it.

"Maybe the money was too good," she said.

Dino started drinking at the bars after work with some of the guys. First, it was in the Flats. She didn't like the idea of him hanging out in those college bars. She told him to come home if he had to unwind in bars.

"Maybe that was my mistake." She blamed herself. Raimo understood; as the years passed, he kept blaming himself for his scars. *Why that night? Why under that tree?*

Dino reconnected with some of his high-school friends at a local bar on the east side of the lift bridge. The Suomi Café was split between a horse-shoe bar and a dining room.

"I don't drink," Irene said. "I've seen what alcohol does to parents and their children. I didn't want that for me or Cassie."

Raimo had to train himself in a mirror to look at people directly, not look down in shame whenever eyes bored into his, as if an "explanation" for his pitiable face could be exchanged in a glance. But it wasn't that that kept him from looking at her. He wanted to see if she would hold that same gentle expression as that time she led him out of history class.

A vestige of Raimo's sickbed reading came to him in a flash. What had Wittgenstein said?

A confession has to be part of your new life.

Raimo despised Dino. Part of it was guilt by association. "Brian's bootlicker," an expression his younger brain coined, stuck. He was sorry he'd allowed the bully's persona to invade his being for a moment when he saw Dino, cringing from Rikki's wrath and whining outside the building. Dino was no match for him now physically. Then the shame for wanting to thrash a boyhood tormentor evaporated in the light of Irene's revelation about her marriage.

Cocaine soon replaced Dino's beers at the Suomi. He still drank and he still went there four or five nights a week. He told his wife the sixty-mile drive home on Route 90 entitled him to a little down time after the stress of the job. The Warehouse District of Cleveland catered to a young nightlife crowd unlike the crack-ravaged inner city. Cocaine gradually moved down to the riverfront college bars. Like most fads arriving in the Midwest from either coast, it happened later. By the time New York and Los Angeles returned to cheaper heroin and meth after the cocaine frenzy, Midwesterners were just getting comfortable with their blasts.

Dino developed a real monkey, she said. Had jitters and couldn't sleep, even developed nosebleeds at work, not to mention the money being burned up inside his nostrils. She took the little girl and moved back home.

A year later, a sweep of the maintenance lockers by drug-sniffing dogs ended his fat paychecks. Amazingly, he wasn't arrested because of some technicality but he and three other techs were wedged out by union pressure. He kept his licenses, barely, and he promised Irene he was through with drugs. She returned home and they started over.

Gradually, he got back on his feet after a stint in rehab before the insurance expired. He went cold turkey on cocaine but he said he still needed to "decompress" and reverted to his old habit of drinking. Without the time-consuming drive back and forth to Cleveland, he could drink earlier and stay longer at the Suomi. His job driving a forklift was a snap compared to his previous work and sometimes he'd go in hungover or come home after his shift reeking of booze. He used beer as a chaser for the shots of cheap rye. The good looks and "guinea charm" that had won Irene and other girls before her was spoiled by a stooped physique, bloated face, half-moon bags under the eyes, and a fast-receding hairline.

Then Cassie started to have trouble. First in kindergarten and then in her elementary school.

"I blamed her teachers at first," Irene said, "and then I badgered them for more help with Cassie. They started to dread the parent-teacher conferences with me instead of the other way around. "Needs improvement" and "not making progress" evolved into "uncommunicative," "refuses to participate with other children," and "fails to grasp key concepts."

Dino, who had never been more than a middling student, started to attend the sessions with Cassie's teachers. Soon, he was asking most of the questions.

Irene, at first, was glad to have her husband aboard with something so important as their child's education; however, it soon became clear that Dino's interest was grounded in something else—fear he might have caused it with his drinking and drug-binging. At the urging of a compassionate third-grade teacher, Irene had Cassie tested. The results showed Cassie's lack of focus was a result of hyperactivity. Heartache at the diagnosis was mitigated by the doctor's assurance that Cassie could lead "a completely normal life." He prescribed Ritalin. At first, the dosage was the problem rather than the cure. She was aggressive toward the other children, wouldn't sit when the teacher asked, and refused to do anything but draw and color all day.

Irene consulted another specialist. This time the verdict was autism.

Dino took another path. He was convinced Cassie's autism was caused by the decades of environmental pollution of the harbor. Irene scoffed at Dino's nightly rant about "the filth in the air and water." However, it was not unfounded as theories go, only a bit more offbeat than the theory in vogue about vaccines and autism. For one thing, there was a history of pollution that bore witness to a dozen rare forms of cancer. On the ride home from Cleveland after another yet another bout of infections and surgeries, Raimo looked out the car window and noticed a trail of small black pennants planted in front of people's houses. Each showed an upside-down smiley face that seemed to pop up everywhere. By the time his father had turned onto Columbus Avenue from Route 11, he noticed a black flag in front of every third or fourth home. When he asked what they were for, his mother told him they were put there by some people who'd come to town from a Greenpeace ship docked in the harbor. One flag for every family where cancer had struck.

"Dino looked up statistics and reports all the time," she said. "If he wasn't drinking, he was at the Northtown Public Library scrolling through microfiche searching out articles on diseases. She remembered one time he came home and announced that Northtown County had "the highest incidence of mental retardation" in the entire Midwest. The same factories that had polluted Love Canal in New York *were here first*, he exclaimed.

"Did he act differently toward Cassie or you?" Raimo asked.

"He was more doting than ever, but I think he feared I blamed him. He grew more distant. He drank more when he did go the bars. Once or twice, Jerry—do you remember Jerry Schroeder?"

"From grade school," Raimo said.

"Jerry always called me to come get Dino whenever he was too drunk to drive home."

Irene said things got slowly better but Dino clung to his obsession harder whenever the subject came up. She refused to discuss it with him because he would get so angry. "A vein in his forehead bulged," she said. "I was afraid he—might try to do something—"

Raimo thought suicide but it wasn't that.

One day she found sketches lying on the coffee table. He'd passed out on the couch the night before. She drove to the address he marked on one of the sketches. A big Tudor-style brick house overlooking the lake with expensive landscaping.

When she asked Dino what he was doing, he got mad at her for snooping in his things and wouldn't say. She learned it was the house of a man who owned one of the chemical factories on Middle Road near Lake Shore Park.

"You think Dino was planning to stalk the man—maybe confront him?"

"I don't know. It scared me. I was afraid he might want to hurt the man or his family. I couldn't bear thinking of it."

Then, without explanation, everything changed.

"Dino came to his senses," she said.

The drinking tapered off, he stopped moping around the house, looking for arguments with her. But the one thing Irene didn't approve of was the fact that Brian Kevin Tuomey was back in Dino's life. She remembered how Brian used to treat Dino.

"It was almost an abusive relationship," she said. "I really hated Brian whenever he came around and after he left town, I told Dino I hoped he never came back."

Then the twentieth reunion announcement in the mail from Ginny Dyson. Brian called Dino a day later and the two met after almost twenty years.

"It was like Brian just resumed his relationship to Dino as if no time at all had passed," Irene said. "One day, he showed up at the house. Same old cocky B. K. Tuomey just dressed in more expensive clothes and driving an expensive foreign car. Dino was his lapdog all over again."

He risked a look: her lovely face careworn by her marital hardship and anxiety for her child. But not so much as a particle of disgust or pity. Raimo exhaled a deep breath.

"It was that bastard Brian," Irene exclaimed, her bosom rising, hazel irises going deeper, "who got Dino hooked up with that slut Julie DeMarest."

Chapter 5 – August 5

His father was a bigger sentimental packrat than his mother. Raimo discovered three boxes in the attic full of memorabilia, one devoted to his marriage while the other two were reserved for his two boys. Bronzed baby shoes, toy soldiers, and blankets. Raimo's Halloween Superman costume, which he refused to wear after a neighbor known to be a man who kept too many dogs, dropped a single Tootsie Roll mini into his open bag and asked him if "he'd flown into a building."

Rikki, by far, had more items, mainly newspaper clippings, a couple framed certificates honoring Rikki as Athlete of the Year, and other tributes to his sporting days at Sts. Stephen and Basil. At the bottom, Raimo found Rikki's old letter sweater. Beneath the felt letters were a pair of balanced rows of footballs opposite track shoes that reminded him of the god Mercury with wings sprouting out of the heels. Raimo remembered how proud his father was at the celebration dinner and then upset when the family got home because his brother's name was inscribed as "Richard" Jarvi.

His and Rikki's senior yearbooks were wrapped in cellophane. Raimo's contained just his single class photo, and he winced at the memory of it. His scars were evident in the unflattering light, and he remembered the embarrassed awkwardness of the photographer that day.

Rikki's yearbook was more like an homage. The adolescent gush of some of Rikki's classmates in faded ink in loopy handwriting on the blank pages reserved for writing showed time's ruthless capacity to expose what was hollow and insincere in words like *forever* and *never forget* and *always remember.* Six of Rick's female classmates, their names slipping through memory's surface, wrote what appeared to be cryptic references to "shared moments" in their mutual past. Raimo wondered how his brother, with the sensibilities of a copulating Neanderthal when it came to romance, reciprocated in their yearbooks.

Tuomey had written: "To the greatest running back at S & B High—from the greatest quarterback."

Dino's was less ostentatious: "To Rick Jarvi, Number 22, a great football player and terrific classmate. Good luck in the pros."

There were a couple photos of all three in group shots. Laughing it up in the cafeteria, decorating for the prom, and in the largest one on that page, Tuomey and Rikki standing in front of the microphone at a pep rally in the gym. Dino, the set-up man for anything involving mechanics, stood off to the side grinning beneath a pompadour of hair. Raimo recalled the longer sideburns sported in that era. Dino's "dago ducktail" was rigidly maintained. Raimo remembered how the harsh light from the building that night penetrated to expose Dino's scalp.

Good luck in the pros . . .

Raimo wondered if Ricki's failure to get on at a big school was the turning point in his brother's life. No more adulation, no crowds cheering. It would explain his desire to leave town after it was clear there wasn't going to be any future gridiron glory after his return from Michigan. His father might have thought so too. The strangest piece among the boys' keepsakes was a partially burned jersey, the top half of a scorched pair of two's, which his father must have found in Rikki's secret backyard fire. Rikki never spoke of it nor did anyone else in the family. All Rikki's sports trophies disappeared from the shelves in their room on the same day.

Dino didn't head for the Suomi Café after work as he had the previous two days Raimo had him under surveillance. No sign of Julie DeMarest with Irene's spouse, either. Her maroon Vibe sat in the hospital parking lot when it wasn't in her driveway in Conneaut.

Raimo emptied the last of his bottled water. His shirt was pasted to his back despite the rattling air conditioner on high. Even in the early evenings, the temperature hadn't abated. The heatwave produced gorgeous sunsets; mountainous clouds along the horizon's edge made it appear as if jagged islands existed just a few miles beyond the breakwall. Overhead the canvass of pastels and swirled shades of primary colors backlit a giant crimson disk of sun and spread elongated fingers of light down to the water. The drone of millions of muckleheads from a second hatching resonated in the air in the evenings and in the mornings plastered the sides of buildings, cars, and houses in the harbor. They swarmed at sunset creating huge columns that undulated with a lakeshore breeze and offered diving swallows targets of opportunity.

Raimo in his youth swam and fished from the Pyramids, a place he and the neighborhood kids named for the stacked piles of massive cement blocks once used to support the cranes that unloaded the wooden ships. The outline of a sunken wooden vessel lay just beneath the edge where Raimo and his friends used to run and dive into the slip below. Raimo hadn't been swimming in years and he wondered if the big golden carp still cruised between the gaps in the rotten hull. Sedge grass grew to the lip of the dock's edge.

The notepad resting on a thigh recorded the lack of progress so far:

Wed. 7:27 a.m., DC left house. Arrived work, 7:55.
Left work, 6:09 p.m., drove home, 6:33 p.m.
Talked to co-worker in parking lot, 5 mins (6:04).
Thur. 7:14 a.m., DC left house. Arrived work, 7:45.
Left work, 6:14 p.m., arrived Suomi 6:52 p.m.;
Left Suomi 9:42; drove home, 9:55 p.m.
Fri. 7:31 a.m., DC left house. Arrived work, 7:51.

Last night, after seeing Dino back to his house, he swung back to the bar in case Julie DeMarest was not working her shift at the hospital at Northtown General as the helpful nurse in ICU had said.

He kept his cell phone charged. Irene said she'd ring his cell if Dino left the house. He didn't. He thought of Jack Nicholson placing a watch under the tire of the man he followed in *Chinatown*. With all the gee-whiz stuff available, he could surveille Dino from the comfort of his office computer with a GPS tracker—if he had the money to spend.

Maybe, Raimo thought, the weekend would ignite the philandering bug in Dino. He didn't want to take Irene's money, and he argued, but she insisted.

Dino came out with his shift. Two men lit cigarettes and a male-female couple stopped to chat near the loading dock. Raimo's field glasses had a good view from the street across from the factory. Somebody had put a double-wide on a lot and then decided to abandon it. He was out of range from the nearest houses and no one in the company lot could spot his car from this distance.

Dino headed casually to his car and got in. Raimo checked his watch and entered the time in his notebook.

Maybe something here—

Instead of taking the U-shaped Benefit Avenue to the harbor, Dino headed west.

On North Bend, Dino drove down Ninevah, a curved and hilly road that made it easy to keep Dino's burgundy Malibu in sight. Ninevah deadheaded at the tee into Lake Road connecting Northtown to Jefferson-on-the-Lake, a once-fashionable spot for working-class vacationers from the steel mills of Youngstown and Erie during the swing-band era until the biker riots of the seventies. It was, the chamber-of-commerce brochures promised, "a family-oriented magnet for young and old."

Clusters of small rental cottages dotted both sides of Lake Road. Many others of uniform shoebox size were lined along the small dirt roads aimed for the lake's edge, the older ones in danger of falling over the cliff from subsidence. In recent years, a Cleveland development company had sniffed out potential in the market and soon a pair of white-stone condominia were constructed overlooking the lake. Dino crossed Lake Road and parked near the main foyer of the nearest complex.

Raimo waited until he saw Caddio trot toward the lobby before he pulled into the lot and parked a couple rows behind Dino's Chevy. He noted the locale and the time. Raimo didn't expect this. It wasn't an expensive love nest he was contemplating but, more likely, Tuomey's summer residence.

Irene's outburst wasn't altogether the abused wife's wrath coming to the fore. Julie DeMarest was notorious in high school for "collecting virgin cards," as the girls in her wild set referred to a contest among them of having sex with the most virgins. Bart Massey's gossip mill barely kept pace with stories of Julie after high school, but he claimed she ruined a couple marriages, caused a suicide by one discarded male—a prominent doctor at the hospital—and was rumored to be involved in everything from swing clubs to BDSM lairs. She was a junior when the Tuomey-Jarvi tandem ruled the school.

"So much for nurses as 'enablers,'" Bart scoffed. Raimo thought of her as the female equivalent of Brian Tuomey. In fact, she had been his girlfriend for a time. Her own domestic situation was a hot mess by any objective appraisal. Married the summer after her high-school graduation, she had a daughter who got pregnant at fifteen. By then she had divorced the girl's father, married a doctor a year later and produced a son who wound up in juvie hall and was taken away by family court and raised in foster homes until his majority. She married husband number three before his incarceration for domestic violence, which was followed by an adjudication of insanity by the courts and Julie's speedy divorce from him, yet he was ultimately returned to the care of his ex-wife. Somewhere along in this menagerie, she managed to procure a degree as a med-surg nurse.

Julie herself occasionally popped up in local gossip for

other reasons besides her sexuality. One rumor had her as a Wiccan who practiced as a midwife in ritualized pagan ceremonies. Raimo was incredulous whenever Bart dropped yet another fabulous story of Julie DeMarest over coffee. The woman either had one of the best blackmail networks ever devised that involved police, judges, and doctors, or else very little said about her was true.

What wasn't in doubt was that she had once been Tuomey's girlfriend and she was still beautiful. Raimo knew her by sight from the few times he'd seen her. Julie's love for Brian Tuomey was borderline psychotic in those days. Even in a sexually permissive era, her passionate kisses and embraces in the halls were a scandal in the school's corridors.

Tuomey bragged to Rikki what he could make Julie do sexually and described in detail how he debased her when the mood struck. Raimo didn't believe his brother until the day Rikki showed him a photograph from a cheap instamatic camera. Julie was tied hands and feet to bed posts with a ball gag tied around her head. Dildos were inserted into her vagina and anus. When rumors went wild about "the photo," Tuomey shut down the gossip by fiat and was not seen at school events or in public with Julie again.

When Irene said Dino was cheating with Julie, Raimo had a hard time picturing the voracious Julie DeMarest with Irene's lackluster husband. Take Tuomey out of the equation, a young and virile Dino Caddio might have attracted Julie back then—but not now. Even if the rumors were right about her promiscuity, one factor remained to contradict Irene: Julie didn't fool around with mechanics. Her stomping grounds were populated with professionals, mainly doctors, especially surgeons, and plastic surgeons at that.

Still, he wasn't paid to speculate. He had a job to do: get out of the car, see if he could locate Dino in one of those expensive glass chicken coops and confirm his presence. He was almost at the front door when he caught a glimpse of a figure inside. It was someone, possibly a concierge, talking to Tuomey.

Raimo turned on his heel and scooted back to his vehicle. Fifteen minutes later Dino emerged from the lobby and crossed in his odd skip-trot gait to the Malibu. Again, Raimo noted the time.

Dino stopped off at the Suomi and Raimo sat in his car, sweating and cursing himself for failing to provide enough water for the surveillance. Two hours passed before Dino came out. He was drunk and gesturing wildly, shouting curses, back toward the tavern. Raimo watched, intent, not sure what was going on until a big man charged out and bore down on Dino.

The man clipped Dino like a linebacker knocking him sideways into the asphalt. His attacker sprang up, launched vicious kicks into Dino's stomach and back. Dino curled up but he was taking some hard kicks. More men exited the bar with their beers in hand to watch the beating; Raimo held his breath. *Sit, get out, sit. Not my—*

Fuck. This wasn't the job, he thought.

Something about the beating being dished out made Raimo nauseated. It wasn't even a one-sided match; it was a beat-down methodically dished out by a much larger man egged on by a circle of friends, screaming for the big man to *kill him, kill the fucker!*

One of the tools from his father's garage he held back from storage was a pry bar for tearing up flooring tiles. Raimo grabbed it from under his seat.

He flew into their midst. He swung the bar right and left, connecting with the backs of knees. Men jackknifed and stumbled as if a bomb had detonated.

Dino, half-conscious, dripping blood from the mouth. The big man leaned over him, a fist balled and the other bunched into Dino's shirt front. Raimo put his hips into the swing and brought the bar down on the man's broad back. The man seemed to freeze with his fist still cocked, a punch telegraphed from on high that stopped in mid-air. Magic.

Raimo scooped Dino under one arm and dragged him across the pavement, still brandishing the iron bar. The circle of men closed around their stunned alpha male. It was that moment of indecision before action coalesced into total chaos and those same drunken males focused on him, and it saved Raimo from a beating just as bad. Caddio was semi-conscious, a stuporous glare coming over his eyes. Raimo shoved him across the front seat of his car so hard Dino's head dipped forward and banged the glove box. Raimo slammed the door shut just as a bottle smashed against the back window and shattered glass and beer all over everything. He cranked the engine, slammed the gear into reverse, and squealed tires exiting through the adjacent lot.

More beer bottles smashed against the sides and roof of the car. More bottles hit his car until he was speeding up Bridge Street.

". . . the fuck, fuck're you?" Dino gurgled. A bloody gob drooled from his mouth. He wiped it with his hand and stared at it.

Raimo kept his eyes trained on the rearview in case he was being chased. Not until he reached the top of Bridge Street did he feel his breath release again. His hands shook on the wheel.

One of Dino's eyes was shut tight in a puffy slit. He drooled more blood and spat onto the floor mat.

"Go back, kill him. Lemme go . . . kill the . . . bastard."

"Shut up," Raimo said.

Raimo busted through a couple stop lights driving to the emergency room. He pulled into the half-round hospital driveway and slammed the horn a couple times. No one came out. He raced around to Dino's side and pulled, dragged him out of the car. Dino resisted Raimo's efforts to get him moving toward the double doors by assuming the belligerent drunk's aggressive stance. Raimo slipped behind him, draped one arm around his neck and hip-bumped him through the pneumatic doors.

The receptionist's mouth formed a pear-shaped silent note at the sight of them coming through the lobby. A pair of drunks in a chorus line with leg kick, swing! Leg kick, swing!

She must have hit an emergency button to signal help. In a few seconds, a male nurse and an intern arrived and took command. Raimo helped them get Dino on the gurney; he had to be strapped in.

"He smells like a brewery," the doctor said. "What happened to his face?"

"Some guy was hitting him," Raimo said. "His name is Dino Caddio. I found him in a parking lot at the Suomi Café."

"What was he hit with? A bottle, bat, a rock—what?"

"Just the man's fist," Raimo said.

"That guy'll probably show up later with an infected hand," the doctor said. "The human mouth's a cesspool of bacteria."

"That'll please Caddio," Raimo said. "By the way, he's concussed. He wasn't making any sense on the way."

"Wait in the lobby," the doctor said.

He sat down in the lobby to fill out forms and wait for the police. He was certain he'd just ended his career as a private investigator. Lose his newly minted license to boot. He'd probably go to jail for aggravated assault and battery. *What else?*

That should do it, he thought.

He called Irene from the hospital and left a voicemail on her cell. The same intern stepped out to take a more detailed verbal report. Raimo gave him the shortest version he thought would make sense and disguise the fact he was working surveillance on the victim.

Irene and the cop arrived almost at the same time. Her eyes were big with concern. Raimo pointed toward the metal swing doors where a series of cubicles with beds were ringed off by green privacy curtains.

The officer led Raimo to the back row of plastic seats. A family of relatives were seated nearby all talking at once to one another and a few mumbled into their cell phones. The cop looked at them with disgust and drew Raimo off to the opposite corner.

Raimo told him he'd driven past the parking lot of the

Suomi just as a fight broke out in the parking lot. He saw one man on the ground being beaten by another man. He drove them off.

"How did you drive them off?"

"I found a small branch lying on the ground."

"Did you hit anyone?"

"No," Raimo lied.

"Good Samaritan with a stick, huh? Just driving by?"

"That's me, Officer."

He wrote down Raimo's name and address.

"Hold it," the cop said. "You're on Bridge Street, right? Give me your license and don't say another word of that bullshit about driving past."

Raimo watched the cop write down the information on his Ohio private eye's license. He handed it back. When Raimo tried to pull it out of his hand, he held it tight. "I blocked for your brother," he said. "Starting right tackle, two years. Tell Twenty-Two he owes me one."

Irene came out and the officer signaled her over.

Raimo didn't make eye contact.

"This man," the cop began, "he said your husband was attacked by a man from the Suomi Café."

"That's what my husband told me just now," she said.

"Wait here with him," the cop said.

He went through the double doors.

"Dino told you that?" Raimo asked her.

"No," she said. "He's barely coherent. They're taking him for an MRI upstairs."

"Thank you," he said.

"I want to know what happened," she said. Her eyes were a gold over brown.

They sat together. The raucous family, dysfunctional and full of bile toward an unnamed party apparently not present, vented and stormed in and out of the lobby. No one behind the glass window paid them any attention. Twenty minutes later, the cop came out. He looked once in Raimo's direction and left.

Irene looked at Raimo and without saying anything, she got up to go see her husband just as the doctor came out to wave at her to come inside.

Another half-hour passed before Dino and Irene emerged. Dino was in a wheelchair, a compress held to his face and a butterfly bandage across his eyebrow; he was pushed by a different nurse to the exit. Irene flashed Raimo a *call you later.*

Raimo took the opposite way home so he could pass the Suomi. Nothing, no one, the rabid circle of men nowhere in sight. Just an empty parking lot. Back in his upstairs, he paced for a while, unwilling to face more bad news on his downstairs office phone. Stiffened with a Tom Collins, he headed down around the corner and opened his office. The recorder's red light semaphored as he unlocked and entered.

"Dino says he doesn't want to press charges," Irene said as soon as he hit Play. "He won't tell me what happened."

Raimo decided to intrude; he had to know. She picked up on the first ring.

"Irene, what exactly did he say?"

"Just some loudmouth in the bar picked a fight with him. That's all."

"Is he going to be all right?" Raimo asked.

"He's sleeping right now. The doctor gave me a prescription for Percodan."

"I'm sorry," Raimo said. "I should have—"

"I'm too tired to talk, Ray. I'll call you tomorrow. Let's let things be for now," she said.

He didn't say anything. Raimo wrote out his notes and locked up but returned to his chair and sat down staring out into the night. A few cars passed but Bridge Street's bars were winding down. He still expected the cops to come for him. He wanted another drink but he didn't keep a bottle in the drawer like a TV private eye. Lethargy overwhelmed him and he shut his eyes.

He'd spent three hundred dollars on a workshop that taught him how to use "a tactical pen" to defend himself against an angry aggressor, how to defuse a violent situation with an angry mob, how to break free if he's duct-taped to a chair, even how to disappear, which, at that moment, seemed like his best option. He thought of that bull-sized man thumping Caddio like a rag doll against the pavement and how he blinked like a stunned ox in a kill chute when Raimo brought the tire down on his thick back just missing his head.

He groaned. A millimeter or two difference, he thought, and he'd be looking at a manslaughter charge or worse. Little things, big differences.

An hour later he woke from his doze. Raimo stretched, checked his watch: three a.m. He locked his office and walked around the corner against gravity, his thighs burning from fatigue that seeped into every joint and tendon. He risked insomnia with a cold beer from the refrigerator. It was too hot to sleep. He put on the TV and caught a nature program on simians. "Too bad for the development of human beings that the violent chimpanzees, with their sharp incisors, violent ways, and cannibalistic tendencies were the ones to come down from the tree first instead of the pacific bonobos, their cousins," the smug narrator intoned.

Sprawled in the La-Z-Boy, he flipped the channel past an infomercial for diets, an auction where a woman was asking about a samovar's value, a commercial for diet supplements and settled for a show on quantum mechanics. He flipped back to the nature show but the monkeys were gone. Instead, he saw a bunch of baby Geckos high-stepping on back legs from the eggs they'd just hatched from. CUT TO a ball of racer snakes fling from crevices in the rocks where they hid, waiting for the first sign of the hatchlings to emerge. He turned the channel, sickened by the image of the snakes uncoiling and straightening into bronzed spears flashing in pursuit, their diamond heads locked onto their targets. A physicist was trying to explain how Schrodinger had a cat inside a locked box with a vial of cyanide that was either going to kill the cat—or not. Somehow the cat was alive and dead at the same time, he said. He called it the "uncertainty principle."

"That's me, too," Raimo said to the TV. He fell into a deep

black vortex listening to the caterwaul of siren screams racing past his building.

Chapter 6 – August 6

"Funny."

"What is?"

"I wanted to smash your face in when you got here," Ron Radebaugh said.

"Now you don't?"

"Don't push your luck with me, Jarvi," Radebaugh said. "I figure I can get one good punch in before that pot-bellied bailiff in the corner can waddle over here in time."

Raimo wondered whether the man's clout extended here, too. Why wasn't he talking to him through a plexiglass window instead of over a small card table in the prisoner rec room?

Raimo was edgy. He'd slept badly. Images of Irene and her battered husband kept recurring in different places in his dreams. He opened doors in a long empty corridor and there one or the other stood gazing at him with a look of pained surprise or contempt.

"So why am I here, Ron?"

It seemed odd calling him by his name. Kristine never had a problem referring to her "Ronnie" throughout their year-long affair. Sometimes it seemed as if Kris Radebaugh wanted to conjure her husband into the room with them. Having him there, hovering like a vanquished shade, make him witness their most intimate moments in the bed they shared. It always struck him as strange she had no remorse about betraying him as if he were somehow a willing party to their adultery.

"I want to know why," Radebaugh said.

He had suffered, and Raimo hated himself for recognizing that in the man. He destroyed a beautiful woman, his own life, career, and reputation. It was a lot for any man to lose in so short a time.

"You mean, why *me*?"

"OK, why you? Why someone like you—"

"Someone as ugly as me," Raimo finished.

"Yeah, you put it like that. Why not? She could have had her pick of men to go to bed with. Younger guys, rich guys, anybody she wanted. You got a freak-sized cock to go with that face, is that it?"

"You're being disrespectful to her memory," Raimo said.

"'Disrespectful to her memory,' he says." Radebaugh's booming laugh echoed. "What the fuck."

Radebaugh looked around the rec room to see if any of the other men were as stunned by Raimo's hypocrisy. A couple black males in their twenties played table tennis. One shouted "Way to go, soldier!" at match point. A group of older men, mostly black, talked over a sports program. Two Hispanic-looking males, one old and the other young, slapped dominos on a table with a flourish.

"You lousy shit," Radebaugh said. "I can't believe you said that."

"This might be cathartic for you, Ron, but it isn't doing me any good."

He stood up to leave.

"Wait, fucker, you just wait a goddamned second!" Radebaugh hissed.

Raimo stood, turned, looked at him. No question about the sincere hurt and the utter bafflement etched on his face. He didn't understand how his sexy, knockout wife could have sullied herself and her marriage to *him,* a man with everything going for him—with a man like Raimo.

Raimo, in truth, didn't understand it well himself. He knew she scored channels in him that would never close, unlike the wounds she liked to inflict. Not all of what she left in her wake wanted to be brought up into the light anyway, he knew.

We were both of us sick with something neither could explain to the other.

Raimo sat down. "Talk."

"I—she never said—she was unhappy," Radebaugh said, almost pleading now. He looked at Raimo defiantly as if his manhood were the topic, not his wife's infidelity.

What did it matter now?

"She didn't think she was ever good enough for you, Ron," Raimo said. "She thought you put her on a pedestal too high. I was someone she could"—*had to be careful here*—"go slumming with. You know, without the pressure of being the perfect, country-club wife."

Radebaugh seemed dazed by the words, fighting a trance so deep at that moment, absorbing Raimo's words. "The perfect wife," he repeated. "She was . . . perfect. He raised his eyes to meet Raimo's. He whispered, "Except for you, you scar-faced freak."

Enough masochism here, Raimo thought. *I fed you a morsel, now take it and leave me alone.*

"I've got to go. So long. Be careful where you're going."

"You be careful, fuckface." Radebaugh said to his back. "I'm not done with you."

Under yet another day's broiling afternoon sun, Raimo headed for his car across a parking lot shimmering with heat mirage that looked like a flat pool of soothing water in the distance. He stood outside, waiting until some of the trapped heat dissipated, his clunky, overworked a/c on the fritz for good.

Raimo didn't believe in love—at least, not among the human species. It never worked and when it seemed to, you just had to scratch the veneer with your fingernail to watch it bleed its true colors and smell the odor of sulfur it left in your nostrils.

Kristine's body was like that—a mirage. She was beautiful, Ron wasn't exaggerating, and he didn't doubt for a second that she merely needed to crook her little finger to bring a man slavering to her feet like rattling a stick in a swill bucket.

That's where Raimo spent most of his time: at her feet, adoring her. Her long legs and thighs meeting at the bump of her sex, a thick tawny bush spiraling like a curl of fire from beneath her cleft. A translucent blonde with high cheekbones and irises the color of sea ice. He was her slave, her disfigured dwarf kept at court to entertain nobility. He meant nothing to her. Without his damaged face, she would never have given him a second look.

She chose him, however. His was a hunger starved for sex because of the burn scars that made women instinctively recoil. Yet he knew he satisfied a dark need in her, too. Such outward beauty belied her core, what people called a soul. Like that twisting, writhing ball of snakes let loose at once with a single purpose: to gorge. Kristine Radebaugh had a worm gnawing away inside her black heart long before she picked him out of a crowd to seduce.

He found Rikki awake but morose when he arrived. The stubble around his brother's jaw was grown out enough to show the red running through his beard; the bags under his eyes lent a bluish cast to his deep-set eyes under the fluorescent lighting. Rikki was lucid despite the morphine drip but he wasn't inclined to talk much and at one point, he asked Raimo "if he was writing his fucking biography" with all the questions.

"I just want to know what happened, Rick," he said. "You could have been killed."

"I was drunk, I crashed, go fuck yourself," Rikki said.

He turned his head away but Raimo remained where he was until a nurse came in and asked Rikki if he wanted to defer his sponge bath seeing that he had company. Her smock had tiny cat faces all over it.

"Give one to him," Rikki said. "He'd love to have a woman's hands on him. Did you check him out yet?"

When she'd entered earlier, her gaze had passed over Raimo's face and taken it in with a single clinical glance. Her twisted smile invited Raimo to share a moment of sympathy for their ill-tempered patient. *He didn't mean it,* her look said. *It's the pain talking.*

"I'll go and let you get your bath now," Raimo said.

"Yeah, fuck off, Mister Twenty Questions."

Crossing the lift bridge, glad to be back home from fighting the traffic on Route 90, Raimo wanted nothing more than a cold shower and a cold drink. He berated himself. He knew he should check his office recorder for Irene's call. Six messages stacked.

He pressed Play. "Mister Jarvi. Hello. I am Leotis Pennimann." Long pause.

Always that identification, as if he were establishing his existential being on the planet. "I want to make an appointment."

Raimo groaned.

"I want to pay you the rest of what I owe you, also," Leotis said. "I'll come by next week. Thank you, Mister Jarvi."

The second one was a half-minute's worth of white noise.

The third was Irene's tremolo voice. "Ray, I don't know what's going on. Dino left this morning. He's not supposed to go to work yet the doctor said. I don't know where he is. Call me. Please."

The fourth was more white noise, briefer than before.

The fifth was from the Prophet Ezekiel, or so the voice claimed to be. He recited his own verse in a melodic tenor voice: "For everyone belongs to me, the parent as well as the child—both alike belong to me. The one who sins is the one who will die."

Raimo waited for the send-money pitch but it never came.

The final message covered the two empty ones: another male voice, white, maybe thirties. No one he recognized. "We know who you are. You better watch your back, motherfucker."

Raimo heard pounding. He thought it was Rikki coming home

from one of his late-night dates and his father had accidentally locked him out. He'd fallen asleep in his father's chair again. One Tom Collins led to two more to ease the pounding of a sinus headache brought on when weather hit an extreme at either end of the thermometer.

Raimo kept one of Rikki's old aluminum bats beside the door. He kept a small Ruger .38 in a drawer in his office. He never removed it from its case. Bart nagged him to go for a CCW and he relented despite the expensive workshop on how to "disarm anyone, talk your way out of any bad situation, and pick any lock in five minutes."

"You can't be a proper gumshoe without a roscoe on your person, man."

"Dino."

"Jarvi. Can I come in for a minute?"

Raimo opened the door. "How are you feeling?"

"Like an asshole casserole, man. What do you think?"

Caddio looked worse in the light. He revealed one vampire eye and a face misshapen with lumps from the blows he'd absorbed. The narrator's voice warbled in his head from last night's nature program: "The male's face, his cheeks, are designed for punching."

"Hell, I'm starting to look like you," Dino said. ". . . Sorry."

"Forget it."

"I wanted to stop by and say thanks for helping me out. I was drunk, you know, or else—"

"Sure. Who was he, the guy wailing away on you?"

"Nobody, some lunkhead. Never seen him before last night. Nothing, it was nothing," Dino said.

"Didn't look like nothing to me," Raimo said.

"Hey, Jarvi, I said forget it, OK? Let it go."

"Is that why you came over?"

"Yeah—no. I want to tell you there's nothing wrong between me and Irene."

Raimo didn't respond.

"I mean, she's—we're fine. She ain't looking for nobody else. That's what I'm saying."

"I'm not sure I understand."

"I'm saying Irene is my woman, man. Stay away from her! I know she's been down here to see you. I don't know what's going on between you two—"

"Nothing going on, Dino."

"Better not be."

"Anything else?"

"That's it."

"Good night."

During the worst period of his convalescence when the risk of infection was too high and he was forbidden to go outside, he read Shakespeare and the Bible, the latter a gift from his mother. He remembered the superstitions attached to Sirius, the Dog Star, brightest star in the night sky. He added up the day's bitter tally and saw himself as a Jonah in other men's lives, a reluctant prophet who had nothing good to say. A brother who ignored him, a man whose wife he shared despised him; another feared what he intended with his wife. Toss in the anonymous threat on his machine below—lagniappe, as they in New Orleans—a little extra for the taking, a baker's dozen of hostility, unhappiness, misery.

Attachment is the cause of all suffering. Wasn't that Buddha's first law? Raimo tried to recall.

Around three in the morning, that time medieval monks called the dark night of the soul, Raimo threw the damp sheets off his body and went into the kitchen to make coffee. The bottle of Beefeater on the counter appealed more; he fixed a small drink and swallowed it. Masochism and self-obliteration on display here, too. The scorching path of the gin down his throat was a reminder of the toxic smoke inhalation that damaged his lungs and sidelined him from any sport for years. *I wear my self-contempt like a badge.* He pondered Ron's question from the county lockup. *Why you? A freak . . .*

Raimo decided to do some work in his office now that sleep was out of the question. Bridge Street was deserted, all the bars closed and no one left on the street. The smell of baking bread hit him just as he left his apartment and turned the corner. The sidewalk next to his building was so steeply inclined that no one not three sheets to the wind would even attempt going down it in winter.

Raimo had just put the key in the door when the gunshot blew out his plate glass window. Huge shards of glass and diamond-sharp pieces shattered over him as he flattened himself to the ground, looking up in time to see a long-barreled weapon withdraw inside a dark SUV racing across the bridge.

Was it a *trompe l'oeil* of the sodium lights overhead or did he catch a glitter from the arm as it pulled back inside the SUV—like the flicker of light from a gold bracelet?

Chapter 7 – August 7

"Where's a cop when you need one, right?"

Raimo stared at him.

Bart said, "Why didn't you call them, then?"

The diner was full of early risers, clusters of women shop owners and working men stoking up on caffeine for another too-warm day ahead. If the clatter of silverware on tables and the subdued conversations around them were an indication, people were becoming testy in the heat.

Raimo could answer the question as simple as it was. His body, for one thing, was still jazzed from excitement, a lack of sleep, and the effects of alcohol. He'd stuck some salve on a gash on his neck and made another drink back in his apartment to steady his nerves, he said, but one-drink-too-many made him lightheaded and reluctant to make a report, especially after Rikki's old teammate had cut him a favor a few hours earlier.

"It was birdshot," Raimo said.

"Could have been vandals riding around shooting out store windows," Bart said.

"If I believed that—"

"Yeah, right. You believe that, you'd be dumber than a bag of dicks."

Raimo swept up the glass, picked out some pellets for the insurance agent, and found a plastic tarp in the back of his office. He spent an hour cutting and taping it to the window frame. That ancient glass had survived a shootout between cops and robbers a hundred years earlier when the current law office was a bank. Thicker than modern window glass and warped in the middle, it produced a soft emerald glow in the late afternoons that gave it character unlike the tattoo of pock-marked BB holes along the upper left of the facia.

"I'm about to crash," Bart said. "I'm going home."

"A long night writing tickets to those speeding buggies?"

"That ended last night. I'm back on days, thank God."

Raimo wanted to go upstairs and catch some sleep, but the glass company said they'd have a man over in the morning to measure the window.

The gun was a shotgun, that was clear from the birdshot. Raimo didn't think the shooter wanted to kill him or he'd have used a deer rifle and buckshot would have sent a stronger warning or done the trick if it was meant to be fatal, not a warning. He recalled Ron Radebaugh's words from yesterday. What message was he supposed to infer from being shot at? Radebaugh could have arranged it. He seemed mad enough, Raimo knew. Dino could have followed up his warning to stay away from Irene by blasting out his window, but that didn't jibe with the man or the tone of his conversation let alone the fact he was seeing out of one eye these days. But he also remembered Dino bragging in school about his "annual" three-day detentions for skipping school to go deer hunting on opening day.

The SUV was one of those cookie-cutter ones with sloped rear ends, and late model, but colors at night under Bridge Street's arc lights were deceptive: blue cars looked white; green cars looked brown. It was too dark and the vehicle was gone before he had more than a glimpse of the arm pulling the weapon back. Definitely the passenger was the shooter, which meant two people and that was as much as he recalled clearly from a split-second glimpse after he hit the deck. The caller on his machine said "we." *We know who you are.*

That's better than I can manage, Raimo thought, *because I'm beginning to wonder myself.*

Being a freelance private investigator in this boondock was

going from pipe dream to nightmare. He faced a pile of utility bills on his desk and the monthly statement from his bank said more was leaving than coming in. Today was the day to officially vacate the house. He had to get the rest of the contents packed and into storage. Rikki was being discharged at noon and that meant a couple hours on the road listening to his brother gripe. Sleep would have to wait.

He was more like Jonah than he first realized. He didn't know what the divine mission was but he wanted to escape it anyway.

Raimo sat in the chair Rite-Aid provided customers while prescriptions were filled. A small queue of people lined up behind a sign that stated STAND HERE FOR CUSTOMER PRIVACY. Half were retirees, half looked to be males in their thirties. The older males tended to be impatient and rude to the clerks, who forced smiles on their faces and ignored them. The younger males were scruffy, mostly unemployed, and seeking the solace of opioids.

He'd gotten Rikki squared away in his upstairs apartment with some difficulty. His brother was silent on the drive back, a small blessing, but getting him out of the car and situated was anything but quiet. Rikki cursed every time he had to move and, since he outweighed Raimo by thirty pounds, helping him maneuver from La-Z-Boy to couch and back again to chair when his brother complained of the pain was a workout. The casts on Rikki's leg and arm were cumbersome obstacles to work around, and the air conditioning wasn't working right in the onslaught of rising heat as the day warmed to unbearable temperatures.

Raimo adjusted his leg an inch too far.

"Fucking watch it, you clumsy fuck!"

"Sorry."

"Fuck you, sorry."

"Here." Raimo handed him the remote.

"This TV's a piece of shit," Rikki hollered. "Go get an air conditioner that fucking works!"

The temperature was forecast for the high nineties again. Bart liked to cite statistics correlating the heat index to certain crimes like rape, domestic violence, and homicide. "That ninety-three-degree thing's an urban myth," he said. "It gets hot, people like to have sex and do stupid shit. Get the temperature up around a hundred and it's too hot to do anything including crime."

"What about winters?"

"Below twenty, people fornicate like sewer rats and do less crime."

The rest of the afternoon was spent at the house. He piled everything into a rental truck. Checked the garage and decided to leave some old tools, plywood sheets, a rusted push mower, and some jars containing nails of different sizes. Maybe the next owner could make use of it. He drove to a storage facility in Saybrook Township and unloaded everything: furniture to one side, boxes of memorabilia and dishes to the other.

He'd come across papers his mother had squirreled away in a secretary with a hutch she'd inherited from a great aunt from County Mayo. He remembered that piece of furniture well. When he was a kid, he'd found a secret panel and placed his favorite toy soldier inside the compartment. That soldier was unarmed and molded for lying prone on a stretcher; his bandaged head and arm in a sling spoke of combat valor. Raimo prized him above all and wanted to protect him in his battle scenes with his other soldiers. One day he found the wounded soldier missing and knew his mother had discovered it and thrown him away. He understood that piece of furniture was her property and to be left alone.

By the time he had finished unloading the truck and returning it, it was late afternoon and he was soaked in sweat. He'd have to get home, shower, and make supper for Rikki and him. He was exhausted, weary. It seemed someone had shot at him a long time ago instead of just that morning. So much for the glamorous life of a private eye.

After supper, he did the dishes and told Rikki he was going out.

"Where?"

Raimo was surprised his brother cared. He hadn't spoken ten words since he had the remote in his hand and that was to complain about Raimo's cooking.

"Out," Raimo said. "I'm working a case."

"Ray Jarvi, Northtown's answer to Magnum P.I."

"That's me," Raimo said.

"Fuck off, Columbo."

Raimo felt more like Inspector Clouseau. He had no cases to work, and the one he did have was suspended when Irene told him to lay off.

It's too late for that now, Irene. That shotgun blast had changed everything.

The concierge told Raimo to wait in the lobby. She called up to Tuomey's condo, said he had a guest below. She said "Raymond Garvey" into the phone, looking at him the while.

"Mister Garvey, Mister Tuomey says to go up. He's in Room Three-Fourteen. Take the elevator at the end of this corridor, turn left. You'll see."

Raimo thanked her and walked down plush carpeting thick enough for a cat to curl up in. The décor was a play on gold and white. Pillars that didn't seem to be holding up anything were veined with marble glitter.

Tuomey was leaning against his door jamb when he got off the elevator. His shirt open to the waist. A bronzed tan too even for Northtown's erratic sunlight and current brutal heat. Raimo caught the gold chains from his chest that looked polished and realized he'd shaved it. More gold dangled from a wrist. People fried themselves like lobsters at the beach, peeled, and reverted to their usual pale tones by autumn. Tuomey had the toned body of an avid gym rat. Up close, he was almost Rikki's size.

"Rai-moe, what brings you here? Collecting for the hospital's burn unit?"

"Rick is staying at my place," he said. "I want his clothes."

"You want his clothes," Tuomey repeated, as if it were

worth repeating.

"I'd appreciate it."

Raimo cautioned himself not to overreact. Tuomey baited people for all kinds of reasons besides boredom or malice.

"You'd appreciate it," Tuomey said and let his gaze settle on Raimo's face.

"Stop clucking, Tuomey," Raimo said, "and get me his clothes."

"I heard Rick had a bad accident. That's too bad."

"Any chance I could have his clothes now?"

"Sure, there's a chance," Tuomey said. He cast a look behind him into the room as if some confirmation of that prospect was about to come from a third party.

"Today, if you don't mind."

Raimo inched forward in a casual, nervous shuffle of feet until he was in Tuomey's space.

"What's your hurry, Rai-moe? Got a date with the bearded lady at the circus?"

"Your act's stale, Tuomey. Get some new lines."

Tuomey, palms striking Raimo's shoulders, threw him off balance. Agile as in his playing days, he chest-bumped Raimo several feet backward until he collided with the opposite door.

"Watch it, asshole," Tuomey said. "You might be Rick's brother, but I'll kick your ugly face in."

"Rick's clothes. Get them. I'll wait here."

"You're fucking-A right you'll wait in the hall," Tuomey said.

He turned around casually and walked into his condo's living room as if giving Raimo a target.

Raimo throttled back. The palms of his hands were wet and he was shaking with unspent adrenalin. He'd forgotten how much he hated Brian Kevin Tuomey.

Twenty seconds might have passed before the door opened again and Rick's clothes came flying out pell-mell, the shoes last, one aimed at Raimo's head.

"Tell your brother he needs to call me," Tuomey said, one hand on the door jamb, waiting for Raimo to charge. "I thought so. Now fuck the fuck off, you Finn motherfucker."

Caddio left work at 6:09 p.m. He took North Bend but instead of crossing Lake Road to the condo's parking lot, he drove west toward Jefferson-on-the-Lake. Raimo expected him to pull off somewhere in the resort town and find a new bar now that the Suomi was hostile territory.

Dino slowed to 5 m.p.h. as the traffic flow became bumper-to-bumper once he turned onto the main drag, a half-mile of concession stands, parking lots, miniature golf, rides that ranged from a mini-Ferris wheel through dodgems to gas-powered racers on a dirt track; the latter end held the new water slide, several arcades, and bars. Mostly bars. Stephen and Basil's upperclassmen spent whole summers cruising the streets looking at girls, pining for their twenty-first birthday so that they could drink legally, and walking the Strip from one end to the other. His brother and Tuomey were regulars from the age of 19 on. Brian clouted IDs for both that stood up to checks at the door.

Despite the occasional stare by pedestrians at crosswalks who could penetrate the windshield reflecting the Strip's neon lights bouncing off cars, he managed to keep low behind the steering wheel, enjoying the crowds and savoring the aromas of frying donuts, pizzas, and vinegar-laced French fries.

He took his eyes off Dino's Malibu and glimpsed the sun between rooftops, blooming over the lake in a huge red ball.

Someday, ninety-million years from now, it will nova, he thought, and cover the entire horizon.

Dino passed more arcades, bars, and food stands and people walking everywhere like giant ants at a picnic. What was left at this end of the Strip was a seedier slice of offerings—biker bars with Hogs lined up, another nondescript, cement-block bar favored by the year-round locals, a fortune-teller's window, and an ancient arcade with flaked paint. Vacant and boarded up over the windows, it used to feature tiny cranes with shovels and four buttons for control. The sand inside the glass cases was littered with junk like packs of cigarettes or Gillette razor blades, and party whistles. The prize Raimo had focused on was 1950's cheesecake photos of women in bathing suits or daring two-pieces of the day. Raimo spent a small fortune manipulating the claw shovel. Rikki discovered the cards tucked in his tennis shoes and gave them black eyes and clown faces or inked vees of hair under their arms and between their legs.

The Malibu turned right down a narrow gravel road lined with small cottages on both sides. Raimo parked on the street and kept the rear of the Malibu in view.

Dino parked at the end cottage but didn't get out right away. Raimo kept him in sight from a pizza stand across the street. Caddio got out after another minute and headed around the side of the cottage. He had something in his hands, possibly a cell phone or it could have been a pack of cigarettes or a folded roll of rubbers. Raimo saw zero chance of not being seen by strolling down to the end for a casual look. Dark was still hours away.

He left the cover of the pizza stand and took one of the benches opposite the lane of cottages. No one paid much attention but sometimes the other end of the bench was occupied by a stroller or a couple. Children stared at him until their parents distracted them with cotton candy or a powdered waffle.

In the course of an hour, he shared the bench with mothers pushing strollers, teenaged girls out with a boyfriend or girlfriend, red- and blue-haired goth kids, a straight-edger with X's on the backs of his hands, men ranging from retirees with thin Q-tip hair and pants hiked up to their nipples through college males in baggy shorts and frat insignia to their counterparts from the lower classes who lived rough and carried their travails in the helter-skelter tattoos on as much flesh as they could expose without drawing a Lake cop over. Now and then, someone would look his way. Raimo was no longer offended if that person suddenly had an urge to vacate the bench.

When he saw Dino's Malibu back out of the slot, he swung

around on the bench and waited until the car turned onto the Strip and turned back in the direction of Northtown. He wasn't going to make much progress; nightlife was commencing and the crowds were thick on the sidewalks and in the street. Pedestrian crosswalks were no longer more than a suggestion as people strolled between stopped traffic. A signal had been sent and received: the watering holes were filling up and pre-mating rituals were in full effect. Music blasted from the open doorways of bars close by, their siren songs luring the different cliques by their preferred sounds. A steel guitar riff competed with the percussive drum thump of EDM.

Raimo got up, stretched, and crossed the street to his jeep. He drove down the gravel road, stopping midway and turning into an empty driveway next to a cottage. The black Jag's coupe wheel rims and the double set of exhaust pipes were unmistakable from this distance. He remembered the grin Tuomey flashed as he extended the middle finger.

Decision time. Raimo doubled back, found his former spot taken by a 60's Impala with the historic car license plate. He drove fifty yards down the street to a parking lot that charged fifteen dollars. Raimo paid the bored kid who seemed reluctant to get up from his Chief Wahoo folding chair to take money. Another teen with a shag haircut that covered both eyes flicked his flashlight to the end of a row where Raimo barely squeezed into a spot beside an Escalade and a dinged-up Nissan slathered with decals protesting various causes.

His former bench was fully occupied so he drifted up and down with the press of the crowd. There had to be a good reason why a snob like Tuomey would forsake his ritzy complex on the lake where condos started at fifty thousand for tiny, déclassé digs like this cottage on a side street favored by bikers, runaways, and transients looking to score drugs.

Raimo could give it an hour but he had to get back to check on Rikki even though the Hydrocodone and Percodan were strong enough to knock him out until morning. Raimo walked down to Freddie's Grill on the lakeside and crossed over to the Swiss Chalet where standup comedy was billed. He knew he could commandeer a bench and wait for the flutter of nervous movement, and soon he'd have it all to himself.

He kept walking. It felt good to move. The air was tangy with scents and he didn't mind the stares from pedestrians.

He lingered by the crosswalk opposite the lane as if unable to choose a direction but counting down the minutes until he felt time to leave. People passed around him, headlamp beams swirling up and down the Strip while the mobs of people blurred and shimmered past his fixed position. He was a rock in a stream.

"Let's see what you're up to, Tuomey."

A man passing by gawked at him. He'd spoken it aloud.

Crossing the street in the tumult of the crowd, his ears picked up the roar of the Jag's pipes. A quick look over his shoulder and he spied Tuomey at the wheel, shades on despite the hour, revving the engine.

Raimo could have stared right at him from that distance because Tuomey was busy soaking up the envious stares of people moving past his gleaming, expensive ride, reflecting daggers of neon across the hood.

Tuomey made a deftly-handled turn into heavy traffic forcing an oncoming Porsche Diablo to hit its brakes. The driver waved Tuomey in. *Money calls to money.* Tuomey waved a hand back in appreciation.

As the Jaguar merged and the Porsche closed ranks behind it, Raimo saw her. He knew her by sight as well as the mental image of her draped all over Brian Kevin Tuomey, senior class president and prom king. No mistaking the hair, the face caught in the light of bar signs and arcades: Julie DeMarest.

The baby fat cheeks were replaced by the woman's mature, sculpted cheekbones. The make-do hair for the hospital job was replaced by a coiffed and styled cut; she looked like a model posing for a car magazine. So much for Irene's fear of her husband cheating on her with Northtown's notorious homewrecker. Any possibility of Julie and Dino as a couple was dispelled by that single glance. Raimo had never inspired that look on a woman's face and knew he never would. Brian Tuomey had it then and he had it now. It was the face of a woman content to be with the man she loved above any other. A traveler facing the sand seas of the Empty Quarter of the Arabian Peninsula understands water differently from the man lolling in an infinity pool with a cool drink in hand.

He told himself it wasn't hatred for Tuomey, the showboat, that prodded him into this gamble. He would admit, if asked, his contempt for the man garnered a big percentage. His license could be suspended for it, but he'd mentally packed in his career by now anyway. Trespassing and the burglar tools fetched from a lock box in his trunk would be enough to get him hauled in on the spot.

Raimo checked his watch for the third time. Tuomey and Julie had passed him on the Strip thirteen minutes ago. The crowd frenzy increased the decibel level and offered better cover despite the incipient dark. Faces glistened under neon lights, eyes bright with expectation.

Raimo's neck itched from anticipation. The cottages were old, post-WWII and all built from the same architect's blueprint where "cozy" and "quaint" were the guiding principles.

He walked down the gravel road, a little wider than a path, and saw lights in every other cottage. Having a distinct face like his was a disadvantage if anyone parted the curtains to take in a stranger walking past.

He was right about the door placement. It was on the lake side and that would allow for time and privacy. As he turned the corner, his peripheral vision took in the cottage opposite. No lights on.

Raimo pulled open the screen door and saw at once the main door lock wasn't an old-fashioned pin tumbler kind. Someone had replaced the door lock with one built into a handle and it looked formidable. He set to work but when he managed to get the jim in place, the pick wasn't set right. In minutes, he'd worked up a sweat and perspiration dripped from his forehead into his eyes and stung. His fingers became thicker instead of more agile. A passing gull's overhead scream startled him and he dropped the jim. Nothing worked. The keyhole was scratched but intact.

He never planned to use it but brought it along as a last resort. He didn't know how much time he had, and he didn't know if the practice with his lock picks and a video from *YouTube* was going to pay off.

Raimo jammed the beveled edge of the pry bar into the upper corner and tugged. The jamb cracked and wood chips flew back. So much for subtlety. He threw more weight into the next effort. It bit off more chunks until he had a purchase in the corner. One more good pull and the door splintered along the edge. He put a shoulder to it and he was inside.

The room smelled of must and stale perfume. He took everything in. Nothing that implied a lived-in look other than a pizza box on the small table, two tumbler glasses. Four bottles of liquor and three cans of beer lined up on the counter.

He moved to the bedroom.

His nose wrinkled in disgust at the musky tang of recent sex. The bedsheets had spilled to the floor. Full-length hanging mirrors leaned casually against the walls. A Sony camcorder rested on a tripod and was aimed at the foot of the bed. The lovers liked to admire themselves in the act.

The room held nothing else of interest or indicated anything that might relate to Rikki. Other than the fact he or Julie or both were messy housekeepers, the room spoke of no ill intent to anyone. It could be that Tuomey wanted to keep Julie away from his condo because he didn't want her to get comfortable with being there in case he brought other women over. Or he didn't want to be seen with her on the condo's CCTV system. Either way, it had nothing to do with his brother.

He found a laptop under the bed. Failing to crack a simple lock didn't give him much confidence he could get in without her password. He planned on an hour inside at most and figured he might as well try a few. He used several combinations of Brian and Julie's names. The names of Julie's children, even her husband. People still used password as their password no matter what the security experts said. He put in *briankevintuomey* and it booted up.

She liked porn sites and "bisexual" appeared in several ULRs when he typed a few words into the search bar. He clicked on the *Dr. Tuber* and *YouPorn* sites. Two women and a male cavorted in both but neither looked as kinky as the pop-ads that barraged the margins selling sex toys and Viagra. Each ad was replaced in a sequence that reminded him of nesting dolls or a magician's playing cards thrown into a fan on the table. One asked if he wanted to have sex with "a pretty bi-MILF named Katya just 3.6 meters away" and offered him a pair of boxes marked Accept and Decline.

He scrolled through several Wiccan sites and one, *paganfriendly.com*, that Julie must have used often. He opened her Instagram file and found several of her family, domestic scenes featuring a dour, nervous-eyed male in his forties and a sullen-faced youth in his early twenties. Julie seemed to be the only one smiling. Another file held naked selfies, some obviously taken in the cottage bathroom. She locked her hands in front of her to push out her breasts. A third file contained dick photos, not all the same size, race, or girth.

He pulled up her calendar and found dates and abbreviations. Some looked to be motel rendezvous and men's names or initials, Phil, Ted A., Alex, G.W. He found 5 meetings with D.C. noted overt the past three weeks, including today's with 7:30 p.m. underlined for "mtg w/ BTK." D.C. was Dino Caddio, obviously. But why the formality of separate meetings with Dino and the one with Tuomey present? That ruled out sexual liaisons. Caddio wasn't in the cottage more than a few minutes. Some of her abbreviations defied logic but nothing struck him as bizarre. He saw the numbers 275 but nothing to explain them. Phone prefix?

He wrote down a week's worth of these scraps. She had a

pdf file of monthly credit statement that showed a consistent pattern of deposits and withdrawals but one figure stood out: a $2,000 monthly deposit on the third. There was nothing noted for this day except the inevitable BTK adorned with a girlish heart encasing the letters.

No mention of Rikki. No other references to Dino, none that looked even remotely intimate. He wondered if Julie simply transposed the letters BKT, or was it deliberate, an inside joke, maybe? It had been years since the story broke in the national papers but Raimo suspected most people would remember that BTK was the signature of Dennis Rader, a mild-mannered Wichita family man and church leader who murdered ten people some years back. BTK stood for "Bind, Torture, Kill." He shut down the computer and replaced it under the bed. There was no hiding the break-in, but the computer's presence under the bed would reassure her.

Julie was hiding something, though. Maybe a boyfriend she was cheating on while Brian was in town. Brian must have installed her here for a reason and it wasn't for the convenience of a fuckpad or because he feared a rival. Tuomey didn't change spots. He didn't show up for his class reunion to resume an affair with an ex-girlfriend. Tuomey lived and worked in Columbus and kept the condo in Northtown for short vacations, according to Rikki.

Where did Rikki fit into this cottage liaison and the meetings with Dino Caddio? He needed more information. Raimo selected an unopened bottle of Courvoisier and looked around a final time.

"Brother, what have you got yourself into?" He pulled the door as tight into the jamb as he could. He descended the steps and headed down the gravel road to his jeep.

Whatever it was, Raimo thought, *he suspected it was more than a torched bar in California.*

He found 3 messages from Irene on his recorder.

Dino was drunk and he was violent. She didn't want to call the police. *Would he come over?*

By the time he played her third and longest message made twenty-two minutes after the second, she sounded more subdued, less distracted.

Raimo checked on Rikki again. He'd gotten into the liquor and seemed half-drunk, slurring words. He was sitting in the La-Z-Boy flipping through channels with a fervor that suggested he couldn't concentrate. He was surrounded by a pile of newspapers including the *Plain Dealer*, which he insisted Rikki get as opposed to "Raimo's local rag." Raimo pointed out the *North Coast Tribune* was good enough when its sports reporter covered his games. He told him there was food in the fridge.

"What is it? You kept me up all night with your shitty cooking."

"Meat loaf," Raimo said.

Their mother was a lousy cook. To say she was raised on the meat-and-potatoes fare of an Irish-American background was true enough, but their grandmother was a wonderful cook by all accounts. His mother was uninterested in food; everything she made was burnt or raw. Pork chops sat in grease until they had to be scraped free of the gray congealed fat with a knife. Hamburgers were tough as shoe leather. He used to wonder how Rikki ever acquired his muscular physique from their mutual diet. Raimo vowed to be a better cook than his mother and managed to acquire a repertoire of simple dishes in bachelorhood.

"You'll make a great wife someday," Rikki jibed, "if she can get past your face. Of course, she can always put a bag over your head . . ."

Raimo was getting used to Rikki's bad temper, but he knew there was something else gnawing at him other than having to accept charity from a despised younger brother. He left Rikki sulking in his chair.

Shortly after they married, Irene and Dino had moved into Dino's parents' house. His parents downsized to an apartment. Dino's mother died of breast cancer and the father had a stroke that put him in the county nursing home. Like most of those tough old Italian men, they came home from factories that sprouted up in the nineteen-forties for the war effort, stripped off their shirts, and headed out to their backyards where they vied for best gardener title of the neighborhood.

Raimo knocked on the door. Dino's Malibu wasn't in the driveway. Irene had to be aware of his suspicions.

She opened the door. Her dress was ripped at the shoulder exposing a bra strap. She held a wash cloth packed with ice over her left eye.

"It's nothing," she said.

"Irene," Raimo said, "tell me."

He stepped inside the foyer and closed the door.

"Where is he?"

"I don't know," she said.

"Let me see," Raimo said and approached her.

He put a hand on the wash cloth to pull it away but she reached up with her right hand and clasped his by the wrist. Neither said anything. Then she let go.

He gently pulled it from her face.

"Nice shiner."

"You should see his eye," Irene said.

"I hope you left some good, deep scratches, at least."

She mimed coming at him with cat claws but the charade fell apart and she started crying. He had her tight in his arms and he was rubbing her back, making soothing sounds, while she sobbed.

Whoever put love in the mind of us animals should be shot, Raimo thought. When she'd calmed, he warmed a cup of coffee for her in the microwave. Her cheeks held a brushed pink, like smears; the tears had stopped and her face set into a bleak mask of resignation.

"Aren't you having any?"

"No, thanks, not now," Raimo said.

He tried to find the right tone for comforting her, but everything he said landed with a clunk between lighthearted and grim.

"I suppose I nagged him," she said after a while.

"No, no, you didn't. Don't say that," Raimo said. Blaming herself for his brutishness.

She didn't ask more than a couple questions after Raimo told her there was nothing between Dino and Julie DeMarest. He didn't mention his B & E job at the cottage or what he'd discovered on her computer.

"Ray, I don't understand why he's so tense and short-tempered all the time."

"I'm going to find out," Raimo said.

She looked at him.

"Don't worry," Raimo said. "It's not—I'm not doing this because you hired me. That's done, we're square. I think my brother is involved in something going on between him and Tuomey. It might involve Dino, too. I'm doing this for me."

"I didn't mean that. I meant . . . I don't know what I meant," she said. "I hate Tuomey. He's like poison when he comes around."

Raimo helped her straighten up. Most damage was to furniture from the rampage. He picked up a shattered salad bowl and lettuce greens on the floor. The wall panels were stained with what smelled like vinegar and oil.

Irene was picking up a chair and looked over at him. "I did that," she said.

"You do know how to toss a salad," he said with a deadpan expression.

It was the wrong thing to say, once again, and her pretty face swelled up from the effort to hold back tears.

Raimo insisted on taking her over to her sister's. When she refused, he told her he would report Dino to the police if she didn't oblige him in that one thing. He waited in the driveway while she packed some clothes.

"I wrote him a note," she said. "I left it in the fridge next to his beer."

"He'll come home and sleep it off," Raimo said. "If you want, I'll go look for him. He's probably getting drunker and he's sorrier than ever right now."

Why apologize for him? he wondered. *Raimo Jarvi, unlicensed marriage counselor.*

"No," Irene said. "You're the last person he'd want to see now."

Back in his apartment, he found Rikki sound asleep, zonked on a cocktail of booze and opioids. The TV was blaring. He hesitated with the remote in his hand. He remembered it from the hours of dull television watching he'd logged while recovering from his burns. Two pretty women, both bored housewives, wanted to go to a Chippendale's gig without their husbands finding out. The husbands weren't playing poker as they had told their wives; instead, they were carousing at a strip club where they got drunk and then arrested for touching the girls and punching the bouncer. All the couples met up at a police barracks. The dialogue was full of *double entendre*. The happy ending had domestic bliss restored to all households. The segment ended with one wife doing a strip-tease for her chastened but appreciative hubbie. Even at that age, Raimo knew what a crock of shit that was. He thought of the angry, tight-lipped silence of his mother and his brooding father, weeks at table where no one spoke. Little wonder Rikki got out as soon as he did. He resented Rikki for leaving him trapped at home *with them.*

The actress who played one of the wives married the husband with an IQ so low it beggared belief. She faded from sight after the series had run its course. Some recent tabloid show featured her as one of the sitcom stars from the eighties. Three bad marriages later, several drug rehab stints, arrests for shoplifting, public drunk and several DUIs, intoned a British female host with a plummy accent, she was found dead of an overdose in a car packed with junk on Wilshire Boulevard across the street from the La Brea Tar Pits.

Raimo was forced to cultivate a sense of life's irony in youth because life marked him one day and it set a governor in his brain that made him assess everything afterward against that one random event.

He waited for the closing music, a simpering mash-up of

piano *glissando* punctuated by the triple notes of a flute, as if a mourning dove had interrupted the composer's happy creative process with a reminder that—domestic TV bliss notwithstanding—all is not good, all is not well.

He covered Rikki with a light blanket. The pills and booze had a bad effect last night. He groaned periodically until dawn when the moans turned to deep snores.

When the doctors were trying different dosages and combinations of drugs on him, Raimo remembered a bad week of fever dreams, full of sex and violence. He didn't know that kind of horror could even exist in his mind. The next time he heard *made in His image* during religious class, he shuddered, thinking of those awful dreams.

Chapter 8 - August 8

Irony, again. He never got to use much of the expensive equipment in his year of playing detective, such as the stereo and shotgun sound boosters, the action ear, a "dark invader" for amplifying light, and a parabolic mic, all of which sat useless in various drawers in his office. Now that he was through with the business, he might actually require some of it.

More irony: anything he used to eavesdrop or record would constitute a gross misdemeanor of privacy laws if he got caught using it. He had no client or reason to spy on private citizens. The expensive directional mic would finally get into the game. He needed to catch Tuomey and Julie in conversation and that, for him or anybody nowadays, was a snap with all the cheap bugging equipment available from Radio Shack and Amazon.

It wasn't much of a decision this time because he'd crossed that line when he jimmied the cottage door open last night. Too late to plant a voice-activated listening device. A pinhole night-recording camera would be risky until he knew something more. A second break-in on consecutive nights would spook Julie and alert Tuomey. He was guessing they'd already dismissed the first as some lowlife prowler looking for easy targets. Leaving the camera and computer behind would have reassured them. Tuomey's expensive cognac missing would mean a thief with low ambitions. Raimo didn't have the skill to break into Tuomey's high-end condo without outside help. He had to keep them right where they were.

He had no idea how long Tuomey intended to stay in town. Brian was a marketing big shot in a pharmacy company. DeMarest had her daytime shift at the hospital. When he'd asked his brother if he'd heard from Brian lately, he got a noncommittal shrug and a curt "What do you care?"

Raimo parked in the lot behind Freddie's Grill and walked the three blocks to the water slide, which was doing daytime business with a pre-teen crowd. From the top of the slide, he'd have a view of the cottages at the end of the gravel cul-de-sac and Julie's cottage.

He gave the teenage attendant a ten "to check out the height" because he was afraid his young daughter might be afraid and he wanted to see for himself before he let her on.

"I don't know, man," the boy said. His cheeks were blue from acute acne-scarring. He gave Raimo a hard look, a flicker of kinship passed between them. Raimo encouraged it with an extra five.

"It would mean a lot to me," he said, aping a concerned father.

"Yeah, OK, but be quick, like. I ain't supposed to let anybody in without a bathing suit."

Raimo took the metal steps three at a time and reached the top, panting slightly, and had a good view of most of the Strip. From behind the platform leading down to street level was the chute resembling a giant turquoise intestine. He had a vantage of the cottages and the surrounding area. The lake resembled a flat dull mirror.

As soon as he passed the kid taking tickets, he called Irene's number from his cell but it went to voicemail. Time to go home and face another bout of Rikki's temper for leaving him alone. Raimo more than once volunteered to hire a part-time nurse but that was met with scorn: "You'll do anything to get a woman in here."

"We can't all be sexy ex-jocks like you."

"And just how many smoke alarms do you need in this three-room dump?"

"That's called a non-sequitur in logic, Rick."

"What's it called when you ask your brother to keep a few beers stocked in the fridge and he can't fucking remember to do it?"

"*Delinquent, barbaric, evil* all come to mind."

"Fucking retard, it's a hundred degrees in this brick shithouse."

When Raimo opened the door, he saw Rikki asleep in the La-Z-Boy again. He was getting better at maneuvering himself into it with less help. A sheen of sweat covered his forehead and Raimo went to check the second window unit he'd installed. His brother was right about the nighttime heat. Sweat pooled in the hollow of his Adam's apple; damaged nerves in his side, back, and torso sparked like downed wires.

Steady thrum of motor and the knob on high.

He risked waking his brother with a palm set lightly on his forehead. Rikki told him the first time he did that he'd pull back a bloody stump if he tried it again. Broken body or not, Rikki was still formidable.

He wasn't asleep, he was semi-conscious—burning up with fever.

"What are you doing?" Rikki gasped out, his eyes snapped open.

"I'm calling for an ambulance," Raimo said. "You've got to lay off the alcohol—"

"Go. . . fuck. . . yourself," Rikki moaned.

That was the extent of Rikki's reaction. Raimo made the call and stepped outside to his walkway to smoke and wait for the ambulance. He was full of bad habits now. He wondered if getting shot at counted like some Hollywood action film with an inane PG-13 rating below the trailer: "Some Violence, Language, and Cigarette Smoking."

The ambulance arrived before he'd finished the cigarette. He watched them load Rikki into the back. The driver spoke a few words to him. He was an overweight, cheery fellow with red spots on his cheeks, and a thick beard like a young St. Nick.

"I remember your brother," he told Raimo. "He was a jock, wasn't he?"

"He was a jock," Raimo agreed.

Raimo looked about the half-filled parking lot under a white-hot sun beating down from a cloudless sky. Gulls whipped past on thermals high overhead, no need for a wing flap for speed. A speckled Cooper's Hawk sat on a broken limb in a dead tree just beyond the lot where a strip of land was fenced off from the Point above, overlooking the entire harbor. It stretched its wings as if they were too hot to lift. Men in tall hats and women in crinoline carrying silk umbrellas sat on the long porch of the Point Park Hotel a hundred years ago and fanned themselves from the intense daytime heat.

"You can ride along in the back," the cheery paramedic said.

"No, thanks," he said. "I'll follow you in my jeep."

He watched the ambulance drive off with his brother.

He knew he should have gone in the ambulance. It was the first time he had betrayed his brother in even this small a way. Maybe the heat was getting to him, too.

He thought about the ambulance man's lackadaisical memory of his brother's fame. That, in the end, might have been his brother's curse, he thought. You weren't meant to peak at seventeen and see it all go downhill from there.

The hospital had Rikki hooked up to an IV drip. The doctor told him his brother was dehydrated and he looked at Raimo. "You know, alcohol doesn't rehydrate the body or restore electrolytes like you might think."

The Army-Navy store downtown was in its last week before going out of business. Raimo scored several bargains at once: camos guaranteed to wick moisture, a pair of steel-toed boots, a Macassar skinning knife, and a thermal sleeping bag "tested in the Yukon wilderness."

Back in his jeep, Raimo called Bart. "I need your camper tonight."

"You woke me up for that? Just take the goddam thing,"

Bart growled and clicked off

He swung by Bart's on the east side and hooked the fold-up camper to his Wrangler's trailer hitch. He was cruising the Strip in forty-five minutes and coming up on the street where he needed to turn past Julie's lane.

Less a street than a zig-zag of footpath, overgrown in places, between a paved road where a row of newer cottages occupied a lake view. The right-hand side comprised seven log cabins with a similar angled driveway for parking a single vehicle.

At the end of the road, as Raimo had seen from the top of the slide, a patch of scrub trees, bent by the winds off Lake Erie, remained as cover. But not much of that before it dropped sheer to the lake a hundred feet below. Enough to squeeze Bart's camper into it. The Jeep had no difficulty punching over the rough ground, slewing in swamp muck once he left the gravel road.

Visible in daylight, it was a risk if one of the Lake cops got curious. It wasn't a designated camping site even if Lake cops weren't known for their investigative skills. Law enforcement agencies used them in their workshops as whipping boys for inferior policing. Back in June, a runaway from Pennsylvania was found decomposing under a rotted lifeboat on the beach. Raimo's police scanner turned out to be as useful as a glass ashtray, but he picked up the code for "dead body found" when a tourist from Michigan reported it, and an off-duty Northtown cop made the discovery.

On the way, Raimo concocted a story about being a novice birder and hoped to spot a rare egret. He'd stopped at the library in the harbor for a few books on bird-watching and memorized a few species while he drove. He took out the directional mic and attached the audio camcorder to the shoe built for it. He had a straight sightline to Julie's kitchen window and he swung the microphone right at it. If he needed to, he could bounce a laser beam off the glass for greater accuracy. He didn't have to worry about ambient noise like the din from the Strip or the wind soughing off the lake. He was well within optimum range.

He'd have plenty of time to hide his equipment if he saw anyone coming. The cabins closest to him were too far off to worry about being mistaken for a window peeper. Raimo took out the sleeping bag and unrolled it. Plenty of time to read up on species while he waited for dark.

As if on cue, a pair of grackles appeared over the lake and mobbed a turkey buzzard drawn to the beach by the dead fish. The shad die-off wouldn't stop. The tiny fish continued to beach themselves along Erie's shoreline all the way to Toledo, where a foul-smelling green alga had reappeared for the second year in a row. Ohio's Fish & Wildlife Service had never seen anything like it. The *Tribune* said 62 people had died in the heat wave smothering the Midwest, many indigents living in cardboard boxes or squatting in Detroit's abandoned houses, while the majority were elderly holed up in tenements in Chicago and Cleveland, baking all day in the murderous heat. Local churches were inviting their congregations to start prayer vigils for rain.

Raimo's capacity for stillness was an attribute learned from countless hours of bed idleness. He was put to the test once the chiggers attacked his ankles and the mosquitoes found him a delightful target for donating blood. His bird book said mosquitoes liked to attack sleeping birds, too, nailing them in the feet and eyelids. The sleeping bag was a temporary escape. His body temperature soon drove him out of it. He reverted to some of the games he played in his youth like naming the kings of England, hall of famers with batting averages over .300—*Sorry, Mick, two-ninety-five excludes you*—and car models between 1945 and '59 with fins, gills, and hood ornaments. The sound of Tuomey's Jaguar and his hi-beams slicing through the dark of Julie's road jerked him out of a sweat-drenched nightmare in which Rikki had him by the legs and was pulling him back into the burning tent.

He grabbed his field glasses, put on the earphones, and shot a laser beam at the window before Tuomey was out of the car and inside her cottage. He could just make out the top of

Tuomey's head in front of the kitchen window.

Muffled sounds, a door shutting. A feminine voice: Julie greeting him.

Tuomey: Dino here yet?

Julie: No. I've been in the shower. This fucking heat.

Tuomey: Relax, babe. It'll be done soon.

Julie: When, hon, when?

[Sounds of kissing. Mumbled words, unintelligible. A door shutting, the refrigerator.]

Tuomey: . . . that fucking Dino . . . panic . . . he's . . . [unintelligible].

Tuomey: . . . [unintelligible] . . . shower.

Julie: Want to fuck first?

Tuomey: Pope shit in the woods?

Raimo took off the headphones and wiped sweat out of his eyes. His hands and back of the neck were favorite targets.

Twenty-five minutes later, Dino's Malibu turned up the drive. Raimo put the glasses on him. His face had lost some of its swelling but one eye was bruised.

[Sound of door opening.]

Tuomey: ". . . door doesn't close now."]

Dino: ". . . who [something] . . . did it?"

Tuomey: ". . . fuck should I know . . . junkie asshole."

Julie: "Hey."

Dino: "Hey."

Julie "Drink, Dino?"

Dino: "Naw, I'm good."

[Tuomey laughs.] "You had a few already you mean, lying ass dog."

[Voices escalating, unintelligible. Moving away from the window.]

Raimo had nothing but garbled words, a scrambled syntax, words clipped. Tuomey's curses were the only words he could pick out clearly, but there was some fun at Dino's expense for his beating. The voices drew down again. Silence. Tuomey moved back to the window.

"Have a drink, Andino. Calm the fuck down, for Christ's

sake."

"When do I get my money, Beak?"

[Glass breaking, something crashed to the floor. The sounds of a fight. A body slamming into the wall. Julie's scream above it for them to stop it.]

Tuomey spoke to Dino at the doorway. Raimo adjusted the mic's arc, although he could have heard and caught every word if he knew how to read lips:

Tuomey: "Caddio, get a fuckin' grip! Think of Irene, your little girl."

Dino: "Look, I need money to go away, all of us! Get out of here for good!"

Tuomey: "That's what we all want, babe. Keep it together a little while longer. That's all I ask. You did—look, I can get you some more stuff. Now relax, for Christ's sweet sake. You'll get what's coming to you. I promise you."

Dino: "All right, all right, all right. Fuck, man. I don't know."

Tuomey hands Dino something [money, pills?]: "That should tide you over. Now take it easy, OK, Dino? You're running around, getting your ass kicked—"

[Dino mumbles] ". . . care of myself."

Tuomey: "I hear things."

Dino: "What—things? You mean, Irene?"

Raimo watched Dino get into the Malibu and peel off spewing a rooster-tail of stones behind him all the way down the street.

Tuomey, still in the doorway, watched Caddio drive off. Julie's hand came from inside the cottage and rested on Brian's shoulder.

Julie: "C'mon, babe. Come inside before someone sees you."

Tuomey uttered the last words Raimo recorded.

"That fucking moron," Brian said, placing his hand over hers. "If he doesn't calm down, and I mean right fucking now, he's going to get me and Jarvi—[unintelligible]."

Raimo packed everything up, moving as slowly and silently

as possible in the darkness. He knew the way back to the gravel road and risked driving without his headlights. Once on the Strip, he seemed to feel his breathing return to normal. He wanted to play the tape over until he captured as much as possible. Had it not been for the last word he understood plainly, his brother's name, he would have packed in his snooping career then and there.

Chapter 9 – August 9

Raimo looked up from his computer screen in time to see his bearded, pony-tailed Bridge Street veteran aping another show in front of his new plate glass, another expense in a growing list of bills bombarding him with more frequency just as he'd planned to end one profession and search for another. This time, it was possible to see in and out clearly. The old man still wore his black-and-gold tee shirt and he looked scruffier than ever in the heat. His thin lips moved against the glass but Raimo couldn't make out the words.

The message from the hospital must have come just as he left for the Strip. Rikki was being released in the morning but the attending physician would like to speak to Raimo personally.

Raimo waited in the lobby while the doctor was paged.

He knew a few of the doctors at Northtown General from his days of in-patient care after the burn unit in the Cleveland Clinic released him. Some were entering their long internship phases, others had moved into private practice, and a few had since retired. Dr. Kudret Arzu was an ENT specialist who had treated Raimo for throat infections. His thinning black hair had made a full retreat in the years since; he was bald except for a Caesar fringe but his eyes were the same, kind and yet searching. He spoke the most precise English Raimo had ever heard and it was always in his mind to ask him how he had become so accomplished in a second language when most of the people Raimo knew were barely literate in their native tongue.

"It's good to see you, Raimo."

Dr. Arzu was the only person outside his family who used his given name.

"Good to see you, too, Doctor."

"I wanted to ask you to see if you could persuade your brother to see a colleague of mine."

He handed Raimo a business card.

"This says he's a psychiatrist, Doctor Arzu."

"I believe your brother needs psychological counseling to assist his physical rehabilitation," Dr. Arzu replied. "I realize I'm poaching on another's territory to make this assertion, and I hope you'll forgive my intrusion, but I know you want the best for him."

"Has Rick been acting up?"

"No, I assure you, Ray, he's most lucid and obliging. However, it would be wise, I think, to intervene before some of those tendencies he has expressed to staff become acted upon. Perhaps you could push him in another direction for his own good. That is all I wanted to say. It's good to see you again, Raimo. You are looking well."

Raimo didn't know what to make of it. Rikki was sullen, moody, and hadn't said much to him that suggested anything other than boredom and disgust with his current situation. Coupled with what he had overheard with the mic last night, he wondered if Rikki had been in contact with the West Hollywood Sheriff's office in his absence. *Was Rikki expecting trouble out there? How did he tie into what Tuomey said to Julie?*

The nurse wheeled Rikki down the center of the carpeted lobby; she was an older woman with a sour expression. She left him there without a word and turned on her heel before Raimo could say anything.

"What did you do to her?"

"Take these and let's go."

He handed Raimo a citation for a court date, which stipulated a bench warrant would be issued if he failed to attend, and a wad of prescriptions.

Raimo looked at them: steroid medications and amoxicillin, which Dr. Arzu had often prescribed for his throat infections. Another was for low white blood cell count.

"Come on, move it," Rikki said. "Let's get the sheep and get the flock out of here."

"You're regressing, brother. That's what we used to say in high school when we were afraid of our teachers."

"I'm not afraid, dumbass."

"OK, but we're going to have a talk when we get home. I think you're in trouble."

"Kiss-my-ass."

The ride home was silent except for the fidgeting of Rikki's fingers extending from the cast. Raimo walked him a step at a time down the walkway and helped him to the chair. He put the a/c on high.

"God *damn*, that hurt!"

"We need to talk," Raimo said.

"Fix me a drink," Rikki ordered.

"Fix it yourself."

"Irene, did Dino say why he's been meeting Brian and Julie DeMarest out there?"

"No."

"What has he been saying about where he's been?"

"Ray, I told you," she said. "He just gets real mad, like, he goes from zero to ninety if I so much as try to find out! I know Brian's got something to do with it. I'm not surprised he's back with her."

"Has he said anything about work lately? Any trouble there?"

"No—no, it's just those people are hounding him and the other mechanics."

Raimo looked at Irene. "What people?"

"It's nothing, Ray. After the crash, the one where that family crashed in the lake. The NTSB investigates everyone at the airport. Dino said it's normal procedure after an accident."

Raimo glanced over at Irene's sister May, who sat in the

breakfast nook with her coffee while they talked. May's house was small and offered little privacy. Her four children wandered into and out of the kitchen, ignoring the adults, opening the fridge constantly in a quest for food or asking their mother for items they'd misplaced earlier. Raimo experienced a pang of envy at their happy indifference. Life was still good and everything it was supposed to be. No deep, dark woods for a Hansel and Gretel to be afraid of.

"He's just—he said he'd like to move out of Northtown," Irene said. "Go somewhere else. Start over. Dino always talks like that. It means nothing. He loves Northtown. He'd never leave."

"Thanks, Irene. Call me if you need anything."

"I will. Thanks again, Ray."

"I'll leave by the back door, if that's OK." He cut his eyes to May, who held his look and responded with a slight nod.

Outside, he made a show of checking his tire pressure. May came out, her face held the same look of concern.

"I sent her to the laundry room for a minute," she said. "I don't know why she's protecting Dino. Irene told me he's afraid, not just angry. Something's going on."

Something bad, Raimo thought.

The Cleveland news stations said the NTSB was continuing its interviews of Burke Lakefront personnel. Irene said *investigate.* Big difference, he thought. Raimo put an image of Rikki in the lounge chair in front of the TV. He replayed it and remembered something from the day he moved him in. Rikki reacted to the news of the crash, the merest flinch of his head moving toward the TV, an alertness he recognized instantly in his brother's mannerisms. It meant nothing then. Raimo tried to recall the news—something about male remains brought up, part of a fuselage—other pieces of the downed plane detected.

Of course, the NTSB would investigate all personnel at the airport when a small plane carrying six people drops from the sky a mile from take-off. The question, if Irene's sister was accurate, was why would Dino be "hounded" any more than other personnel like traffic control in the tower? That supposition made Dino's hurried meetings with Brian Kevin Tuomey at Jefferson-on-the-Lake more interesting. Tuomey worried Dino was cracking under pressure according to the tapes he'd replayed. What if the pressure was coming from federal investigators? The 275 figure on Julie's calendar could refer to a payoff or a bribe.

Divide that by six innocent lives and it wasn't so much.

"You asked my foreman to see me, Jarvi. What do you want? I'm on the job here."

Dino carried a welder's mask he slapped against his leg as they talked. They were in the lunchroom built off one of the hangars for small craft. Dino gave no sign he wanted to sit down for a chat with a fellow Northtowner. It was more than annoyance, however. Dino's eyes flicked nervously from him to the exit.

Raimo threw the dice. "I've got you on a tape out at that cottage where you met with Brian Tuomey and Julie DeMarest."

"What?"

"I know things, Dino."

Caddio's eyes bugged. It was so sudden and involuntary a reaction that it reminded Raimo of Bart's description of a gunshot suicide: "The guy's eyeballs raccooned, man . . ."

"I don't know what the fuck you're talking about, Jarvi, but you better get out of here."

Raimo leaned toward Dino and clutched the fabric of his coveralls.

"I checked up, Dino. Before you got busted for coke you were A-and-P licensed, Airframe and Powerplant. Aircraft maintenance. You need to talk to me or else I talk to those NTSB investigators," he said.

"Fuck off!"

They were standing close enough for Raimo to catch spittle on his face.

"You need to talk to me, Dino. For Irene's sake. For

Cassie."

"I don't have to do shit and I told you to stay the fuck away from Irene."

Raimo unfolded a paper from his pocket. He'd printed it from his computer before heading to Cleveland.

"Elliott Gerrard, age fifty-six," he read. "Mary Gerrard, age forty-nine. Sons Alan and Steven, thirteen and twelve. Their neighbor, Paul Frabuttino, age fifty-two. And his thirteen-year-old daughter, Alexa."

"Jarvi, you better watch your mouth—"

"Your good friend Brian Tuomey works for the pharmacy company Elliott Gerrard owned," Raimo said. "Do you think the cops are going to have a hard time connecting those dots?"

Dino's face was mottled; he was experiencing a flurry of emotions. A vein ticked at his temple like a fat worm.

"What did you do for the money, Dino? Wrap a wire around a hydraulic fuel line and turn that Cessna into a flying bomb? Three children died—"

The welder's mask caught Raimo under the jaw and he flew backward, where the corner of a table caught him below the ribs like a hard punch to the liver. He lay stunned against one of the stools unable to get his breath back right away. Like the tables, they were bolted to the floor.

He didn't remember seeing Dino leave the lunchroom. He didn't see the two men who came in but they were lifting him to his feet asking him if he was all right.

"Sure, thanks. I just got faint for a second."

Raimo thanked them again and waved off their concern with a grimace meant to be a laugh. His jaw and backside ached with ferocious pain; walking was torture. Like a toddler, he put one foot in front of the other. He managed to get a look inside the hangar where Dino had come from but he was long gone. The foreman who had allowed him into the lunchroom came to escort him out with two security guards. His two helpers must have reported him.

"This area's off-limits to the public," he said. "You'll have to leave."

They had his name and license number at the front gate when he'd driven up and asked to see one of the employees "on a personal matter."

Raimo wasn't sure how much he could report factually if the NTSB got wind of the ruckus and sent an investigator around. But his gamble with Dino paid off. *What part had Rikki played in this horror?* It was a question that roiled in his stomach like hot bile; ugly emotions awoke, stirred in his mind. He'd opened a box of sad memories he thought he'd buried long ago. He didn't know the answer. But he knew someone who had all the answers.

Northtown General was aging like its elderly patients. The whole first floor was once taken up with polio victims in the 1950's. Now it was a family-friendly lounge area with a hi-def TV and comfy chairs, a flower shop, and another for knick-knacks to bring patients on the upper floors.

Raimo smoked while waiting for Julie to leave. Her Vibe sat in the employee lot at the back under a pole light. He remembered the same swing of the hips as the evening he'd snapped her on the way to her Vibe. He got back from Cleveland limping from the excruciating pain of being confined in a hot car for the hour-long drive. His jaw was sore but none of his teeth were loose. His planned tête-à-tête with Rikki, now a showdown, in effect, had to be postponed when he arrived home and found Rikki snoring, zonked to the gills, in the bedroom. Rikki could be faking it, he thought. Either way, Raimo didn't want to be in the same space with him. He'd gone down to his office to ponder a next move, which he knew would be crucial for his brother's future.

Complicating all the uncertainties, he didn't know whether he could, or even wanted to, keep his brother out of what was coming, tempting as it was to lay off all responsibility on the other three. He hoped in the deepest cockles of his heart that the fight at the reunion was because Rikki was appalled at what Brian Tuomey, a lifelong friend, had engineered with that sad sack Dino Caddio. The motive could only be greed, but how, exactly, Raimo didn't know. Killing the executive and his sons gave the ambitious Tuomey a straight path to the top of the company. Yet, from all Raimo gleaned from his sources about Gerrard Pharmaceuticals, it was just a small, family-owned company staffed by a few executives, including Brian Tuomey in marketing. Raimo knew that vice-president titles were given out like candy in academe and business as feel-good measures when the salary was less than eye-popping. Gerrard Pharmaceuticals, Inc. wasn't listed on the stock exchange and existed as only a two-line listing in standard business references at the Northtown libraries.

He thought of Irene, and what he ought to tell her about his suspicions of Dino. None of his sympathies for her or his brother could undo the unbearable image of a plane carrying two families, celebrating a ball game, and then, in a flash, being forced to confront their own awful death when the plane plummeted from the sky. That was the horror of murder: it took the second most scared act of your life after your birth away from you.

Raimo watched the cars pass. In the white-hot light of midday, all he saw was a steady ribbon of flashing chrome and sunlight glinting from windshield. No chiaroscuro effect of twilight or the color-switching of shades under arc lights. Julie's maroon SUV could have possibly appeared black that night. It wasn't worthwhile waiting for dark to test the hypothesis by watching cars pass.

Raimo knew with no doubt whatsoever now that the arm pulling the shotgun back inside the vehicle belonged to Brian Tuomey. So vain, he kept his gold bracelet on his wrist when he went to commit murder, if it was more than an attempt to frighten him off. Raimo replayed it again: the merest wink under streetlights, like the flash of green light people claim to see at sundown.

That light was no myth, a real optical effect. But the sun itself was a mirage. Its burning image hangs above the horizon but the actual sun itself is below earth. *We spend our whole lives trying to figure out what's real,* Raimo thought. *What is a monster to us?* The Greeks called their monstrous hybrid creature with its lion body, goat's head, and tail ending in a snake's head Chimera, sibling of Cerberus, the three-headed dog guarding the gates of hell. They should have named those heads *Certainty, Truth,* and *Knowledge.*

He saw groups of young women leaving in twos and threes as mostly elderly patients and visitors entered by the front lobby. They made a contrast of youth and health, old age and sickness. Old, tired, and obese—most of the patients—they went in with somber faces unlike the nurses leaving who found a spring in their step, their workday over, even though the blast of heat coming fresh from chilled air would guarantee the thin fabric of their blouses and cotton pants would be sticking to their skin in seconds.

Walking by herself, Julie drew eyes from the men, furtive glances from the men with their wives, bold assessments from single males of every age. Her sensuality wasn't disguised inside the cotton uniform but on a muted display. She had what the boys in her class called a sweater-stretching physique long before breast enhancement surgery trickled down to the middle classes. The long, sheep-dog hair style she affected in high school was gone with disco. She wore it in a practical bun loosely tied off in back.

Raimo crushed the cigarette into the coin holder and started up as Julie left the lot; he waited at the intersection for the light change and stayed a few cars behind. If she took Carpenter Road, he hoped she'd make a beeline to her lover at the cottage, not his condo. So far, it was all cottage. Dino had plenty of time to call Brian and tell him. They could all scatter like fish at this point. If that was the case, Rikki would have to take his chances with the rest.

He was close enough to see her talking on her cell phone the whole time. Julie drove past Brian's condo and gave a couple blasts of her horn as she passed and drove toward the cottage, as he'd hoped.

At the Strip, she slowed to the posted 15 m.p.h., Raimo two cars behind. It was too early for the mass exodus from

Northtown to go cruising, but the heat was wreaking havoc on everything, including people's normal habits. The bars on both sides of the Strip hummed with business. People mobbed the sidewalks moving like cattle to the watering holes. Few looked like tourists or families, a normal sight at this time of day. Bikers, college kids, some of the rougher-looking nighttime crowd were evident, probably forced out of their cramped quarters by the heat to seek solace in the bar of their choice.

If Julie's horn blasts meant more than a lover's ritual, he'd be on his way to see her. Raimo didn't have much time.

Raimo pulled up behind her Vibe, blocking her in as well as taking up that end of the road. He went up the steps and knocked. She couldn't have been inside longer than a minute before he pulled in.

The door was new, more solid than the plywood one he had smashed. Raimo had a transcript of Dino's visit from last night on the passenger seat and the disk copy he made; he intended to play it for her if she balked.

He twisted the knob, the door opened immediately. He had a foot inside when an overpowering odor of gas assaulted his nostrils.

His heart thumped in his throat—

Oh shit, go—

Raimo didn't remember much after that, not the bright flash or the concussive *whoomph* like gas poured on fire. The explosion blew the cottage into splinters and set a fire on part of the roof on top of the cottage opposite. He didn't remember flying, being airborne, a wingless human projectile launched from the concussive force of the blast. He would tell himself he knew it was happening but that was the mind trying to fit the picture-making mechanism of the brain with a narrative that made sense. It doesn't. A two-hundred-pound man doesn't fly like a gull on his own, inside one moment, aloft, viewing the cliff edge below the next, Raimo told himself. *It can't happen again*—while it was happening.

This is what death feels like and then he went black.

Chapter 10 – August 10

The force of the explosion blew him out the door and should have catapulted him over the cliff onto the rocks below—except for the jerry-built fence someone had erected at the cul-de-sac to keep drunks from driving over the cliff edge. Raimo's body shattered three boards and lay with his head and one arm dangling over the edge by the time he came to rest. The paramedics found him dazed, conscious but incoherent, lying in the weeds. If his right foot had not been sticking out on the gravel road, he might not have been seen. If he'd rolled the wrong way, he'd have gone over.

They examined him in Jefferson Memorial. Except for his hearing and his clothes partially shredded in the blast, he was groggy, disoriented, but not seriously damaged. The door had acted as a shield. Sitting up, he felt nauseated, short of breath, and a full symphony orchestra was playing inside his head. Hospital staff talking to him sounded as if they were speaking underwater. Raimo's vision had cleared but the ringing in his head would go on for a while, they told him.

He found out that night from the detective assigned to the case via a state arson investigator, along with a tidbit later contributed from Bart Massey, vacuum cleaner of station gossip—the replacement door installed by the manager of the cottages had been a mistake. He was a regular at the Lake, a known bar fly and part-time biker, who ordered the most expensive door in the Lowe's online catalogue. The owner of the cottages was a retired insurance executive in Sharon, PA, who told him specifically to get the cheapest replacements for all repairs.

"That door saved your life," Detective Dave Nolan said. "Here's what it looks like now."

He handed Raimo a photo taken by the arson investigator.

The inside of the door was cratered and pockmarked, riddled with shrapnel and debris. It looked like the side of a barn after a passing tornado.

When they first brought him in, one of the nurses started to hook up an IV line until she realized his facial scars were old ones covered in dirt, not results of the explosion and the fire that consumed what was left of the cottage. His hair, kept short since high school, hadn't burned except for a patch on the back that gave him a monk's tonsured look; his eyebrows were singed and his face smeared with soot as if he'd dabbed and streaked himself with greasy smoke.

He told the detective he was "visiting a friend from high school." The cop didn't react when he gave Julie DeMarest's name as the friend.

"Where is she?"

"I don't know," Raimo said. "Maybe the draft from my opening the door caused an arc to ignite the gas."

Like the arc caused by a wire in too close proximity to a fuel line, he thought.

Nolan said they'd run her plates from BMV, make some calls, trace her phone. If they had to, issue a BOLO.

"There's no body in the cottage," Nolan said. "We made sure."

He was in dangerous territory, covering for his brother in a second attempt on his life. Nolan was noncommittal when Raimo told him he was a private investigator. "But not working a case, purely a social visit," Raimo insisted. Nolan mentioned a suspected gas leak as the cause of the explosion but said BCI from Columbus would be called in if the county sheriff's department decided to turn it over. The Lake cops weren't even mentioned as investigating.

Raimo told them he'd come down to the station to make a

statement as soon as he was cleared by the doctor.

"It'd be a good idea to let local law enforcement know," Nolan said. "If you do work cases around here, I mean. We don't like amateurs pissing in our territory. Things can get rough if you bypass that little courtesy."

Rough? What part of rough was he missing so far?

Victims of blunt-force trauma and bad concussions often don't remember much of the actual events that precede the incident that clobbered them. It's a blank slate; the screen goes black and then, as more memories pile in, the jagged sequence of narrative tapes itself together like an old 8 mm film strip.

Raimo recalled all of it from the moment he placed his hand on the door and opened it. He still had the distinctive olfactory sensation of gas in his nostrils to bring it right back. But not the explosion itself—no flash, no sound. Raimo credited his flight-or-fight instinct for kicking in a nanosecond after the odor registered and a fraction of a second before a stream of exploding debris struck the door behind him at Mach 1 speed. He was hypersensitive to fire like a deer that had escaped one forest fire and was always on alert for the next.

Back home, Raimo found a note from his brother on the counter beneath a glass in crabbed, unfamiliar handwriting. "Gone out," it said. Signed with Rikki's R in the middle of the water mark. He started for the door when he realized Rick wouldn't have attempted to go out walking by himself. He noticed the pile of Marlboros smoked down to the filter. One Winston in the pile suggested a visitor.

He was planning on a long nap to clear his head and ease some of the ache in his bones. The physician at the hospital wrote him a prescription for pain which he folded up and put in his pocket. On the way down Lake Road, he drove to the storage facility in Saybrook.

He went to the secretary resting against the back wall. He tripped the wooden plug that released the catch and popped out the secret drawer. Where once he had hidden a wooden soldier, instead he found a wad of folded papers. A newspaper article was folded around a small square piece of blue-tinted paper. He set the clipping aside to study the flimsy blue square of paper; its blocky typeface produced in the era of electric typewriters with fly wheels in the decade before computers took over the world's writing tasks.

Rikki's birth certificate. It had been folded and unfolded so often it had worn thin along the creases. Raimo could have pulled it apart as easily as the wings from a cabbage moth. Everything on it made sense with one notable exception: the father's name, which was not Raimo's father's name. The man's name on the paper was Kenneth M. Gilles. For most of Raimo's youth, he was a coach and later athletic director for another school district his high school competed against. The paper always called him Mel Gilles whenever he was named in a sports article. He was a four-sport athlete in his day. Raimo had seen him several times in town, sometimes within a few feet and often when he was out with his mother, who didn't like to drive alone. He never saw her speak to the man and never thought much about him one way or the other. He died of cancer five years earlier because Raimo remembered reading the *Tribune*'s gushing, half-page tribute, noting Mel Gilles as one of the first Northtown athletes elected to the county's athletic hall of fame. And that same article he was holding in his hand. Raimo superimposed an image of Rikki in football uniform scoring one of his many TDs over the paper's sepia photo of Mel Gilles as a running back for his high school.

The other paper bore the letterhead of the California Bank of Commerce in Chino. It listed monthly deposits totaling $55,700 dollars and corresponding withdrawals of the exact amounts within a couple of days. The first deposit dated fourteen months after Rikki had moved to California, staying just ahead of an investigation into a boxcar theft in Northtown. One of Mel Gilles's accomplishments was election to county commissioner.

He refolded the papers as they were and replaced them in

the not-so-secret drawer. He wondered why his mother had kept them. Maybe she wanted to atone for the betrayal of her marriage vows in her Catholic guilt. Maybe she wanted to stick a finger in the eye of anyone who survived her. With his mother, it was hard to say which she preferred. The thought of his own mother writhing in illicit, passionate embrace in some squalid motel like the ones he staked out made him sick. *Who was he to judge?* He had put cuckold horns on a man's head and it led to murder. Rikki had the benefit of his doting mother's best love, not to mention the reverse mortgage payout all along.

The retirement bash he promised to treat himself to at the Wyandotte Club would have to wait. He was engulfed in questions. No one told him when he became a private investigator his biggest mystery would be himself.

Raimo went home to wait for Rikki. He could hold back the last bombshell discovery of his brother's true father but the rest—Dino, Tuomey, the reunion, Julie and the cottage, whatever conspiracy lay behind it all—all that had to come out. It was time his brother learned what he knew because it was just a matter of time before law enforcement pieced the whole story together.

Whatever part Rikki played in the plane crash, and he still assumed it was more willful ignorance than active participation, he would do what he could for him with the money he had left from his trust fund. In life, his mother failed to pry it loose to hand it off to her beloved older son, but in death, he would oblige her by seeing Rikki got enough to rent the services of the best trial lawyer he could afford.

No phone message, nothing on his cell's voicemail. Raimo had another thought that kept him uneasy and restrained him from mixing the Tom Collins he started to make. Tuomey had shot at him, whether intending to kill him or scare him wasn't the point but there was no more doubt. Dino had rigged the cottage to blow up when he entered, and it was orchestrated from the moment he followed Julie to the cottage. Raimo dead meant all three—or four, counting Rikki—remained in the clear. Tuomey wasn't known for moderation. Until he could get a fix on Tuomey's whereabouts, Raimo wouldn't feel safe no matter where he went.

Raimo drove back to his office when his call to Irene on the road went to voicemail. He wasn't sure she could help at this point but maybe Dino had called her. If the man had brought down a plane, jury-rigging a gas line to blow a cottage to smithereens would have been child's play. Unless he had acquired the sociopathic personality of his two partners in crime, it had to be eating at him; some of his erratic behavior of late could be attributed to a man laboring under a weight of guilt. That might also explain Rikki's morose behavior around the apartment since the reunion and his scuffle with Tuomey.

Raimo was sure Tuomey got to Dino with his lifelong influence, much less the money he offered, and he was equally certain Dino had been told the only person on that plane would be the company executive. Whatever else Brian told him to justify the "accident," only Caddio would know. Manipulating Dino to do the unthinkable was a shock to people with middle-class sensibilities, not to cops who saw evil on the job. Raimo wasn't used to it. He didn't like its proximity to him through his only brother. On the other hand, this was a day of surprises about things he used to know that it turned out were never true in the first place.

Bart was grooming for a date.

"I don't have much time, Ray."

"Did Julie DeMarest come down to give her statement?"

"Nolan was showing off her paragraph in the muster room. One paragraph full of misspellings, this little-girl handwriting with circles for dotting *i*'s, yet, man, this rack like Milena Velba—"

"Who?"

"Forget it."

"She mention me in it?"

"You? No, why? She told Nolan she was at Annie's Bar drinking with a girlfriend. No one back there, no one expected. The girlfriend confirms she was at the bar. Ditto the bartender. Julie's hard to miss even in a shithole bar—"

"What about people in the cottages?"

"The neighbors all confirm—at least the ones who weren't high or blitzed."

"Tell me about Nolan."

"Made detective sergeant last year. Good copper, a hardass. Why?"

"He gave me a friendly warning," Raimo said.

"Take it seriously, bro. You damn near had to testify in Radebaugh's trial. Old Ronnie Radebaugh had a lot of friends in the department."

"Your prosecutor didn't want me on the stand," he said.

"Before you ask," Bart said, "Radebaugh's assigned to LECI. His lawyer angled for the honor farm in Columbiana County but the state said no dice, murder and all that, not jaywalking or kiting checks."

LECI was in Conneaut a dozen miles east of Northtown on the Ohio-PA border. Lake Erie Correctional Institute was a private prison, medium-security, with inmates on good behavior assigned community service work.

"Nice," Raimo said. "He'll be out shoveling sidewalks in Conneaut with the other cons this winter."

"Winter's never coming back, man. This heat wave is God's punishment."

"It's not right, Bart."

"If it bothers you, don't go sticking your fishing pole in strange waters next time."

That was what Kristine née Levesque Radebaugh had been reduced to now—a smutty cautionary tale.

"Speaking of poles," Bart said, "I'm on my way out the door. Wish me luck."

"You should practice what you preach, hypocrite."

Click. Gone.

Not thinking about Kris Radebaugh four times a day was

like not thinking about food, water, rest. He never kidded himself about love in her case. She wasn't made for it. Yet she dazzled him from that first moment he saw her at a political fundraiser for her husband. He'd gone along with Bart, who called him his plus-one, but it was Raimo's notion to start going out into public. He was like a baby reptile breaking through its shell. He hadn't gone anywhere in years where people met and spoke. He wasn't introduced because Bart was eyeing his own political prospects, trying to grease some wheels for his future run at the Sheriff's job. Her eyes met his and held his stare, daring him to break it off first. He never gave her a thought except to note how lucky Radebaugh was to find a trophy wife that pretty.

Two weeks later, he had a message on his cell to call her. He didn't know how she got his number unless it was from Bart, always with his eye on the main chance, and he would have obliged her in a heartbeat and never thought to tell Raimo. His directory at the time wasn't exactly full: Bart, Rikki in California, the trust lawyer in Jefferson, and a specialty meat market in Kingsville.

Days passed before he called her. Two days later they were lovers in her bedroom. When he entered her that first time, he said something like "Kristine, we're making love," as if his brain couldn't process the fact because it had happened so fast. From a gentle touch of her hand along his scarred face, to cupping his chin, to a pull of his neck down to her breasts. Raimo had never kissed a girl, let alone a woman. He'd accepted the fact that he was condemned to celibacy as if he'd taken the vow.

When she stepped out of her lace panties, and he glimpsed her tawny pubic ruff, he knew that they were going to be lovers and it made him crazy with expectation and something he had never experienced in life before: bliss.

How it degenerated from there seemed to happen unconsciously between them as if their brains communicated without words. He would have done anything, said anything. She wanted the sex rough, not tender, and it was his pleasure to oblige her wishes. His back, thighs, and chest bore the scars of her nails. The breasts she let him kiss after a beating had the tiniest blue veins below the areolar tissue, and she allowed him to place his mouth on them while she panted, drawing her breath in for the next assault. She never asked if he was in pain or should she pull her punches or kicks. She never marked his face, however; that was reserved for her to grind down on him, panting, gibbering an onslaught of bedroom filth with spittle covering her face while she worked on him, cursing her freak, until she orgasmed and collapsed over him.

Bart used to laugh at him for his clumsiness, the bruises, and the cuts in his flesh. He didn't realize how bad his need for her was until he urinated blood. Mirrors were banned in his place so he had to buy one from an antique shop to see the grapefruit-sized bruise on his back near his kidneys.

She never spoke of her sexual relationship with her husband, and he never asked about it. She was the epitome of the upper-middle-class wife and there was never a question of abuse. Ron spoiled her and she accepted it as a lovely woman's due. They never spoke about anything that had to do with the world around them because small talk would have broken the spell he was under. He had no doubt she was in control.

When Ron became suspicious she was having an affair, he felt a mix of emotions that ranged from profound sorrow to relief. Kristine was descending into murky depths and he didn't want to follow her there. He knew she was on the verge of something far darker than their relationship provided like a drug that has to be increased in potency to get the same effects; it was coming at any time, but what it was, she wouldn't reveal until the day she said Ron was thinking of having her followed by a private investigator.

"We'll have to stop seeing each other," Raimo said. "You have too much to lose."

"I don't care about that," Kris said. She brushed the scars along his face with her long fingernail. Until she'd achieved orgasm, she was incapable of rational thought or speech. She was all hunger and appetite. His pain was her bliss.

"I want you to do something for me," she said.

"What is it? You know I'll do whatever—"

"Die for me," she said. She kissed his scars.

She wanted him to die for her. Not a suicide but a murder she controlled.

A normal man would have cut and run at that point. He told himself that was the absolute end point and omega of this crazy, intense one-sided relationship. But he also knew a part of him wanted to acquiesce, *would acquiesce*, the part of him she controlled. That knowledge from the abyss terrified him, woke him up with night sweats and a dream of Kristine, mouth red as a cannibal's feasting over his guts. He felt as if he'd been on a three-day binge and woken up in a parking lot. He could almost hear himself agreeing to it. An ugly, evil dwarf, a homunculus curled up in his brain and waited to be let loose.

Kristine tapped into his psyche. In those long months after his return from the burn unit, he couldn't bear a human being's touch on his skin. He regressed, unable to sleep, clumsy in basic things. His father wanted to bring him to a speech therapist because he rarely spoke. His parents talked to him and he understood what they said, but he didn't feel a compulsion to respond. Words were unnecessary, a torment. It wasn't a vacuum so much as a state of doldrums, a windless, empty, flat terrain with no features and nothing on the horizon but more of the same until the next round of *blitzkrieg* pain radiating like the sun that racked him in spasms of agony.

He turned the corner physically long before his mind found equilibrium. Rikki had stopped speaking to him. It was the only time his parents were angry with his brother for the name-calling.

"He doesn't say shit, why bother? Look at him sitting there at the table. Hey, space monkey, wake up!"

When he saw his father weeping in the garage one day, he made a conscious effort to return from that place.

Grade school wasn't so bad. His classmates at Our Lady of Sorrows knew him and pitied him. Some didn't speak to him at recess. Always, the covert stares, the open-mouthed gasps. He learned to shield his face from view with his arm until his eighth-grade teacher pinned his elbow to the desk and told him to straighten his posture.

That, however, was a prelude to what was coming for the next four years. High school was a rapid descent into self-abnegation, abasement, and humiliation. He became a master at invisibility, absenting himself from class discussions, and avoidance of anything that drew him into the light, a hideous moth fearing all flame. He was grateful for Rikki's athletic glory. Without that protection—a brother feared and admired equally—he would have been lost. Being known as Rick Jarvi's brother saved him untold amounts of shame and grief.

But the day Irene Donovan pulled him out of his desk and led him from their history class marked a day as special as if the mighty angel of death had flapped his black wings overhead, looked down, and spared him.

Chapter 11 – August 11

"I want to pay you," she said.

"I don't want your money," Raimo said.

"Find him, Ray. I know he's in trouble. His job called today. He's fired. He hasn't shown up but he's been leaving the house at the same time every day. I never knew."

"I'll do my best, Irene. You know that."

"I trust you, Ray. I always have. How's your brother doing? I heard he was in a car accident."

"He's—he's fine."

"Are you OK? The *Tribune* said you were hurt in the explosion at the Lake."

Her eyes could shift color like taupe. He couldn't read her.

"I was there, yes. I was visiting a friend. Bad luck."

But good luck that Julie DeMarest wasn't named the cottage's renter. The man in the two-paragraph article besides him was a JOTL resident who transacted the rental agreement by phone and paid two weeks in advance—Tuomey covering his tracks. If Julie DeMarest didn't have a party-girl reputation, she wouldn't have been recognized as the one occupying the cottage at the time, but the reporter didn't follow up.

Raimo turned to go, but he felt the soft pressure of her hand on his shoulder.

"Ray, I never thought—"

"What is it?"

"I never thought any less of you over that—over Kris Radebaugh. That wasn't your fault."

"Thank you."

He'd abandoned the hope she wouldn't have heard the gossip about him. Rumors were as common as songbirds in Northtown.

"You know our reunion's coming up in ten days?"

"Is it?"

"You know it is," Irene said. "Fifteen years, a long time. I'll make sure you get an invitation."

"I'll be sure to read it," he said. *And throw it away like the last one.*

"Be sure you RSVP it or I'll come get you."

He looked at Cassie playing with plastic dolls on the floor. Tawny sweat curls ringed her forehead. A coloring book and crayons lay beside the doll house. The only difference being she played in a kind of intent silence, whereas most little girls would chatter happily at their dolls moving them back and forth in the room of the open-faced dollhouse. He risked a look at Irene, smiling at her girl. *Tenderness,* Raimo thought. *Attachment. They're the cause of all our suffering.*

Most men his age had girlfriends or wives, families, kids who were growing up and looking forward to high school. Careers with meaningful work to do every day. Lives with order and purpose, if not much privilege in a small Midwestern rust-belt town. Those things mattered. They helped you weather the storms life was going to throw at you. *You can't miss what you never expected*, Raimo always told himself.

He tried the Suomi, thinking it doubtful Caddio would go back there so soon. He was drenched in sweat after checking three more bars on Bridge Street. A few others wouldn't open until late afternoon. Two more, he was sure, Dino wouldn't be caught dead in, the cowboy bar and the latest bar to open that seemed to be flirting with an art crowd. He passed the coffee shop, a curio and antiques store, a chocolate store, and the internet café. The Vapes shop was the latest newcomer to the street besides his offices. No one had seen Dino or remembered seeing anyone who looked like him.

He cast a longing look across the street at the Wyandotte.

A cold brew sounded good to him just then, but he held on and headed for his office.

Once inside, he realized his error. He forgot to leave on the air conditioner and the tiny office could have been a sauna. He turned on the machine, a futile effort to remove the blast-furnace heat and hoped he hadn't done harm to his computer.

While waiting for it to boot up, he checked his phone calls. Telemarketers, two with thick Indian or Pakistani accents. Someone else wanted to sell him a burial plot at Angels of God Cemetery in Kingsville. He didn't think that a bad idea the way things were going. A booming male voice bellowed "Score!" and followed it with a wolf howl: Bart, *braggadocio* of the successful suitor. Two hang-ups, a person wanting to know if he took cash only, a spoof call from a breaking teenaged male voice, and two robocalls offering him a deal on aluminum siding and hair transplants. Ezekiel called again: "I will carry out great vengeance on them and punish them in my wrath. Then they will know that I am the Lord, when I take vengeance on them."

"You aren't the only one losing patience," Raimo said to the prophet's voice.

The noise behind him jerked him to his feet and sent the chair clattering across the floor.

"I'm sorry," she said. "The door was unlocked."

Jumping Jesus Christ. Not by a long shot—

But absolutely Julie DeMarest. Standing there, in living color, in his cramped office.

"I came in to get out of the heat," she said. "It seemed a little cooler back there."

She stepped forward and offered a hand to shake. "Julie DeMarest."

Raimo shoved her aside and lifted the bat he kept under the desk ever since the Night of the Broken Glass, as he called it.

"Where's Tuomey?" It came out a snarl.

"I don't know what you mean," she said.

She looked calm, not frightened. But she hadn't expected that reaction from a male, even a damaged one. A fact that impressed him considering what she'd been up to lately.

"I'll repeat the question," he said. "Where is that sewer rat boyfriend of yours?"

"Brian, you mean? I have no idea. Why?"

"Hang around. You'll hear me call him plenty more names."

"This must be a bad time for you. I'll go—"

She tried to move past him. He gripped her triceps and halted her in mid-stride.

"Don't play the ingénue with me."

"What—what do you mean?"

"You're involved in a conspiracy that killed six people, almost killed me, and you're about to waltz out of here like it's nothing."

"Are you insane? I'm not involved in anything like that! I have no idea what Brian said to you about me, or what he did, but I am not involved in anything like that. That is bullshit."

"Then we can go right to the cops," Raimo said. "I'll drive. Let's go."

"Get your fucking hand off me. Just let me tell you why I'm here and if you want me to go to the police, I'll do that."

He dropped his hand. She stood still, facing him, breathing hard, eyes glittering. Her upper lip trembled, the philtrum glistened from sweat. She wore her green scrubs. A silk underwear shirt covered her cleavage. She was ringed with sweat from the tops of her shoulders to the vee of the neckline. He might have left his office door open. He was distracted and tired from a week like no other in his life. But that back room was dark and empty—why hide there waiting for him? The temperature would have been a few degrees short of oven heat compared to the front part of the office.

Raimo, shiny with sweat, uncertain what her presence signified, was tense—anything but the stereotypical wise-cracking gumshoe of pop culture.

He pinched a finger and thumb together and said, "I'm this close to calling the police. I have one question. Answer it and I'll listen."

Raimo dialed nine-one and hesitated. His finger hovered over the button, and he looked at her.

"Answer it any other way, you and that shitheel will do the perp walk in front of cameras at the Sheriff's precinct."

She stared, lips forming a pout. He pressed the last digit.

Ambulance, fire, or police. What is your emergency?

"Ask your question."

"Where is Dino Caddio?"

What is your emergency, please?

"I'll take you to him," Julie said. "That's why I'm here."

"Give me your key," he said.

She reached in her purse, and he panicked. He grabbed the bag from her and dumped out the contents on his desk.

"What the fuck," Julie said.

He spread out the contents. Her keys were in a leather pouch. He picked up her driver's license, noting the DOB. A crumpled monthly bank deposit statement showing a $2,000 deposit on the third. He saw a couple prescription bottles and read the labels: Vancomycin, for treating staph infection and another antibacterial he recognized. Nurses worried about nosocomial infections, an occupational hazard. He shook out a couple pills from each bottle. He recognized the markings for schedule 1 drugs.

"What's this? Oxycontin. Are you addicted to hillbilly heroin?"

"Fuck you."

"You're a junkie nurse," he said. Another occupational hazard of the medical profession.

"Go fuck yourself, you creep. Get some plastic surgery while you're at it."

"Dino asked you to get me and bring me to him, and I'm supposed to believe Tuomey didn't send you?"

"Go take a flying fuck at the moon. I don't give a fuck what you believe."

"You and Tuomey are a good match. Products of a good Catholic education."

"Go fuck your mother."

Her anger didn't seem real, but there she stood, big as life, bosom expanding with indignation.

"Why are you here?"

"I told you that twice," she said. "'Bring Ray Jarvi,' he said. He's been doing coke—"

Julie wanted to drive. He told her to park her SUV around the corner behind his building. He'd meet her up in the parking lot behind his office. While she was out, he slipped the Ruger into his belt. Closed-circuit cameras from the law office across the street would keep her SUV in view.

"Pop the hood," he said.

"What—what did you say?"

"Pop the hood."

She climbed back in and reached down to the floorboard and pulled the lever.

Raimo lifted the hood and loosened a couple distributor cap wires.

"I'm driving," he told her.

He had to stop playing checkers to Tuomey's chess. He was gambling Tuomey wouldn't make a pawn of his queen—but with Tuomey, who knew? The man sent two families, deliberately or not, into the lake without remorse. Unrecognizable body parts were all that the Coast Guard had dredged up so far. More would wash ashore in the coming days, the news channels predicted. That made everyone around Tuomey a pawn.

"Take Lake Road," she said.

"He'd better be there," Raimo told her.

"You gonna hurt me if he's not, creep?"

Some of her confidence was back. The kind attractive women took for granted around men. Her body heat and citrusy perfume wafted in the chilled air pumping through the vents. He felt dizzy from anticipation and the eight cups of coffee he'd gulped so far with little food to keep down the stomach acid.

Northtown ended past the abandoned illuminating energy

company building. Weeds overran parking lots that used to handle hundreds of vehicles parked by men and women working the factories nearby. The first building across the township line was a ramshackle gentleman's club called Queen of Hearts. An old-fashioned garage sale sign with missing block letters had stood as a local joke for years: D NCERS WE COME AT 4:00.

The lake swung into view on the left. He saw a Canada Steamships oreboat heading uplakes, its broad silver and black band across the port bow. Raimo's father had told him how the oreboats traveled through the Detroit River, into the Soo locks and the upper lakes, Michigan and Superior. The giant thousand-foot freighters hauling coal and taconite from the Mesabi Iron Range in Minnesota used to be a common sight. It was his boyhood goal to sail on those boats when he recovered until his father told him, as gently as he could, he had to pass a physical to get an ordinary seaman's license. But his condition . . .

Julie snapped him out of his reverie. He was aware of her body, curved like a capital S; she exuded a tangy perfume that mixed with the scent of her flesh. Raimo banished a wickedly acute image of her long legs locked in coitus around Tuomey's midriff.

"Dino said you hate women because—"

"—I look like a freak?"

"—because you got burned when you were a kid," she said.

"He ever tell you how it happened?"

"He said you were playing with matches or something." Julie spread her legs and aimed the vent at them. "Fuck me, it's so goddamn hot."

"Why are you still in scrubs?"

"Double shift," she said. "I switched with another nurse so I could have more time."

"For Brian, you mean."

"Yeah, whatever, asshole."

"Your husband mind?"

"He don't fuckin' care," she said, lapsing into a familiar

Northtown locution.

Lake Road passed through Kingsville, a notorious speed trap, and ended in Conneaut ten miles ahead.

"Are we going into Conneaut?" Raimo asked her.

"Almost, slow down."

Houses began popping up on the lake view side and were either grand manor houses with spacious yards of several acres, all built by Northtown's gentry within the last decade or were tumble-down, rinky-dink houses falling apart with children's toys scattered around the yard and Harleys and four-wheelers out front with 4 Sale signs. Unlike the cottages going west toward the JOTL resort, these were laughingly small, some spavined like old horses, and neglected, abandoned with sumac growing through broken windows, or painted in faded Jamaican colors.

Julie suddenly perked up and stretched toward the windshield, intent on the roads shunting off to the side oblivious to the enhanced femininity on offer—*or was she?* wondered Raimo. Tuomey was smart to use her as bait if this was a trap.

Julie deflected his attempts to get her to talk, answering with a "You'll see" or "Ask Dino that." He failed to goad her with Tuomey.

"Tuomey's using you and Dino, Julie. If you're smart, you'll go with me to the cops and cut a deal."

"I've done nothing, fucker, so I don't have nothing to worry about."

"What about Brian?"

"That's Brian's business."

"You're with him every day. I've seen his car at the Lake."

"So what? I haven't seen all that much of him since his class reunion. He keeps putting me off, says he's got to work the phones, blah-blah, work the phones, every day when he's in town. Then he's back home to Columbus for his work."

"You think there's a future with him?"

"No, and what do you care anyway?"

"You'll have time, all right. Years of it. Be smart, Julie.

Don't take a fall for him. Maybe you don't know how big this is, what he's involved you in."

It was tossing chum in the water, but she didn't bite.

"What about your brother?"

"What about my brother?"

"I know what Brian told me. Him and Rick are a trip. They're into some big deal. 'If I go down, Rick Jarvi goes with me,' he says, so whatever deal those guys got going, they're joined at the hip and you better think about that, little brother."

Little brother—Tuomey's voice echoed from her lips.

Raimo did think about that. Tuomey's words on tape: . . . *he's going to get me and Jarvi* . . .

It was the missing, garbled portion Raimo needed to be sure of before deciding what to do about his brother. Julie confirmed what he suspected in his gut: Tuomey masterminded the plane crash, Rikki was in on it somehow, and that meant he was responsible for two dead families no matter what Tuomey told him. He needed time to find something to exonerate his brother. If not, he promised himself, he'd do all he could to sink him and Tuomey together. None of that Arab bullshit: *My cousins and I against the world, my brothers and I against my cousins.*

"What do you know about me anyway? Brian says you're full of negative energy. Turn here!"

He swung hard left and nearly sideswiped a reflector pole.

"Fuck, man, slow the fuck down!"

"Where?"

"That blue cottage at the end, see it?"

"This one going to blow me up when I walk in like your other one?"

"Whatever."

He pulled up to the front door, shut off the engine and stared through the windshield. A pair of curtained windows on the second story. Nothing moved behind them. Julie started to get out. He grabbed her arm and held her back against the seat.

"Wait."

"Wait for what? C'mon, man, Dino's waiting inside."

"You first," he said.

The two-story house, not a cottage, was invisible from the road, a simple prairie style, once popular in the twenties. Well kept, however, with flower boxes of day lilies in the windows opposite the door. The grass around it recently cut; dried clumps traced the rows of the lawnmower. Most of the lawns around were burned brown by the heat. No alligator flaking like the houses and cottages they'd passed coming down the lane.

In front of the door, he touched the fleshy part of her right hip with the barrel of his Ruger. She jumped as if bit.

"Small barrel, Julie, but it'll make a big hole."

"That you? Small barrel, big mouth?"

"Let's go."

Julie rapped a couple times on the wood and then pushed the door open.

Raimo kept her in front of him as he took in the room. The big pieces of furniture, chairs and couch, were draped in muslin cloth. A flight of stairs bisected the downstairs.

"Call him," Raimo ordered.

"Hey, Dino! It's OK. Jarvi's with me," Julie said.

"Tell him to come down," he commanded.

"Dino, Jarvi says come down!"

She turned to Raimo. "He's paranoid as hell."

"He ought to be. He tried to kill me and he may have done a lot worse."

"He's afraid of cops."

"What's upstairs?"

"Two bedrooms," Julie said. "Dino's in the second one. He's out of his gourd on dope."

"Up. Real slow," Raimo said and nudged her with the gun.

Raimo let her get a few steps ahead as they went up; he kept one hand rucked in the fabric on the back of her pants.

"Copping a feel?"

"Keep moving, not so fast."

She put an exaggerated emphasis on her hips, bumping him in the crotch, her body's rejoinder.

"Like that?"

"Stop here," he said.

The narrow hallway was covered by flocked wallpaper featuring blue velvet deer and birds. Both bedrooms had old-fashioned transom doors. The second one showed light. As they approached the first door, he used her as a shield, kicked the door open, and swiped along the wall for the switch.

A small bed with spiraling posts ending in finials that looked like pineapples and a patch quilt coverlet. No pillows. A dresser with a cracked mirror. Old prints of bewigged gentlemen and ladies swinging under massive oak trees. Leaf corbels in each corner. The room had a funky smell like greens cooked too long.

"C'mon, the next bedroom, I told you. Hey, Dino! We're coming in!"

"Shut up," Raimo hissed.

She turned around in the middle of the hallway. Raimo had to jerk the barrel from sticking her in the belly.

"What the fuck's wrong with you? He's right in there, don't be such a coward!"

Raimo punched her on the jaw, one short looping chop, stunning her, not knocking her out. He spun her around and pulled up the material from her waist and threw his shoulder into her back propelling her the few yards down the hallway. Julie as battering ram was effective; the door blew open and she hit the center of the floor like a diver who fails to correct in time and does a belly flop. The smack of her full weight hitting the floor was the only sound. The impact of her fall exploded dust from the carpet.

No one popped out from a corner or a closet to kill him. Raimo slid his back to the near wall, gun close to his body in a two-handed grip, so could swivel the barrel in any direction.

There was no need. Dino lay naked on the bed with a shotgun lying across his body. The headboard and wall spattered with fresh blood, bits of bone, and chunks of brain matter.

Julie struggled to her feet, gasping for air, a battered fighter making it up before the referee counted ten. She threw her fists up to charge Raimo, spitting a fusillade of curses, but stopped when she saw the gun. He had not moved since he noticed the body on the bed.

Julie half-turned to see what he was looking at.

She threw a hand over her mouth and wailed. "Oh God. Oh God. Oh God." The mantra accelerated until the syllables cascaded and became a single guttural cry.

OhGodOhGodOhGod . . .

Julie ran out of the room and down the stairs. He didn't try to stop her. He could hear sobbing downstairs.

Raimo approached the foot of the bed. Only Dino's lower jaw was visible but there was no face to recognize because there was no head to recognize. What hadn't exploded out of his skull was a matted and stringy ragout of shreds with flaps of skin and bits of head hair. No eyeballs or teeth evident in the carnage.

I found him for you, Irene.

The single light in the room came from a lamp on a nightstand. Raimo was suddenly aware of flies buzzing. Several ticked against the glass of the window pane but he couldn't see them because the shade was pulled down. One marched across the dripping mess above Dino's shoulders and disappeared.

He had the sickening feeling he was playing a part. He was meant to stand here and see this. After a while, when the drone of flies became unbearable, he left the room, went downstairs and collected a wet-faced Julie DeMarest, cheeks smeared from running mascara. She stood bent over the fender vomiting beside the car; dry heaves racked her body and, finally, sobs bubbled up from her throat punctuated by hiccups. She stepped to the passenger side door like someone caught in a dream where feet are stuck in quicksand. Like someone blind she moved around the jeep to the door, reaching out a hand to steady herself.

Raimo watched her intently looking for the signs of acting but all he saw was a woman knocked senseless by a vision she did not expect to see, ever.

Just beyond the tiny blue house, the bluer expanse of Lake Erie stretched to Canada and a horizon scraped of clouds. Just blue sky and blue water. He remembered when his father used to tell him about sailing on the Great Lakes ore freighters when he was a young man. The water, he said, was a filthy brown in those days; flies used to come out to the shipping lanes where the lakeboats went up and down between Buffalo and Superior, Wisconsin. "Bats came for the flies and hung from the radar mast like upside-down Christmas tree decorations."

Bats for the flies, bacteria for the flesh. We think we are unique. We think a loving God keeps all of us in his gigantic pocket, warm and safe.

What else are we to think?

Chapter 12 – August 12

A grueling five hours later, Raimo walked out of the Kingsville police station, a low-slung brick building that resembled a county library in a farm town. When he asked about the woman he came with, the police sergeant, who seemed to be a jack-of-all-trades in the tiny department, even interrupting his session with Raimo a couple times to handle dispatch for a late employee, told him she had left two hours earlier.

Raimo wondered if grand masters at chess felt this kind of mental exhaustion after a match. He had to think every question two or three moves ahead so that he didn't get tangled in something he'd said ten minutes earlier. It was not untruths he feared, because he avoided outright lying, but the omissions. He never mentioned Brian Tuomey by name, but expected the officer assigned the case from Sheriff's to bring it up. He was grateful it wasn't Nolan—cops view coincidences in witness statements as hamster wheels; subjects work themselves dizzy trying to get out of them. Kingsville's version of every police department's "box," the interrogation room, was an empty carrel with a screen to set it off in a corner near the coffee machine. Another officer frequently popped his head around to bring updates to the detective asking him questions. When Raimo wrote down his statement, the muscles in his hands were so tense that the papers he wrote on curled up and met in the center. He flattened them out as best he could and handed them to the cop who interviewed him on his way out the door.

"We'll be in touch," he said.

Julie's Vibe was being towed when he arrived back at his office. Raimo hadn't eaten in twelve hours and his stomach let him know it. The image of Dino Caddio on the bed was burned into his retinas, but his appetite clamored for attention. He was dehydrated and light-headed from sweating all day long in and out of cold rooms.

He didn't blame DeMarest for fleeing the precinct. Having a gun held on you and seeing a corpse would unsettle even a surgical nurse. Julie DeMarest was either innocent of everything, a pawn of her lover, or she was being strung along by Tuomey because he found her useful in other ways besides sex.

It was that same wretched streak of masochism that compelled his next move. He knew he had to go see Irene. The death notification was only hours old. He couldn't hide behind the police and he couldn't point them in any direction that wouldn't drag his brother headlong into it. Knowing his adversary meant everything now. Rikki's friendship with Tuomey went back a quarter of a century. But Rikki was out of his depth, Raimo suspected. Tuomey would throw him to the wolves the same as he had every other obstacle in his path.

May came to the door but said Irene was lying down and didn't want to see anyone. He tried to form words for her sister to pass on but she seemed eager to get him off her doorstep.

A middle-aged couple pulled in behind him, family coming to comfort. They looked at him and walked past without a word.

Raimo drove through the harbor wishing he were a stranger just arriving in town, looking it over for the first time. His office was cooler than he expected; he had just turned on his computer when Det. Nolan and another cop in tow walked in.

"Jarvi, mind if we ask you a few questions?"

It wasn't a question, and it wasn't politely asked.

Raimo recounted the airport "confrontation" with Dino Caddio, trying to keep it confined to the purview of his job: looking for runaways included runaway husbands, he said, and sometimes they didn't want to be found. Raimo gave them the gist of his conversation but left out Tuomey's name once again.

When he probed for information with a question or two of his own, it was batted away.

"Julie DeMarest isn't your client, Jarvi. It would be a good idea to tell us how the two of you happened to be involved in two crimes within forty-eight hours."

"Is the cottage explosion a crime then?"

"Our arson investigator thinks so."

"I'm sorry, but I don't feel comfortable talking about the case in much detail. Mrs. Caddio is my client," Raimo said.

"Who the fuck do you think you are?"

"Easy, Frank," Nolan said.

He placed a restraining hand on his colleague's arm. Raimo was mildly impressed; most strangers were shy around him until they adjusted to his scars.

"You're a person of interest in a murder investigation, Jarvi."

"You think I murdered a man I was paid to look for by his wife, a lifelong acquaintance, a man I was brought to see by a mutual friend? I then murdered him with a shotgun I don't own, stripped him, and laid him on the bed with the weapon and then called the police?"

"Let's talk about this mutual friend of yours," Nolan said.

Frank looked up from writing in his notebook, waiting for him to respond.

Raimo mentioned knowing her from high school and had seen her "to wave to," he said, but it wasn't until she came to bring him to see Caddio that he'd spoken more than "hello" to her in a decade.

"You know who she's dating?"

"I understand she's married," Raimo said.

Frank barked a laugh.

Raimo was surprised when Nolan's questions circled back to repeat what he'd asked earlier checking to see if his responses varied. TV, like a broken clock, could get things right on rare occasions.

An hour in to it, Raimo disciplined his answers to avoid a curtness; they were reacting to tone and body language more than his replies. Frank's scribbling was a give-away; he made timed scratches at regular intervals. Doodling, applying psychological pressure.

The cops left without saying anything much other than Nolan's stare, which said all it needed to about his performance.

Raimo knew they'd find the connection soon, whether he was cooperative or not. All the arrows pointing to Dino Caddio from the NTSB investigators, BCI, the Sheriff's detectives, and ATF, if they got involved, were going to bring Tuomey into it, and once he was implicated, Rikki was handcuffed to him.

Raimo saw fireflies in his office hovering against the big window. *How could that be?*

He heard the door open, he didn't see someone come in but a shade hovered over him and then he felt his head being cradled as he slumped off his chair to the floor.

When he came to on the floor, Bart Massey's face was staring into his.

"Ray, what the fuck happened?"

"I fainted," Raimo said. "I haven't eaten in a while."

"Then I'm the answer to your prayers," Bart said. "I dropped by to collect on my debt."

"What debt?" Raimo asked him. "You still owe me a twenty from the doubleheader."

He stopped long enough to eat with Bart, brushing off the deputy's questions like flies. Columbus was three hours away and Raimo had a little more research to do on his computer. Julie hadn't been forthcoming about Brian. She could be lying about Rikki's involvement solely because Brian claimed it to be true. He was in a bind over that, too. He'd called everyone he could think of in Northtown but no one had seen Rikki since his accident. He called Ginny Dyson but she hadn't seen Rick since the night she put their classmate in a cab. Being gone when cops come around with questions was like sleeping in an interrogation room, Bart liked to say. It meant game over, the verdict's in: guilty.

Raimo tried to sort through the complexities of profit-sharing companies, privately owned businesses, and LLPs with partners, how to divest and sell a business. He went through a dozen FAQs for large and small companies, found several online consulting services and called one in San Diego.

"Ranjeeth Haria, Samjia Services," a lilting Indian voice said.

"Mister Haria, I'm thinking of investing in a business here in Ohio."

"What kind of business, pliss?"

"It's a small pharmaceutical, privately owned."

Raimo hoped the name wouldn't be familiar to California although the national news on all three major channels had given the lead or the second spot to the plane crash.

"Is your company privately owned?" Haria asked.

"It is but family circumstances are requiring it to be put up for sale soon, maybe within a few months. One of the prospective owners told me he intends to file articles of organization as per instructions from the Secretary of State's office within six months."

He hoped that sounded like good business jargon.

"How much do you intend to invest, sir, if I may ask?"

"I'm thinking of a million dollars, assuming of course the bank will lend it to me," Raimo said.

As near as he could figure from a comparison of other pharmacies across the Midwest, Gerrard Pharmaceuticals was worth about six million.

Haria gave him a synopsis of privately owned enterprises versus profit-sharing.

"It comes down to how much capital is invested if the

theoretical value has already been determined for these—these future partners—based on the existing value of the shares?"

"That's right," Haria said. "Sole proprietorship is the easiest way to go, legally speaking so if there is profit-sharing, that would have to be established up front by the controlling partners."

If there was one thing Raimo felt sure of, it was that Tuomey wasn't going for a larger share of the profit-sharing with new owners of Gerrard; he was going for a majority ownership that would increase his value of the shares exponentially. He'd need the biggest bank loan he could get and to arrange for that, he'd have to have sizable collateral as well as a silver tongue.

Raimo checked his watch. Time to hit the road. The memorial service for the two families was scheduled for this evening. He'd need to shower and change. He wondered what mask Tuomey would put on for the grieving family in the Gerrard reception line.

The portraits of the father and his daughter were set in the center of a table displaying photographs and keepsakes of the family. She liked animals and pets. She was in the band. He was often caught with a grin or a grimace on the links after a shot went awry or sailed true to the green. A nice family, decent people with well-ordered lives perhaps cajoled into taking a trip to Cleveland in Elliott Gerrard's plane with his wife and sons. Raimo saw the stern expression, forcing back tears, as she hugged and kissed the people coming through. *She still wishes she had gone with them*, Raimo knew.

The daughter was a popular girl in school. Many of the teens who showed up were openly crying. Raimo saw the widow surrounded by her family in the greeting line and he felt anguish for her.

Raimo had to disconnect the sleaze button in his brain so that he could assume the role and shake the woman's hand. He mumbled his condolences and passed on, another friend of her husband from the business.

He scouted potential faces in the room for an opportunity to butt into a conversation or eavesdrop.

He shook hands with several people and introduced himself as "Gordon Drake," a pharmacy rep from Gerrard who also knew the family slightly.

Raimo finally settled on a potential prospect. He was a man in an ill-fitting suit whose wife ignored him and spent most of her time greeting people, reading the cards from the flower donors, and assessing who was related to whom in the crowd wherever she saw a familiar face. Some people thrived on the funeral ceremony. Death, the aphrodisiac. He'd seen several people at both of his parents' funerals act the same way. By that point in the evening, the teens had come and gone.

Raimo approached the man and offered his hand. "Gordon."

The man shook hands, a wet fish shake. He cracked a nervous smile. "My wife worked with Cheryl at Mary Alice's school. Our kids take—took band together," he said.

"I used to work for Gerrard," Raimo/Gordon replied. "I hear the company's going on the block."

"Probably, I guess so," he replied. "Elliott died intestate, Rita said. Hard to believe, isn't it? A man that successful. My wife said the company's being sold. Seems a shame the state will get the money but there's no family left on either side. Her parents died of cancer within a year of each other and now this."

"I know this sounds crass, and forgive me for asking," Raimo said, "but does your wife know if the employees will be kept on? I have a good friend who's almost sick with worry."

"No idea," he said. "You can ask her, though. She knows every darned thing about everything. She's over there glad-handing with some people. See her? She's looking right at us."

Raimo had caught her eyeing them while they spoke. Her husband waved her over.

"Oh my God, were you in that plane, too?"

"No, these are old scars from an accident a long time ago," Raimo said.

"Lord God Almighty, Rita."

"I'm so sorry," Rita said.

"Think nothing of it," Raimo said.

The husband, embarrassed, excused himself to go outside for a smoke.

Raimo fully intended to capitalize on the wife's gaffe. "We were talking just now about Elliott's company. I have a friend there, as I told your husband. He's an executive in one of the departments. He's very worried he might lose his position if the company is sold."

"You know, that's funny. Cheryl told me just last week about some executive Elliott had to fire or was about to fire. He said the man was embezzling. Something to do with missing drugs or accounts not balancing. Oh dear, I hope I'm not gossiping."

"Not at all," Raimo said.

"I can't recall his name," she said. "He was in marketing, Cheryl said. Who was your friend?"

"My friend's in accounts receivable," Raimo said.

"Who did you say you are, Mister—"

"Drake," Raimo said, and looked at his watch. "I'd better hurry. I want to pay my respects at the Gerrards' service and it's getting late."

Raimo, in fact, was sorely tempted to take the Westerville exit to the memorial service once back on the Columbus innerbelt. It wasn't worth the risk. He doubted Tuomey would show. For another thing, if law enforcement connected even a couple dots linking Dino to Tuomey, he'd already be under suspicion and law enforcement could have a plant there to watch and film; that's all he'd need to try to explain away to Nolan.

Irene wasn't returning his calls, not a surprise.

Julie DeMarest wasn't his preferred option, but Tuomey was too risky to surveille until he knew more; she, however, was mixed up in it no matter what she said. That figure on her calendar wasn't evidence of a bribe or a payoff, and it could easily be explained away by any defense lawyer. Add some zeroes and it's the realtor's price of a house she was looking to buy or the value of her retirement portfolio. Julie was Tuomey's go-between as well as his lover; that was certain. How far did it go? The better question was how far Brian trusted her before she, too, became a liability?

Bart called.

"I'm not picking up a thing around the station. If Nolan thought I was talking to you about his case, he'd ream me."

"Caddio's autopsy is what I'm curious about."

"His head was blown off, Ray. What the hell else is there to know? You saw it."

"No, anything the pathologist might have to say about the manner of death. Could he have fired that Remington with his big toe that easily? What about the angle? Would the shotgun recoil knock it off his body?"

Bart said, "I don't need to see the autopsy for that. There's less recoil in modern rifled slugs. I hunt with those shotshells myself."

Bart also told him those were heavy lead projectiles, sometimes copper-covered with plastic tips, and came with rifling striations designed to deform the slug when it passed through a tight choke. Nothing left for a ballistics comparison. They were meant for bringing down bigger game at as much as 150 yards.

He still paid for a monthly subscription to a couple of aggregate databases and he fed DeMarest's DOB into both. She was a scofflaw fined $500 for unpaid speeding tickets by Kingsville police two years ago. Over the last ten years, she filed three insurance claims to three different companies for stolen or damaged vehicles, she had her water turned off last April, and a lawsuit had been dismissed against her five years earlier involving a charge of criminal mischief. Hardly a candidate for the FBI's Most Wanted list but she was no model citizen either. A background check in April cleared her for gun ownership and—a little surprise there—she possessed a CCW license. No weapon in her purse when Raimo searched.

Her bank statement was a thin reed to hang anything on but that figure Raimo remembered from his B & E job at the cottage might have another interpretation other than Tuomey's paying off his mistress in installments from a hefty salary as a marketing executive. If you were enamored of a woman like her and could afford it, $2,000 on the third of every month might be a reasonable trade-off. He knew a couple reputable men in Northtown who made no secret of doing something like it, as he'd had interesting, off-the-record conversations with wives inquiring into his services about just that. Ambitious girls signed up on some of the darker dot-coms all the time to get their college expenses paid for by a sugar daddy. If Julie had a habit, she'd need more than her nursing salary to accommodate that house in Conneaut full of dependents but no breadwinners.

He didn't want to assume Julie was in on Tuomey's scheme to acquire Gerrard's from the outset. If that was a wrong assumption, Julie might be vulnerable. Her reaction at the house could have been good theater but Raimo doubted it. Tuomey wouldn't send her to the cops with everything riding on her ability to convince police she was merely doing a favor for a depressed man with a drug problem whose life was crashing down around him. Throwing him into it for the cops to look at made sense only if he assumed one more thing: Dino was murdered in that bed and made to look like a suicide. Send a patsy to fetch another patsy. Tuomey rolled them out like circus clowns tumbling out of a Volkswagen.

He drove back down Lake Road looking for the possibility a closed-circuit camera might have caught Tuomey's Jaguar but the nearest CCTV was three miles away in Conneaut at a small grocery store. He noted the crime-scene tape wrapped around the little blue house in passing; the whole lane was blocked by a pair of sawhorses with a No Trespassing sign strung between them.

Back in the office, he searched some online public records. A search of reverse addresses and property ownership showed all seven houses and three cottages on that lane were owned by a single development company: J. Enright Associates of Columbus. It was a thin line to Brian Tuomey.

He did some research on the company and didn't find Tuomey's name anywhere on filed documents or as a silent partner. The company claimed more than physical property but had a hand in consulting because its website offered expertise in "power and management," whatever that was.

Eleven Enrights were listed in the Columbus directory; three had call blocking. He called the remaining households with a story about being hired to survey adjacent property in Northtown County and eliminated them.

The numbers that blocked him belonged to a dentist, a college recruiter, and a vice president of a pharmacy company.

Bingo. John Enright was vice president of Gerrard's R & D.

"Jack's out of town on a business trip," a woman's voice replied. Raimo thanked her and said he'd contact her husband at his office in the morning.

He's on a trip, all right, Raimo wanted to say. *You just don't know what he's tripping on.*

Raimo checked the time. Julie's shift ended ten minutes ago.

He grabbed his ball cap, shades and "Sam Spade" newspaper, he called it, the weeks' old edition of the *Tribune* for hiding his face behind the windshield. He did fifty up Bridge Street, a 25-m.p.h. zone, and blew through the red light at the Lake Avenue intersection. Cops were nocturnal animals when it came to patrolling the harbor district.

He let out his breath when he saw the Vibe sitting a couple cars distant from the same light pole.

She came out, flipped a cigarette butt at the pavement, and popped her locks. She looked frazzled in the harsh light. *What woman wouldn't if her man was whoring her out,* Raimo thought. It was hard to despise her though every fiber of his being ordered him to. Anyone within a degree of the nightmare those people endured for the long minute it took for that plane to plunge was pure scum. The NTSB and the Coast Guard were still hauling up pieces of their remains and wreckage. A formal report wouldn't be issued for another year, if then.

Raimo followed her, praying there would be a love nest at the end of it. When she bypassed Tuomey's condo, he felt the odds improving with every mile. No shortage of hook-up motels on the Lake.

She drove through the Strip and kept going. Jefferson lay ahead but hope rekindled when she made the turn into the lot of the state lodge. Far ritzier digs than anything the resort town could offer. Gourmet meals, a walking path along the lake with spectacular views of the sunset—that is, if the clouds of midges and mosquitoes weren't out and you didn't mind the stink of dead shad and carp littering the shoreline.

He followed her into the lobby and felt the staff's eyes pick him out among the tourists clustered at the lobby desk. He smiled at the irony. He would always be remembered for his face whereas fewer people remembered his hero brother with every passing year.

Except he's not my brother . . .

Julie bypassed the elevator and took the stairs. He closed in behind a family going up behind her. The wife dug her elbow into her husband's ribs when she noticed her husband's eyes mesmerized by Julie's fluid bottom ahead, twin glutes alternately racing for the lead and falling back. The husband laughed at himself and threw an arm around his wife's shoulder.

She turned right and went for the second door on the right. Raimo halted, no longer covered by the family going the opposite way. He retreated a few steps back to the elevator doors, unfolding his newspaper, although there was little he could do if she returned. He heard the knock again, a triple rap on the door. He heard a stranger's deep male voice and then a door shutting.

Got you.

Raimo went back down the stairs, crossed the lobby, and headed for one of the benches with a lake view. The temperature was keeping activity down but he saw bikers, walkers, and even a brave middle-aged couple in tennis whites battling each other and the suffocating heat.

He called Irene.

"Irene, it's me," he said.

"What do you want, Ray?"

"I just want to know, to see how you're doing."

He winced at the stupidity of the cliché.

"I'm doing OK," she said. "It's been rough. The police keep coming around. I don't know why."

She sounded dopey, maybe tranquilizers, but she sounded—functional, if that was the right word for the yawning abyss that opened beneath her feet.

"Look, I don't blame you for anything," she said. "I'm still trying to figure it out."

"I know," he said. He didn't but he felt out of his depth with other people's grief.

"I've got to go," Irene said. "I hear Cassie crying upstairs. She cries for her daddy and there's nothing I can say or do."

He heard the distinct sound of a sob before she hung up.

He sat in the sunlight and looked at another bench under the shade of a maple; it was just twenty yards away. He couldn't have gotten up to go to it if he tried; he was bolted fast by her sorrow, clamped down by guilt. Weary of being too little, too late.

Two hours passed, then three. Raimo stretched his legs twice, walked around the lodge, and fetched a bottled water, the "spy camera," and a voice-activated pen from his car. His ears attuned to the throaty purr of the Jaguar but nothing as exotic entered or left the lot.

The couple playing tennis abandoned their game and walked past him holding hands into the icy lobby. The man's stare lingered longer than his companion's. Raimo's flesh had knitted long ago into the unsightly ridges and purple-gray spider webs of his scars but for years he had to avoid direct sunlight.

This was masochism sitting here instead of inside the relative comfort of his vehicle where the a/c could give him some protection. Yet he stayed put, not thinking of anything, which wasn't strange for him, because he cultivated "null states," as he called them. Places he could go in his mind like a traveler seeking relief in the shade of a tree. He disciplined his mind to relax, free itself from the terrible stress of the last few days, open itself to images other than the ones that wanted to barrel in and force him to relive the ugliness of that bedroom, a lachrymose Irene thrust violently into widowhood, Kristine's last moments, their bizarre relationship, his boyhood of isolation and pain. Six people, three of them so young they barely had a sense of their lives to be in a future time, gone, taken from them, all gone. Raimo never had the epiphanies that people who meditated achieved, or the Japanese *satori* of insight. He considered his sudden moments of inspired thought more mundane, less mystical, like some underground creature. Like a vole digging a new burrow where it could escape danger.

Julie and her new man left the lodge at seven-forty-eight, hip-bumping, rubbing each other and laughing like teenagers. She had exchanged her hospital get-up for a short-waisted black summer dress. Raimo had read the same article thirteen times by then but the words didn't register. He watched them go to the other end of the lot.

He was balding, paunchy, unremarkable. Another middle-aged man in polo shirt and khaki slacks. Closer, the image exacerbated the contrast between her sultry beauty and his mundane ordinariness. He was short, stocky with a comical simian look behind the aviator sunglasses. Julie DeMarest on his arm was the only thing that made anyone want to look his way.

They climbed into a pearl-gray Lexus. He watched their heads move together in a kiss as he passed. He aimed the camera discreetly beneath the newspaper.

Ten more minutes of fondling and kissing. It was too far for a clean shot, but when she got out and leaned over to kiss him goodbye through the driver's window, he had a view of her skirt hiked up in the back to reveal the edged furrow of her sex. She gave the stranger a long kiss and one hand sneaked down past the wheel to his crotch. They remained like that for a minute, oblivious to the cars entering or leaving.

Raimo had everything in view: the man, the girl, the license plate. He sped across the lot and waited, a predator watching a pair of lesser mammals in a crude mating display.

Julie stood up, adjusted her top, and tucked herself back in. She was as *brazen*—a favorite word of the teaching nuns from his Our Lady of Sorrows days—caressing her lover in a public parking lot as when she used to rub herself against Tuomey in the halls. Why not? No one had stopped her then, either.

Raimo punched the accelerator and came to a few feet of the nose of the Lexus before the squeal of brakes from both drivers avoided a collision.

Raimo waited for the man to get out of his car but he sat there, shocked, gesticulating with his arms and his lips moving in what were undoubtedly curses aimed at him.

Raimo exited his car, camera dangling from a strap against his leg, and a regretful smile creasing his face. The driver got out, inflamed by the near miss and asked Raimo if he was drunk to be driving the wrong way in an exit.

"No," Raimo said and smiled again. "But you must be."

"Wha—what are you saying, fellow?"

Raimo smiled and shrugged, "I mean, to be conducting an affair in the wide open like that. Man, some nerve you got there, pardner."

He lifted his camera to show the man.

"What—what . . . who are you?"

"I'm a private investigator," Raimo said. He flipped his license open with his other hand.

"My wife—did she—"

"We should talk somewhere more discreet," Raimo said.

"I'm a reasonable man and I'm sure you are, too, Mister Enright. May I call you 'Jack'?"

"Oh, fuck me," Jack Enright said.

But his long exhale told Raimo he was relieved. It was a bribe and he could deal with that over a messy, sordid affair made public any day of the week.

"Come on, Jack," Raimo said. "Let's have a drink and a quiet chat. We can come to an agreement over this. . . misunderstanding."

Enright looked up, his mind focusing again. He sensed he was being thrown a lifeline before he went over the cliff.

"All right," he said, finally. "There's a bar inside."

"After you, sir," Raimo said.

Enright muttered something like "sleazy bastard."

Raimo found it wasn't all that hard to act like a gumshoe with his hand out. He once thought he'd take a bullet for the people he loved, but so often, they turned out to be the ones behind the trigger.

Chapter 13 – August 13

Jack Enright came clean. His furrowed brow unknitted when he found out Raimo wasn't going to develop the prints and put them in a manila file folder for his wife Susan. Gratitude lit his face. He wiped a sheen of perspiration every couple of minutes with a cologne-soaked handkerchief. Raimo changed his mind about the man's simian features; he reminded him of Pépe Le Pew. *A pitiful case, am I not?* Too much time bedridden in front of a TV, Raimo thought. He could have asked Enright to kiss his ring and the man would have leaned over the table to do it.

The bar was cool, nearly empty. They had a booth to themselves. The same motif as half the restaurants in Northtown catering to retirees evident on the paneled walls and behind the bar: a Jacob's ladder descended from the ceiling between a pair of metal wheels from a pilothouse. Raimo stared at a ten-by-ten print of the *Paul R. Tegurtha*, a "footer," going through the lock at Sault Sainte Marie, but the painter made a slight error: the thousand-foot *Tegurtha* was one of a very few Great Lakes freighters that had to use the Poe Lock at the Soo because of their length and girth. Even before he succumbed, Raimo's father kept up with traffic on the lakes. Bookend brass chadburns stood at each end of the curved walnut bar.

"If you're not working for my wife, who are you working for?"

Raimo sipped his Tom Collins while Jack worked on his

second bourbon.

"That shouldn't concern you, Mister Enright," he said. "Let's say the people who hired me are interested in the future of Gerrard's and they're looking at the organizational structure."

"You want to buy us out?"

"I can't discuss that," Raimo said. "It's confidential."

Raimo hoped he wasn't being too ham-handed with the crumbs he was dropping. He counted on Enright's near-miss from a marital collision being an advantage along with the liquor for loosening the man's tongue. Enright was so comfortable with his illicit amour just concluded that he took a call from "Susan" as soon as they sat down. He spoke in monosyllables and rolled his eyes at Raimo.

"She thinks I'm here on business," he said and laughed. "She's right. That DeMarest woman is some business." His wife Susan, on the other hand, was a boring shrew, but they made a good combined income between them.

"Look," Jack Enright said across the table, thrumming his fingers nervously on the tabletop. "There is something going on, and you can tell your people that from me. It has nothing to do with a reorganization. We're close to acquiring the company. It's a question of funding."

"Perhaps we can help you with that, Mister Enright."

"Call me Jack, will you? For Chrissake, you caught me with my pants down. We ought to be friends, right?"

"You said 'we,' Jack. I take it you have partners?"

"Just one," Enright said.

Raimo sensed he wanted to say more about his partner.

"Any problems there? My associates have vast resources."

If a couple hundred empty shoe boxes counted as resources. . .

"No, no," Enright said. "Nothing I can't handle. My partner's slicker than cat shit on a marble floor, but I know how to handle him."

I hope you do, Mister Enright, Raimo thought. He thought of Dino Caddio's penultimate resting place on the soiled bed.

Raimo took a flyer with his next question. "I understand

you guys in R and D are close to a big one. Rumors are you're going to the FDA for permission to test within a couple months."

Enright blanched. "Who told you that?"

Raimo hoped his smirk counted as coy. "People I know."

"That cocksucker Tuomey," Enright said and slapped the table.

Raimo said nothing.

"That—that *fucking idiot*," Enright fumed. "We're so close now!"

"I know," Raimo said and nodded, commiserating.

"He signed the same confidentiality agreement I did," Enright fumed hypocritically.

"It might be worse than you think, Jack," Raimo said. "We hear he's moving on a separate loan as we speak. You could be cut out by the time the ink's dry. Oh, you'll keep your same profit-sharing deals in the reorganization, whatever that might be, but he's going ball's out for sole proprietorship—"

Enright's face blanched in front of Raimo's eyes. From toad-belly white under the dim lighting to crimson. He knocked back the dregs of his bourbon and lifted his sifter in the direction of the bartender.

"He can't do that," Enright said. "We agreed."

"Share and share alike," Raimo threw out. "Like the lawyers say."

"Screw the lawyers," Enright exclaimed.

"It sounds like socialism to me," Raimo said. "But Brian Tuomey is a die-hard capitalist."

"That's why he set me up with that slut," Enright concluded. "'A great girl in town I know,' he says to me." He drew air quotes around Tuomey's part. "I let my cock do my thinking."

Raimo nodded, allowing Jack time to spin a way out of his dilemma. No honor among thieves.

"That drug you're working on—" Raimo began.

Enright looked at him and for a moment Raimo thought his sham was exposed. Enright pondering how much to reveal, wondering if he'd gone too far already. Then he said, "That drug is going to change everything, you better fucking believe."

"Drug?"

Enright leaned toward him, drawing him closer into confidence. "Before Elliott's big splash, he gave us the green light for human testing. He said his FDA contact green-lighted the fast track. No two years' bullshit, full speed ahead."

"Alzheimer's," Raimo said, guessing.

"Alzheimer's, hell. This drug—you've heard of CTE?"

"Chronic Traumatic Encephalopathy," Raimo said. TV wasn't always a curse.

"Even better," Enright bragged. "Alzheimer's shrinks the hippocampus. We're going after white-matter brain disease. Much more widespread. The potential market is *worldwide*." Enright gloated like a parlor-trick magician with jumping knots. It wasn't the bourbon talking but greed, as in Seven Deadly Sins caliber. Raimo tried to imagine the worth of a company that had the cure for a brain disease that afflicted vast portions of the world. Even more in Gerrard's case: a company where the principals no longer had to worry about a succession of sons taking over the family business.

"We can free up nutrients to arteries deep in the brain hardened like cysts. Do you know what means? Full-blown stroke, early-onset dementia. Cured! Fucking cured, man. This is Nobel Prize territory."

Enright's eyes were bright, smeary, as he ticked off the wonder drug's capacities: "We can improve every executive function of the brain—thinking speed, general functioning, language, immediate memory, delayed memory, working memory and visuo-spatial construction. Improving thinking speed alone, like those herbals all the aging hippies go for in vitamin stores will be *clamoring* for the drug. Hell, improving thinking speed alone would make us richer than Croesus."

"I can understand why Brian's so excited about it," Raimo said.

"How often has he been in contact with you—your

people?"

"You know, Mister Enright, I just can't say that."

"Wait until I see that filthy, lying prick myself."

Enright placed his empty glass on the table and glowered, looking about for the absent bartender.

"If people think that CEO with the Narcan syringe got rich, wait'll you see what our IPO offering will make us."

"Is Julie involved beyond—?"

"Hell, no, she's just a cunt. Why?"

"She might have a problem with medications herself, you know," Raimo said and shrugged his shoulders, the all-knowing company mole. "A little midnight requisition from one of your drug rep's stock."

"I don't know anything about that. Tuomey says he keeps her on a leash with pills. That bitch can suck the chrome off a trailer hitch."

"Jack, let's say we keep our conversation between us for the time being. Is that all right with you?"

"What's in it for me?"

"I'll make it worth your while with my people."

"Sweet. Have you got a card? A number? Somewhere I can reach you?"

"Jack, we don't operate like that."

"I understand. Of course, of course. Julie, she's really quite a girl," Enright said.

His hairy fingers resumed drumming on the table.

Raimo was more astounded than pleased Enright bought his high-stakes espionage scam. He could see his mood swing like the silver-ball pendulum he probably kept on his desk—greed to lust, lust to greed, *ad nauseam, in perpetuity*. Julie had swung from "cunt" to "quite a girl" in less time than it took him to sip his bourbon. Revolting human nature dispensed through a dark bar.

"I'm sure she is," Raimo agreed, nodding.

"You get those wounds in Iraq or Afghanistan?"

"Ever hear of a place in Pakistan called Abbottabad?"

"You're shitting me."

Raimo slugged back his drink and left John Enright, VP, sitting there, one hairy paw around the glass, thick arm hair curling into his polo shirt and gray-black tufts spilling from his chest. It reached down to the second knuckle of his fingers. Quite a contrast for Julie on her own pendulum, swinging from the hirsute lover to the smoothly shaved one.

From scummy private eye to Seal Team Six in one fell swoop. Raimo knew he had a belly full of the trio of Enright, Tuomey, and DeMarest; it sounded like a law firm, one of those that specialized in tort law.

Raimo was back in his sweltering office listening to Ezekiel's latest prophecy decrying the wickedness and the abominations of a sinful people. His Bridge Street window peeper stared through the glass the entire time Raimo sat there listening to his messages.

A car honked behind the peeper and Raimo straightened up in his chair to look. Raimo had never noticed the baldness before; wild gray locks cascade down his shoulders as he returned to viewing Raimo. The banker's lamp ensured he was completely visible to the man yet his expression remained the same. Raimo wondered if *he* had ever wondered what he looked like to Raimo staring back at him. Raimo associated Ezekiel with fire, earthquakes, hail.

Maybe the coming solar eclipse was the end, he thought.

The night before Rikki disappeared, Raimo was irritated that his brother never noticed his condition from the explosion at the cottage. He shoved a hastily prepared meal of macaroni and cheese at him, expecting to hear him complain. Instead, Rikki held the plate in his lap untouched, his eyes glued to the ranting preacher thundering away about apocalypse or end of times. He remembered hearing Ezekiel's name.

Raimo ignored the old peeper. When he went for another refill from his coffee machine, the man was gone when he turned around.

He was too buzzed on coffee to sleep. He wrote down

everything he recalled from his conversation with Jack Enright in pencil and put asterisks at those places where he thought Enright was being deceptive. Then he read it a couple times in his head for accuracy before he composed it on his computer.

Around ten-thirty, he looked up at the clock. His vision was blurred so he looked away from the screen and stood up to stretch. He had the distinct sensation he was moving while standing still and almost teetered into the monitor. Stepping back abruptly, he knocked his chair behind him; it squealed noisily across the floor. He laughed, thinking the castors were loose or he needed to cut back on the three-in-one oil next time. He fumbled in one drawer where he thought a certain paper was he needed—but he couldn't remember what the paper was or why he was looking for it. He thought his brain was caving in from sheer exhaustion. That struck him as amusing, too.

"The squeaky wheel gets the grease," he said aloud, repeating another old cliché of his mother's. He said it at the dinner table. Rikki always got to choose which shows the family watched.

His vision clouded. He blinked several times trying to clear his vision.

"Cataracts," he said to himself, "I've got cataracts." He thought that funny, too, but he didn't think you could develop them in a day.

What he remembered occurred through foggy vision: his office was dark, but he didn't recall turning off the lights. The banker's lamp was switched off. He turned his head to see the digital clock's LED numbers: 10:39.

He closed his eyes again. He figured a little cat nap at his desk would snap him out of this funk. A busy day, a long week. When he opened his eyes again, the clock said 10:42, which was odd.

Brian Tuomey stood in front of him. Raimo had to raise his head from the desk to see him. His head weighed far more than the average thirteen pounds of a human head.

Tuomey looked down, a wide smirk covering the lower half of his face.

Until it twisted. He slapped a black tear-drop shaped object in his hands.

"You fuckfaced putz. Who told you to get into my business?"

He hit Raimo in the temple with something hard.

Raimo thought he was having one of his boyhood spells. His family, mainly his father, were anxious because of his withdrawal and the long periods of silence. It lasted months and when he returned to "normal," that being a much different existence from what it had been before the fire, he was grateful no one spoke of it. Even Rikki managed to curtail his tongue when it came to their brief talks in their shared room.

He knew he was in the back of a vehicle, a camper or a van, because it was spacious and he was spread-eagled on a plywood floor, gagged, beneath a blanket, so it had to be something big. Whenever the vehicle made a turn, he felt the pressure of the nylon cuffs securing him as his body leaned into the curve. He tried flexing his fingers. Whatever the drug was, it was wearing off. He knew he was in trouble and he knew who was orchestrating it.

By moving his mouth against the gag, he managed to lower it enough to speak.

"Tuomey!"

Nothing.

"Tuomey, let's talk!"

That sounded lame.

From the driver's seat, noncommittally, "Got it loose, did you, you fuck?"

"Talk about . . . this isn't going . . . to work." He hoped to get a reaction, buy time, distract—he didn't know what else to do. Words spluttered.

Silence. Then, Tuomey's bored voice:

"I'm tired of you, Jarvi. That's as simple as I can say it."

Raimo sucked in as much air as he could and bucked against the restraints. The pain in his wrists and ankles made him choke on spittle. His right foot moved a few inches and connected to something.

He gave another heave from the floor, telling his mind to get ready for the knife-like pains shooting in to his brain from all four quarters. This time, his left foot clicked against something.

The blanket moved halfway off his face to give him a view of the driver's seat. He strained his neck to look down his body to see what his shoes had touched: two red plastic jugs of gas containers with yellow spouts, one on each side of the back door. He twisted his neck to the right and left using peripheral vision to spot two more identical containers placed at his head behind the front seats. Surrounded by gasoline . . .

"Why not rig . . . a shotgun . . . like Dino?"

"Not as much fun," Tuomey said.

The van bumped along. Fear welled up in his throat. *Stay calm, stay calm* . . .

"Why . . . kill? . . . not pay him?"

"Speak up, you're mumbling."

He had no idea what good it could do to goad him. Sweat oozed into his eyes and ran down his face into the gag, sopping it more. His body seemed to spring a leak from every pore. Pure animal fear, he told himself. *Calm, stay calm* . . .

Tuomey spoke: "You probably have him on tape, that fool. He said we should offer you money. I said you were too fucked up in your ugly *cabeza* to take a bribe."

Raimo croaked out, ". . . sure . . . take a bribe. How . . . much?"

Tuomey laughed.

They were driving over rugged terrain. He strained with every limb to stretch the nylon, maybe snap it. His feet were reinforced with bindings that led upward to an eye bolt. His hands were completely numb, the fingers almost useless. He jerked harder abrading the wrists until he felt blood slip. Tuomey could see what he was doing if he turned his head slightly. The sloping turns and bouncing of the van kept his hands on the steering wheel and his concentration focused. The interior was dark—no streetlights or other sounds but the noise of stones kicked up under the chassis.

Raimo felt his body weight shift to his back and shoulders. They were going up. He tried to activate the GPS in his head to tell him where they were going.

Only one answer from the geography made sense: the gulf. His father used to take him fishing and hunting for arrowheads down there. But they went upward, which meant he'd been unconscious long enough for Tuomey to take them to the overlook.

". . . drug . . . slipped . . . coffee . . ."

"You think, genius?"

"Same as . . . Dino."

"No, not the same as Dino, stupid. A toxicology report would show it."

Julie—had to be. She'd know what drug to use, being a surgical nurse. She probably provided him with the hospital gowns after he pulled the trigger. The blood and gore would have spattered him from head to toe. He'd have to be wearing earplugs as well as the smock. Raimo thought of Tuomey methodically stripping his friend's inert body, fixing the shotgun, lifting his head to place the barrel just so . . . No forensics would be able to reconstruct the aftermath of that mess, and he knew in his viscera the same would be true for his.

The van slewed right then left. Raimo craned his neck but the windows were blacked out. Raimo figured Seven Hills, heading toward the highest point of the gulf overlooking the Northtown River. When the van clattered across what sounded like railroad ties, he knew exactly where they were: the wooden bridge in Plymouth Township, and his senses quickened with the realization of what Tuomey intended—a long fall over the cliff to the riverbank below. The van would compact like an accordion. He'd never survive it.

But the gas was not meant to ignite on impact; he was going

over the edge in a ball of flame.

"What did you say, Jarvi? Speak up."

"Sheriff's deputy . . . patrols these hills . . . lover's lane."

The isolation and the view were favorite trysting spots for teenagers. Massey did double duty in uniform chasing the cars away and brought his own dates here.

"Keep dreaming, Rai-moe. There won't be enough left of you to fit into a cereal box. Besides, I'm just finishing what your brother started long ago."

. . . *Rikki, no. Not possible. Rikki saved him from the fire.*

It was an ice dagger plunged deep into his heart. Raimo always suspected something. For a while, he believed Tuomey set the fire and blamed it on a bottlerocket. He'd been there with Rikki all the time . . .

"What, Jarvi? What was that, tough guy? Better save your breath," Tuomey said.

They van bumped over ruts, going slower now, about 5 m.p.h., and lurched to a stop that threw Raimo against the seat backs. Tuomey cursed. The gas jug near Raimo's head gurgled when it slid into his shoulder.

Raimo figured the van was inching toward one of the sheer drop-offs rimming the gulf.

The van stopped. Raimo was aware of a deeper blackness. Tuomey struck a match and Raimo's heart went wild until he realized it was a cigarette; he was smoking. Seconds later the smell reached him.

"A short reprieve," Tuomey said. "Some kids up ahead, fucking."

Raimo heard Tuomey twist around in the seat. He saw only the crimson tip of the cigarette arc from Tuomey's hand to mouth in the thick blackness.

"That old pile of broken concrete's still up here. Nothing like tradition, eh, Jarvi? But you never came here with a girl. Did you, Handsome?"

Raimo twisted his body and strained, biting into the rag to stifle sound, working his wrists like a saw blade against the nylon straps. *Keep talking, Tuomey,* he prayed. *Keep reminiscing about your sex life. I need time, more time.*

No moon to see by. Not so much as a breeze. His whole body was wet from the heat and the exertion. The whirr of a window going down. The *chirr-chirrup* of insect life. Out here in the palpable dark, the glowing tip of a cigarette could draw hundreds to the windshield in no time.

He hoped it was too dark for Tuomey to risk driving off to try another spot. With a little more time, he might manage to work his way to the spout of the gas jug. Raimo's fear of fire had become so pathological after his burns healed he had refused to ride in the family car for months afterward. He would not go anywhere if he was confined to a single exit or had to come within ten feet of anything that could ignite. He overcame his revulsion and clamped his teeth on it. The weight strained his neck hard enough to make the strap muscles of his neck bulge.

"I used to bring Julie here, too," Tuomey went on. "We'd fuck like rabbits. She let me do anything I wanted to her. If I told her to pull a turd out of my asshole with her teeth, she'd have done it."

Raimo sank back exhausted, a muscle in his jaw quivering and the tendons on the right side of his neck throbbing. He had to breathe open-mouthed and suck in air like a fish starved of oxygen to keep Tuomey from figuring out what he was up to.

"You never had a girl with that monster face, so I'm assuming you beat off all through high school. Rick and I fucked more girls out here than you've passed by in the street. You probably pay for it, am I right?"

"Your mother . . . gives best head . . . Northtown."

Tuomey snorted.

"As soon as those lovebirds up there get their rocks off, I'm turning you into a Roman candle, motherfucker. I've got that fucking Enright to deal with now because of you."

". . . two suicides . . . cops . . . get curious."

"No more jokes about my dear old mom sucking cock, huh?"

"Dino . . . your dog." Raimo tried not to gasp the words but he used every ounce of his strength to force the spout downward so he could get it locked between his jaws. The spittle he'd slimed it with was mixed with gas that made his eyes burn and dried his throat.

"I wanted him to rig your office but he lost his nerve. You have to be a wolf in this world. Rick's a wolf—I thought he was. You, you're a fuckfaced sheep."

"Where . . . Rick?"

". . . about time," Tuomey said. He started the van.

Raimo heard a car start in the distance. Headlight beams sliced through the van and passed on, blackness returned. For an instant, he'd had a glimpse of Tuomey, alert in the driver's seat, his face intent staring through the windshield. A fresh cigarette in his fingers.

The idea of his flesh melting again hammered Raimo with such force he urinated. *Can I pray*, Raimo thought; *can I pray now? Pray now, pray . . .*

He reared up popping air in his vertebrae to get the handle into his mouth once more and work up the spout, millimeters at a time, gagging on gas-flavored saliva, up, up the narrow spout until he had the small cap clenched in his teeth. With a twist of his neck, he shook it like a terrier with a muskrat in its teeth.

Got it. Loose. He had to keep his stomach from spasming.

Tuomey drove slowly in the direction the spear of headlights had come from.

Raimo upended it and used his head to butt it sideways. He spat out gasoline. The skin inside his mouth burned as if he'd sucked fire. He almost passed out. He lay back, a sob from the effort broke from his throat. He was done. His brain wanted to shut down, abandon the citadel.

Tuomey swung the van around in a three-corner turn and was slowly backing it up.

Gas fumes overpowered the front of the van with a vapor stench. He heard Tuomey slam his fist against the side of the door, pounding it, trying to hit the window release button.

Sparks flew from his cigarette.

A mumbled curse. Raimo hyperventilated, entered a state of full, animal awareness. Sounds of kicking, slapping. Light flickered on the van's ceiling above the windshield.

Fire.

A scream followed by a gibbering. Raimo heard the door flung open. Flames snapped and crackled, louder, curled up to the steering wheel. Light danced on the roof, big flames he could see by arching his back. The fire was a living thing now, too big for Tuomey stamping and swearing like a lunatic up front, hissing like a basket of snakes.

Alone.

The side panel door swung wide.

"Jarvi, you fucker! You're going over now!"

Tuomey was a demon in firelight. The front of the van burned over the seat and flickered among the wheel rim. Tuomey kept trying to reach the gear shift from outside. More gas pooled under the carpet beneath the driver's seat. The back of Raimo's head was growing warmer by the second; so far, the flames burned sideways and forward compelled by the draft from the driver's open window. Raimo saw flames licking backward to enfold the tipped container.

Tuomey cursed, thrashed about in knee-high dockweed for something to jam down the gas pedal.

The flames met in front of the container. An orange jet of flame erupted along the driver's seat, extending a couple feet close to his head, scorching his ear. Raimo tugged harder at his chafed wrists. He bought an inch of slippage along the upper eye bolt where an orange flame appeared.

Tuomey appeared again in his peripheral vision, a wild-eyed Neanderthal with a club. Enraged, he brought it down at the panel door in an overhead swing that sheared off the top portion before the blunt end slammed across Raimo's abdomen, knocking the air out of his lungs.

Tuomey screamed, "You're not getting out of this!"

The nylon popped and Raimo rolled to the other side of the van as Tuomey's second swing angled off his shoulder and back, just missing his head. Raimo's vision went grainy, a black melting curtain descended over his eyes.

Don't faint, he ordered himself.

Tuomey, a shapeshifting beast became once more a fallen angel backlit with flames. He kept popping up in Raimo's vision all around the van, seeking a way to get at him before the flames reached the back. Raimo noted a new weapon in Tuomey's hand, a bent rebar. More range for his swings now. Raimo felt it land just above the knee and he almost jackknifed upright.

"No escape, motherfucker!"

Tuomey slavered, full of rage. Raimo was a mouse in a maze, rolling from one side of the van to the other, to avoid the blows. He was caught between two terrible deaths.

Raimo swung his body high enough to catch hold of the eyebolt pinning his other arm.

"No, you don't, fucker," Tuomey said.

Tuomey only played zero-sum games and he intended to win. The whole front of the van was burning seats and steering wheel wrapped in flame, black roiling smoke like thunderclouds filled up the ceiling. Raimo was near total exhaustion. His bruised legs were tucked against the cords and every muscle strained taut.

Tuomey, a ravening beast, climbed into the van. Raimo forced himself to look at the knife in his hand.

"You know I'm going to kill you. Look at me, Jarvi."

The van lurched backward, slipping gears into Drive, suddenly bulling through the thick weeds, tossing Tuomey from side to side.

Going over. . .

Tuomey crab-walked to the open back door and flung himself to the grass as the front fell and the back wheels lost contact with earth; the van tipped up and hung there, rocked like a diver flexing for the final spring from the board. Both gas containers skidded across the plywood and smashed into the seat backs.

The front of the van angled thirty degrees off the ground

with a roiling, black smoke and orange-yellow fire taking more open space and filling the inside of the van. Behind and below him, the black void. Ahead nothing but flames and smoke fed by the shaft of air funneled into the van's interior. The gas had burned itself out but the seats, dashboard, and fabric was smoldering or burning steadily. He'd die choking inside this chimney of toxic smoke before he'd burn to death. Or the van would slip its slender tether to earth and plummet hundreds of feet to the rocks and shallow river.

Raimo's amygdala was even then conditioning him for his death. He stopped fighting. The blood poured down his wrist would never grease the nylon enough for him to slip his hand through. That moment of reconciliation came a split-second before his brain registered the glint of light playing off the blade on the floor. Tuomey dropped it when he jumped. Raimo slumped down to the floor and reached his flopping fingers as far as he could across his body. It might as well have been on the moon.

Another lurch and the knife slid a few inches closer. How many degrees higher could it go before gravity won? Raimo strained again but it was magical thinking, not reality. He closed his eyes and slumped against the seat back.

. . . let it happen . . .

Another jolt skyward, an impossible angle. He opened his eyes. The knife was touching him.

He used his heel to drag it to his fingers. He sat upright and sawed at the straps, dropping the knife several times because of his hand's numbness, every second pounded against a vein in his forehead.

Too long, too long, too long—not going to make it. . .

Raimo heard the cord part and was in motion, rolling out the side door into a thicket of nettles. The van slid past him, the friction of its slow descent picking up speed as the battle for gravity finally won by the center of the earth drawing all things to it. One pant leg was shredded by an edge sticking out as the van went by gathering speed, a ship going down stern first into the vortex.

Raimo had nothing beneath his feet and two hands buried in the pricker bushes to keep from being pulled down with the burning van. He was in total blackness, sobbing with the skunk smell of burned rubber in his nostrils and the taste of gas in his mouth causing him to burp fumes. But alive. He would wait here all night until dawn if he had to. He would not let go. They would have to saw around him to remove him.

Not let go, not let go. A mantra until he knew he could not dangle over the edge of the cliff all night nor wait for dawn because no help was coming. He climbed, struggling to gain an inch or two, losing one, pantomiming the doomed van from moments ago—or was it days? His mind was pinwheeling, and he had to focus. Pull, strain, pull. Keep going. Don't stop. One inch, one more. Teeth clenched, back muscles on the verge of spasming, Raimo, a six-foot inchworm, finally reached the top. His thighs were caressed by earth now, not the open void. He had made it.

A bird watcher sitting on a bench near a landscaped portion of grass by the Smolen-Gulf Bridge, hailed as "the longest covered bridge in America," noticed billowing smoke from the gulf and called nine-one-one when he got home. He was having coffee with his wife, who just came downstairs. A sheriff's deputy investigated an hour later, pried off the vin tag, although it was too burned to decipher. He told dispatch the van was torched, empty. Probably some hillbilly who didn't want to pay the tow decided to junk it. Northtown's white trash being infamous for dumping sofas, busted fridges, crapped-out washing machines, and junk cars on every dirt road in the county.

He had a hunch where the van must have gone over, he said, that place being familiar to every swing-shift deputy as the site for rousting horny teenagers.

That's where he found Raimo, shivering in the dew, incoherent, stinking of gasoline, filthy and soot-covered and bearing bloody ligature marks on his wrists. Try as he might, he couldn't get him to make sense so he drove him to the emergency room. A mean-looking cherry stripe in the back of his triceps and along his thigh looked especially nasty and he was bruised all over, the deputy reported.

After his wounds were cleaned, and he was salved and bandaged in several places, he was given prescriptions for the pain and infection. The deputy drove him to the Rite-Aid down the street.

"You don't have to wait," Raimo said. "I'll be fine now."

The deputy didn't move. He had his orders, he said. There was nothing Raimo could say that would keep Det. Sgt. Al Nolan off his neck for the next six hours at the precinct's interrogation room and that's all she wrote about that.

Chapter 14 – August 14

"Any word from Rick?" Bart asked.

"Not yet," Raimo said.

Raimo was stone cold sober. Bart seemed to be getting drunk for the two of them. The Wyandotte was packed once again in the middle of a hot day. When Raimo finally told Det. Nolan he'd had enough, he was exhausted, needed a shower, something to eat and some sleep, the cop backed off and let him go.

It was good timing. Bart had just pulled into the precinct parking lot. He was packing in the double overtimes for a new camper, a Silverstream. Raimo could get a ride.

"Have you seen Ahti lately?"

"Whoopie left town three years ago," Bart said. "I heard he bought some property in Antelope Valley, lives there now. Got a wife, a kid and everything."

Raimo wasn't sure how living on the edge of the Mohave comprised "everything," but he was glad to hear he was doing all right. Like Raimo, Ahti Wuopio was a shy kid from his neighborhood, and he was sorry they'd lost touch in the mêlée of their high school years. For some, like Rikki and Tuomey, it had been a high point, for others a speed bump. For anyone small or vulnerable like Ahti or him, it was running backwards up the Empire State Building. Raimo's name in Finnish meant "protector"; that was a joke.

"I can barely keep my head off this bar," Bart said. "What's keeping you awake?"

He gave Bart a skeletal version of last night's ordeal, leaving out everything but Tuomey's admission of responsibility for Andino Caddio's death and his attempt to send him into the gulf riding a flaming chariot.

"You have really set off a shitstorm," Bart said. "Nolan hates your guts. He doesn't know which end is up right now with all these federal yahoos and alphabet agencies coming at him. He was talking to Columbus PD when I left the station. They want more info on your Enright."

"My deepest sympathies when you see him," Raimo said.

"Yeah, I know," Bart replied. "He went to the waterboarding school of suspect interrogation."

"At least Tuomey's going under your white-hot interrogation lights," Raimo said.

"Not—exactly."

"What do you mean?"

"He came in 'of his own volition,' to quote his lawyer, an hour after you went home," Massey said. "Then he lawyered right up. In and gone. Adiós." He made one of those empty-handed magician gestures.

"Tell me you're riding your lie bicycle right now," Raimo said.

"I shit you not, Jarvi," Bart said. "May the tattoo on my shoulder become infected and I die of blood poisoning if I should lie."

Raimo sat quiet while he pondered the news. He was certain his statement, not to mention turning over the tape, with the photos and the recording, would sink Tuomey—or at least bury him in legal problems and lawsuits for years. It had to kill his deal to take over Garrett's Pharmacy with Enright, at the very least. Never mind what would happen when the NTSB investigation concluded. They'd tie Dino Caddio's murder around his neck and put him away forever or, with luck, send him packing to Lucasville with a fifteen-year countdown clock before he took the needle. That was one ticket Raimo planned to wangle from somebody in the penal system bureau.

"It's called corroboration, my friend," Bart pronounced and upended his beer. "Mother of God, this heat won't let up. Look at my hand, I had to break up two bar fights in a couple redneck joints."

"That's a terrible boo-boo, Bart. Look, you cracked a cuticle, too."

"You shock me, Ray. You aren't known for sarcasm."

"Try a week without sleep, being shot at, blown up, poisoned, and hit with a steel rebar, not to mention having to suck down a couple shots of gasoline—"

"Leaded or unleaded?"

"Go to hell."

"You are in a bad mood."

"Patrolling towns with one stop light doesn't equate to the same scale of violence as Kashmir, Bart. Give me credit for something."

"I do beg your pardon," Bart said.

Raimo had managed three hours of blank, dreamless sleep after getting home. He checked his messages: nothing from Rikki or Irene. He stepped out of the shower and fell across his bed without shutting the blinds. He sat upright, wide awake, as if hit with a cattle prod; his whole body ached and there were massive purple bruises on his back and shoulder where Tuomey struck him and an ugly crimson lump surrounded by a wavy pus-yellow ribbon across his leg just above the knee cap where the rebar landed. It looked like a 10000 x magnification of a virulent virus under an electron microscope.

"If you have any pull with Nolan, tell him to go hard on Enright," Raimo said. "He'll cave. He won't take a bullet for Tuomey."

"Do I stutter? When I said Nolan hates your guts, what part of that did you miss? You came within a whisker of being hit with obstruction and a dozen other charges for withholding evidence. He wanted to keep you there but the Sheriff said to cut you loose."

"I turned over everything I had. I didn't have to do that.

What about Julie Demarest?"

"What about Julie DeMarest?"

"Shouldn't you guys be trying to turn her?"

"You're picking up cop lingo nicely," Bart said. "I might have a shorter learning curve with you than I first thought on that happy day when that window across the street says Massey and Jarvi, Private Eyes. Villains Beware."

"Nolan must know she's vulnerable while Tuomey's out," Raimo argued. "Send a cop around or give her protection. He won't try anything if he sees she's got protection."

"Ray, I have to say this. Brian Tuomey isn't the spawn of Satan as far as people in this town are concerned."

"What are you saying? People will believe him over me—why? Because he was a popular kid in high school and a big shot quarterback twenty years ago?"

"You just answered your own question. Him and Rick, they walked on water."

He didn't feel loyalty to Julie DeMarest. She deserved whatever was coming to her, legally speaking. But Tuomey's maniacal visage, a savage with a stick tromping around a blaze, would stick in his mind for a long time. Raimo wondered about the evolutionary progress of human beings from fish with spines to a rampaging psychopathic biped like Brian Kevin Tuomey.

"I don't know," Bart said. "Maybe you've noticed she lands on her feet whenever she's not on her back. Besides, I've got more important worries like how many more meals I can cadge out of you by the end of the month before you step in it so deep no one in Northtown ever sees you again."

Exhaustion, the heat, his worry about Rikki was taking a toll. Raimo sagged on the bar stool, could have slumped to the floor and squeezed between the chrome stools and fallen asleep as easily as a house cat in a ray of sunlight. *Sagging*, one of his father's favorite terms. A vessel *hogged* when its keel ends bent lower as a passing wave peaked amidships. Over time, this caused a warping of the bulkheads so ship builders in the days of wooden ships designed braces to counter it. *Sagging* was the opposite, a wave's trough peaking amidships. Women and animals found their way into sailors' talk: a cunt splice or a cuntline for an eye-splice or the valleys between strands in a rope or cable, catting an anchor. . . How furious his mother was when she heard her husband teaching Raimo the language of the sea. . .

"Hey, Ray, you OK, man? You look like you're about to fall off that stool."

"I'm keeling," he said, feeling wobbly as if the drunk fairy had smacked him on the temple with her wand, and climbed off the stool.

He walked across the street at a lope. His bed never beckoned so much as at that moment. Whatever chemical discharge his body gave him after last night's roller-coaster was gone, dissipated in the alcohol and the heat falling around him under a cerulean sky.

More a seesaw with him on one end and a two-ton safe dropped on the other, catapulting him into the abyss, Raimo thought, picturing the burning van lifting upward, breeching, his mind yanking him back to a time when he felt secure from things that could reach out of the dark and pull you into it. He remembered his dad one time telling him about a mythical gnome in Scandinavian lore—just a head inside a shoe who peeked at you from around corners but whenever you turned to see him, he was gone.

He slept the sleep of the dead, an expression of his mother's, not his father's.

In his dream, he was looking for Rikki but he kept bumping into old Finnish people from the Harbor, acquaintances of his father mostly, men his father had sailed with when he was a wheelsman for a Great Lakes freighter. Raimo couldn't recall much of their faces but he remembered their names: Saari, Karhonen, Heikki. An old man named Oscar who smelled bad and used to spit on the sidewalk. Before he got burned, he and Rikki used to run around the neighborhood together exploring in "Bumstown," their name for the couple hundred acres of wetlands stretching between Walnut Beach and the cyclone fences of the railroad yards, and swimming at the slip off the Pyramids. Rikki used to fish on the breakwall in those days; it was the last summer before Rikki discovered girls and found older boys from high school to hang out with.

He spotted Rikki up ahead, running like a deer, in the old abandoned factory they called "the Ice Cream Factory," for no logical reason whatsoever. It was a textile factory in the earliest days of Northtown Harbor and it made sweaters, not confection. The giant gear machines and black spindles on the second floor stood in their rows under broken fluorescent lighting as if waiting for the laborers to come back and replace the spinning frames.

As boys, he and his friends from the neighborhood climbed through broken windows from the fire escape behind the building, shaded by sumac that grew between the hand rails. On the bottom floor, they crawled like miners on hands and knees from one floor to the next, oblivious of rats. Rikki was always just ahead, out of earshot, but Raimo knew he had to catch up—something Rikki said he'd never do.

High on the rooftop, the boys could see from one end of Bridge Street to the other. The boats passing under the lift bridge heading out to the breakwall and the lake. Rikki, agile as a monkey despite his adolescent bulk, jumped from the top floor to catch branches of trees. He dared Raimo to jump. Raimo wanted to take the dare but he was terrified of the fall. Mounds of garbage, rusted metal and broken bottles from the bums who used to slip off to drink their Thunderbird wine and fall asleep under newspapers were left by men their parents told them to avoid.

Raimo knew he couldn't do it. He didn't have the strength.

"Coward," Rikki called out, shimmying upward like a python wrapped around a banana tree, bicep muscles flexing.

He jumped—too short by a foot. He saw his fingers reach out for the branch and miss it while Rikki teased him. "Grab it, dummy, come on!"

He fell—

Raimo jolted upright in bed for the second time in less than a day.

He thought he was sweating out the booze from the Wyandotte until he realized the air-conditioner wasn't humming in the window. He got out of bed and hit the light switch, another power outrage like yesterday. People were consuming more electricity in the heat wave and the power company was running out of joules, amps, watts—or whatever it was they produced and sold. Raimo couldn't beat Rikki in anything that required physical prowess, but he had one thing going for him when it came to heat or cold. He could endure both better. His father was still sailing when the *Daniel J. Morrell* went down on Thanksgiving Day, the lone survivor, another watchman his father's age, endured three days in a life raft in freezing temperatures when a Coast Guard helicopter spotted him. "You be like that brave man," his father said. "Don't give up hope. Never give up hope."

He showered, made coffee and toast.

The sweat began pouring off him while he stood eating the toasted bread and thinking, watching the traffic on Bridge Street. It was over. His part was done. He slipped on a pair of shorts and walked out back to fetch the paper.

The *Trib*'s headline belabored the obvious: *IT'S HOT!* A man in his eighties died of heat exhaustion on the west side of town; he was found dead in the upstairs bedroom when his dog wouldn't stop barking and neighbors were alerted. He landed with the first wave of Marines on Iwo Jima. The "burning van found in the gulf" was demoted. Police were not revealing further details while the investigation was ongoing. His name wasn't connected to it and an unnamed officer from the Sheriff's was quoted once: "We traced the van to a previous owner in East Cleveland, who claimed he sold it last March to a neighbor."

Nothing on the plane crash or Dino Caddio's suicide, a headliner yesterday, now another back-page item of three sentences. Fifteen minutes of fame was going at a discount nowadays. It didn't matter; he was out of it, all of it. He'd done his bit for justice and all it got him was banged up, nearly killed—and all minus a fee.

He had called half the motels between Erie and Cleveland. Today would be another day of calls hoping somebody remembered a man with two casts checking in.

His cell trilled Lisa Stansfield's ringtones on the counter. Phooey on Adele, he thought, true to his first and only English songbird.

"Ray? It's Irene. Can you come over?"

"Sure," he said. "Everything OK?"

"Yes," she said. "My sister's getting tired of me. She's been so good. I thought I'd bend your ear a little—if that's all right with you? I'm home now."

She sounded good, her voice stronger, no more catch in the throat, that tiny vibrato that indicated a sob coming on. He thought that might be too judgmental considering. Grief found its own equilibrium like water. It seeped, sometimes it poured, but it made you remember you were a human being and you had to live in this world until your own time was up. Time healed. It just wasn't much of a beautician.

"I'll be right over."

The dog returneth . . .

Something Kristine said to him after one of her late-night summons while Ron was on a business trip and she needed him. Her legs splayed exposing the silky thatch; he laughed then, but what had she meant? Was he a dog? *Yes, for her, anywhere, at any time she called.* When he hadn't heard from her in three weeks, he stood in a thunderstorm on the edge of her property, hapless peeper, risking a lightning strike under a Gingko, leaves falling like gold coins around his head in the wind, one hand caressing the cell phone as if rubbing it would make her call. Even when he caught Ron's lumbering shadow pass by the curtained bedroom window, he still didn't leave.

He didn't want to lie to her, but he wasn't going to be the one to tell her. That was Nolan's job or one of the NTS people, not his. *I'm out of it,* he said, again, while listening to her.

"They asked to search his room. I said fine, whatever," Irene said.

Her coffee was horrible, watery, and, worst of all, decaf. All she had.

Raimo couldn't look at her long. She was breath-taking in her mature loveliness. Not Kris' blunt sensuality or Julie's dirty sensuality. He remembered a time when Rikki and Tuomey, wearing their letter sweaters, sat in his parents' kitchen and compared different girls at school for beauty based on race. They agreed Scandinavian blondes should be at the top. Rikki said he was going to California for that "sweet blonde pussy" when he graduated. When he singled out Irene Donovan for "Irish beauty," Tuomey scoffed. "Watch, she'll turn out like my aunts," he said. "She'll develop a belly like a Ben Franklin stove after she knocks out a few babies."

Irene's face was the first thing you noticed. Raimo could stare at her eyes all day like some love-struck kid. Irises the color of tea that shifted with the light. Her face still had the firm bone structure of their high school days. "Every girl in the world has a fox face or a pig face," Rikki once told him. Hers remained fox. Yet the lips were fuller while the cheeks had leaned, more womanly, the skin was every bit as unblemished as the symmetry of her eyes, nose, mouth was striking for its perfection. Pretty women like Kristine made him feel the shame of his own face that much more, yet she had the opposite effect. Deep down, Raimo had come to believe that a large dollop of guile was implanted into humans no matter what the mask of the face presented to the world. It wasn't innocence or naiveté but a charm in her case. From her silvery laugh to the delicacy of her hands, she was enhanced by time whereas he felt the subtraction faster than most as his scars seemed to take on a deeper discoloration like the tattoos of elderly people's skin.

She talked for a long time about Dino, the early days of their marriage and how things went well until he tried cocaine and grew angry because she wouldn't.

"I smoked some marijuana a couple times with him, but it

made me sick. I don't see how people can stand smoke in their throats," she said.

Raimo tensed.

"I'm sorry, Ray," she said. "I forgot—"

"Forget it. I don't think about it anymore."

"More coffee?"

"I'd love some," he said.

He felt like an old perv watching the back of her long thighs and her round butt stretch the Levi shorts when she stretched for a Sweet-'n-Low packet in the cupboard. Women always knew when you watched them. They had to, he suspected. The world made them learn about sex faster than boys.

The phone in the other room rang. She poured his coffee and went to answer it.

He was left with a hand shaking the cup because of the perfume from her warmed skin. Unlike the nose-stinging tang of Julie's, hers was a scent that bypassed the nose and went straight to the neocortex. He knew he should leave.

He couldn't hear what she said but her responses seemed all one or two words and a sentence at the end.

She came back into the kitchen and that change on her face would have told him she'd been given bad news if he'd met her only once.

"What is it, Irene?"

"That was an FBI agent. They want to interview me right now," she said.

"Would you like me to stay?"

"No, I'll be fine," Irene said.

At the screen door, she pulled him to her and hugged him. He could feel her warmth flood into his body as if they'd been nude, freezing, cuddling for warmth. Her breath on his neck was an aphrodisiac and he flushed crimson. He'd seen the notes on the scratch pad when he came into the house; she was making plans for her husband's funeral, selecting a casket from a brochure.

When they separated, he saw tears welling in the corners of her eyes.

"Irene, I—"

Too late. The door closed on him slowly. She stood there behind the mesh, a shadow Irene, while he stood rooted to the steps looking back at her.

"—I'll see you," he finished.

She thought he meant the funeral service. An awkward moment; then she nodded and was gone.

He should donate his brain to the Smithsonian, he thought. How many awkward, ill-timed things do you get to say to one person in a lifetime?

Driving home, he convinced himself he could do nothing for her. She would have to bear the shame and horror of what Dino had done—for money—with or without Brian Tuomey's instigation. Nobody would care about motives. Dino had stuck her in a lifeboat in a winter gale, she and her young daughter both, and they were left to bear the stigma of disgrace along with the snubs and provincial contempt of a small town's hostility.

"Be strong, Irene," he said.

Chapter 15 – August 15

Baseball fans cling to their myths. There's a widely believed one that says a line drive on artificial turf accelerates despite Newton's law of entropy saying the opposite. Things degrade over time. Just looking into a mirror means you're a split-second older by the time the light bounces back into your brain camera. Twain said a lie travels halfway around the world while truth is still putting on its shoes. Sometimes news travel faster than at other times and it seems to speed up everything around you, heightening your senses, making you feel vulnerable to the forces of randomness.

Bart's news at the diner caught him like that.

"Julie DeMarest is dead."

Tuomey, he thought at once: cleaning up another big loose end.

"How?"

"Overdose. Alas, yet one more sad statistic to keep Ohio leading the nation in opioid fatalities."

"That's harsh," Raimo said. "She was more than a statistic."

"Tuomey's off the hook anyway," Bart replied. "He was sitting at the precinct with his mouthpiece and Nolan when the call came in."

"How'd he take it?"

"Tuomey cried like a bitch."

"Massey, for Christ's sake—"

"I detected a flinch. A very noticeable . . . shrug of the

shoulders," Bart said. "Tommy Harris confirmed it. He was standing right next to me in the A/V room."

Some deputies disputed it. Some were angry that a favorite son was being dragged into the mud. It was a remark aimed toward Raimo, who was said to be acting on a personal vendetta over his brother's accident, blaming him, and making wild accusations all over town. His lawyer interjected to say they were contemplating a lawsuit for slander against Ray Jarvi Investigations when this "so-called" criminal investigation was concluded.

"That's all?"

"Our high-and-mighty Sheriff offered him coffee and a stale croissant."

"Our tax dollars at work."

"There's this, too. On his way out of the room, Tuomey said he'd volunteer to take a polygraph," Bart said.

"Tell me you hooked him up on the spot," Raimo said.

"Fat chance. With his lawyer right there to put the kibosh on it? That was for show. Besides, we don't have a machine. Harris took a workshop on voice-stress analysis."

Bart and some deputies coming off shift had watched different portions of the three-hour interrogation tape "given voluntarily," his lawyer insisted on noting. Bart said Tuomey's lawyer nipped off every other question. Tuomey provided what sounded like a rehearsed statement and looked to his lawyer for coaching when he had a tough question. Nolan lost patience and another detective took over.

"He's faking it," Raimo said.

Brian Tuomey had faked and charmed his way past a lot of people by then. Bart said the guys at the post loved to mock perps on tape in the interrogation rooms. "If you're thinking he had it done, you could be right, Raymundo."

"Just leave me out of it from now on," he said. "I'm too tired to care anymore. I just want to find Rick."

"I was just about to say something like that. Look, we're friends, Ray. We go back forever and all that shit. Our daddies were friends, blah-blah. But you know I can get fired for talking to you about a case. Shit, guys have seen us at the Wyandotte."

For a man who often whined about his job at that very bar in front of anyone, not just the bartenders, and claimed to be on the verge of quitting, Raimo thought he sounded suddenly paranoid about losing it.

"I understand," Raimo said. "You know I'd never say anything to anybody."

"I trust you. I do. But you're deep in this thing with Tuomey now, and I don't know how it's going to shake out. If Nolan or my boss get wind of me even talking to you about the heat or the cure for a sweating toilet tank, I'm a goner. Man, you dropped yourself into it at the station with that story about Tuomey and being poisoned, it's way different now."

Dropped myself into it, Raimo thought. *Tuomey tried to drop me over a cliff.*

"Better steer clear of me for a while then."

"Thanks, Ray. I know I can count on you. Good luck."

People always said that to you when they saw stones piled up to your knees.

Tuomey had already tied off some big loose ends: Dino Caddio's death was still "under investigation," according to the *Trib,* quoting the county medical examiner's preliminary report. Enright remained *stumm* and stonewalled behind his lawyer. Rikki was gone, disappeared like smoke. And Raimo felt the whole town turning against him as the gossips unleashed their tongues. He was getting hate mail on his voice recorder and in his email. He had to remove the Contact Me box from his website because of comments from trolls.

Cat's-paw had more than one meaning besides a person used to gain an end: it could mean a hitch thrown into a bight, the loops resembling cat's "eyes" for hooking up a tackle or it could mean a patch of rough surface ruffling smooth water, as if a cat had pawed it. Words were shapeshifters just like people.

Why did he find it so hard to be anything other than one

person, the man with the scarred face, when everyone around him seemed able to switch personalities like throwing on a shawl or taking off a ball cap? He'd known Bartolomeo Massey since they were in kindergarten at the old Jackson Elementary School. His father and Bart's worked on the docks together. Bart's dad was built was like a fireplug but agile enough to climb and work the gigantic Hewlett ore unloaders that scraped thousands of tons of the taconite from the cargo holds of the ore boats berthed in the Northtown docks. Raimo's dad left sailing, abandoned his boat in Duluth at twenty-five, and settled in Northtown and married Nora, Raimo's mother. He never said why he gave up his home and family back in Duluth or his Lutheran faith. Bart took after his short, dark father, had his exact stevedore father's physique. Pour a few shots of Old Forester down his gullet and egg him on as his deputy buddies did every so often at the Wyandotte and you'd see him transform himself from cop to actor in an eyeblink. He'd hop on the bar and imitate a Northtown junkie in withdrawal, kicking over beer bottles, clutching his stomach and moaning, "Gots to have my *hay-rone! Gots to have my hay-rone!*"

Raimo kept a dictionary and his mother's bible on his bedside night table along with bottles of Ibuprofen, Naproxen, Ansaid, and Anaprox while his mother changed the gel sheets at night. Looking up words helped take his mind off the stinging pain as his nerves sparked back to life like inverted hair follicles, but far more painful, and reconnected to pain neurons in his brain. He loved the strange words and their concepts like "morgellons," a neurological disease where red and blue "fibers" grow out of the skin on the palm of a person's hand. "*Calliphora*," a pretty-sounding name for blowflies. He stopped reading it for a long time when he came across *transmogrify:* "to transform appearance in a surprising or magical manner, especially strangely or grotesquely."

Dictionaries, like children, could be cruel.

Chapter 16 – August 16

It wasn't all bad news, however. Getting blown out the door of a cottage and dangling over a cliff might even be good for business. Erasing the nasty ones left four messages from people inquiring about his services and asking for callbacks. Two of them he declined outright, one asking if he would break into his ex's house to see if she had his Keurig and favorite power saw, the other prospect wanted him to follow a man she was convinced was beaming signals to her though her television set. The third was a "friend of a former client of his," whom Raimo suspected to be Leotis Pennimann, and his concern was expressed in formal diction up to the point where he professed to discovering "a dick photo" on his wife's cell phone. The fourth, however, came across as a welcome respite from the week's craziness, violence, and hustles: an insurance company wanted proof that someone they'd insured was legitimately handicapped and asked for three hours of surveillance and mentioned a handsome fee per hour.

He'd spent the last three hours calling motels and getting nowhere in his search for Rikki. He'd called a lawyer, who agreed to make the court date for Rikki. The case officer at West Hollywood Sheriff's provided him with a few places to call out there. He was locking his office door when the hairs of his neck bristled.

"Hello, fuckface."

"You've got nerve, Tuomey."

Raimo took a step toward him when a towering black man the size of a granite block appeared behind Tuomey with a grin on his face. Bulk aside, he was noticeable for the twin gold incisors. He was dressed all in black from a knit tam to high-top sneakers.

He flashed a smile at Raimo.

"Let me guess," Raimo said to Tuomey. "Gerrard's changed the locks on the drugs cabinet so you had to call Rent-a-Thug."

The big man took a step toward Raimo but Tuomey placed a hand on his massive chest.

"Relax, Mikel."

To Raimo: "Mikel Moore here's my bodyguard. He's my protection from you."

"Michael Moore?"

"He spells it 'M-i-k-e-l,' right?

Mikel grinned, a pet Sumo wrestler.

Tuomey pulled a paper out of his pocket, unfolded it, and held it up. "A restraining order signed by the Honorable Judge Patrick Fingal Shannon of the Western Court himself this afternoon."

"And they say we Finns are clannish," Raimo said, perusing it from a yard away, not wanting to touch anything from Tuomey.

"Finns, Irish, Italians—that's the past, man. Look at Northtown now."

Almost on cue, an overweight white girl in tight slacks with a nose ring and dirty-blonde hair pushed a pair of biracial toddlers, slumped over, their small arms hanging loose over the stroller, around the men blocking the sidewalk.

Tuomey smiled at Raimo, said: "See?" He looked at the girl as she circled to the curb, wary of the three men standing stiffly like giant garden statues.

"Kind of hot to be pushing the kiddies around Bridge Street, isn't it, Mom?"

"Fuck you, asshole," the girl snarled.

Mikel's pasted-on grin split into a wide smile. In his black get-up, black tam cocked over his bald head down to one ear, ropes of gold chain circling his chest and gold studs in each lobe to balance the teeth, he glittered. His eyes fastened on Raimo, a hooded cobra watching a mouse.

"Did you come here to discuss social Darwinism?"

"No, just a friendly visit."

"Sorry I can't offer you any coffee to dope. I just emptied the pot."

"Hang on a moment, Jarvi."

He took out his cell phone and spoke into it, asking someone at the other end if he "got it."

Tuomey squeezed the phone in his back pocket and looked at Raimo. "There's a guy with a telephoto lens across the street in front of the Wyandotte," he said. "See him?"

"What about him?"

"He took a couple snaps of you lunging at me a moment ago," Tuomey said.

Raimo felt heat rising up the side of his face; he wasn't supposed to be the one photographed in a compromising situation.

"Where's my brother?"

"Fuck if I know, Handsome."

"What do you want, Tuomey?"

"Delivering a message. If you had anything done to her, if that was you, I swear I'm going to make you pay for it. You'll think that purple mess on your face is a beauty mark by the time I'm done with you."

"That's good acting. It's also a threat I can report. But, then, you've had a lot of practice fitting in with normal people by now, haven't you?"

"What that supposed to mean?"

"I mean you're a bona fide psychopath."

"You hear that, Mikel? This circus freak calls me a psychopath. That's not what the sheriff said to my lawyer. He promised he's going to take a closer look at you."

"That's your message?"

"Part of it. Stop talking about me, Jarvi. If I see my name

in the paper, if I get a call from the police again, or if I ever hear my name's put on a police report again, it'll go really hard for you."

As if to reinforce the message, Tuomey put a cigarette in his mouth. Mikel's arm appeared and snapped a Bic under it. Tuomey sucked on the cigarette and took it out of his mouth and studied the tip before blowing on it until it was the size of an eraser tip.

A lit cigarette smolders at 1100 degrees Fahrenheit. A two-second puff reaches 1600 degrees, which is higher than gas' autoignition of 500 degrees. Raimo had once studied combustibility thresholds of everyday items the way a fanatic studied the surahs of the Qu'ran.

"Be careful, Jarvi, I'm watching you."

He flicked the cigarette at Raimo's feet where it exploded in sparks on his shoe.

When he felt stress in the past, especially when he was convinced everyone who saw him recoiled in disgust, he would find calm in his habit of locking himself in the bedroom and reciting the trivia he'd memorized during his idle periods. He thought of one now, an old standby when someone hit his internal distress button with a look or a word: the hierarchies of angels with their three embedded choirs. From Seraphim to mere angels, he put them in their boxes the way he used to tidy up his toy soldiers in battle lines. Counselors, governors, messengers, they served in their capacities much as the dark spirit world of demons served their lord in the house made for them by God and coined by Milton, the blind poet: Pandemonium. The whole universe was a *pas de deux* of dangerous partners—matter and antimatter, light and dark, good and evil.

It seemed clear to Raimo the forces of darkness were on the upswing in Northtown.

Chapter 17 – August 17

"If you can make chocolate chip cookies, you can make meth," Bart told Raimo.

Deputies prowling city and county backroads for the telltale, cat-urine odor found carboys full of explosive liquid in campers and cars parked on side streets in front of schools, in abandoned houses and houses where small children played on the floor. Once, infamously, in a nursing home in downtown Northtown that exploded injuring two and making one late-night talk show where the host had the camera zero in on the *North Coast Tribune* headline in type font just shy of a World War Three declaration.

The hallway outside the Sheriff's Office featured a wall of fame with framed photos, articles from the *Trib*, certificates and plaques of appreciation testifying to the agency's success in the war on drugs. One showed a grinning Bart Massey along with another deputy standing in front of some 15-year-old *wunderkind*'s confiscated homemade lab in his backyard surrounded by a 5-gallon carboy, plastic Keck clips, rubber bungs, pipettes, amber Boston round bottles, and bottles of hard-to-find Red Devil lye. Bart and his colleague held the porcelain mortar and pestle the lad used to smash Sudafed tablets.

If the southern counties of Ohio were in active competition for marijuana growing sites, Northern Ohio remained true to its love affair with opioids with a notable exception: Jefferson-on-the-Lake was awash in meth, either manufactured and sold by cooks from so-called Nazi labs stuck in the nearby woods or imported from Mexico, and it was easily available. Emaciated addicts scratched invisible crank bugs as they wandered the Strip or waited in Northtown's county offices for their welfare recertification.

Raimo's anonymous caller claimed to be "a decent-sized" distributor of that product.

He sounded high—or jittery. He claimed Raimo might be interested in a video he "acquired" that included some people he, Raimo, knew. These people were recently deceased and not in good ways.

"Name them," Raimo said, "or I'm hanging up."

"Dino Caddio and Julie DeMarest."

"Why tell me?" Raimo asked.

"It involves your brother," the voice said. "The famous Rick Jarvi, number twenty-two."

"My brother's lived in California for the last three years-"

"I'm talking about the last three weeks," the voice said.

"I'll ask it again. Why tell me? Go to the police."

Raimo was packing up his office, storing away his expensive and mostly useless electronic gear when the man on the phone called to say he had some "valuable" information about the recent murder of Andino Caddio and "that other one, the woman with the ass you could eat lunch in."

"I heard they're both suicide," Raimo said with caution.

DeMarest's death hadn't made the paper yet, and without his unofficial pipeline in Bart, he knew from a source he used before in Conneaut what the obituary notice was going to say when it came out, which was that she died at home. Along with the euphemism of "died after a long illness" for cancer, "died at home" was becoming vogue for "suicide via accidental overdose."

"Suicide? They calling that a suicide, too? That's like calling Jeffrey Dahmer a chef."

"Look, whoever you are, I'm no longer in the business. If you have some information about my brother's whereabouts, I'm interested in hearing it."

"I don't know where your brother is," the voice said. Raimo could hear sniffling or snorting in the background.

"Then I'm hanging up," he said.

"Hold on, homes. Wait a second, man. I called you because I need someone to . . . to run interference for me, like."

Raimo was used to roundabout conversations. People called him but they rarely showed up with money to pay for his services. He felt more like a telephone therapist.

"I got a little problem with the courts right now," the man said.

Raimo rolled his eyes and waited for him to get on with it.

"I'm thinking, like, someday, maybe sooner than later, there's going to be a big reward offered."

"A reward for what?"

"Information," he said. "Details, man. *Crucial* details about things related to those people."

Raimo tensed, waiting. *Those people. The families in Lake Erie's murky waters?*

"You there, man?"

"I'm here. Say what you have to say."

"I know who did it, man. I was there. I mean, I was kinda there, like, you know, *observing*."

Like pulling teeth. . .

"Observing what?"

"Fucking."

Raimo slammed the phone down so hard he cracked the cradle. A sordid and fitting way to end his career, he thought. Beat to a pulp, harassed by the man who nearly killed him, and now pranked by some drug-addled jerk with too much time on his hands.

The phone rang again. Raimo ignored it and resumed his packing.

His back, shoulder and leg still ached and had turned the colors of rotten bananas. He looked at the expensive lettering on his plate glass; he was talked into something called Hanzel Extended by a professional engraver. Not a week old and he'd have to pay someone to remove it. He'd even purchased some prints to take away from the impoverished look of the whitewashed brick interior. Two Ansel Adams prints faced each other: a moonrise over El Capitan in Yosemite and a clutch of snow-covered birches. Balancing them were a pair of color prints, one by French photographer Jean Guichard of a lighthouse being slammed by monster waves, the tiny figure of the keeper in an open door at the base seconds from being swept away by a colossal wave crashing against the lighthouse from the sea. The other was Raimo's favorite, *Gulf Stream* by Winslow Homer.

The phone rang again.

"Fuck you, Jack," Raimo said to it.

He left his office for what he expected to be the last time as a working professional private investigator.

Upstairs in his apartment, he fixed a Tom Collins and took it to the La-Z-Boy. He plopped into it, spilled some over his chest. He set the drink on the floor, spilling even more of it. He peeled off his shirt, balled it up and tossed it at the door. He decided to spend the afternoon smoking cigarettes and getting plastered. If Bart wanted to buy him out, he'd give him a good deal, take the money, and leave this shitty town forever. Disappear like Rikki.

By two in the afternoon, he was well along in that process, one bottle of gin destroyed, a fresh one cracked open and at his service. He was feeling—not good—but freed from the weight pressing down on him ever since Rikki came back to Northtown.

Rikki burned him . . .

He couldn't drink that thought out of his head.

The cell phone rang; he expected Bart, eager to collect on yet another dinner. Raimo had a craving for food, mainly so that he could continue drinking throughout the afternoon.

"Don't hang up on me, man," the voice said.

It was the same anonymous caller. The thinnest trace of a lost Hispanic accent in the *n*'s pronounced farther forward as if the tongue were touching the top of the teeth rather than the ridge between the teeth and the roof of the palate.

"I'm busy," Raimo said. "I haven't got time for this bullshit."

"Fuck, man, you high? You sound high? Look, listen to me for one fuckin' second, all right? I need somebody to. . . hold this tape for me. I'm going to court tomorrow for a stupid drug beef. I've got information, like I said. Brian Tuomey, you know him?"

"I'm listening."

"I videoed him," he said. "He's been using my cottages."

"Using? How using?"

"Swing parties," the voice replied.

Raimo had this bizarre image of people swinging from balconies on ropes.

The man said, "I taped the dude's swing parties. I got 'em all on disk."

"Tell me who's on these disks," Raimo said.

"That girl with the boobs, Julie. She's in there, and so is that guy who blew his brains out. I seen him one time. He shows up, he don't fuck, though. Your brother, too. Only he gets it on."

Raimo straightened up in the lounge chair. "You called them swing parties, why?"

"They ain't just fuck parties. They have couples come over, you know, wife-swapping or whatever the fuck."

"Why haven't you told the police?"

"The cops—fuck them, they'll jew me out of any reward once they get their hands on my collection."

"You want me to hold these disks for you? For how long?"

"I want someone, you, for a fee. So it's legal and all that shit. I want you to make sure when a reward comes out, I'm the one who gets the money."

The NTSB investigation was ongoing, no word in the *Plain Dealer* for days now, and when it was concluded, it might not be available to the public for a year or longer. No agency, federal or state, was putting out an offer of a reward for information leading to convictions at this stage because no one was suspected of sabotaging the plane. The families of the victims weren't suspicious; in fact, no one was until he handed over his material from his surveillance of Julie's cottage and Jack Enright.

"I'm still confused," Raimo said. "What does my brother have to do with the plane crash?"

"What plane crash? I'm talking about two people dead in a week, man. Your brother and this other guy, Tuomey, signs his name on the hold-harmless rental agreements, 'Jack Mehoff' like I'm some moron, they were having sex parties at the Lake."

It finally clicked: Raimo's caller wasn't talking about the plane crash but a pair of suspicious deaths.

"He's right there with Mister Jack Mehoff and the other one, that short guy looks like a friggin' ape. Your brother's in the middle of this clusterfuck with those bitches they're banging. Then this guy dies. You tell me that flies? Even lake cops aren't that stupid."

"What did you plan to do with it, I mean, otherwise?"

"Upload it to *PornHub*. Who gives a shit? The point is I got them freaks talking when they ain't jackhammering bitches."

"What's your name?"

"Fuck you, I ain't giving you my name until I know we can deal on this thing."

"OK, Mister Fuck-You, let's meet."

He couldn't picture Rikki involved with a lowlife meth dealer, but he could see his brother going along with Tuomey's sexual escapades. He'd been doing that since high school, the two of them *primo* studs, Cocksmen of Saints Stephen and Basil, as they billed themselves. Rikki once complained toward the end of senior year he couldn't get a date with a decent girl anymore because his reputation was so trashed from hanging out with Brian. It was widely gossiped and believed that every girl's mother had taken her daughter aside for a lecture about going out with Brian Tuomey or Rick Jarvi.

Drugs were another thing Raimo had a better-than-average knowledge of through the forced lesson of his experience with the fire that consumed his flesh and the litany of esoteric pharmaceuticals that followed in its wake. He had a prudish contempt for the illicit kind. The idea of methamphetamine alone made him recoil. It was 100 times stronger than the typical dopamine flush the back brain rewarded the body for pleasurable achievement. It was therefore a great enhancer of sex first in the AIDS crisis of the eighties in the gay community. Everything drifted to the Midwest from the coasts eventually.

His caller had the unlikely name of Kornbluh. He was a dozen years younger, olive-complected, part-Puerto Rican and "part yid on my old man's side."

Raimo had to press him to admit his name when he sat down opposite him at the Mud Turtle in Jefferson-on-the-Lake.

"Eddie," the man said. "Edgardo, really, but my friends call me 'Poke' or 'Poken.'"

Short for "Poken Beans," he said, a tag the older kids in his neighborhood saddled him with because his mother had called him in for dinner one night with that call. The moniker stuck.

Edgardo's hands and forearms were slathered with tattoos of the jailbird kind. He seemed to have two different faces; a soft, full-lipped mouth; gold loop earrings gave him an epicene cast, but beneath the thick lashes, a pair of intense blue eyes stared. He had the high cheekbones of someone from the steppes of the Caucasus. He wore the obligatory outfit of the TV gangsta rapper: gold chains over a LeBron James jersey and, tilted precariously sideways, a pristine baseball cap with the New Orleans Saints fleur-de-lis emblazoned in sparkling silver glitter.

"My mom's family name is Alarcón," he said. "I go by that. It avoids a lot of unnecessary explaining." He drew out the word as if he was beset daily by people clamoring for information.

The lighting was dim on one side of the bar; they sat in a booth. On the opposite wall was a single window with a neon sign of a turtle dragging a large spiky penis behind him. The surrounding window bricks were new. It had once been a Jehovah's Witness congregation building. Like most, they were built to formula over a weekend by volunteers and windows were sacrificed for speed of construction.

"I don't mean to stare, man, but what the fuck happened to you?"

"I was sleeping in a tent that burned down. I didn't get out in time."

"Dog, that is some evil-looking shit. Check this."

Edgardo turned his head sideways to show Raimo the faint outline of a triple crown above his street name inscribed in italic script.

"Lasered it off. Hurt like a motherfucker, man. Cost me four hundred rupees."

"Rupees?"

"Dollars, homes. You no speaka da English? I did a stupid thing when I was fourteen." He'd been enamored of the gangs in Compton, LA, and Chicago depicted in rock videos. "But I wasn't in no gang, see."

He lowered his voice to a discrete whisper despite the fact the only other customers were two middle-aged men in plaid shorts sitting at the bar. "Fuck, the only gangs at the Lake are bikers and who wants that crazy peckerwood shit, right?"

Raimo thought that ironic because they were sitting in the one bar at the tail end of the Strip notorious for bikers. The JOTL chamber of commerce tried every year to find a way to get rid of it through code violations. They even tried a GoFundMe page to buy it out from the current owner, an ex-biker named Curly Jones.

The Mud Turtle's name came from a smutty joke by the first owner, a second-generation Swede, that had to do with "sticking your turtle in the mud." The Mud Turtle Bar was a cement-block biker hangout at night, but it was relatively safe up until dark when the clientele changed drastically to black leather-vested types in beards. The owner had to sell it when the law enforced too many violations of underage selling and was now doing time somewhere. Curly Jones was a former Bandido who used to come through town with some of his chapter brothers on a ride on Interstate 90 that diverted to the Lake on their way to an annual club gathering in New York State. After several fights that tore the place up, he managed to get the officers of the various gangs together to declare his bar neutral. But the peace was often broken and the Lake cops were called out in the early morning to subdue fights while classic Stones' tunes blared from the speakers.

"I want to see the cottage myself."

The cottage was in walking distance down a winding dirt road that abutted an overgrown golf course. A rusted cart lay smothered in weeds. A white flagstick missing its flag canted drunkenly from the putting hole of a nearby green.

"Here it is," Edgardo said. He pulled a key ring from his pocket, fingering them rapidly in rotation until he found the right one.

"I manage these five places for the owner," he said. "He lives in Youngstown, a lawyer."

"Why not ask him?" Raimo asked.

"Why not ask him? Well, let me see. My father's a real Jew. That guy's a fucking Jew. You know what a *schmuck* is?"

Alarcón was looking at doing for a second offense for manufacturing and distributing, he'd said back in the bar. He wanted to secure his "investment" before he went away. When Raimo asked why he thought he'd be a safe risk despite the fact his own brother might be involved with Mehoff/Tuomey, Edgardo told him, "Someone I know said you could be trusted to do the right thing."

"How much did he tell you about me?"

"He didn't tell me about your face or nothing like that. He just said I could trust you. He said you were one-hundred percent on the level. 'An honest man,' he said, and smart, too.'"

The only client Raimo had ever done business with more than once was Leotis Pennimann and Leotis knew next to nothing about him. He recalled Leotis asking him once how he got his education, and Raimo told him he dropped out of college when he was a sophomore and decided to stay home and read books on his own.

"Show me how you did it," Raimo said.

Edgardo took him into the cottage, a surprisingly spacious and attractive one despite the general neglect of the surroundings. Pink and white Angel Trumpets hung from bushes planted on either side of the door. He saw Mosquito Shoo geraniums lined along both sides of a flagstone walkway.

"Back here's the bedroom," Edgardo said. "I got it rented out for tonight."

He showed him where he had the cameras secreted in the wall. The bed was covered from three angles and a sound enhancer was hidden in a floor vent.

"In case, you know, for marketing reasons. The cameras are high quality. I get stuff from a guy who boosts from boxcars at railroad sidings in Cleveland."

"Show me what's on the tape," Raimo said.

"We got to go next door for that," Edgardo said. "I keep all my electronics there. The shyster gives me a place rent-free."

The vehicle parked in front was a late-model cherry Subaru with a broad racing stripe down the hood.

"I keep it parked here, man. Those biker assholes don't care whose car they scratch when they start up their fuckin' hogs. I got nitrous oxide tanks for street racing, too. I'm gonna have to put my baby in storage if I go away again."

His was the biggest of the cottages with a loft. A mattress and tangled sheets were visible from below. Beside the bed was a hookah, a stereo system, small TV, and stacks of CDs in stands. Except for that, the furniture of his cottage was identical: the same polished blonde wood on walls and counters, furniture that looked like shipping crates nailed together. Edgardo turned on a laptop and slid a silver disk into a laptop tray.

"Take a seat," he said.

Raimo sat down at the kitchen table. Alarcón hit a few keys

and swung the monitor around.

The clarity was good but the sound faded in and out.

Two women stripped down to panties. One, large breasted with dusky areolae, was kissing a smaller blonde on the mouth, shoulders and armpits. Her haircut as familiar as the caduceus tattoo on her right shoulder. Her hand played lightly over the woman's crotch and then slipped her fingers under the elastic. He didn't know the woman Julie DeMarest was fondling. Their kissing and moans were picked up by the hidden mic. A videocam pointed at the women just out of frame.

"I didn't put a bug in the kitchen," Poke said, "Those walls in there don't absorb and I was worried it might pick a squawk from the speakers. I wasn't the only one filming the action."

The sound of male voices coming from the other room weren't recognizable nor the words spoken.

"I can't hear what they're saying," Raimo said.

"Wait for it, man," Edgardo said.

Two men, nude, walked back into the room. Tuomey and Rikki had finished their confab in the kitchen.

Tuomey: "Starting without us, you sluts."

Tuomey flung himself between the women. Giggles. Rikki moved around to the blonde's side of the bed; he was semi-erect.

"Let's get past this part," Raimo said.

Ed put the cursor on fast-forward. The two couples on the bed appeared to be tossed up and down, back and forth, by an earthquake. Positions were switched at lightning speed and the juddering of frenetic sexual motion looked comical.

"Like rabbits, huh? Right about here, yo," Edgardo pointed. He slowed the tape to Play. Rikki and Tuomey had switched partners.

Voices. Laughter. A third couple entered the cottage. Dino Caddio had a bottle of liquor in one hand and his other hand on the buttock of his date. Her hair was long, raven black and she wore a short skirt and sandals. The girl immediately stripped. Caddio moved off to a corner and drank from the bottle, content to be a voyeur. His date moved over to Julie and began fondling a breast rubbing the nipple to erection.

"I said I don't want to see this," Raimo told him.

Alarcón shrugged. More earthquake sex with Dino's date proving she possessed an eclectic and gymnastic bisexuality.

"It's when these freaks get done sucking and fucking. The girls lie around on the bed fingering each other's pussies. Your brother, he goes off with Mister Mehoff into the kitchen again. Your brother gets pissed off at something he said to him. Listen." He slowed the tape again.

Raimo could pick out some words, such as "solo," "Gerrard's," and "Dino"; a word that might be *money* was repeated many times. The growl must have come from Rikki out of range. At one point, Dino walks over to stand in the doorway. He sees Tuomey's arm shove Dino backward, and he hears the words "*private conversation, Caddio*" distinctly.

"See that? They were planning to do the little ape-man right there in the kitchen. Betty Boobs, I don't know what she done, but she turns up dead next. Suicide, my ass. It ain't like a cold, you don't catch it. But there you go, man, two of 'em deader than Julius Caesar. You tell me that shit don't stink?"

A first-rate lab like the BCI's could probably clean it up, but there was nothing overwhelming to incriminate Tuomey in a court of law, and, if anything, it seemed to exonerate Rikki if what he was thinking was true. Brian was putting his plan into motion: Dino would sabotage the plane at the hangar. What part did Tuomey expect Rikki to have?

"This guy with your brother, man, he's a player, for sure. He loves to watch the girls bump fenders. And that chick with the boobs, she ain't the only one, man. Got a whole bunch of Northtown gash all summer long."

"How long?" Raimo asked.

"Oh, maybe, like, twice a month up until Fourth of July. I told him some dude from Pittsburgh had a standing reservation for all the cabins. So he gets all pissed off at me and never called for a cottage again when I call him up, tell him I got openings again."

"Listen to me, Edgardo. You do not want this man to find

out you've been filming him."

"Fuck him."

"How many people besides you know about these?"

"Me, my posse, you. If I need to plead down, I can use this to get a reduction," Edgardo said. "Thing is, I don't want to waste it if there's a reward posted."

"Why not?"

"Because cops and lawyers, they got this rule about doubling-down."

"Double jeopardy," Raimo said. "It doesn't apply. If this helps you in the sentencing, it'll help you get any reward later, if one's posted."

"Whatever, man, but you wait for my call, see. Sentencing hearing's day after tomorrow. I'll call you right after," Edgardo said. "My lawyer knows his shit. He said it's a thousand-dollar fine, ten days in county suspended, and a year probation. No sweat."

"Look, I can take it to the detectives for you. They'll keep your name out of it if they can," Raimo offered.

"No, we gonna do it my way first," Ed told him.

"You'll take my warning about Tuomey seriously, right?"

"He's just a silk suit, a pair of Ferragamo shoes. Check these, man."

"Congratulations," Raimo said. "You're wearing high-tops."

"Shit, man, these are Louboutin, cost me two racks. Hey, your bro, man, he's got a fan club out here. He should be out in Hollywood making money with that block and tackle."

Raimo remembered the day he drove him to the Cleveland airport. Rikki smiling, gleeful, happier than Raimo had seen him in months. He took all his frustrations out on a heavy bag their dad hung in the garage for the boys. Rikki punched holes into it over time and covered the holes in duct tape. Poken Beans was right: Rikki had dreams of making it in Hollywood.

"Man, I am never coming back to this third-rate shithole," Rikki said to him. "I'll send you money when I get settled out there. You can join me."

"No, thanks," Raimo said.

"You idiot," Rikki said. "You can't cross a street without seeing beautiful women everywhere you go."

"That's what they tell Muslim suicide bombers when they lock them into their vests. Seventy-two virgins in paradise. It's just a dream, Rikki."

"That's your problem, kiddo. Ever since you got burned, you've stopped living."

Rikki was right about that. He thought of Dino slugging down booze in the corner watching the action on the bed. He left Irene alone just to be Brian Tuomey's court monkey all over again. High school never ended.

But maybe it wasn't too late to start living again. *There are moments when courage and daring are the only acceptable forms of caution.*

Parti Québécois founder Réne Levèsque had said that, but last time he checked his Atlas, Quebec was still in Canada.

Chapter 18 - August 18

The heat at the cemetery was pulverizing—a heating iron pressed down on the heads of everybody who ventured outside. One old aunt of Dino's dressed in black and wailing her grief like an old-country Sicilian *matri* fainted and had to be carried off by three husky men to the shade of an oak and revived.

Irene was surrounded by women in black and held by both elbows by two more of these bookend aunts. Her long chestnut hair was combed severely down her back instead of the jaunty horsetail she normally wore. Raimo recognized several people from the reunion. Everyone wore shades and most of the older women silk scarves out of deference to the family. Everyone looked exhausted. Raimo saw Detective Nolan at the back of the crowd when the Our Father was recited, signaling an end to the chapel prayers.

It all seemed unreal as if staged by some invisible director offstage.

He thought about Dino and wondered what he knew of him. It was the same with Rikki. The priest had talked about the Holy Ghost's purifying fire. He knew fire another way. Something he remembered from Nietzsche: "There are no facts, only interpretations." Tuomey wasn't at the mass or at the cemetery. No one spoke his name.

Raimo went straight to the Wyandotte after the casket lowering. Irene might have seen him but she didn't acknowledge him and he didn't want to intrude. In a few days that burning disc was going to be blocked out and the people of Northtown would get to experience that eerie sensation of the sun going full dark, a palpable blackness, not a mere shadow. Raimo's father told him his people used to believe a wolf was eating the sun. Dragon, bear, something was said to dine on the sun during an eclipse. He knew from his reading that the Greeks believed the gods were angry. The paper cited some superstitions from the past like banging pots and pans to drive away demons or not cooking food during an eclipse because it would be poisonous. Children and pregnant women were to be kept indoors. But it wasn't all bad. Italians believed flowers planted during an eclipse were brighter and more colorful than at any other time.

Raimo drove by Tuomey's condo and spotted the gleaming black Jaguar. For someone who was supposed to be employed in Columbus, he spent most of his time in Northtown.

In the office, he made some calls to Gerrard Pharmaceuticals, LLC, purporting to be a drug rep for another pharmacy looking for work one time, a fiduciary expert another, trying to elicit whatever information he could about the company's status from anyone he could cajole the receptionist into patching him over to. He gleaned nothing useful and didn't want to press his luck by persisting with questions. He called Gerrard's asking to be connected to the marketing director whose call he was returning but was told "Mister Tuomey was on vacation" but would he like to speak to one of the other vice presidents? He wouldn't "but thanks for asking."

Julie DeMarest's obituary in the *Tribune* that morning consisted of a couple lines announcing the date of her death and which funeral home was making arrangements.

That old cliché about mad dogs, Englishmen, and the noonday sun should be expanded to include amateur detectives working feeless, he thought. Lake Road East was bare of traffic except for gravel trucks avoiding the main route through Northtown and was populated with mini-tornadoes of swirling bugs that smashed themselves against cars and smeared windshields with snot-like goo. Midges, Canadian soldiers, mosquitoes, and mayflies were enjoying triple harvests of birth rates in these endless days of bountiful August sunshine.

Buffalo Street in Conneaut qualified for the *Trib*'s jargon as being "no stranger to the police." Domestic violence, drug abuse, menacing, receiving stolen property, child endangerment, and a variety of drug offenses were steady fare in the police-beat section. Julie's house was a 1930's Craftsman, brown trim over white, shingle roof feathered and covered in moss. A mangy, postage-stamp of lawn bisected by a flagstone walk, a porch with missing rails, and a couple shagbark hickories out front. Fried oil wafted across the street from a Chinese take-out.

The county nurse met him at the door. City workers were hauling green garbage bags to the curb. Lying on the phone was becoming a skill. He said he was "assisting" another investigation with Det. Sgt. Nolan of the Sheriff's. The nurse explained they were waiting for a second ambulance, which was delayed en route. Both father and son were being transferred from home care to the county nursing home until the court adjudicated on mental fitness.

Raimo found them sitting side by side on a couch. The son wore a Guy Fawkes mask and didn't take Raimo's hand when he was introduced by the nurse. Julie's husband wore a faded blue terrycloth gown and pajamas with slippers.

"It's only temporary," he told Raimo. "I expect to be back to work next week."

"What do you do?" Raimo asked.

"He's a surgeon," the son said. His words sounded mushy behind the mask. "He cuts out parts of people and puts them in their heads and sews them up again."

"Be quiet, John," the father said.

"Mister DeMarest—"

"Vandenhyden," he corrected. "Julie uses—used her maiden name."

"Some maiden," Johnny said. "She was a whore with a tail

like Jezebel's."

The nurse sitting across from them looked uncomfortable.

"He knows," she said.

"I'm right here," Vandenhyden said.

"Mister Vandenhyden, I'm sorry if this sounds abrupt. Were you home when Julie died?"

"Yes," he said.

"Was she alone?"

"You mean was she upstairs fucking someone?"

Vandenhyden slapped his son's face and knocked the mask sideways; the boy was years older than Raimo thought. His face was tear-streaked and his eyes red-rimmed.

The nurse walked over to Johnny and picked up his hand as if it were a dead bird. "Let's go into the kitchen, sweetie. Come with me."

"Go!" his father ordered.

Mask back in place, he shook off the nurse's hand but meekly followed her into the kitchen.

"I'm sorry," Raimo said. "I didn't mean to cause—"

"She *was* a whore," Vandenhyden said. "John isn't wrong about that."

He took a prescription bottle out of his pocket and shook two pills into his hand. Raimo watched him wash them down with water.

"Lord help me," Vandenhyden said and rubbed his temples. "Life is so. . . sometimes."

Raimo could agree with that, whatever the unspoken word implied.

"Do you know someone named Tuomey?"

"Toomey?"

Raimo spelled it for him. "Brian Tuomey was a classmate from Julie's high school," he said.

"Was he someone she was screwing?" Vandenhyden asked. "I don't know. I stopped asking her. She'd have lied anyway."

"I'm sorry if this sounds indelicate. Did Julie see other men with your permission?"

"She doesn't—didn't tell me anything," Vandenhyden said.

"She went out the door to work, she says. She came back late. Sometimes she didn't come back for a couple days. She left in her uniform and sometimes returned wearing a dress. She said she was with girlfriends but I never believed her unless girlfriends have a habit of taking off your panties and putting them into your purse."

"Do you have any reason to believe Julie's overdose was anything but an accident?"

"Maybe you've noticed. We're a pill-taking family. That's how we cope—or don't."

"Do you remember what Julie said to you before she went upstairs . . . the last time?"

"No. Don't ask me another question. I don't care what your reasons are or what you told the nurse."

The nurse had told him Julie's body showed rigor in the neck, back, and upper arms when the husband entered the room. He had to break one of her firmest "rules" about never disturbing her when she was in her bedroom. The hospital called to find out why she didn't show for her shift. Vandenhyden knocked and paced outside the door for hours until he gathered up the courage to break inside and find her. Her room was a hoarder's pigsty, the nurse said. Stacks of magazines reached the ceiling so that first responders had to wend between them to get the body out. Even then, Vandenhyden insisted she be given first aid but she was cold and liver spots were evident on her breasts and back. The police collected the bottles of prescription pills, baggies of marijuana and pipe.

Raimo's disfigurement sometimes produced an extraordinary effect on people. Strangers who weren't initially repulsed by his face seemed drawn to him, and he often found the whole ice-breaking stage bypassed. In its place, an unwarranted confidentiality was presumed. The county nurse was one of these moths drawn to a sympathetic response with no prompting and little ruse up front when he asked to "have a few minutes of her and the family's time." She told him what she picked up from hospital gossip: Julie found a simple way to bypass the check system of the hospital's policy regarding removal of controlled substances from the locked cabinets. The two-person check system sometimes had a big flaw when the colleague holding the key was in cahoots with you. She said the other nurse was exposed and now all the drugs were being counted and the morphine checked to see if it had been diluted.

Raimo left the husband sitting there on the porch, smoking and trying to keep his hands from fidgeting in the pockets of his frayed bathrobe.

The ambulance pulled up to the curb out front.

"Time to go, Frank," the nurse said.

She led the masked son past Raimo out the door. He suddenly stopped, turned around, and took off his mask in front of Raimo. He handed it to Raimo.

"Here," Johnny said. "You need this more than I do."

Raimo was standing on the porch when he heard Vandenhyden call him. He found the husband sitting on the couch smoking a cigarette in an odd way, holding it between the last two fingers so he seemed to be slapping his mouth whenever he drew on it.

"You called me, sir?"

"I'm diagnosed paranoid schizophrenic," he said, "so take whatever I say with that in mind."

"All right," Raimo said.

"She said—Julie said, 'If I suddenly turn up dead, you'll miss me, won't you, Frank? Even after all this?'"

Raimo thought he understand the last part—*all this*—her history of infidelity and drugs, his mental condition.

He asked, "Did she say who wanted her dead?"

"No, she didn't. She was just heading upstairs like always. I knew she was going for her 'medicine.' She said it like a joke, but I saw she was afraid. If you knew my wife, you'd know she wasn't afraid of anything when she was manic."

He looked at Raimo. "My ex-wife was bipolar as well as a sex addict. She kept the one a secret from everybody, not the second."

"I'm sorry, Mister Vandenhyden."

"We made a terrific couple. She was wearing this. I found it around her neck upstairs. I didn't give it to her."

He opened his fist to reveal a thin gold necklace with a curved horn dangling from it. Raimo had gone to school with plenty of Italian kids from the east side; he recognized the golden horn as a charm against the *malocchio*, the evil eye. It was supposed to protect you from the envy of another.

"She used to say my cum tasted like butter cream," Vandenhyde said.

"Smart idea, Jarvi," Nolan said.

He looked around Raimo's office as if he'd never been there before. Raimo's desk was clean except for the nicks and gouges, the phone, a desk calendar, mostly blank, and the computer.

"What is?" Raimo replied.

"Getting out of the private-eye business," he said. "You're not cut out for it."

Nolan set the disk on his desk and spun it like a top.

Raimo put a finger out, stopping it mid-spin at a tilt; he used to hold a football that way waiting for Rikki to kick it.

"It's not evidence, Jarvi."

"Is that your professional opinion or the prosecutor's official determination?"

Raimo flicked it with his fingertips toward Nolan.

"Keep it," he said. "I made a copy in case this gets buried like everything else in Northtown."

Nolan shrugged. "Suit yourself."

Raimo noticed the disk was a copy, not the original with Edgardo Alarcón's writing on it.

"We went over the gulf with metal detectors, above and below. We didn't find that piece of rebar you said Tuomey hit you with."

"You think I beat myself black and blue with a steel rod?"

"Tuomey said you always had this inferiority complex about your brother, and you look for ways to bring attention to yourself, like this private investigator gig."

"You're taking Tuomey's word over mine? Did you get the toxicology report back?"

"Not yet. We took a sample of yours at the hospital and sent it in, too. What do you suppose that'll show?"

"Have them check for propofol while you're at it," said Raimo, recalling the Michael Jackson drug they'd found among the bottles on Julie's nightstand. That logy feeling could have come from a dozen drugs, but the anesthetized effect from a couple sips was instant; even its milky-white color would have gone undetected in the coffee he doused with instant powdered creamer.

"Look, Jarvi, you're rattling a big stick inside a small bucket. We found nothing on Tuomey and we did a deep search. No criminal record, not even a traffic ticket—unlike you, I might add. He's financially solvent and pays his taxes."

He'd checked those same properties on a Google Earth map himself. Tuomey had two rentals in Columbus, as well as a summer condo on the lake in Saybrook. One was a townhouse in New Albany. The other was a huge colonial that sat back on a couple of landscaped acres in Powell, a tonier suburb yet with a median income of $135,000. The rental sat back on bucolic Olentangy River Road, away from campus traffic, and was leased to visiting professors, thanks no doubt to his alumni connection. Tuomey was a dues-paying member of The Ohio State Alumni Association.

He was relieved when Nolan left. He could only expect so many visits before the cuffs were slapped on. Some criminal law of diminishing returns at work there, he supposed. He couldn't keep crossing Nolan's path without an obstruction charge resulting. But his clipped responses to the cop's questions stemmed from the discovery of a phone bug, by pure accident, when he returned to the office. He removed the cracked plastic casing after noticing hairline fractures along the seam that weren't there before. He left the bug but put a strip of electric tape over the Skype camera lens as a precaution, although that wouldn't help if Tuomey paid someone to hack his computer.

It was all-out paranoia time; he was the one surveilled and bugged. The biter bit. If his phone was tapped, what else? Wouldn't there be a tap on his cell phone, a hidden lens somewhere, a GPS tracker on his jeep, bumper beepers, spy cams in his apartment, too? He remembered Gene Hackman's character in the final scene of *The Conversation* sitting on the floor with his entire apartment dismantled and stripped down to the floorboards.

Raimo had Edgardo Alarcón's disk of Tuomey talking to his brother; the words could fit a puzzle that formed a conspiracy to tamper with the Gerrard Pharmacy's executive's plane. *Gerrard flies solo to Cleveland. Dino is bribed to tamper with the plane while it's in the hangar. Gerrard dies in a tragic accident. The company goes up for sale. Tuomey and Enright maneuver to buy a majority share at fire sale prices, no sons to inherit. The new miracle drug, once approved by the FDA, will make them both fabulously rich.* He'd saved the disk in a file and burned a copy, which Nolan rejected as evidence. Where did that leave him?

But it wasn't enough, and he knew it. Even a *pro bono* lawyer could poke holes in that theory big enough to drive a truck through. It would look like what Nolan called it when he first valked in—warped sibling jealousy by someone with a endetta against his brother's longtime friend.

The urge to drink was on him, but there was Rikki to think Raimo needed more and he knew who had it. Edgardo ıld have burned other disks besides the one he gave him safe-keeping. He remembered what Edgardo had said t uploading the disk to a porn site. That meant he had s. Maybe he made copies for friends or sold them with homemade porn out of his trunk.

doubted Tuomey made one attempt to get Rikki d. Tuomey did nothing by halves.

eft the office with his gun stuck in his waistband; , after all, was just heightened self-awareness.

swung by the McDonald's on Lake Avenue. He had to eat something but food sickened him lately.

He stopped cooking for himself and he no longer went to the diner in case Bart was there. He was losing weight and he had deep bags under his eyes. Noise made him jumpy and falling asleep terrified him. Every stir in the muggy night air of Bridge Street meant one of Tuomey's hired killers was coming through a window for him.

The Strip was beginning to pick up action; the dinnertime crowd and the sunburned vacationers were giving way to the younger, more serious crowd there for the real excitement on offer. The morning's *Tribune* said that crimes at the Lake were up by 40% at this point with Labor Day still weeks off; the spokesperson for the Strip's businesses said it was the heat. People weren't handling alcohol as well as they did in cooler weather. More fights, more vandalism, and far more drunk-and-disorderlies. The Lake hired extra off-duty Northtown cops and Jefferson sent over four additional deputies to he' patrol the Strip. A record number of people were expected the end-of-summer holiday, which always included a through by one of the outlaw motorcycle clubs, which the stakes for trouble.

Raimo drove past the Mud Turtle, noting the l black Harleys out front. He'd try there if he Edgardo's vehicle at the cabins.

He pulled in front of the cottage and felt guilt his mud-spattered, dented vehicle next to E shined Impreza tricked out with racing strip bars and LED underglow display lights. E lights were visible. Raimo heard the soft r idling beneath the repetitive thump of ba obscene chant about cars, money, sex. F was inside getting the place ready for th

Raimo planned to brace him har before he had time to think. The c what he would do if he found participation.

He knocked. He couldn't see t

blinds over the windows.

He knocked again.

He figured Edgardo spotted him and wasn't coming to the door.

Raimo decided the door wouldn't give if he rammed his shoulder into it and went back to his jeep for the pry bar. It had worked once before. At the last second, he decided to try the lock pick. The practice paid off or he was lucky; either way, his fourth attempt worked. He eased the door slowly open.

Edgardo wasn't avoiding him, although he seemed to be mocking him, kneeling on the floor with his arms dangling at his sides and a swollen, blackened tongue sticking out of his mouth.

The rope from his neck led to a balcony rail where it was tied off with a knot Raimo could have done in his sleep—a half-hitch his father taught him before the harder ones like a bowline or a sheepshank.

Edgardo's knees pressed together. They cleared the floor by an inch and his body weight rested on his haunches. His toes bent from the weight pressing down.

Sexual asphyxia—another suicide? Not likely.

A struggle had occurred downstairs, but it didn't last long. One table shoved to the wall but not smashed, nothing else knocked over; a throw rug tossed or kicked out of the way. The refrigerator door left open and, in front of it, a green bottle of Heineken lay in the center of a pool of beer on the floor suggesting Alarcón might have been blindsided by his attacker. The ball cap with the fleur-de-lis lay on its side by the far wall. He knew who he let inside, might have gone to the fridge to fetch a cold brew when the attack came.

Raimo stood in front of the body and looked for signs of bruising. Edgardo's tee-shirt was rucked up in back. His boxers exposed down to the buttocks; he noted the dark stain over the crotch where his bladder released. They'd been pulled down, not off. The killer's clumsy, last-minute staging interrupted perhaps by evacuated bowels.

Maybe not so clumsy, Raimo thought. He could be identified as someone seen with the victim recently. He was in this cottage. That meant his prints might be found here; if no prints he left, then Tuomey's access to his office meant he had no difficulty planting them here along with a phony attempt to cover it up by the murderer, him. He had no time to search the premises for anything incriminating. His racing mind tried to help him by playing devil's advocate: *What motive would he have for killing Alarcón?*

The answer came back in Bart's voice, something they'd talked about at the diner many times over coffee: *Prosecutors don't need motives. Juries do.*

Raimo touched an arm below the elbow—no rigor, the arm not yet cool to the touch. Abrasions and nicks in the skin above the rope revealed Edgardo had thrashed and clawed at his neck fighting the rope, so he was conscious while it was happening. Had he been thrown over the iron railing above, his neck should have snapped and the wrought-iron scrollwork didn't permit a body to be rolled underneath the bottom rail. He was raised from the floor and tied off when his feet cleared the floor. Then he was lowered to this position when he stopped struggling. That took someone with more than average strength. Raimo squatted down and felt along the floor over the polished wood and felt smudged places where Edgardo's heels must have pounded the floor while he was being hoisted.

He climbed the winding stairs to the loft and stepped gingerly around a dozen CDs scattered around. The Bose stereo system, headphones, a small TV, and stands of CD holders looked as if they'd been handled and roughly replaced. He lifted the mattress. Edgardo put all his money into his car. No furniture besides the mattress but three garbage bags of clothes, one for dirty laundry. No extra disks secreted inside, no laptop.

He took a last look around for places he might have touched. Edgardo's eyes were slits, looking away to the left as if embarrassed by the pungent odor of voiding.

No, that's wrong, thought Raimo. *The dead don't care about anything anymore.*

He drove down the strip back down Lake Road surprised at his calm even when he passed a Lake cop sitting at the curve where youth liked to punch a last burst of speed out of their fast cars before the inevitable logjam ahead.

Raimo passed Tuomey's condo but didn't spot the Jaguar under the high-masted parking lights bathing the cars below in a white sheen while the others were merely tinted in the surrounding umbra.

Raimo didn't turn off to Bridge Street. The thought of being observed or listened to sickened him. It wasn't pique that held him back from calling Nolan but the need to clear Rikki from any association with Tuomey's madness. He slammed the jeep to a halt in the middle of the Lake Avenue and Walnut Boulevard intersection. Walnut Beach hill beckoned from his left; he could drive down and watch the moonrise over the lake or go home and get drunk. He swung the jeep left and aimed straight for the breakwall. He could look at the water and watch the stars come out. He had to think. He had to have a plan for Tuomey before he found himself wrapped in a cocoon of evidence that all pointed to him.

The public beach was off to his left, a pewter disc unbroken to the horizon. A dozen cars remained in the lot and some kids rode their boards at the skateboard park the city built for them when every sign in town marked No Skateboarding was defaced by Day-Glo colors. A few straggling beachgoers were on their way back to their cars on the boardwalk. Ghostly echoes of voices calling from the beach carried all the way to the top of the hill.

The Wrangler was his father's last purchase, a bequeathal on his deathbed. His father died before he had 5,000 miles on it. Raimo replaced the ragtop because of hail storms, but it drove through deep snow and plowed through mud like a warhorse. He loved moonlit nights in summer or winter where he pushed the vehicle to the top of second and third gears, running dangerously close to the granite slabs. In winter, he drove up the breakwall's beehive-shaped ice dunes formed by the relentless wave action; in summer, he took the top down. The big tires slewed and fishtailed through sand as soft as slurry beside the stagnant pools behind the breakwall. A spin-out was inevitable but he almost tipped the jeep onto its roll bar a couple times in winter. The challenge was to take the jeep up to the top of the wall. The risk was to avoid careening over the wall into the lake crashing with eight-foot waves. Therapy, he called it.

Raimo drove off the pavement into the sandy, pot-holed dirt road leading to the giant slabs that kept the shallowest of the Great Lakes moving sluggishly eastward toward the harbor's mouth and beyond to Niagara Falls at the same pace since the last ice age when the giant skyscraper-sized glaciers carved it out.

He parked and got out. He didn't see anyone else on the wall but a couple older vehicles parked nearby and some LED camping lights a half-mile distant suggested some fishermen were enjoying the night as well.

The old crescent moon had just begun its eastward climb through the sky. Cassiopeia's bent W beneath the pitched tent of Cepheus led him to Polaris rather than the easier way from the star Dubhe in the Big Dipper bowl.

He loved the vastness and darkness of the night sky. It reduced the Earth and its humanity to such puniness that even murder seemed to lose perspective. Most people see death in the painted colors of a funeral home casket's display. He had seen two living, breathing human faces reduced by obliteration and suffocation in small empty rooms in a week.

He found handholds and climbed to the flattened granite top, where the blocks were laid a hundred years ago like giant, ill-fitting puzzle pieces that stretched a mile to the lighthouse. He had walked that distance once with his friend Tony, who stole a *Playboy* pinup one sailor had taped to his locker.

He stood there looking at the stars, naming the constellations. After his father ended his sailing days on the oreboats, he taught him how to read the sky. Nights on the water were so black the running lights of a ship were pinpricks in a vast black blanket and that blanket stretched from bow to stern and from horizon to an invisible shore with every star crowding the night sky from all points of the compass. Raimo knew his father was hurt he could not share that experience with his damaged son but he made every effort to bring him what he could from his time on the water.

Raimo felt the warm wind wash over his face. It should have been a cool breeze by this time of the summer, but everything was off, murder was commonplace. He smelled odors he was familiar with since boyhood. The lake was black at the horizon but frothy gray where it broke against the bottom slabs slimed with seaweed at his feet.

He shivered from the knowledge punched into his brain's neurons from the body's danger sensors: *Not alone . . . someone close—*

He saw a glimmer of metal from below. Mikel's face looked up from the base below to orient himself to Raimo's position.

Mikel charged up the rocks with the speed of a linebacker. Raimo's gun was in his hand one moment and then it was clattering over the rocks into the water the next. Raimo didn't know whether it was a fist or a foot that swung out of the dark, but the lump of ice in his belly told him it didn't matter.

"Make you a deal," Mikel said. Incisors flashed as he spoke. "I'll be quick about it. You won't feel it." Another glint at his beltline: a long straight blade, a filleting knife held loosely in his hand.

The people left at the beach when he arrived were gone. No one to hear him. Raimo risked a quick look down the breakwall where the distant lamp of a fisherman glowed. Too far. Running in the dark over these rocks, each one canted at a different angle from the next, and sometimes exposing gaps of a couple feet, wasn't much option. "You won't make it," Mikel said, reading his mind.

"You're right," Raimo said. He lunged toward Mikel, ordering his brain *don't look at the blade, don't look . . .*

The sheer unexpectedness of being charged by his prey caused the big bodyguard to hesitate a second too long before reacting. He swung the knife up but Raimo was already within kicking distance and caught Mikel under the chin with his foot hard enough to make him grunt from the blow but not hard enough to move him so much as an inch backwards.

Raimo crouched and ran past him, blindly, unsure of his footing but able to launch himself in the air just as Mikel twisted to slash at him with his knife hand going by. Raimo's back felt the knife score a channel alongside his backbone that burned like acid but by then he was rolling over in the sand coming up to his feet and running hard in the direction of the jeep. The two halves of his shirt flapped behind him like a torn sail until blood stuck them to his back.

The force that drove him headfirst into the sand-covered road knocked the air out of him and made him gag on the sand that got into his mouth. It felt like one of the breakwall slabs was sitting on his back.

"You're making this difficult," Mikel said. He wasn't even panting.

He jerked Raimo to his feet. A fist smashed him in the nose and he dropped. Mikel jerked him to his feet again and hooked an arm under him.

Raimo couldn't see from the tears and sand but he could hear every word. More sand stuck to the blood from his nose and was smeared over the lower half of his face.

"Keep walking, that's a good little white boy," Mikel said. "Not long now."

Raimo walked drunkenly, escorted by the brutal strength of Mikel more than his own legs.

"Get up on the wall," he said. He threw Raimo face forward onto the sand at the granite base.

Like a kitten in its mother's mouth, Raimo was hauled up, airborne, and dragged over the rocks by Mikel's hand hooked in the back of his pants. "Up you go," he crooned.

On top of the wall, Raimo looked about for help. No one, nothing—just that fisherman's light teasing in the far distance.

"No one's coming," Mikel said, reaching the top and standing to his full height. "Just accept it."

"Who are you?"

Stupid question, under the circumstances, but he asked it anyway.

Mikel sang: "I'm a motherfuckin' starboy."

Raimo weaved on his feet. Mikel held the knife in one hand and gripped his shirt collar in the other to steady him. Raimo tried to headbutt Mikel but that only made him laugh and bunch the material of his collar under Raimo's neck tighter. It was like having a forked tree branch jammed under his neck. He couldn't move. Blood was pouring down his throat choking him. He was too dizzy to try another kick and Mikel's strength and size made that futile.

Raimo tried to hook a leg behind Mikel's knee. The effort was so pathetic Mikel laughed as he put the point of the blade under his eyeball. "I could have made this easy but not no more, fool."

"Talk is cheap," Raimo said. "It takes money to buy whiskey."

"I'm in control here, little man. I'm going to open you up for the fish. Slice your motherfuckin' stomach open so them eel things can swim inside your belly and lay babies."

Raimo spit a gob of bloody phlegm into Mikel's face. Maybe that would work better than his father's saying.

Enraged, the bodyguard took a half-step back to swing the knife with force instead of plunging it in where they stood—so easy to do—but Raimo used Mikel's own shifting momentum against him and threw his body in the direction of Mikel's arm. They teetered along the edge, Raimo gaining a purchase and wrapping his arms around Mikel's massive torso, dancing him toward the lip of the granite's edge. Raimo had climbed these rocks with the agility of a mountain goat as a boy but there was no muscle memory left, just blind, dizzy luck. The bodyguard understood Raimo's intention and over-corrected his own movement, which put one foot in jeopardy.

Losing balance, an odd couple close dancing on a slab, they

went over sideways, sticking together down the slope, tumbling toward the water in a lover's suicide pact. Had the rocks been jagged or uneven, it would have made little difference. Gravity was going to win where the rocks were flattened, smaller than the massive slabs above; their combined weight created a toboggan in a chute all the speedier as they neared the thick seaweed that flowed like hair with the water's motion.

Once his head hit the water, Raimo propelled himself with his feet against the rocks and pulled free of Mikel's grasp, his ripped shirt coming loose.

Raimo swam underwater, unable to see anything in the dingy water. When he came up for air, he was twenty feet from the breakwall, which was just a darker line in his vision. He could make out Mikel thrashing in the water just feet from the rocks. Water erupted from his hands, pounding and slapping just feet from the evenly breaking waves against the breakwall. Mikel flailed at the water, still clutching his knife. Raimo watched from a distance treading water, unsure if the big man was feigning. White bursts exploded around Mikel's head like explosions of baseball-sized hail falling into a swimming pool.

Raimo heard him gasping for breath, his cries of fear climbing the scale to ever higher notes from the basso-profundo of his threats with the knife while they stood locked on the wall.

He was in no hurry. Raimo knew he wasn't badly hurt and his limbs were intact. The searing pain of his back was nothing compared to the exhilaration of surviving.

Time didn't seem to have any meaning in the water—seconds to minutes passed. Raimo couldn't see Mikel's head without intense concentration. He stopped thrashing and moaning. His head disappeared and bobbed to the surface.

Raimo moved closer to him, soundlessly, in no rush.

Mikel's head disappeared again from view and this time it barely broke the surface. Choking sobs came from his throat. He went under again, and the return to the surface was slower yet.

Raimo moved in, ever cautious of the man's brute strength. He did not want to come within reach and be pulled in by a drowning man's frenzy, especially one the size of Mikel.

When Mikel surfaced again, he was face down. Raimo covered the distance in a few strokes. He had him by the belt, swimming hard to cover five feet to the nearest slab of rock. It seemed to take long minutes to move Mikel's bulk, a tugboat trying to maneuver a four-story cruise liner into port. Raimo climbed up on a small shelf near the place where they had gone in. He could get the big man's arm out of the water at first but not much else. He struggled to turn him around so that he wasn't floating face down.

Once he made it out of the water, he found he could pull and drag the bodyguard if he timed his efforts to the slight swell of the waves rolling in. It was dead lifting from a sitting position while trying to find purchase for his feet on the greasy seaweed. Each effort yielded a little more of the floating bulk visible above the waterline, but it was like trying to push a canned ham into a chipmunk hole. Putting his back against a rock, he managed to get Mikel's torso free of the water and wedged into a crevice between a pair of rocks. Bigger waves would dislodge him, but for now, that was the best he could do.

Raimo went through Mikel's vest and pants pockets and transferred everything but a soggy pack of cigarettes into his own pockets. He clambered over the rocks to the other side, a human crab, unwilling to trust his footing in the dark. The only lights visible came from a distant lakeboat and the lighthouse's sweeping beam snatching objects out of the pitch black like the canopy of trees in the surrounding wetlands, and then returning them to their position.

He walked off the breakwall on rubber legs, his breath coming in harsh whistles in counterpoint to the squishing of his wet shoes dripping water.

He drove to a Dairy Mart on Lake Avenue and called nine-one-one from the pay phone built into the wall. The youth using the phone immediately gave it up when he saw a dripping, half-nude Raimo approaching him like the creature from the black lagoon.

"Ambulance, fire, or police. What is your emergency?"

"Ambulance," Raimo said. "I want to report a drowning at Walnut Beach."

The dispatcher had a hard time believing him, thought he was a crank caller when he said the victim was "alive, still clinging to the rocks" on the other side of the breakwall, but she agreed to send an ambulance to the exact spot Raimo described.

When asked how the victim got there, Raimo told her he pushed him off the breakwall because the man tried to rob him with a knife.

"Sir, do you want the police too?"

"Not yet," Raimo said and hung up.

That might be up to Nolan and his boys anyway . . .

Chapter 19 – August 19

Ezekiel called again. "The path of the righteous man is beset on all sides by the iniquities of the selfish and the tyranny of evil men."

It clicked: Jules in the restaurant scene from *Pulp Fiction* by Hollywood's *enfant terrible.* Rikki came home raving about the film's embedded story-telling technique. Raimo said nothing but held up his copy of the Conrad novel he was reading and said it was no big deal. Every story, he would learn later, was an embedded story, fat lies wrapped around a kernel of truth within a bigger, more elaborate lie, every beginning and ending shirred like the ribbon decorating a birthday present.

Not a word about Tuomey or Tuomey's half-drowned bodyguard. Nothing on any investigation other than con men passing through town and selling phony cable deals or painting roofs with Silver Brite. Almost everything disappeared from the front pages, the Tribune not known for follow-up investigations. One back-page report mentioned more pieces of wreckage detected at the bottom of Lake Erie in a wider pattern suggestive of a mid-air explosion rather than an impact crash. The smoldering ruin of the van in the gulf never merited a mention after its debut paragraph. Andino Caddio was buried in a closed casket *sans* the three pounds of pulp that constituted his brain. Julie DeMarest lay on a steel table in some mortuary with a trocar sticking in her, exchanging her blood for formaldehyde and waiting for the last cosmetic touches to be applied to her dead face.

An envelope with his name on it was shoved through the

mail slot. He counted $42.00. No note. Leotis Pennimann's final payment on his bill. If he called again, Raimo intended to refuse any further assignments. He was bordering on existentialist despair, a hair's width from surrealism, and he had no desire to resume his theater-of-the-absurd life. Geography is history, Raimo read. What, he wondered, if missionaries had come to the Western Reserve first? In the first year of the nineteenth century, a man named John Young bought the future city of Youngstown for $16,000 from the Connecticut Land Company and platted the town for farmers and merchants. Northtown was settled by whiskey-drinking adventurers, hard men, sailors, escaping slaves, and indentured servants running from their owners.

Raimo doused his back with gin in the shower and screamed; he turned both faucets on full to dampen his cry of pain. His bed sheets were ruined—dried blood formed craters of brown at the edges where the sere had separated.

He stepped out of the shower and wrapped a towel around his waist when he heard a noise coming from his living room.

Idiot, fool, he called himself. No weapon in sight other than the empty gin bottle on the sink. What if that receptionist at the hospital was wrong, mistook the name? What if Tuomey's bodyguard came back to finish the job? He thought of smashing the bottle against the sink but carried it into the next room; it would be handier to throw if Mikel came in armed.

Irene was standing in the middle of the room examining his books on the shelf.

"I'm sorry," she said. "I knocked and called but you didn't hear me."

"I was showering," he said.

"I can see that, Captain Obvious." She smiled. "I thought I heard you yelling in there."

"I accidentally turned the cold water on full blast," he said. "I'll change, Irene. I'll be right back."

"My God, Ray!"

"What is it?" Raimo turned around fast, one hand clutching the towel, the other raised the bottle by the neck, another jolt of fear that someone else might be hiding in the room.

"Your back," she said. "What happened?"

"I slipped on some stairs," he said.

"Let me see."

"I'll just change first—"

"Ray, come here, damn it. Right now."

He walked toward her. The adolescent shyness was foolish but he couldn't control it. He had never had any other feeling with Kristine other than animal lust, not once, as if she controlled what he would feel too.

"Let me look at your face," she said. A phrase that would have wilted him from anyone else but her. "Step over to the window."

"Do you want me to get arrested? I'm wearing a towel."

"Don't be silly," she said. She cupped his chin and turned his face this way and that. "Your eyes are puffy. The skin under them is discolored."

Mikel's big fist. He hadn't noticed. He avoided looking at his mirror until it was steamed up after a shower. That way he could control how much of his face to see at one time.

"Turn around."

He did, grateful he could hide his growing erection.

"You need stitches."

"It's fine," he said. "I doused it with gin."

"Is that why you screamed just now?"

"Private eyes don't scream. Besides, cowboys do it all the time," he said. "They get shot and bit by rattlers and stabbed by Apaches. Then they pour booze on the wound."

"Not all at once, I hope. Cowboys on television never get staph infections, either. Real people do. Besides, I don't think you're a tough guy, are you?"

"So very true."

"Where do you keep the band aids?"

"Bathroom cabinet. First door to the right," he said.

Raimo saw a new pair of pants hanging over the chair next to his bed. How to get past her? Mortified, excited, and ashamed all at the same time. It was a new feeling for him.

How many times had he heard it said with brutal honesty or gentle persuasion that he was doomed to live a life without love? Even his mother had tried to prepare him by showing him a mirror when he was seventeen and working up the courage to ask a girl to the prom.

Irene came back while he had his back turned pretending to look out the window at Hulbert Avenue as if he'd never seen a brick road before.

"Hold still, please."

He felt her fingers applying three butterfly band aids to his back. The seconds elapsing between them made his priapic condition worse.

"There, all done," Irene said.

"Thank you, Doctor Donovan."

Idiot, he accused himself, *you used her maiden name.* First an awkward and puerile shyness, now an adolescent glibness. He felt himself regressing by the second. Soon he'd be gibbering. He bunched the towel at his waist with both hands. *Worse and worse . . .*

When she reached out to stroke his forearm, he shivered from the touch. Then she was in his arms and they were kissing, their mouths locked. Between them, the bath towel remained like some modern version of a sword between a knight and his chosen damsel in bed to maintain their purity—until Irene slipped her hands to his waist and pulled it away.

Raimo had been led to Kristine's bedroom the same way and the anticipation of sex with her was always keen. Irene stepped back and looked at him. He picked her up—another dumb move—and carried her to the bedroom, setting her down gently as if she'd break or he'd wake up and find it all a mirage.

It wasn't the same rough sex with Kristine because they were new to each other, and it was all discovery and little mistakes like a knee to the stomach that made him gasp and her laugh out loud. A kiss that missed its mark and hit teeth, a little clumsiness here or there that smoothed itself out as they touched and moved together or separated at arm's length to enjoy each other's body. Raimo thought he might have to do math problems in his head to keep from ejaculating prematurely. But they found the rhythm, at last, and it made for the exquisite pleasure nature intended.

It was slower the second time and when they both climaxed it was like falling from a great height and being pulled through the bed, bodiless wraiths, dropping through the mattress, into the floor, and floating downwards through Raimo's empty office and coming to rest on the wooden floors in each other's arms.

Later, she asked him if he thought she was "a horrible person."

"Why?"

"I just buried my husband and here I am in your bed," she said.

Raimo moved onto his elbow and put the palm of his hand gently over her mouth. He kissed the strands of hair at her temple, her ear, and then her cheek. They were both covered in a sheen of perspiration. Raimo had never felt this good, not in years, not ever.

"You're coming to the reunion tonight," she said simply.

"I think I'll pass," Raimo said. He was still wearing a goofy smile on his face. He didn't mind anymore if he looked and sounded like a teenager. Bliss makes its own rules.

"I want you there with me," she said.

"Then I'll go," he said. "I'll go with you if you insist and if you want to be seen with me."

He reached over and kissed her hand. That kiss led to another on her nipple and then he moved down her body to the spiky hairs of her pubic ruff and kissed her there and lower down until she made those same moaning sounds that throbbed in his inner ear in a better and more fulsome way than all the notes in Chopin's Etude in C Minor, which he remembered, smiling, was all about the fall of Warsaw.

Raimo Jarvi's fall, too, he thought happily.

She was beautiful. She made Raimo's heart sing watching her

move among the tables, talking and laughing with the classmates. She wore a bright print dress with pearls and sandals. Raimo thought of her breasts under the dress.

The reunion was a lite version of his brother's class from a couple weeks ago—same dim lighting, tables and set-up. Even the caterers were the same. Irene laughed and slapped him on the shoulder when he said her reunion committee had simply recycled his brother's reunion plastic cups and streamers.

"As a matter of fact, I did call Ginny Dyson when we were putting this together."

The music was different. Three years in rock music was a lifetime, like politics. *The Anthem*, *Hollaback Girl*, *Shape of My Heart*—Raimo recognized one or two.

"I'm sorry to tell you this. You're a failure at pop culture, Ray," she said. "Those are on every millennial's must-have mashups and mix tapes."

"A totally misspent youth," he said. "What's a mashup, by the way?"

"I believe it. I saw your book shelves. Sartre, Camus, Kierkegaard, Solzhenitsyn, Nietzsche. Am I saying those names the right way?"

"Right as rain, every syllable of every one nailed to perfection," Raimo said.

Peace, Albert, he thought. *You can be Cay-muss for just tonight.* He'd toss every book into the trash tomorrow if it subtracted an iota from the happiness he felt at that moment being near her.

"What's that song?"

"*Say It Right*," Irene said. "We did that today, didn't we? I mean, it was right between us, wasn't it? Not a mistake—"

"No, it wasn't a mistake," Raimo said. "I've never been happier."

Gushing again, the schoolboy back, all shiny and polished, Raimo Jarvi point two.

He smiled and had to restrain himself from touching her. He was afraid that, once she'd endured just so many condolences from well-meaning classmates, their spell would be broken and he'd lose her forever. It was like watching a magician spin plates on a stick.

He tuned in to hear her talking music with another male classmate who wandered over, a moth to her flame. He remembered him for the portraits he drew of him in study hall that he left behind for Raimo to find: a Frankenstein head without the bolts.

"Everybody knows the best music was produced between ninety-seven and two thousand-three, right, Ray?" she turned to him.

"I stand in awe of all tonight's music selections," he said.

She pinched his arm and waved at a couple entering the cafeteria.

She and the woman squealed at the sight of each other. Raimo beamed with pride as if she were his date, his woman.

Raimo watched her circulate, tried not to stare. A few of his former classmates acknowledged him. He had brief conversation with several who vaguely remembered him from their honors writing classes.

"Jarvi, holy shit."

"Hello, Arnie."

Raimo shook hands with Arnold Chismar and nodded to the wife standing beside him.

"Babe, this is Ray Jarvi."

Chismar agreed to take over as yearbook editor senior year when Raimo was told he'd have to attend the spring banquet and present certificates to his staff.

"I almost didn't recognize you," Arnie said. "For a minute, I thought you were your brother, the football player. You got big."

Arnold, on the other hand, had changed in the normal way for men fifteen years out of high school. Once an energetic and wise-cracking classmate who had no problem overlooking Raimo's appearance and wasn't ashamed to be seen with him in the cafeteria at lunch, he was jowly, pasty-faced, and three or four belt sizes bigger than when Raimo had last seen him at graduation.

Irene invited Raimo to sit with her at a table but he found excuses to avoid being seen too long in her company. He thought, if he could last another hour, he'd be able to leave without causing her concern. He watched the cafeteria fill up and observed some of the same antics and cliques he remembered and was uniformly ignored by. Raimo stayed near the drinks table and wandered into the hallway frequently as if fascinated by the trophies in the display case. The photos and letters from classmates who could not attend and teachers who had retired littered the tables, much as with Rikki's class. *Ritual, ceremony*, Raimo thought. *We move in the same circles, say the same things, do the same things . . .*

He was about to leave, confident Irene would be happy inside without him hanging around. If Bart could see him now, he'd accuse him of mopery with intention to gawk.

"Hey, Handsome," a voice called out. "Holy shit, is that you?"

Raimo had a frisson of irrational terror. He thought Tuomey was here.

He peered into the glass's reflection to see three men standing nearby off his right shoulder talking. None of them Tuomey. He recognized one right away, an obnoxious former jock named Jimmy Nazwisko, but the other two required a moment's more time to recall from memory cells. All three were basketball players. Nazwisko went out of his way to harass Raimo with sly remarks in class or the halls.

It was odd, too, because Naz had one of the worst cases of acne he ever saw. As he approached, Raimo saw the right side of Naz's face was dented with hollows left by the acne as if he'd taken a load of BB shot on that side of the head.

"I'm Ray, Jim, remember?" Raimo said.

Nazwisko had not gained any height but his mousy hair had thinned back to a combover look. He had once thrived on his status as an athlete. Raimo could not recall a girlfriend during their high school years despite the lewd commentary Naz inflicted on every attractive female in his classes. He thought for a time during their freshman year they might be friendly to each other, if not friends, as they shared a common schedule, and Naz was star-struck by Raimo's athletic brother. As the years passed, however, he turned on Raimo with a surliness and hostility that had no cause unless it lay in the fact that Naz was a starter on the basketball team and Raimo was lumped into another category altogether: he was an Untouchable.

"Hey, Handsome, how you doin'?"

Naz looked back to see if his two ex-teammates appreciated the show unfolding at Raimo's expense.

Raimo caught Irene coming into the hallway out of the corner of his eye.

"Hey gorgeous, look at you," Naz crooned. He embraced her with a bear hug that lifted her off her feet.

"I was just catching up with old Handsome here," Naz said to her.

"What—what did you call him?"

"Handsome. That's what we all called him, remember?"

That awful, ugly, shriveled-up feeling like vomit rising in his throat came welling back as if he had just come out of third period and bumped into Naz in the hallway, willing victim for his jibes.

"I don't believe you said that, James," she said.

She pulled away from Naz and cut her eyes to Raimo in a glance that scorched him to his soul. They watched her walk back into the cafeteria.

"What the hell's got into her?"

"She didn't like you calling me that name," Raimo said.

"Too fucking bad," Naz said.

He left Raimo there and started walking back to his friends.

Raimo hadn't moved a muscle the entire time he saw Irene approach. As soon as he saw her reenter the cafeteria, he walked over to the group and stood behind them. The incident forgotten, they were reliving some distant ballgame from their glory days. One of the men stopped talking when he noticed Raimo standing there. His face lit in that grimace Raimo had no trouble recognizing because he'd seen it on so many faces during those four years and after.

Naz turned around and sneered, "What are you looking at, Handsome?"

Ten thousand punches thrown at a heavy bag had given Raimo all he needed to throw a short right hook that traveled flush into the side of Naz's jaw and snapped his head back. Raimo never looked to see where Naz's body wound up because he was there and then he wasn't. Raimo found himself close enough to the classmate who had eye-fucked him in that way he hated, the way that made him feel disgusted with himself, a bug, not a person.

Raimo stared into his face very calmly the way he'd seen Rikki do whenever he got up from a tackle where an opponent played dirty, tried to gouge his eyes under his facemask. Rikki never had to say anything. He just looked at him that way.

Raimo chest-bumped the man out of his way and walked down the corridor.

His face burned with shame all the way to the door. He heard a commotion behind him, shouts. A woman's piercing shriek—*Nazwisko's wife, someone else, please God, not Irene, not her* . . .

Every heel-tap on the slick parquet floor told him he was a joke, unworthy of her, a vile, sucker-punching bully. The very thing he despised most in the world—what he had transformed himself into because of a rude, stupid comment from a man half his size.

Still the adolescent, his inner voice chided. *Always an adolescent. Go home, Ray Jarvi*, it said. *Run home, you slimeball coward piece of shit.*

He fired up the Wrangler, checked his face in the rearview mirror, the livid scar winding and twisting down the side like a lamprey with its sucker mouth. The throbbing in his hand was growing worse, maybe a fractured metacarpal in there behind the purpling of the knuckles.

All those hours, thousands of them confined to a bed where he could do nothing more active than hold a book up in front of his face and absorb wisdom—and what good did that do? Like a knife, a phrase whiplashed across his memory: "Those who prevail over their opponents do not get involved."

Even a centuries-dead Chinese general could scold from beyond the grave.

Chapter 20 – August 20

He awoke at five slapping at invisible flames on his chest. His eyes itched from a fretful sleep, disturbed by every sound including the air conditioner fighting its losing battle against the unrelenting heat. He threw open the window at a quarter to three and stared at the deserted street below.

No call from Irene all night. He picked up and put down his cell a dozen times, unsure what he'd say if she did answer. He cracked open the Laphroaig he'd bought for Rikki and downed a couple shots. Other than accelerating his body temperature to overdrive, he couldn't shake the feeling churning in his guts that he'd spoiled the one thing he should have preserved at all costs.

He made a call to West Hollywood Sheriff's asking to get a message for Det. Fanducci to call him back in the morning.

He took a shower and came out feeling better but the air in his apartment was already stuffy. He shut off both air conditioners and decided to endure the heat, a small punishment for last night.

The hammering at his back door made him jump and slop coffee on the floor. He fetched the gun and jacked the slide.

He undid the top chain lock and cracked the door a couple inches, gripping the butt and keeping a finger on the trigger guard.

A middle-aged man with a manila file folder and a nervous expression asked if he had time.

"Time for what?"

"My taxes," the man said. "Isn't this LaSalle's Accounting?"

"Take the next walkway over," Raimo said.

His heart pounded with relief. He felt like a lab rat in a maze with no escape door, no goal or reward for making the right turns. In his case, every turn was a potential catastrophe and he had himself to blame. He'd failed to get a lead on Rikki and knew he wasn't working as hard at that task as he should. Tuomey was out there plotting somewhere and he was likely to be under surveillance wherever he went. Nolan didn't trust him as far as he could throw him, and he expected cops with a warrant for assault to show up at his office any minute.

He made more coffee and laced it with whisky—just to take the edge off, he told himself. He might as well go downstairs to his office, defy any bugs Tuomey's men had planted, kill time, wait for the cops. All the moves he knew he should be making fell apart like a house of cards under strobe lighting. Until he knew where he stood with Irene, nothing else mattered and that thought scared him more than a little: he'd been shot at, witnessed two death scenes, been nearly thrown over the gulf in a flaming van, attacked by a thug big enough to eat apples off his head, and heard from Vandenhyden's own lips that his wife was murdered.

The street was busy with the boating crowd and shoppers milling on the sidewalks. He saw Bart leaving the diner at the end of the block, running at a good clip to avoid traffic. The pedestrian walkways that the merchants' association demanded from the city worked like Russian roulette. Raimo stopped in case Bart looked his way but he didn't.

He unlocked the office and pushed the heavy door open with his foot. He exhaled slowly, gripped the automatic beneath the folded paper in case Tuomey had another surprise waiting for him inside. He remembered Bart's FBI man telling him PI work was boring, just skip-trace jobs, chasing runaways to Florida, and tracking deadbeat dads. "All that lethality," he told Raimo, "was TV stuff." Now, Raimo wondered if he could get through the month.

Nothing. Stale air, sunshine streaming through the plate

glass, refracting into fat columns of drifting motes.

He tossed the paper on the desk and flipped the a/c knob to high.

He booted up his computer and shoved the paper aside when some words struck him: *Body Found in Lake Cottage.*

What about the body found *in* the lake? Raimo wondered.

The details were skimpy but the on-scene detective did not think "foul play" at this time. "We're investigating all leads," said Lieutenant Gary Bryce from the Jefferson Sheriff's. The victim, a young male in his twenties, had not yet been identified. Bart Massey told him Bryce wouldn't recognize a fight if it broke out in the back seat of his cruiser.

The brief article at the bottom of the page, a trio of skinny columns squeezed between the obits and the index, did surprise him. *Man Found Dead in Apartment.*

Leotis Pennimann had hanged himself in his shower with his belt. The suicide letter was folded inside an envelope and *Nisha* written on it. Leotis pinned it to his shirt pocket before he stepped into the shower, fully dressed, and looped a leather cord around the shower head. Neighbors were called because of the odor of decomp. Raimo got as far as "believed estranged from his wife" and stopped reading. He paid his debt to Raimo and killed himself.

Raimo was caught in his stupor by the Bridge Street drunk. Raimo looked up and saw him staring at him through the window.

Before he knew what he was doing, he bolted from his desk and flung open the door.

"What are you looking at?"

"It's coming tomorrow," the old man said. "The Path! . . . Of! . . . To-tal-ity!"

Path of totality? Then it clicked: the solar eclipse. Northtown swathed in darkness. Why not?

"All dark . . . end of time. . . Northtown . . . extinguished, over, *kaput.*"

He stuck his tongue out and blew raspberries at the window, a toddler discovering pleasure with his mouth.

"What the hell are you talking about? Get the fuck away from my glass!"

"The path of totality," the drunk repeated.

"You'd better fuck off, old man, or—"

Hadn't he just put on the sack cloth and ashes for bullying a man? Now he was at it again. Maybe he'd never learn to be a decent human being.

"Sorry," Raimo said. "Thank you. For reminding me."

Softer, thinking of his father's heavier drinking toward the end, before alcoholism itself couldn't compete with the ravages of dementia. "You're blitzed, old timer. You should go home now."

"Shouldn't talk to me. . . like I'm a child," he said. He shook a fist at Raimo. "Going home . . . home," the old man said.

"Good, you should go home. Wait for the end," Raimo said. He watched him stagger off, impossibly drunk in the morning heat and weaving like a man who kept bumping into a wall next to him.

The solar eclipse. He'd forgotten all about it. Northtown was due for a treat: a hundred-mile-wide black arrow crawling across the continent. It would dip from Oregon, swath Pelee Island in its path, black out Northtown county and cut across Lake Ontario on its way to the St. Lawrence Seaway and the Atlantic Ocean beyond. A darkness so primitive it was visceral, atavistic, that only those between the Moon's umbra and penumbra would experience. It was a chance to feel what our earliest ancestors felt like when they used to paint their faces blue and bark at the moon.

Raimo watched the old man stumble on in his zigzag fashion until he disappeared up Bridge Street.

Maybe he is Ezekiel, Raimo thought. *Come back to earth. Warning us. He's been warning me all along what was coming.*

Things are never that simple. Think of a burning match. The match head comprises antimony trisulfide and sulfur as fuel and is ignited by a mix of chemicals such as red phosphorous, powdered glass, a binder, neutralizer, a small amount of carbon black and potassium perchlorate. The head oxidizes rapidly, red phosphorous becomes white phosphorous and reacts with the perchlorate to create heat and ignite the trisulfide and the sulfur; then the resulting flame burns through the wood treated with ammonium phosphate. Then consider the flame's yellow and blue color. That's a separate study in convection, combustion, heat gradients, and the concept of black bodies, that exist only as an ideal, not in reality. The human body, for example, emits warmth from infrared radiation we cannot see with our eyes.

Raimo had studied the physics of fire when he realized he was going overboard with his phobia, waking up with nightmares of burning, running from his house in the middle of the night, as if everything in it was lying in wait to self-ignite in a perfect storm of chemicals to create the all-consuming holocaust that would burn everything in the world.

Maybe for opposite reasons he had found safety in water. As soon as he was able, he learned to swim. The deeper the water, the better. On a dare from his friend Tony Kantorak, he swam out into Lake Erie from the breakwall one summer day like this and didn't look back until the breakwall was a bump with stick figures on top. The water turned rough, lake chop, the kind that made summer sailors sea sick. He kept treading, not ready to swim in, even though he could see Tony hopping up and down on the wall waving frantically to him.

He stopped treading and looked over his shoulder at the cobalt sky in the north and the massive thunderheads boiling up from Canada. By the time he was within shouting distance, the waves had heightened from wind shear and the sudden drop in pressure. Lightning forked crazily against the black curtain of sky. Rain pelted him so hard he thought he was breathing water; white caps broke over his back and submerged him a couple times. Once he made it to the rock, he could not hear Tony screaming at him from above *to get back, hurry up, let's go!* He threw up some water, climbed up to the top, and laughed at his adventure. Tony's eyes bugged in his head, rain poured down his hair flattening it around his ears like a sleek fur hat. After the fire, water and rain were nothing to him.

His haul from Mikel's pockets was a bonanza. He sorted and lined up the items on his counter top. A traveling man's essentials: cell phone, key ring, money clip, a notebook and pen, Bic, penlight, Swiss knife, flask, half-empty baggie of marijuana wrapped inside a Mighty Black Sabbath Motorcycle Club patch, nail clippers, and a triple pack of Trojans. The name on his California driver's license was Mikel Charles Moore. The last number in the waterlogged notebook, barely discernible, was Tuomey's condo number. Below it, he could make out the faint outline of some words or abbreviations:

Ex Chart Ex

War – Yng

08/20

It took a few minutes playing at the computer before he had it: Exclusive Executive Charter Flights, out of Louisville, Kentucky, Warren-Youngstown airport. Tomorrow.

The airport was in Trumbull County on Kings Grave Road, fifty miles south on Route 11. He checked out the website. It offered a variety of exclusive jets for the busy executive who preferred the comforts of flying in a private plane. The headquarters promised to put a plane at your disposal anywhere in the country and would cater to your tastes in food, wine, and other "creature comforts." It had to be extremely expensive and far beyond typical business travelers. No prices listed on the website but were "negotiable on contact."

Raimo tossed condoms, flask, and everything that could hold a fingerprint into a paper bag and shoved it behind some cans in the pantry. The rest except for the smudged notebook went into the trash. He counted the money: $6,000, mostly in hundreds. He separated the bills on the counter so they could dry out. The notebook was mostly illegible, but he could make out parts of phone numbers and area codes for other states.

Three were numbers for Indiana, the Indianapolis code. One was Pennsylvania, the Erie area, and another dozen were

California numbers for Los Angeles with street names, like "Popcorn" and "Cake," sounding more like confections in a vending machine than names for people. Four turned out to be for prisons: Corcoran, Folsom, Pelican Bay, and a final number for the ADX in Florence, Colorado, the male supermax. Friends in low places.

One was pure gold: D. C. and a Los Angeles number that Raimo had called before: Darlene Cook, the buxom blonde owner of several rental properties and a bar in West Hollywood that burned down under suspicious circumstances.

The phone, however, was useless. It must have cracked while Raimo was lugging him up onto the rocks. He took out the SIM card and tossed the plastic shell into the basket.

He took a chance and called Irene's cell but it went straight to voicemail. He asked her to call him "as soon as she had the time. . . please, Irene." The whiny, insecure boy back in the citadel. He craved her touch, her scent, the tenderness he thought was always beyond reach. The uncertainty was a madness storming around in his mind.

He called Northtown General and asked about "the status of Mikel Moore."

"We have no one by that name, sir?"

"He's the drowning victim. He was brought in two days earlier."

Raimo wondered, with all the violent deaths and OD's happening around town nowadays, if that was enough information.

He was put through to ICU and was told the patient *Charles* Moore was listed in stable condition.

"Will Mister Moore be able to make his flight this afternoon?" Raimo asked. "I'm calling from Exclusive Charters. He's scheduled to fly out today."

She told him pneumonia from the water he'd taken into his lungs was still a danger but he was being prepped for a lifeflight to St. Elizabeth's."

"Nurse, who gave the order for that transfer?"

"That's confidential hospital procedure, sir," she said.

"Can you tell me if that's routine procedure?"

"We don't have information on Mister Moore. Would you be willing to provide us—"

He broke the connection.

Tuomey pulling strings to get his thug out of town.

Before he left his office, he made a call to Gerrard Pharmacies, asking to speak to "anyone in HR."

"Hiroshi Teshigahara, speaking."

"Sir, hello, my name is Garvey. I've worked for Pfizer for fifteen years and I learned yesterday I'm being transferred to North Dakota. I've already had my share of snow squalls living in Indiana, ha-ha, and I was wondering if Gerrard's has an opening for an experienced drug representative with fifteen years' experience."

A long pause. Finally, Teshigahara broke the silence. "Right now, we're on a hiring freeze."

"Oh dear, I'm sorry to hear that. Business downturns happen to us, too. I'd heard such good things about Gerrard on the road."

A longer pause. "You have?"

"You know, we drug reps meet up on the road, friendly conference chat, ha-ha."

"Actually, we're doing extraordinarily . . . fine," Teshigahara said. "We are reorganizing at this point in time and we are—who did you say this is?"

Raimo hung up. No fishing with this guy. He picked words like a jeweler looking at facets through a loupe.

The SUV behind him had tinted windows and out-of-state tags. Raimo figured he'd acquired a tail and there was little he could do about it. He was pushing luck in all four corners but impersonating someone over the phone wasn't a worry compared to everything else. Cops lie all the time, Bart used to tell him. It's legal. Private eyes don't get that privilege.

The Lake was jammed with people. He'd never seen anything like it. Traffic was stalled on the Strip before he made the turn from Lake Road. The lake was packed with wind surfers, jet ski riders, and multitudes of charter boats as well as recreational vehicles. People were celebrating the sun instead of complaining about it. Or maybe it was tomorrow's eclipse.

It took him twenty-five minutes to make the turn to Edgardo's cottages. He couldn't see the dark SUV behind him in the crush of traffic.

He drove past the cottage with the crime tape, noting its droop across the front as if the heat were affecting inanimate things too. He parked and kept his shades on. He couldn't tell if the other cottages were occupied. He saw no cars parked nearby.

He took out Mikel's key ring and went through each key until he heard the familiar click.

Inside, the air was fuggy like rotting fruit, but the cottage was clean. All the furniture was missing. The rope was gone. Police dealing with hanging victims ordered forensics people to take sections of the rope in case the knots turned up in other crimes.

The floor had been polished to a waxy shine. The stainless-steel refrigerator was left in place but emptied out. He walked behind the wall to the single bedroom identical to the one in Tuomey's sex film. No bed or furniture; it was pristine, undisturbed. A wooden blind was pulled down over the window.

Raimo headed up the loft stairs. Everything was packed up in cardboard boxes. The laundry and clothes bags were lined up and looked untouched. The CD stands were in one box and the disks in another, all tossed together. He found some porno DVDs with titles like *Poker Her Face* and *Cum-Swapping Sluts*. The music CDs were all rap or hip-hop—Chris Brown, Bruno Mars, other names he didn't recognize.

Some disk covers showed numbered song titles on the front of the cheap vinyl holders written in blue ink on white unlined paper in a small, neat, precise handwriting. He recognized some names: Keely Smith, Betty Hutton, Kay Starr, Lena Horne, and Martha Tilton. Oldies from the fifties, a post-swing-band America growing up fast in the Eisenhower years. His parents loved that music.

He couldn't see Poken Beans listening to this saccharine music. Rikki used to curse and leave the room whenever his mother or father put in a CD and their parents danced to Nancy Wilson's "My One and Only Love" or Dinah Shore's "Love Is Here to Stay." The disks inside the holders weren't Read-Write but DVDs. He gathered these and left, thinking of Mikel ransacking the loft, looking at the covers and tossing them aside.

No sign of the SUV with the tinted windows. The sweat dripped from his face and neck, his skin itched all the way back to the harbor.

He parked in back behind his apartment walkway. He strolled down to check the office for any sign of entry, resorting to the John le Carré trick of sticking a wedge in the door, which was intact where he jammed it.

Upstairs, he stripped off his shirt, pulling the scab free again. Still crusty with dried blood but no sign of pus. He was lucky considering what was floating in Lake Erie nowadays. He took his assortment of disks into the bedroom where his laptop was and inserted one into the tray. More sexual rendezvous by Tuomey and company. The girls varied in age and look—some could have been runaways from out of state. Julie DeMarest was the staple, however, in every scene; she was a voracious lover of Tuomey and the other girls or women. No more Dino Caddio. Or Rikki, which fact eased the knot in his shoulders.

No talk except for love moans and the uttered commands of Tuomey, sexual ringmaster. The camera at the foot of the bed filmed everything, unaware of that fact.

He fast-forwarded to the end. Another disk, the same results except that the action was restricted to Julie and Tuomey. He sped the film even faster, assuming Tuomey would not talk murder or conspiracy with her in the throes of their energetic humping.

Two more DVDs followed the same route as the others.

Sometimes different couples, attractive people in their thirties and forties, enjoyed swapping mates. Brian, the gracious host, invariably undressed last once the action commenced, choreographer and sexual glutton all in one.

He put in the last disk, shut off the sound and went to make a drink. What the hell, he might as well start early like the rest of Northtown. Raimo's mouth tasted of ash. Watching the antics on his bedroom screen was anything but prurient.

A knock at the door.

Irene. Dressed in a bone-white blouse and short navy-blue skirt. Hair fixed in French twist behind her and her face made up with an expert touch of cosmetics and sheer natural beauty.

She rushed into his arms and they kissed. He forgot about the drink and it hit the floor slopping gin over their shoes. Irene pulled away and laughed. She grabbed his hand and turned it over.

"It looks painful," she said.

"It is," Raimo said. "I should have kicked him instead."

"You're lucky we're not greeting between a sheet of plexiglass," she said. "Everybody wanted Naz to file charges. His jaw's badly swollen. It looks like he tried to swallow a balloon."

"I'll call him and apologize," he said. "I'll even let him take a swing at me if you'll forgive me."

"There's nothing to forgive, Ray. I'm on a mission of mercy here. I want to check your back and make sure it isn't getting infected."

"Not a bad idea, come to think of it," Raimo said. He'd had to peel shirts off the scabs every time he came home to change or shower.

"Let me get my stuff out of my purse. I'll need your bathroom again. Take off your shirt while I'm gone," she said. Ray caught her sweet smile flashed back to him. "This might get messy."

She stepped into the bathroom and shut the door. Raimo felt a rush of erotic bliss overwhelm his senses. Blood went south as if it had a separate command from his brain. From the verge of despair to a rocket blast to the moon. He was dumbstruck with happiness.

Then he remembered—*the DVD's still playing in the bedroom.*

He tiptoed past the bathroom door and reached for the laptop.

That's when he froze. An image pounded him into the floor. He was lead. From tumescence to zero in a heartbeat. Irene was performing fellatio on Brian Tuomey. Julie DeMarest leaned over her back, cupping one breast and kissing her neck. Julie stroked her back and reached to take his swollen penis out of Irene's mouth and put it into hers.

No, no, no, nonono—

Raimo reached out to steady himself against the dresser. He had to sit down on the bed or his legs would give in. Too stunned to reach out his hand to slam the laptop's cover down. He felt nauseated, as if the bile lumped in his throat was forcing its way up his esophagus. Veins pounded with blood in his forehead.

He felt a firm hand clamp his shoulder. Involuntarily, he swung around, startled, as if Irene's touch had come out of the screen and lacerated him with white-hot fingers.

His eyes flooded over with tears. She stood there silent, looking down, and then took a drunken step backward.

He saw it in slow-motion. A syringe dropped from her left hand so slowly Raimo could track its fall with his eyes and brain. It was like having the photographic capacity of a fly's brain. Then he saw what she looked at: a dot of ruby blood popped on her inside wrist.

"Oh God," she said. "Oh God, no."

Raimo, still sitting. His brain tried to put the pieces of the garbled scene together and failed. He watched her stagger back to the living room, touching the walls as if she'd drunk the whisky in the bathroom in a matter of seconds and come out intoxicated. It made no sense.

She looked at him from ten feet distant, her mouth opened and worked to form words but no words came out. Her face had gone leprous-white. With a loud moan, she dropped to the floor before Raimo could propel himself off the bed to reach her.

He cradled her head until she came to. Her eyes blinked several times but not at him, trying to take in whatever was storming inside her. When she could sit up, he left her to get a wash cloth for her face. He soaked it under the faucet.

"This is cold water," he said. "It'll help."

Irene's laugh was an eerie ripple in the air that gave him gooseflesh. Her legs were splayed, one sandal off, the other hanging from her toes. She scooted around on her rump to face him; the skirt rode up her thighs, exposing her, and he glimpsed she was naked underneath.

She laughed again but it came out a sob. "It'll help . . ." she repeated dully.

Raimo was panicking. She'd seen him watching the film. There had to be an explanation.

But his mind told him that wasn't it—

When it clicked, it was like a punch.

Not the film. Not the film, he realized. *The needle.*

He watched her back standing at his sink pouring the half-bottle of gin over the puncture. She threw open his cupboards looking for more alcohol to pour. She ran past him to the bathroom and opened the medicine cabinet. She knocked his and Rikki's prescription bottles to the floor, cursing, found a bottle of rubbing alcohol and doused her wrists and arm with it. She was crazed, a woman possessed by a terrible fear.

"What—what's it got?" Raimo asked her when she calmed down.

Her hazel irises, so quick to shift in light, were thick with color, yellow now, a malaria victim's.

"AIDS," she said, her tongue thick, barely getting it out.

Her laugh this time was full of bitterness and ended on a shrill note of despair.

"He kept saying you had more lives than a fucking cat," she said in a low, anguished voice.

He looked over to where the syringe lay on the floor. Such a small thing. Julie could easily have obtained it in the hospital.

A little thing with an adder's bite at the tip.

"How long have you and Brian—"

"Oh fuck, Ray, does it really matter now?" Exasperated, her eyes zeroed on him like a target.

"It matters—to me," he said quietly.

She went back to the chair. Placed her hand on the arm rest and slowly, like an 80-year-old, reversed her body into it.

"I have to sit. My legs won't work."

Raimo said nothing. He stood near her and waited for the rest of it.

"Help me up, please," she said.

He caught her under the arms just as she was about to fall again. He led her to the lounge chair in the middle of the room.

"Can I get you something to drink?"

"Whisky, if you have it, not beer, please."

So polite. 'Hello, Irene, how are you, would you like a drink?' Never mind the needle on the floor over there you just tried to destroy me with. Courteous acquaintances.

In fits and starts, between bouts of crying and softer whimpering and wiping mascara that smeared worse despite the towels Raimo fetched, she told him.

Rikki was involved in part of it.

"It was the one time, the only time," Irene said. "I had a goody-goody reputation but I wasn't what people thought. I was more careful than most girls, that's all. Don't look so. . . forlorn, Ray. Girls like sex, too."

"Sorry, I didn't mean—"

"Ray, shut up. I tried to kill you and *you're apologizing to me.* Just shut up."

She was double-dating with his brother, Brian and another girl from the public high school. She couldn't remember the other girl's name. Raimo doubted Tuomey would either. Irene said they'd gone down to a spot at Lake Shore Park where the kids often went to drink, do drugs, or neck. A few "went all the way," in that quaint euphemism. The township was in a legal dispute with the city and didn't want to pay for cruisers to patrol, so for a time, it was considered a safe place to go and be undisturbed.

"Brian was having sex with the girl in the back," she said. "Rikki and I were up front. The girl's head was all the way in Brian's lap and he was pressing down on the back of her head. I watched his eyes because I was facing the back seat."

She'd had sex twice before with a couple boys from their class but didn't have an orgasm, thought the whole thing was overrated by pop culture until that night with Rikki when she sat astride his brother and he penetrated her harder and longer than the previous dates. She enjoyed her first orgasm, but it was while she was staring at Brian getting oral sex from the girl that their eyes locked. Unashamed, feeling those waves build inside her, she stared—and he smiled at her.

"I was a freshman," she said. "Those guys were seniors. The big men on campus. You know how that goes."

"Yes," Raimo said, "I do."

He didn't want her to involve him in her narrative but he had to hear it all.

"It was so. . . erotic," Irene said. They were secret lovers from then on, but she had to be careful for his sake. Her parents would go to the police if they suspected and have him charged with statutory rape.

Years passed, she started dating Dino at Brian's suggestion. It was a lucky decision, it turned out, because she would get pregnant by Brian years later and Dino was there to fill in when she started to show.

"Did he know?"

Raimo recalled the slender, blondish girl with Irene's features playing with dolls and her coloring book on the floor. Dino was a swarthy Sicilian-American.

"No, he was convinced she was his," Irene said. "He couldn't see past his drug use and Cassie's autism."

Raimo doubted that was all there was to Dino's erratic behavior at the end, especially with Tuomey pulling the strings.

"Did Dino say anything . . . about the plane?"

"Don't ask me that. My husband's in the grave now."

"Brian told him the president would be alone," Raimo prodded.

"I don't know what Brian told Dino about anything," she said, as if it didn't matter.

"Six people died in that crash, Irene," he said.

"Fix me another drink, please," she said.

Raimo made it and brought it to her, careful not to let her touch him.

"I'm not contagious yet," she said. "You don't have to be afraid."

"It's not that," Raimo said.

"What is it then? The fact Julie DeMarest and I were having sex with Brian together and alone?"

"Julie got possessive," Raimo guessed.

"Stupid bitch with her big tits and that silly giggle," Irene said. "Brian didn't love her, never loved her, not like he did me. He used her. She was helping him with the company."

Julie's hysteria at the blue house meant more than shock at seeing Dino in the upstairs bedroom. She thought she was fetching Raimo so he could be implicated in Dino's death. He sent Mikel to do the same with Alarcón's phony suicide once he'd learned about the sex disks. He must have followed him to the bar or tapped his office phone. But it never occurred to Julie until the moment she returned with him that Brian was throwing her to the wolves along with him. She knew then he'd chosen Irene over her. Hers was the only real suicide of the three.

"Is it done? Does Brian control the company?"

"It's supposed to be. . . happening now. We were going to drive to Columbus right after—"

—after you stuck a virus-tainted needle in me.

"How much will Brian make from it?"

"He said—God, why am I—maybe I owe you this. He's in for twenty-one percent. Enright will get twenty-nine, he's putting up most of the money. Or his wife is, at any rate. The rest will go up for sale when the drug they're working on comes through."

As if she felt the weight of her dream crashing around her, she put her hands over her ears and sobbed. She gulped the last of her drink. Her eyes had dulled to brown mustard.

"What now?" Raimo asked her.

"I don't know," she said.

"Why bother with me at all?"

"He thought Rick might have told you enough to make you a problem when he made his move on the company. If you were following Dino, we could keep an eye on you. Brian doesn't like people beating him. He doesn't let go. Don't you know that by now?"

"People get stuck in him like flypaper and then—does Brian know where Rikki is?"

"No, I don't know. Don't look so sad, Ray. You were in the way, that's all. Nothing personal."

"Brian's idea, wasn't it?"

"You mean the needle? We thought it would preoccupy you with something besides him."

It would have worked.

"Are you going to keep me here?"

"No, Irene, you're free to go."

"Thank you, Ray."

He helped her out of the chair and she stumbled to the door, legs not yet working, and left without turning around.

Raimo stared at the door. The room was changed, he was changed. He didn't know how he felt and that, all things considering, was all right for the time being. But he also knew it wouldn't last and when the full knowledge of her treachery hit him, it would bite with a deeper, lacerating pain than he wanted to shoulder at the moment. When it came, that would be a howling hurt, as the mystic poet Rumi called it.

Chapter 21 – August 21

Bart called with news. "You didn't get this from me. Nolan said the state executor appointed for Gerrard's estate filed an injunction to halt the takeover as soon as the lawyers filed in probate."

"I thought you were keeping a low profile around headquarters," Raimo said.

"You stirred up the pot, man. Lots of people are putting their heads together. The main reason is Nolan stopped using your name as a spittoon."

NOAA was sending a deep-sea research vessel in to hunt for more pieces of the plane. All the human remains possible to collect seem to have washed ashore by this time.

He'd asked about the Edgardo Alarcón investigation. Bart mentioned it could be "folded in" later but right now they were leaving it at sexual asphyxia. DEA, FBI, BCI, and Highway Patrol all had one member on the new task force.

Raimo was relieved that something had been working in the background while he was being followed, chased, thumped about and threatened around Northtown. He'd kept what happened with Irene a secret. Why not one big one to take to his grave? Justice came in other forms than through lawyers. For sorehead prophets, only Isaiah could top Ezekiel: *No one enters suit justly; no one goes to law honestly; they rely on empty pleas, they speak lies, they conceive mischief and give birth to iniquity.*

Irene's motives he could understand but not forgive. She wanted out of her marriage to Caddio, the old-fashioned word *beard* struck him as right—wanted to go off with Brian Tuomey and his money, live on some Caribbean island paradise. Or was that his own secret dream with her?

Rikki was his focus now. He had to concentrate on that. Let the government investigators do their jobs. He wasn't paid to be a bullet catcher. In fact, he wasn't paid, period. He'd mailed an anonymous donation of the six-grand swag from Mikel's wallet to Doctors Without Borders. Dirty money, a clean cause. That was the way of the world.

Ezekiel ran past his plate glass, shaggy hair tied off in a neat ponytail bouncing at his back as he ran, shouting, "It's here! It's here!"

Raimo thought he sounded sober, for once.

Twenty-eight days of sun-scorched pummeling were going to be interrupted by the coming solar eclipse.

Raimo left his office unlocked and ran for his jeep. He hopped in and gunned it for Walnut Beach.

The breakwall was lined with people, all kinds of people—young and old, blacks, whites, and Hispanics. Some alone, most with families. Couples clutched each other, all waiting for the big show in the heavens.

He parked between a Harley and a Jetta and made his way through the crowds to the wall. People came with a variety of devices for viewing the eclipse; some even held welder's glass in their hands. Others had homemade cartons with mirrors. Most had the rectangular eclipse shades being sold or handed out all over Northtown. Everyone, regardless, had sunglasses.

He climbed up and headed down the line of people to find an isolated slab of his own.

The water smelled the same, an olfactory potion of fresh oxygen tinged with putrefaction. Life and death. The crowd noise swelled as soon as the orbital plane of the moon intersected with the sun. A puny thing, the moon. Yet it could block out the sun. Soon the umbra would come, that dark cone of black stretching a tiny path of total darkness across the earth's surface. A happy accident four billion years in the making that would favor those in its sweeping path across the earth and extend to these Northtown citizens a seven-minute experience they'd likely never have again.

Raimo glanced up every so often to check the moon's progress. People behind the breakwall and on the distant beach surged forward toward the water as if a few more feet made any difference to the celestial mechanics above.

Raimo, no longer the bedridden bookworm of his youth, felt a tenderness for all people at the moment of the sun's complete display of its malevolent corona. He knew *eclipse* came from e*kleipsis*, meaning "abandoned." The Greek poet Archilochus wrote about this darkness-at-noon moment in a fragment he'd committed to memory as a boy for whom beautiful thoughts and words in books had replaced ugly reality: *Nothing there is beyond hope/nothing that can be sworn impossible,/ nothing wonderful, since Zeus/father of the Olympians, made night from midday, /hiding the light of the shining sun, and sore fear came upon men.*

Hope and fear. That's all we have, Raimo knew. He climbed down from the rocks.

EPILOGUE

August 22nd once meant something in the Persian world. It was the date the last Imam disappeared and was also the date he would reappear. That was in 1187 when Saladdin conquered Jerusalem.

Flash-forward to the present and Raimo Jarvi, a nobody from the a nothing state in the Midwest, was waiting to get off a plane in LAX along with 178 others aboard, all trying to disentangle their luggage from the overhead compartment at the same time.

It had been a rough flight with turbulence most of the way and children crying. The people around him kept up moronic conversations in relays: first the young couple behind him, then the middle-aged couple in the aisle opposite. A businessman in front of him talked nonstop to the young woman beside him about IPO offerings for several new tech companies in Silicon Valley. The young bearded guy in his row at the window seat kept his earbuds in the entire flight bobbing his head to the music. Raimo sensed the man beside him, a cosmetic surgeon, was itching to talk to him about his scars, but Raimo refused to send any signal he wanted to discuss that or anything. Airplanes were torture. Aside from being jolted up, down and sideways by G-forces, the sardine-packing of passengers, the recirculated air that transferred billions of microbes from the front to tail, there was the incessant pressure in his head aggravated by the passing stares of people boarding and deplaning. He had one thing going for him and that was his innate ability to remain still, be silent, hide within. Wandering talk closes the information flow, but then again, he *was* en route to Hollywood, a city like no other.

He told his Uber driver to take him to West Hollywood Sheriff's.

"Good flight?"

"Fine," Raimo said.

He was thinking the Prophet Mohammad must have had an easier flight when the angel Jibreel scooped him up in Mecca and dumped him at the mosque in Jerusalem on the Night Journey.

"Fuckin' something, huh?"

"What?"

"That solar eclipse yesterday," the driver said.

"Yes, something."

Detective Miles Fanducci was a short, stocky man with long arms and ginger hair that had to be pasted down but managed to stick up all over his head. He was far from the dapper detective Raimo had imagined on the phone from the cop's precise and polished speech. Instead, he found this pleasant, beefy orangutan in a blue blazer and rumpled beige khakis. The striped cream tie with its tiny, short-barreled revolvers all over it was not a *faux pas* but a happy statement of cop fashion.

"Thanks for being helpful, Detective," Raimo said after they'd been introduced.

The detective took him to his desk and offered him coffee. Fanducci told him the arson investigation was still open. He'd appreciate Raimo bringing his brother in "for an interview, not an interrogation," if he located him. It was a gracious way of introducing the *quid pro quo* for his help and time on the phone. Raimo gave him the vital stats and an abridged version of Mikel Moore's abbreviated career in Northtown along with the notebook.

"We were thinking there was more than a case of Jewish lightning here for the insurance," Fanducci said with a wink. "I'm Jewish, by the way, so don't get your Midwestern knickers in a twist."

"I thought you Californians were the politically correct ones," Raimo said.

He thought he should bring Bart out for a lesson in cop courtesy. Bart was reprimanded for telling one drunk in the back of his cruiser "to shut the fuck up" when he claimed to be attacked inside by a man who tried to bite his nose off.

Bart admitted to driving Rikki from his place to Cleveland-Hopkins when Raimo called him last night while packing for his flight.

"How'd you know it was me?"

"I'm a private investigator," Raimo said.

The lonely Winston butt in the ashtray piled up with Rikki's Marlboros told him as good as a signed note.

"He told me not to tell you," he replied, which was all the apology he knew he'd ever get from Bart Massey.

Fanducci gave him a list of homeless shelters, men's shelters in West and North Hollywood, several nearby drug rehab centers, halfway houses, rescue missions, supportive centers, transitional houses, day-only shelters, LGBT shelters, emergency shelters for homeless families, and non-profit centers and peer-counseling places for Jews, Hispanics, Pacific Asians, and everyone else between the lost residents of Easter Island and aging, unreconstructed hippies. California was inclusive if it was anything.

"I put them in a best-to-worst ranking to save you some time," Fanducci said.

"Best?"

"Best odds," the detective replied, "if I was your brother, and I wanted to stay off the grid. Of course, there's Weingart on San Pedro downtown, if all else fails," Fanducci told him, meaning LA's infamous Skid Row.

He handed Raimo his card and wished him good luck. "You got one thing going for you," the cop said. "Your brother's walking around with casts on his arm and leg. Somebody should remember seeing him."

He folded up the paper and Fanducci told him he'd have

to make a call for a ride from the pay phone in the lobby.

"Hello," a rough-timbred female voice responded.

Raimo hung up. At least he knew where to locate Darlene Cook.

Raimo's motel had a neon sign with an orange-and-blue parrot in a palm tree and offered free X-rated movies. He spent a couple hours calling the nearest men's shelters and hit paydirt, albeit several places had provided beds for men with casts. The homeless were prone to more broken bones and assaults than squarejohn citizens. But the description confirmed it was either Rikki Jarvi or he had a *doppelgänger* running around town with him.

He took an Uber car to the shelter and learned that Rikki had not been there in a week but the man identified "absolutely" his brother from a photo Raimo showed him.

"He didn't say much, and he looked like he was in pain, but we don't allow no drugs in here unless they're prescribed, and he didn't have anything like that."

Raimo left him some Xeroxed photos with his cell number. He checked on three more places but came up empty.

Back in his motel, he ate fast food from a nearby Taco Bell and mixed a Tom Collins from a package and a bottle of Seagram's extra dry he bought at the liquor store across the street. The manager in the lobby warned him it was "a tranny hangout" at night. "Some of those bitches will skin you alive, some will blow you away," he said. He hesitated and looked flustered once he caught sight of Raimo's face.

"I didn't mean—"

"No problem," Raimo said.

He found the heat less brutal than back home. The late afternoon sun had dimmed to a golden yellow and his room was cool and the sheets were clean. He pulled the shades and thought of Irene, not anything she said, just the image of her sitting on his floor with tears flowing down her face. She was right to despise him; he was weak. She'd tried to give him a slow death yet he wanted to comfort her. The same warped thinking that kept him chained to Kristine Radebaugh.

He slept for a couple hours and woke with a headache.

He called more shelters farther out on the radius Fanducci had given him. He didn't want to make the amateur's mistake of running around without enough information or a clear direction, but he felt the walls closing in on him and he wanted to be out in the air.

He noted the transvestite gathering at the liquor store parking lot and loped across the street. *Why not?*

One six-foot woman with a black wig and loop earrings smiled at him. She wore a thigh-length miniskirt and black laced boots. Her carmine lips were outlined in the same black as an eyeliner pencil.

"Hey, honey, looking for a date? I'm Miranda Lopez. That's Yolanda Lopez, my sister, and over there's Tina and Salma, cousins, and Tiajuna there is the one with the big booty standing by Dremel, who thinks he's not a pimp."

Miranda and Yolanda Lopez.

Miranda studied the picture of Rikki for a long time before returning it.

"No, I haven't seen him. Good looking dude, though. What the fuck happened to you, honey?"

"Playing with matches," Raimo replied. "I burned the house down around me."

"Well, fuck me, where are you from, sweetie? That accent is a-tro-*shush*."

"Ohio," Raimo said. "Can you help me?"

"Maybe, I don't know," Miranda said. "Girls, yoo-hoo, over here. Look what I got."

Miranda Lopez was no more Hispanic than he was.

A prostitute and a man who might have been her pimp walked casually over. Both eyed Raimo as if they might be smelling a vice cop.

"I'm looking for my brother," Raimo said.

"You seen this guy around, Yolanda?" Miranda appeared over Raimo's shoulder.

"Shit, why you askin' my woman, bitch?"

"He's looking for his brother, Dremel. Maybe she can help.

It's not like she's *busy* right now."

"I'll busy you with my foot up your big ass," the man said. He glared at Raimo.

Raimo was tonight's entertainment, a hick from Ohio. He stepped into their midst and held up his Xeroxed photos. "I'm offering a reward for information. Five hundred dollars, no questions asked. Call me. I'm in that motel across the street."

He handed out the flyers to each girl and woman. The pimp looked at his, wadded it up and threw it across the parking lot into the gutter.

"I seen him," a voice called out from the edge of the crowd.

A girl who looked sixteen. She didn't have the make-up or the cosmetic flourish of the others, and she lacked that hardboiled look of a street runaway. As she got closer, Raimo noticed the telltale flecks of gold paint in both nostrils, a huffer. Aside from the greasy hair and the dirt under her fingernails, she was pretty.

"He was getting out of a taxi on Sepulveda this morning."

"This man?" Raimo held the photo out and watched her eyes.

"Yeah, he had crutches but that's him."

"Did you see where he went?"

"I think he went into the men's shelter down there."

Raimo checked Fanducci's list and found one on Sepulveda.

"Lyin' ass little 'ho," Dremel scoffed.

"Don't pay him any attention, hon," Miranda said. His new guardian angel.

"What's your name?"

"Felicia," she said.

"Where are you from, Felicia?"

"Coeur d'Alene."

"If you and Miranda come with me in a taxi, would you be willing to show me where you saw him? I'll give you each three hundred dollars as soon as I confirm he's there," Raimo said.

"I don't know," Felicia said.

"Baby," Miranda said to her, "we are both of us getting in

the fucking cab because I will beat the living dogshit out of this here Ohio boy if he even thinks of fucking with us."

That seemed to settle it.

In the cab, Raimo sat between Miranda and the whey-faced runaway from Iowa. Miranda looked over at Raimo several times, studying him. "You better not be no damn serial killer," she said.

Raimo barked out a laugh that was half sob. He didn't know why. A stab of anguish hit him at the thought of Irene, and this absurd taxi ride down a twisting canyon road in California sandwiched between a transvestite spangled in leather and costume jewelry and this petite, whey-faced runaway from Idaho.

"What are you laughing at?" Miranda demanded. She turned, squaring her shoulders.

"Nothing," Raimo said. "I'm just clearing my throat."

Raimo paid the $56.27 fee and a twenty tip for the driver; he told him to wait.

"We'll need cab fare back and our money, please," Miranda said.

"As soon as I show the photo inside," Raimo said.

Felicia and Miranda trailed behind him.

At the door, Raimo showed the photo and identified himself as a private detective.

"He was here last night," the manager said. "I can't say if he'll be back tonight. We don't book rooms like a hotel."

Raimo gave Miranda and Felicia their money, counting it out in the palms of their hands. He gave Miranda three twenties for the cab fare back. "Another twenty for the tip," he said and pressed the money around her fingers with a squeeze. "Remember, I'm in that motel across the street."

Raimo watched the cab drive away. He walked a short distance from the shelter and smoked. Men started to appear from different directions as if a signal had been given. Maybe beds were limited in this place. An hour passed and then another. The nighttime traffic picked up. The women who passed him seemed to shrivel, acquire a stern hatchet-faced demeanor as they passed. Older, obese women pushed shopping carts and cane walkers. The sign on the door gave a list of rules of acceptable behavior while a guest of the shelter. Raimo figured it would probably be easier to sneak a weapon past a checkpoint in the Green Zone of Baghdad.

He was about to go when a dented Silverado pickup pulled in front of the shelter. A rosary dangled from the rearview mirror and a bumper sticker said *In Guad We Trust.* Guad: Our Lady of Guadalupe.

The driver got out and opened the passenger door to help him out.

"Rick."

He looked bad—thinner by twenty pounds, scruffy bearded, rumpled clothes that were never in fashion even if they'd been pressed, and both his casts soiled and discolored passing through stages of white to their present dingy and tarnished eggshell.

"Ray."

Raimo walked up to him, unsure what to say, and that amazed him. He'd come this far. What was he supposed to do now? Kidnap his brother and force him to go back with him?

"You need to come home with me," he said. "We have some things to discuss about Brian Tuomey."

The wrong thing to say. He could see Rikki bristle.

Then: Raimo *knew*. It was a chance that would either pay off—or, more likely, end all contact between him and his brother forever.

"I know you set the fire," Raimo said. Unconsciously, he brushed his fingers down the rib of scarred flesh on his face.

If possible, his brother shriveled in front of his eyes even more. A husk, not the bulked-up athlete he used to be. The outrage, whatever he had intended to say, all the years of bullying the little brother into silence or obedience were gone. No more the hero Northtown worshipped. He was a man with broken limbs and broken dreams.

Raimo didn't feel pity for himself or for his brother. He had to think about other things, the future.

After waiting a sufficient amount of time, he asked: "You coming home or not, brother?"

THE END

About the author

Robb White is the author of two hardboiled private-eye novels featuring his existentialist detective Thomas Haftmann, both published by Grand Mal Press: *Haftmann's Rules* (2011) and *Saraband for a Runaway* (2013). His crime novel *Special Collections* was the winner of the 2014 Electronic Book Series Competition by New Rivers Press. "Frotteur in the Dark" was selected by *10,000 Tons of Black Ink* as one of 6 Best Of for 2009. That story was published in the collection "Out of Breath" *and Other Stories* by Red Giant Press of Cleveland in 2013. White also writes book reviews and does interviews for Tom Huff's magazine *Boxing World*.

Also by the same author

Northtown Blitz (Volume 2: Raimo Jarvi Investigates)

When You Run With Wolves

Dead Cat Bounce

Printed in Dunstable, United Kingdom